move ... the
breat...

W... l his
neck ...

H... and
his other held my back to press me to him. He scooped me up off the floor. My feet dangled.

I buried my face into his shoulder, breathless and consumed by his embrace. It was too close and everything I wanted right then. How did he know?

"*Aggele mou*," he whispered, and he moved his face until his cheek was next to mine. "Sang, don't ever do that to me again. Don't you ever fucking wait..." His breath was hot against my ear.

I couldn't speak. Tears stung my eyes. I hadn't realized until that moment that Silas had been holding back something from everyone, waiting until we were alone to tell me this. I swallowed heavily, tightening my arms around his neck. My fingers slipped into his hair, feeling the smooth black locks. I felt so bad. I'd scared him.

The Academy

The Ghost Bird Series

Friends vs. Family

♥

Book Three

♥

Written by C. L. Stone
Published by
Arcato Publishing

http://clstonebooks.com/
Published by Arcato Publishing
http://www.arcatopublishing.com

ISBN: 149290001X
ISBN-13: 978-1492900016

From The Academy

The Ghost Bird Series

Introductions
First Days
Friends vs. Family
Forgiveness and Permission
A Drop of Doubt
Push and Shove
House of Korba (October 2014)

The Scarab Beetle Series

Thief
Liar (August 2014)

***

Other Books by C. L. Stone

Smoking Gun
Spice God

For Chelsea
For Delona
For Tabitha
For Nesha

For what family means

♥

SECRET LIVES

I dreamed a wind swept through a valley, laced with fire and blinding anyone it came across. I was tied to a tree, unable to dodge the fire no matter how I struggled. All I could do was wait for what was coming for me.

Part of me felt like I deserved it.

"Sang?" a voice woke me from my dream.

I sat up in bed, shivering, confused. It was dawn. My alarm hadn't gone off yet.

A knock sounded at the door. "Sang?" my father called. "Are you awake?"

My father never came to my door unless something was wrong. Was he going to the hospital with my mother? I kicked off my blankets, my heart rattling hard in my half-asleep body. I swallowed back my fears, tugging down the hem of my t-shirt on my body as it had crept up my stomach while I was sleeping. When I was decent, I opened my bedroom door, peeking out.

My father loomed in the hallway, dressed in dark slacks, a white collared shirt and tie. A suit coat hung over his arm. If he was going to the hospital, he wouldn't be wearing that. He peered in at me with his dark and tired eyes.

I opened the door more, tilting my head. "What's wrong?" I asked.

"I'm going on a business trip," he said. He nodded

toward the stairwell, in the direction of his bedroom, where my mother was likely still sleeping. "I won't be back for a couple of days. I need to make sure you get your mother to eat something while I'm gone. You know how she gets when she doesn't eat."

I nodded. Since I was about nine years old, my mother had been sick. She first went in for a sinus infection but came back weeks later with bottles of morphine for an illness I wasn't told about. She'd never been the same since, in and out of hospitals almost as often as I went to school.

Her illness was bad enough as it was. The drugs, however, made her paranoid. My sister and I spent most of our childhood and early teenage years at her mercy, isolated in our rooms. She told us that men would rape us; monsters would kidnap and kill us. If we disobeyed, if we left the house and she found out we'd talked to anyone outside the family, she punished us by getting us to kneel on a hardwood floor or sit on a stool for hours at a time. If she didn't eat, didn't take her medicine, the punishments got worse.

"Where are you going?" I asked. It was Friday, and not only did I have school, but I also had something secret to do with the Academy. I'd have to hope the boys were right, and it wouldn't take all day.

"Mexico," he said. "I'll be back soon. Tell your sister."

Marie, my older sister, was probably still asleep across the hall. I wondered why he told me and not her. I couldn't remember the last time he went on a business trip. I usually didn't notice until he was already gone. I hardly saw him anyway, he was always working. It had me wondering why he mentioned it this time. Maybe he expected to be away longer.

He marched down the stairs, turned the corner and was gone. A moment later, the sound of his car starting echoed through the house. His suitcase must have already been in the car. Telling me he was leaving was like an afterthought. No goodbyes. No promises to call.

A hollow household with hollow people. We did what we had to do.

♥♥♥

I got dressed for school in shorts and a blouse. When I was ready, I went to the kitchen downstairs. I found some crackers in the cabinet and grabbed a yogurt cup and a spoon, along with a bottle of water. I tiptoed through the quiet house toward my parents' bedroom.

My mother was slumped over her pillow, her mouth open and she was snoring. Her graying hair was pulled back in a ponytail, recently brushed out and fixed up. If I didn't know any better, she looked almost normal, peaceful.

I didn't want to wake her. I dropped the crackers and everything onto her bedside table. I hoped it would be enough if she woke up and was hungry.

Something glinting under the bed caught my eye. I checked her again to make sure she wasn't going to wake up and then dropped to my knees next to the bed, ducking my head.

There was an open shoebox on its side under her bed. I recognized her handwriting on some of the notes that spilled out. The silver metal glint was a picture frame. The picture was a little faded, and it took a moment for me to realize it was of her. She had to have been no more than twenty or so at the time the picture was taken. Her hair was longer then, and her eyes clearer, sharper than I'd ever remembered.

It was in that moment I realized I couldn't recall ever seeing a picture of anyone in my family. I didn't think she owned a camera. Why hadn't it occurred to me before? It was a small thing, but something that never crossed my mind.

This photograph, as far as I knew, was the only one of

any of us in the entire house. She'd kept it hidden.

The sight of this had my heart thundering in my chest. Why was it under her bed? Did she not like it? She didn't want anyone knowing she had it. Did my dad know?

There were other objects in the box as well, needles and old bottles of prescription medication, some dating back to before I was born.

I didn't want to go through her private things or get caught doing so. I closed the lid for her, slipping the box back underneath the bed again. I scrambled to get out of her room.

I would let her keep her secrets. I had my own to deal with. Adding hers to mine right now was too much. I needed to get to school.

♥♥♥

That afternoon, I was flat on my back in a thin, pale green hospital gown as I waited for the MRI machine to start. The guys had taken me to this nondescript medical building in downtown Charleston with the promise that my parents wouldn't learn about where I was or why. I'd skipped my last three classes to get here, with Mr. Blackbourne covering for me. I wasn't sure how late it was. I was worried we were running short on time for me to get back into my neighborhood, preferably before my mother noticed I was late from school.

"Just lay still for a second, Miss Sang," Dr. Green's voice filtered through to me from overhead speakers.

It was difficult to be still. The room was cold and the table I was on rattled with the movement of the MRI machine. I was naked, except for the thin gown around me. I knew Luke, Gabriel, Victor, Nathan, and Kota were probably watching from the same room Dr. Green was sitting in.

I shifted my head to the side, trying to glimpse through the glass window where I knew they were standing, but from my position, and the glare of the fluorescent lights overhead, I couldn't see their faces.

"I said be still, Miss Sang. You can talk if you want, but don't move."

"You might want to listen to him, Miss Sorenson," said the disembodied voice of Dr. Philip Roberts. I'd met him briefly before they chased me into the MRI room. He was from the Academy, I knew, with white hair and age-spotted cheeks. He was Dr. Green's mentor and residency supervisor. I liked him immediately. "If you move, it takes longer. We might have to start over."

"It's cold," I said, shivering.

Kota's voice cut through. "Didn't you wear shorts and that pink shirt to school today?"

I blinked and worried if blinking counted as moving. "Yes."

"Why'd you take those off? They didn't have any metal. You could have worn them. It probably would have been a little warmer than the gown."

My mouth popped open. "Luke!"

There was snickering in the background from both Luke and Gabriel.

"I hate you both right now," I said.

"Oy, Trouble. You've got to have the full hospital experience."

"Yeah, Sang," Luke said. "Rite of passage."

I grumbled. Earlier, it had sounded reasonable when they told me I *just had* to put the gown on. After all, I was in a hospital and about to go into a very large machine. Medical dramas on television always showed people in the gowns. I'd never been to the doctor before. How was I supposed to know?

Victor's sweet baritone voice sounded through the speakers. "Do you want a blanket?"

"She can't have one now," Kota said. "She's in the middle of the MRI."

"We can start it over," Victor said. "She's cold."

"She's tough. She can take it. Can't you, Sang?"

I sighed. “Maybe.” I knew I could, I just wanted to grumble. It distracted me from the loud machine and moving parts around me. They were kind of scary.

“This machine costs an arm and a leg just to push the ‘go’ button,” Dr. Roberts said.

“I’ll pay for it,” Victor said.

“We’ve already started,” Kota said. “Let her finish. She’ll be fine.”

There was a softly spoken protest from Victor but he quieted.

I swallowed back my complaints. I thought of North and Silas, who were probably getting ready for football practice out in ninety degree weather. They’d probably love to relax in a cool room right now.

Nathan spoke, “Your ankle doesn’t hurt, does it?”

“No worse than usual,” I said, although his question caused me to focus on my foot. After Friday Fall and I’d jumped from the second floor to the first, I’d ended up with what Dr. Green thought at first was a sprained ankle. It’d been a couple of weeks and I was still limping, despite applying ice packs and the boys berating me to sit down and rest it. I couldn’t hide my pain walking through school and Dr. Green insisted on bringing me in for an MRI, since the first X-ray didn’t show a broken bone.

“Give me a few more minutes,” Dr. Roberts said. “We’ll find out what’s bothering you.”

“It’s probably nothing,” I insisted, like I’d done for weeks. “If it isn’t broken, there isn’t much else that will fix it besides resting it, right?”

“Will you let us doctors do the doctoring here, please?” Dr. Roberts asked. “She’s a miss smarty-pants, isn’t she?”

Gabriel chuckled. “If I hadn’t already nicknamed her Trouble, I probably would have gone with Smart Ass. Or Pretty Ass. I can’t decide.”

“Ugh,” I said, grateful the MRI machine was hiding my blushing.

Hidden Bruises

What felt like eons later, I was able to get up, and get dressed. I found Luke and Gabriel and Nathan in a waiting area. They were still wearing their faux school uniforms, although they'd all shed the blazers. Luke's white button up shirt was undone halfway down his chest. Gabriel had removed the white shirt, wearing just a ribbed tank undershirt. Nathan was wearing a white t-shirt. I thought their uniforms looked good on them, but hated that those uniforms also made them targets at school.

Luke noticed me first and whistled a catcall.

I huffed. I put my lips together and blew, only getting empty air and a raspberry at the end.

"Your whistle broken?" Nathan asked.

"Never had one," I said. "I can't whistle."

"Sure you can," Gabriel said. "Put your lips together."

I did.

"Now blow through them."

I blew a raspberry.

Gabriel snickered. "Guess you can't. Come sit by us, Sang." Gabriel patted the empty chair between him and Luke.

"No," I said, tucking myself next to Nathan in a loveseat across from where they sat. Nathan was buried in his phone, punching in a message. He hooked one hand under my thighs, scooting me around until my knees were over his legs so I could prop up my sore ankle. They'd all done the same when they could, and it no longer fazed me that I was practically sitting in his lap this way.

"We were just teasing you," Luke said. "Besides, it was cute."

"Not really worried about what you've already done. It's what you might do," I said. It was difficult to smother my smile, though.

"She's on to you, Luke," Nathan said, finishing his message and putting the phone down. He sat back, his elbows propped up on the low seat cushion behind him. This caused his chest to flex out, and the white t-shirt he was wearing did little to hide the defined muscles. "The only reason she hasn't gotten you back is because she's nice."

"Or maybe I'm not. Maybe I'm just waiting for the perfect moment." I widened my eyes to emphasis my threat.

"Ah ha," Gabriel said, pointing a lean finger at Luke's brown eyes. "Trouble's gonna get you."

My chest started buzzing. I blushed, ducking my hand into the cup of my bra to pull out my phone. North was calling.

I was hitting the button to answer when Luke, Gabriel and Nathan started giggling at me.

"Hello?" I answered, my voice wavering.

"What's wrong with you?" North asked.

"We don't know yet. They're looking over the MRI now."

"No, I mean, why do you sound weird? What's wrong?"

I should have suspected. Ever since the fight, the guys had been more aware of every little thing. I couldn't sneeze without them asking if I had a cold. I glanced at Nathan, narrowing my eyes. "The guys are laughing at me."

"Why?"

"Because I had the phone in my bra."

North chuckled. "Sang Baby, don't you have

pockets?"

"A lot of the skirts I wear don't."

"You were wearing shorts today."

I blushed again. Nathan's amused smile was teasing as he listened in, and he was brushing his fingertips along the top of my knee. It was almost distracting me from what to say to North next. "It's a habit. I'll put it in my pocket."

"You don't want perverts watching you messing with your bra. You get too much attention already."

"How's practice?" I asked him, wanting to stop talking about my bra.

"Hot. I hate this kind of stuff," he said. "How was the MRI?"

"Cold. It rattled. Luke made me wear a hospital gown when I didn't have to."

Luke's eyes widened. "Traitor!"

North grunted in the phone. "I'll give him a good thumping later if you want."

"Don't for a while. Make him sweat it out."

Nathan laughed next to me. "You're mean. Remind me not to cross you."

I got off the phone with North, tucking my phone into my back pocket this time. I made sure my blouse hung over far enough to where, when I did stand, the phone wouldn't be seen. The guys knew I had it, but my mother could never learn about it. I didn't want to forget where it was and get caught with it.

Kota appeared from a door down the hallway. From behind him emerged Victor, Dr. Green and Dr. Roberts.

Luke and Gabriel stood up to address them. I was about to do the same, but Nathan held on to my thighs, shaking his head. "Nope. You sit," he said.

When the others got close, they pulled chairs away from the walls and clustered them around the loveseat Nathan and I sat in together. This made the fact that I was nearly sitting in his lap a little more embarrassing. I tried to sit up to at least create some semblance of professionalism like they were showing.

"Well the good news is, it isn't broken," Dr. Roberts started, winking at me. "No casts for you."

"What's the bad news?" I asked, my eyes flitting from Kota to Victor and the doctors. "Don't tell me you have to cut it off."

I'd said it because I was nervous, but regretted making the joke because they all started laughing, leaving me hanging longer for an answer until they recovered.

"No, not that. Not yet at least," Dr. Roberts said.

"Your talus and calcaneus bones are bruised," Dr. Green said, sitting forward to put his elbows on his knees. "Your heel and the bone right below your ankle."

"They must have made contact when you touched down," Kota said.

"If it's a bruise, why hasn't it healed yet?" I asked. Normal bruises didn't take two weeks to get better.

"Bone bruises are more severe. You're looking at maybe a month longer before it goes away," Dr. Roberts said.

I sighed, twisting my lips. "And there's nothing you can do about it. I'm so sorry. It was a waste of money."

"Hey now," Dr. Roberts frowned, but his eyes betrayed his playful nature. "Don't give me that tone." He raised a hand and waved it back toward the room they had come from. "That was a perfectly brand new MRI machine we needed to test out and you, girl, just gave the training radiologist someone to practice on."

I felt my lips curling up. "Thank you," I said softly.

Dr. Roberts beamed.

Nathan cupped his palm over my knee. "Now you'll have to listen to us when we say stay off your feet."

"I know, and I am trying," I said. "Unless I'm walking to class or going home. I can't do it forever."

"You don't have to go that far," Dr. Roberts said. "You should be able to walk normally. Just no more jumping from balconies for a while."

"How about ever?" Gabriel asked. "Let's go with that.

Never ever jump off the school balcony again. Or any balcony. Stay away from balconies."

The others laughed.

"Thank you, Dr. Roberts," Kota said. He held out a hand for the doctor to shake. "I'm glad the results are positive, but we should get Sang home."

"In a hurry?" Dr. Roberts asked, an eyebrow shifting. He took Kota's hand to shake, but his gaze fell on me. "Have a date?"

The question glued my tongue to the roof of my mouth, and a finger hovered over my lip. Me? He had to be kidding.

"Concerned parents," Kota said.

That was putting it mildly, I thought. Concern wasn't exactly the word I would have used.

Victor and the others stood, except for Nathan. They shook hands with the doctor, and fixed the chairs.

Nathan gathered me, lifting me off of the loveseat and holding me in his arms.

"He said I can walk," I said.

"I heard him," Nathan said.

I grunted, but smirked, shaking my head. They never listened to me.

Dr. Roberts' eyes sparkled and he winked at Dr. Green. "She's cute. Keep an eye on that one." He patted Dr. Green on the back and started down the hallway.

"I should go on to work," Dr. Green said. "Who's going where?"

"I've got Luke and Gabriel," Victor said. "We've got some work to do as well."

"Nathan and I will take Sang home," Kota said.

Dr. Green nodded. "Sang, listen to the guys. Be careful."

"Thank you," I said.

His easy smile and dazzling eyes left me feeling lighter. He turned and walked in the direction Dr. Roberts had gone.

Now the only thing I had to worry about was getting

home without getting caught. My mother couldn't find out.

Kota seemed to read my worries on my face. "We're going now," he said, pulling keys out of his pocket.

There was nothing else to do. At least I didn't have to wear a cast and try to explain that to my mother. Now I just had to handle a couple of bruised foot bones.

And prevent my mother from ever finding out about Kota, Nathan, and the others in the Academy.

Easier said…

Friday

It wasn't as late as I'd been worried about. We arrived back to Sunnyvale Court before the bus was scheduled to arrive. When the bus pulled onto our street, Kota, Nathan and I emerged from Kota's garage. My sister, Marie, started talking to Danielle, the next door neighbor girl. Derrick, Danielle's brother, was already heading up the road. I lingered with Kota and Nathan. No one seemed to have noticed we hadn't gotten off the bus.

Only now, when I knew I had to get going, I didn't want to leave.

"So what are we doing?" Nathan asked. "It's Friday. What's the plan for the weekend?"

"Sang goes home and checks in," Kota said. He put a palm on top of my head and rubbed. "We'll get homework out of the way and figure things out from there. I'm thinking we'll start with self-defense training. Something light though because of your ankle."

I smiled, feeling better. I was welcome back. Hopefully I could get back. In the last couple of weeks, my mother had told me to get on my knees three times and to sit on the stool four times. Punishments lasted for hours and I was often so sore and tired and angry afterward that I couldn't return for a while.

Kota and the others didn't know about the latest punishments. When I was being disciplined and they were expecting me, I would text to tell them my mother was hovering so I couldn't escape. I knew they would be worried if they figured out the truth, but I didn't see a way out of it and the Academy guys had enough problems. They didn't need to worry about me.

It also didn't matter to me. My mother would punish me. I would sit for hours and when it was over, I'd be out the door to Kota's again. I did whatever I had to do to keep my secrets.

If a few hours of punishment was the cost of my friendship with the guys, I'd take every second of it.

"You want to spend the night again?" Nathan asked, looking at me.

I brightened more, nodding. "I'd like to. Can I?"

Kota smiled softly. "Only if..." he made a face, reaching into his back pocket for his phone. He checked the messages, frowning. "We might have to see," he said. He looked at Nathan. "We've got to go."

"Not another fight," I complained. "Did Silas and North get into trouble with football tryouts?"

"Nothing so tragic," Kota promised. "Academy."

I pursed my lips to hold back the buzzing questions collecting on my tongue. Despite trying to keep out of trouble at school, Kota and the others still got called out on occasion for Academy business. "What do I do?"

"Check in," he said, pulling out his keys. "If you need anything, call Victor if it isn't an emergency. Call me if it is."

"Call me if it is," Nathan echoed.

They waved to me and headed toward Kota's old, clunky sedan parked at the corner of his driveway. Kota was still wearing the blue blazer with the faux school badge. Nathan was in his white t-shirt and uniform pants. No time to change. The Academy was calling.

I started down the road, disappointed that the weekend might be delayed. Kota and Nathan were off to work. North and Silas were probably still at football practice. Luke, Victor and Gabriel were busy. I was bummed, already lonely without them and without an idea of when I would next see them.

Marie caught up with me. We walked alongside each other. It felt awkward. She and I rarely talked unless we had to and often times we avoided each other as much as possible. It was completely different than how I felt about the boys. I knew it wasn't normal. Sisters were supposed to be close, right?

"Are you still spending the weekend with Danielle?" I asked. She'd talked about this last week. She was getting good at disappearing and running off to Danielle's house. She never got into trouble like I did, though. I wondered how she got away with it.

"Yes," she said, shifting her nearly empty book bag on her shoulders. Her hair was pulled back in a ponytail. Her t-shirt clung to her tall frame.

"Check in every once in a while," I reminded her.

"Since when are you the boss?" she snapped at me. "Just don't tell mom."

I sighed, rolling my eyes. It wasn't like I wanted to stop her from a good time. I was probably the only one around who could understand. We escaped to be around people that liked us. I didn't want to see her punished like me.

She sped up, heading to the garage door of our house. I hoped she listened to me, but if she didn't, I hoped she wouldn't get caught. There was nothing else I could do.

♥♥♥

The house was quiet. It was then that I remembered that my father would be gone all weekend. I sunk into myself, disappointed. I might not be able to spend the night with Kota and Nathan after all. I felt guilty about leaving my mother by herself all night. Marie would be gone for the weekend. If something happened and I wasn't home, it would be my fault.

I wondered if my mother had eaten. I wanted to change my clothes and planned to check on her after. If she was sleeping, I'd wake her to get her to eat something. It was risky. Depending on her mood, I might end up on my knees again. Still, since Kota was gone, it wasn't a problem now. No one was expecting me.

I skipped up the steps two at a time and walked into my bedroom. I dumped the contents of my book bag onto my bed since I needed to clean it out. I told myself I would get all my homework done like Kota said before I attempted to text Victor or Luke or someone just to talk.

When I was done emptying my bag, I tossed it on the floor. I stripped off my shoes and socks, leaving on the shorts and the blouse I had worn to school.

I went to the upstairs bathroom, turned on the faucet and washed my face. I heard fumbling in the hallway and I thought it was Marie getting ready to go to Danielle's. I brushed my teeth just to feel fresh. I touched the cup of my bra, expecting to feel my phone there but remembered it was in my back pocket. I pulled it out, wondering if I should charge it. I returned it to my pocket, drawing my shirt down far enough so the lower hem hid the bulge.

Out of habit, I tidied the counter, getting rid of a hairbrush and some of Marie's makeup and tossing it into a drawer, wiping down the white countertop and cleaning a smudge from the medicine cabinet mirror. If I left it to Marie, the bathroom would be a wreck.

I opened the bathroom door and crossed the hallway again to my room and stopped cold. My mother was inside, bent over my bed. She was sweating. Her dark, graying hair was matted against her flushed forehead and cheeks. Was this the same person I'd left this morning?

Her face lifted and her gaze met mine. I could have died where I stood.

She crumbled papers in her hands. Blood drained from my face as I recognized the detention slip and the unread notes I'd collected from school.

"What," she seethed, "is this?" She held up the detention slip toward me and the opened notes. Had she read them?

I swallowed, holding my place by the door. "People pass notes to me in class," I said. "I don't read them. I just throw them away."

She narrowed her eyes and her voice gurgled as she pointed at me. "You wear shorts like that to school?" she demanded. "Do you expect me to believe for one moment..." Her breathing sped up. "And you got detention."

She never talked about my clothes before. I was rattled, unsure what to say. "The clothes are within school regulation. And that was an accident--"

"Inappropriate touching," she called out to me, her voice grating in a higher pitch. "You're touching boys in school."

"No," I said. I eased back a step and sighed, not sure if I should fight it. If I started kneeling now or sat on that stool, maybe I could get it over with in a few hours. I swallowed again when I realized my dad wouldn't be here this time to help if she left me alone for too long. At least I had the phone with me. I couldn't believe I'd forgotten about that detention slip. I'd been so busy with the fighting at school and trying to keep up with the boys that I'd neglected a lot of things.

"You wear those clothes. Boys write nasty things to you. I have the teacher's note right here telling me what happened to you in school," she declared. Her fists crumpled the papers in her hands tighter and she let go, letting them fall around her feet. "What else have you been hiding from me?"

I opened my mouth to say something, but she spun toward the bookshelf, yanking novels off of the shelves. She glared at the covers and pitched them to the ground. "Is it these books? Are they telling you to allow boys to touch you? To touch them back?"

"No," I said, trying to look humble, my eyes downcast. My insides quivered. I didn't understand her questions. Did she think books told me what to do? Like demon possession? I was ashamed of myself already and couldn't face her. I was fibbing. Some boys did touch me, but not like she was thinking. She would never understand.

"You're lying," she cried out. She pointed a finger at the papers on the floor and glared at me. "I know I didn't teach you to do these things. Inappropriate touching!"

I bit my lip, closing my eyes. *Please, please just get it over with.*

"Well?"

What did she want? I didn't know how to respond. "I'm sorry," I said softly, unsure what else to say. I trembled. "Mom, you haven't eaten. You should eat something. You don't look good."

I sensed her crossing the room and out of some deep survival instinct, my arms swung up as I tried to cover my head. She grabbed a handful of my shirt, yanking on it until it twisted around my neck, and dragged me out into the hallway. "Shut up. I will not have a child lie to me and think she can get away with behaving like a tramp."

She pushed me through the open bathroom door across the hall. I stumbled onto the tile, standing in front of the tub. She pointed a chubby finger at me. "Stay right here," she demanded. "When I come back, you better be right here."

I shivered, crossing my arms over my chest and nodding. I swallowed back tears, unsure of what she was going to do. Why was I in the bathroom?

She left and she was gone for so long that I thought maybe she had forgotten about me. Did she mean for me to wait in the bathroom all day? Where was Marie? Was she hiding or did she already leave?

Clunking sounds erupted from the hallway. I recognized the sound of the stool scraping against the wood floor as she pushed it forward. I sighed, feeling a bit better. If she wanted me to sit in the bathroom on the stool, that would be better for me, too. She usually made me sit in the kitchen. Upstairs I wouldn't have to be so paranoid looking over my shoulder. I could text with Victor and the others for a while until I was released. I could probably get up and walk around, too. That wouldn't be so bad.

She pushed the stool through the doorway. She threw it at me. I ducked, holding up my arms as the wood hit me across my shoulder. "You will not," she screamed at me, "leave here. I absolutely can't believe you are making me do this." Her eyes were wide and wild. She pointed at the bathtub. "Put the chair in there."

With shaking hands, I pulled back the curtain of the shower, putting the stool on the floor of the tub. It wobbled a little as the bottom of the tub was uneven.

"Sit," she said.

I carefully climbed in, putting my butt in the seat and placing my feet on the wood supports. I was confused as to why she wanted me in here but wasn't sure what else to do.

She held out a couple of thick cords and my eyes bulged out of my head. I remembered them from when we moved. We'd used them to strap a couple of boxes to the top of the car.

She gripped my arm, twisting it around until I almost toppled from the stool. I corrected myself, and she wrenched my hands around my back. She weaved the cord between one of the spokes of the stool behind me and she twisted the rope around my wrists. She tied off the cord around a slat well outside of my reach. I tested the cord, pulling against it. I was tied to the chair and wouldn't be able to get up without bringing it with me.

She used the other cord around my ankles, interweaving the rope on another spoke of the chair. I shivered hard, suppressing tears. Now I wouldn't be able to get up at all. I was already wobbling to keep balanced. If I tilted too far one way or another, I could easily fall over, hurting myself.

When she was done, she stood back. I swallowed, uncomfortable and worried the guys wouldn't hear from me for hours if she left me here as long as she usually did.

I wasn't sure I could reach my phone.

And no one was around to save me. Marie was gone. My father wouldn't be home for days. If she forgot about me this time, I had no one to help.

She stood in silence in front of me, considering, calculating. I pursed my lips, unsure if I should suggest she eat. How would she untie me, anyway? The knots weren't fashioned with expertise. They were a garbled mess. If I could reach them, I could possibly undo them, but from my position, there was no way.

She nodded as if replying to a question that wasn't asked. She bent over and she started the water in the tub, hitting the shower lever.

The water shot out cold. I gasped, crying out. I focused simply on trying to balance myself on the chair and keep my face away from the spray.

"You won't move," she said. "You should have known better. You're doing this to yourself. You will never talk to a boy again at school. You'll never even think about touching one or crossing that line ever again."

She twisted the knobs of the shower until they were all the way on hot. She shoved the stool and I almost toppled over on her. For someone who was sick, it surprised me she was able to hold me up.

When she had positioned me how she wanted, she aimed the shower head. She pushed it until the water was going over my face and shoulders and down my front. No matter how I moved, I couldn't escape from the water spray. The best I could do was cower my shoulders, putting my face down to get some relief from the constant stream.

When the water started warming up, at first I was grateful because the cool water left me shivering.

The water heated quickly.

I started crying. I bent my head forward, toward my chest and trying my best to get my face out of the flow. My voice filled the bathroom as I knocked my wrists and ankles against the wood.

"Please," I cried out. "I'm sorry. I'm so sorry. Don't leave me here." I sobbed, took in a breath. I couldn't see her anywhere. I was facing the wrong way.

No reply.

Was she already gone? I rattled on the stool. I was drowning in the onslaught of water, nearly scalding. My legs cramped already at being in an awkward position and having to force myself to balance. I was tempted to fall over anyway but worried more about cracking my head open on the bathtub. Would it help? Would she leave me mangled and broken in the tub or put me back into place?

"I'm sorry!" I shouted. If I could get out of this, I would do whatever it took to never let her catch me again. I promised myself to be more careful, to get rid of those notes and any hint of the boys. I'd been slacking. How could I have ever known she would go this far?

Panic forced my breath to catch and it was hard enough to breathe under the onslaught of scalding water.

I twisted my head to the left, waiting there for as long as I could stand it. When the water was too hot, I turned my head again to the right, catching a different angle. The water felt like it was burning the tender bits of skin around my eyes, at my ears, and along my lips.

I sobbed. I called for Marie. I called for dad. I knew they weren't there, but I didn't know what else to do. I called for my mother. "Help me," I cried out. "Please stop! Please!"

Motion nearby caused me to pause. She came back! She realized she'd gone too far. I never cried like this for kneeling in rice or for any of her other punishments *Please. Just turn the water off. That's all. I'll stay here for hours. I'll do it. Just not with the water.*

A hand gripped my hair, forcing my head back. A glass smacked at my mouth. I breathed in vinegar and lemon.

I opened my mouth before she had a chance to strike

me with the cup again. I swallowed, forcing back my sobs. I was only halfway done when my stomach lurched and I started purging. The cup was pulled back. I tilted my head away, still with the onslaught of hot water against my tender skin. I emptied the contents of my stomach into my lap. Stomach acid mingled with the lemon and vinegar against my raw skin.

When I was done vomiting, the hand was back and I was forced to drain the cup. When I was finished, the glass was dropped into the tub. It cracked against the basin, shattering. I was puking again on myself, sobbing, feeling my throat scratching. I wanted to take in water but my throat was burning and the water was too hot.

The shower curtain was pulled over, shadowing me against the light. I heard the inside lock flip and the door closed. I twisted around, peeking through the water.

If Marie came looking for me, it might look like I was just taking a shower. She might not think to check on me at all. My mother had thought ahead enough that she didn't want anyone freeing me before she came back.

I was alone.

When the hot water died about thirty minutes later, I was still crying. I felt the phone at my back pocket and I couldn't get myself to even attempt to save it. I was sure it was broken now. What could I do with it anyway? The guys couldn't come save me because my mother would stop them, perhaps even call the police on them and have them arrested. Would they ever forgive me if one of them ended up in jail?

If I kept my head tilted forward, it gave me just enough breathing space that I could take in some clean air without breathing in water droplets. It was extremely uncomfortable. I held it for as long as I could to allow myself to catch my breath.

Soon, my tears died off. My breathing was ragged, my throat stinging. I tried drinking water but I coughed it up quickly and the coughing irritated my throat further.

At least the water was cool.

♥♥♥

I stared off into space a lot. The feather blue paint along the edge of the shower near the ceiling looked a lot like a shirt I'd seen Luke wear to school. I thought of his blond hair and the contrasting dark brown eyes, when my neck started hurting and my face couldn't stand another moment of the constant spray.

The sliver-like gleam of the faucet reminded me of Victor's medallion. I thought of his finger tracing along my skin as he held my hand between classes. I thought of Silas hugging me, strong enough to pick me up off of the ground. Memories swept through me of North's intense brown eyes, and the feel of his fingers massaging my scalp, of Gabriel's curses and stealing my hair clip, of Kota's smooth fingers tracing my cheek, and of Nathan making faces at me when I peeked back at him during geometry.

I even thought about Mr. Blackbourne and Dr. Green. I thought about Greg and Mike and Rocky and other people at school that I'd met. I thought about Mr. Hendricks and Mr. McCoy as little as possible, but when I did, I kept thinking how even though they were faulty in many ways, they probably never had to deal with this. Greg was vulgar, Mike was brash, Rocky was arrogant. None would dare tie me to a chair in the shower.

Most of the time though, I thought of the boys. I wondered if Kota was worried about me. I wondered if they tried to text but I had been shaking and sobbing so badly before that perhaps if they tried, I wouldn't have felt it. Or the phone really was broken. Victor would be so mad when I showed him the phone later. I wondered if they even noticed I was gone.

I wondered when my mother would come back for me.

♥♥♥

Hours passed, I didn't know how many. My back was sore. I was shivering. My skin felt raw and heavy, like clinging plastic wrap covered it. I kept my eyes closed, my head down for as long as possible, and shifted in my chair. I got used to the way it would rock back and forth. At one point, I tried to twist my body so the chair would move. It did, about an inch. The stool tilted so badly I was afraid it would fall over.

I was tempted to let it. I twisted my body to look behind myself. If I fell in one direction, I would crack my head on the faucet. If I went the other way, I would be on my side, still tied up and helpless. If I tried falling out of the tub, I would probably end up upside down and still unable to move.

My hands felt numb. My feet did, too. I wasn't even sure if my feet were still up on the vertical spokes of the stool. I wondered if I was doing more damage to my ankle and the bruised bones. My butt was asleep as well. Every piece of me felt so cold. When the air conditioner kicked on, it got so much worse that I was shivering, rocking precariously on the stool.

♥♥♥

I was slumped over, almost passed out when the chair started to careen forward. With my heart in my throat, I leaned back, trying to balance myself out. I caught it just in time and rattled back into stabilizing. I couldn't fall asleep. I willed myself to stay awake. I bit my tongue, my cheek, anything to force my eyes open. I stared off at the wall. How long was she going to keep me in here?

♥♥♥

More time passed. I tried counting the minutes. My throat was scratchy, and despite sipping the water falling around my face, I still coughed it up. I tried my voice, but I couldn't hear myself.

My skin felt so tight and sore, I wanted to scrape it from my body. Every little drop of water against my face felt like a sting.

I moved my arms, hitting the edge of the stool and slapping my hands against the wood of the chair. I wasn't sure if my mother or Marie could hear me if they were nearby, but I was desperate. Would my mom come back and do something else?

I was desperate enough to take that risk. I wasn't sure what time it was, but it felt late. I'd do anything to get out of the shower.

If I passed out, I knew I would die.

♥

Saturday

I stretched my arms against the resistance of the cord toward my hip pocket. I didn't know if I could reach anyone. I didn't know if the phone still worked. All I knew was that I had been forgotten.

With what little give the rope allowed, I scrunched my biceps and tugged my shorts down to better access the pocket where the phone was. My fingers clipped the edge of the phone and it started to slide out. I clutched it, gripping at it tightly until I heard a crack. With numb fingers, it was hard to manipulate. I was shaking badly, afraid I would drop it. I had one shot.

I bit my lip and held the phone up. I straightened my body against the onslaught of cool water to block the spray the best I could from reaching my back and the phone. It was difficult to not peek over my shoulder to find out if the screen lit up.

I used my thumb to punch at it, trying to remember exactly what I needed to select to reach the guys.

Please, please, someone. Anyone. I don't care who. Please work.

If it wasn't broken, I only had seconds before the water spraying around me might break it for good.

I jabbed the phone with my finger, hitting at random for what I hoped would be the guys' applications, ones Dr. Green had installed on my phone. I jabbed again; aiming for what I thought would be one of four square buttons of different colors, unsure of which one I was pushing. Black, red... Not that it mattered. I thought this constituted an emergency.

I kept pushing, just in case my first attempts didn't work. A ringing buzz sounded, so faint against the fall of water around me. I'd dialed someone.

Please. Please, anyone. Be there.

The ringing stopped. A click. "*Aggele mou*?"

I swallowed, willing my voice to work. "Silas!" I squeaked out. I grasped the phone, trying to be steady. I wasn't sure he could hear me at all. The water was spraying louder than I was speaking. "Silas, Silas... help. Please. Silas."

Quiet. I twisted and a sudden muscle spasm struck me hard against my legs and back. The phone slipped from my hands. I was too slow to catch it. It fell and skimmed down into the tub. It cracked against the basin, sliding toward the drain.

I sobbed, calling out to Silas, crying out his name over and over. I could only hope he heard me. I could only hope he understood I needed him.

I closed my eyes, my heart wild in my chest. I slapped my hands against the chair. I rocked back and forth on the stool until I felt too unstable to do it anymore. If Silas was still on the phone, I wanted him to know I was there. I didn't want this fragile connection severed.

♥♥♥

I was drifting off again when I heard footsteps in the hallway and my head popped up, despite the stab of pain in my neck and the water pouring into my face. I shivered hard, causing the stool to shake underneath. I didn't care who it was, even if it was my mother who would only have me get on my knees or move me somewhere else. I would go anywhere. Had Marie come back? Had Silas heard me?

The footsteps moved away and I cried out in my raspy voice. "Help!" My voice was lost to the stream of water. I called again and again, grunting, groaning, destroying the last of my vocal cords to try to lure whoever was out there to come back. I slapped my hands against the wood of the chair. I rocked on the stool.

Voices sounded. Low and deep. The guys! I rocked on the stool.

The voices came closer. "I double checked, she's passed out," Nathan's voice drifted to me. I quieted to hear. "I've looked everywhere. Sang's not here."

I am here! I slapped, slamming my wrists against the wood. Please hear me!

"Who's in the shower?" Silas's deep voice echoed.

"It's got to be Marie," Nathan said. "I checked her room, she's not in there. Maybe Sang's out in the woods. I told her not to go without me."

No, not Marie! In a panic, I clutched my knees together against the stool. *Please hear me, please hear me.*

With what little strength I had left, I jumped, trying to lift the chair with me to slam myself back down against the tub.

Thunk.

My butt slammed against the flat part of the wood. Pain radiated from my tailbone through my spine. A sharp pang connected against my ankle. I gasped, a wash of red covering my eyes at the agony.

More silence. Were they thinking Marie was finishing in the bathroom and were trying to get away?

"Silas!" I squealed. "Nathan!" I knew they couldn't hear me. I collected myself. I pulled myself up again, twisting my ankle as I drew up the stool and slammed it down against the tub. I rocked forward, and leaned back to stop myself from slipping off into the tub.

"That's not Marie. That's Sang," Silas said. The doorknob rattled and a thud pounded against the door.

I twisted my face away from the door, shaking, crying quiet sobs. *Thank you, thank you.*

The floor shook, a loud crack thundered, mixed with

splitting wood as the door broke away from the frame, slamming up against the wall. I vibrated with shivers so hard against the stool, I was sure I was going to fall over. I was ashamed, cold, tired, in pain. I was embarrassed they had to come for me. I was so sorry to drag them into this. What would I ever do without them?

The curtain was pulled back. Silas loomed over me, his face contorting into a rage so fierce that I wanted to cower but wouldn't allow myself to do it.

♥♥♥

"Fucking shit," Nathan said. He looked confused, disbelieving his own eyes. He reached out for me, diving into the cold water and wrapping his arms around me. "God damn it Sang, why the hell didn't you call us sooner?"

Silas reached down, pulling at the stool. "She's fucking tied up." He growled and helped Nathan, pulling me and the stool out from the shower.

They lowered me onto my side against the floor of the bathroom. I coughed against the tile.

Nathan put his warm hand against my cheek. "Sang?" he called to me. He brushed my hair away from my face.

"Nathan," I said as loud as I could, but there was nothing to my voice.

His blue eyes lit with tears. He shook his head. His eyes drifted from my face to my bound hands and feet. He grumbled something and turned back to me. "I'm going to break this damn thing, okay? Don't move."

I nodded but wasn't sure if shivering counted as moving.

I heard Silas speaking, but I couldn't see him. "Kota? We've got her. No, she's not okay. Bring Dr. Green. We're taking her to Nathan's."

Nathan stood over the stool. Silas slipped down and hovered over me, wrapping his arms around my shoulders. Nathan kicked at the stool. I was jerked but Silas held on.

The wood split. Another kick and my hands in the cords pulled away from the stool. He worked on freeing my legs, breaking the smaller wood slats and sliding the rope free.

Silas pulled me into his arms, picking me up. I was still shaking so bad, but I felt his warmth and leaned against him, burying my face into his shoulder.

The water was turned off and a moment later Nathan held out a towel. Silas readjusted until he had the towel wrapped over my body.

"Let's get her out of here," Silas said.

"No shit," Nathan said.

My eyes closed as Silas thudded down the back stairs.

A second later, I breathed in the night air.

♥

Rescue Party

I woke up to the smell of cypress and menthol. The scents confused me. The sheets were stiff against my skin. Did I do something to my bed? My face felt heavy and thick, like I had the worst cold in the world. My head throbbed between my eyes.

Dry air tickled my throat and a coughing spasm hit me hard. I sat up, and through narrowed eyes, I recognized Nathan's bedroom with karate posters and exercise equipment stuffed into his closet.

My lungs were on fire. I needed fresh air. The menthol was suffocating; I couldn't breathe.

I got on my knees, trying to crawl to the edge of the bed. My whole body rattled as I coughed. I touched the floor and I got one step before my legs failed. I collapsed against Nathan's dresser, knocking it against the wall. I slid to the floor. Everything on top of his dresser dropped to the carpet around me.

The door opened. Kota and Luke hovered in the doorway. There were more faces beyond them that I couldn't make out as my eyes blurred.

I sat up against the dresser. The cluster of people at the door swooped in on me all at once.

Kota reached me first. He put his arm around my shoulders, trying to pull me up. His spice scent around me was too much. I pushed him away. I was coughing too hard to tell him that it felt overpowering.

Dr. Green nudged Kota away. He pressed his palms against my cheeks in an effort to get me to focus. I tried to back up but I was against the dresser and couldn't move. I pushed at his arms but he wouldn't budge. "Sang," he said. "Sang, listen to me. Calm down. If you pass out, I'll have to take you to the hospital."

"Air," I breathed out. "I can't... I need air."

"Let me take her," Kota said. He pulled me into his arms, despite my squeaking protests. I coughed against his shoulder, my eyes scrunched closed. I willed myself to stay conscious. I didn't want to have to go anywhere. I wanted to be with them.

With me in his arms, Kota moved through Nathan's house. The sliding glass door was pulled aside and he put me down on my back on the concrete of Nathan's patio. He took my arms and held them over my head.

It helped. I sucked in air between the raging coughs and slowly started to calm down. He held me like that until it died off and I was drinking in oxygen.

Kota knelt by my head, bringing his face close to mine. His glasses slid down his nose as his green eyes softened. "Sang?"

I wiped my face to clear my eyes. "Kota," I breathed out.

"Want to sit up?"

I nodded. He crawled behind me, pulling me up by the shoulders until his chest pressed against my back. His legs extended on either side of mine. His arms were wrapped around my stomach. I was shaking again, but I was warm and Kota was there.

North knelt next to us. His dark eyes met mine and he frowned. "You okay, Sang Baby?"

"Perfect," I squeaked out.

His eyes glazed and he blinked hard, but he grinned down at me. "You're so full of shit."

I attempted a smirk. He was right. My face still hurt. My throat and lungs felt twisted like knots. I hated feeling so helpless. I hated that I'd brought them into this. I was consumed with worry that my mother was looking for me right now, maybe even calling the police to find me. Still, I didn't want to leave. I wanted to stay with them forever.

"What do you need?" he asked.

"Water," I mouthed. "And to get up."

North held his hands out, palms up. I let go of Kota and clutched at North. He hefted me until I was on my feet. I blinked at the bandages at my wrists. I felt more crunching of bandage seams around my ankles. I was wearing a pair of shorts that didn't fit and a large Nike t-shirt. I wondered who changed my clothes, but really didn't care. My poor brain couldn't handle that thought at the moment.

I wobbled on my feet. My legs didn't want to work. My ankle throbbed. I willed myself to at least stand up straight. Kota rose with me, and wrapped an arm around my waist. North held on to my hands until I was stable.

North stepped beside me, holding on to my left hand like he was never letting go. Nathan and Silas hovered behind him. Their eyes were wide, mouths drawn, terrified. I mustered up another smile, hoping they would know I was okay. Nathan looked relieved but Silas hesitated, his dark eyes narrowing, unsure.

"Let's get inside and sit down," Dr. Green said somewhere behind Silas. "We should talk."

"I think we need to let her sleep," North said next to me. "She needs to recover."

"We need to figure out our next move," Mr. Blackbourne's smooth vocals cut through and I shivered with embarrassment. I couldn't believe he was there, too.

North squared off his shoulders. "What we're doing is getting her the hell out of there," he said.

I squeezed his hand. His eyes glided to mine. "Inside," I whispered. "I want to talk."

He smirked at me. "Baby, I don't know if you've noticed, but you can't talk."

I rolled my eyes. "Never stopped me before," I croaked out.

He and Kota, who must have been the only ones who

could have heard me, started chuckling. Silas finally relaxed his shoulders. He and Nathan stepped out of the way. Behind them stood Dr. Green, with Luke, Gabriel, Victor and Mr. Blackbourne next to him. Nine concerned sets of eyes fell on my face and I shivered under the weight of their pity. Heat clung to my cheeks, but I was feeling too miserable to protest.

It took a little bit of stretching and a few steps assisted by Kota before I was able to break the stiffness from my limbs. The entire lower half of my body felt numb. I staggered toward the house. Mr. Blackbourne held the sliding door open for me.

I stood in the living room until everyone gathered inside. Kota motioned to the large leather chair, but I shook my head. There was a large wooden coffee table on the rug in the middle of the room. I slid onto my knees to the rug and sat with my butt on my heels. I felt the bandages against my ankles wrinkle and a pain shot through my legs. My tailbone radiated equal agony through my lower spine. It was dulled, more like a throbbing ache that eased in and settled into my bones. I couldn't sit on my butt, I knew, not right now. The ankle was bad enough but tolerable. I folded my hands into my lap and I patiently waited, my eyes challenging anyone to tell me to do otherwise.

The others took positions around the table. Silas, Luke and North sat on the couch. Victor fell into the armchair. The fire was gone from his eyes. I only caught glistening and it looked terrible on him. Kota and Gabriel took up positions next to me on the floor. Gabriel chewed on a thumbnail, as if he wasn't sure if he should be near me or not.

Mr. Blackbourne stood by the coffee table, his arms crossed against his chest, looking displeased. Nathan disappeared for a moment but came back with a bottle of water which he handed to me.

Dr. Green plopped down on top of the coffee table in front of me. He scooped a flashlight from his pocket.

"Let me check your throat," he said. He gently placed a thumb on my chin to get me to open up. He shifted the flashlight to let the light glare into my throat. The warmth of the light was surprisingly soothing on my esophagus. I pressed my tongue down in my mouth so he could see better.

"Was it vinegar again?" Kota asked next to me.

I squeezed his hand and nodded.

Dr. Green let go of me and sat back, swinging his eyes to Kota. "This happened before?"

"Her mother made her drink vinegar and lemon juice a couple weeks ago. It burned her throat for a few days so she couldn't talk."

"That's not all," North said, in a quiet tone. I fired off a look at him but he ignored me completely. "She was forced to kneel in rice on the hard floor for a few hours a couple of weeks ago, too."

"And she sat in that stool before," Luke said. "That was several hours, too. Not in the tub though, just in the kitchen. Just the once."

North's face flashed with surprise and he frowned. "That we know of..." He gazed over at me.

There was a stunned silence that fell between them all as they registered the truth. I wanted to tell them that outside of the vinegar and being tied in the bathtub, that the rice and the stool sitting was actually pretty easy. I could handle that. Weren't they ever punished for doing bad things? Didn't parents spank their kids? Somehow I felt that it wasn't the right response. My face flared with heat. I didn't know what normal was.

Dr. Green pressed a palm to his eye. "Why didn't you tell us what she was going through?"

"We were working on it," Kota said. "I didn't know how bad things had gotten. And I didn't want to overwhelm her with… with us."

Dr. Green's head flexed back. "Kota," he said. "This is abuse. You shouldn't have kept this to yourself."

"She wasn't fully with us when the vinegar thing

happened," Kota insisted. "And she was around us so often these past couple of weeks, I didn't realize she was…"

"You know better than that," Mr. Blackbourne hovered over Dr. Green's shoulder. His steel eyes narrowed. "Abuse doesn't disappear overnight."

"I didn't know about the rice or the other parts," Kota said.

"That's not what I mean. You didn't tell us the full truth about what was going on. You brought her to us knowing her home life and kept it from us. We might have prevented this if you had told us earlier. Now we're left without a choice."

I swallowed. They were talking in circles around me. "It's my choice," I said in a whisper.

Mr. Blackbourne twisted his head to gaze down at me. "What are you saying?"

I closed my eyes, swallowing hard again. I knew they didn't want to hear this but I had to say it. "I have to go back."

"No," Gabriel said. He grabbed my hand. He slid closer on his knees near me. His crystal eyes glossed over with tears. "You're not fucking going back there. I'll kidnap you myself and take you home with me."

There was a round of loud talking and it was a mess. I didn't understand what anyone was saying. I couldn't attempt to talk over them. I looked desperately at Kota. He leaned in, holding his head close.

I angled until my lips brushed his ear as I whispered. "I have to go back."

Kota shook his head, pulling away to narrow his eyes at me. "No," he commanded. "You can't. Sang, you were in there for hours. Do you even remember what happened?"

I nodded. Of course I did. I remembered everything. I knew the truth. If I disappeared, there was a lot more to lose than if I went back now.

The others were arguing but it was a blur of noise.

Gabriel squeezed my hand, clinging to me. Maybe he would listen.

I leaned into him. "My mother is ill," I said. "She didn't eat. With the medication she takes, she's probably making herself super sick again."

"She just tied you to a stool and left you to die," Gabriel said. "You want to go back and save her?"

I felt my body shaking as I forced the words out. "She's my mother." That meant something, didn't it? Wasn't I supposed watch over her?

He reeled his head back as if I'd slapped him. His hand squeezed mine again. I clutched it back, begging silently that he might understand. "We can't," he said, though softer.

"My mother probably doesn't even remember what she did. I can slip back in."

Dr. Green's gentle eyes washed over my face. He pressed his palms to my cheeks. "Sweetheart," he soothed. "Do you understand what you're asking? If you go back, she could do it again. She might do worse. We might not make it next time."

"We will make it," Kota said. "We'll be right there. I'm not leaving her again. There won't be a next time."

"This isn't happening," Mr. Blackbourne said. He started pacing the floor, his hands on his hips. His glasses glinted against the light as he turned back to look down at me. "No, I refuse. I can't allow it. She can't stay in that house."

He didn't understand. I needed to go back before she called the cops and they were arrested. I couldn't ask them to take me in. Where would I go? "What about Marie? What happens to her if I leave?" I asked. "What about my dad? Would he be arrested? He didn't know." I hunched my shoulders, swallowing hard, trying to suppress a cough.

"If he doesn't know, it's neglect," Mr. Blackbourne said. "You can't stay in a house with an abusive mother. Marie can't, either. Your father made his choice. You didn't have one."

"I have one now. Where else am I going to go? I have to go back."

Anguished glances were exchanged above my head.

Mr. Blackbourne knelt nearby, his fingertips brushed my arm. The gentle touch forced me to look in his direction. His steel eyes focused on mine. "Miss Sorenson," he said in a quiet voice. "Listen to me. You can't go back. We can't keep you safe there."

"She needs help," I whispered. There was nothing they could say that would convince me otherwise. Where else would I go? Kota was being brave, but he couldn't take me in. How would any of them explain it to their parents? How could I explain everything to them without a voice?

I turned to Gabriel, looking for help. He bent his head over, pressing his ear to my lips. He spoke for me. "If she's not there, her mother may call the police to find her. If the police find out what happened, she'll end up under control of the state."

Kota frowned. He swung a distressed glance at the others.

"We could..." Dr. Green started. He looked over at Mr. Blackbourne intently. A silent communication of expressions passed over my head faster than I could keep up with.

Mr. Blackbourne shook his head. "No approval. It's not a shelter."

"Application?" Dr. Green.

Again Mr. Blackbourne shook his head. "Trial time. We don't even know if she qualifies."

"We could keep an eye on her until then. Special circumstances? Expedited? They can't refuse us."

"No," Kota said. "I don't want her there."

"What?" I asked. I was having trouble figuring out this conversation. Did I miss something? Maybe I did need to sleep.

They all ignored me and concentrated on Kota.

Kota hooked his arms under my thighs and around my

back, lifting me off of the floor and pulling me into his lap. "No, she's not going there," he said. He crossed his legs on the ground and drew me in close to him. His arms encircled my waist. His cheek touched my temple as he talked over my head. "She's right. She has to go back."

"Fucking hell no!" North shouted louder than the others but each of them expressed equal displeasure, all except Mr. Blackbourne and Dr. Green, who only looked curiously at Kota.

"Sang goes back," Kota said in a louder voice. "But not alone. We're going to set security up in her house. We'll monitor her. We'll be close by. Anything she needs, we'll be there for her." I felt his chest rising as he inhaled. The sound of his voice reverberated through me. "We're not prepared to take her out of her house right now. She's right. If her mother calls the police, we're not equipped for it alone."

"We can handle this," Mr. Blackbourne said. "We've done it before."

"We aren't prepared right now, not without asking a favor. Her mother will call the police today if she figures out she's gone. I'm surprised she hasn't done so yet. What are the police going to do? They'll arrest her mom and her dad and they'll send her and Marie to live in a foster home."

"We can't get the police involved," Mr. Blackbourne said.

Kota nodded. "It's too volatile. We'll get her mom treatment. We'll make sure it doesn't happen again. We need a better plan than just kidnapping her."

"It won't be kidnapping," Dr. Green said. "You're underestimating us. If we just call…"

"Not that." Kota said, zeroing is gaze in on Mr. Blackbourne. "She is never going to the Academy. I don't want them knowing any more about her. We're going to do it without their help."

My eyes popped open. Dr. Green and Mr. Blackbourne were going to send me to the Academy? How? I didn't even know it was a possibility.

Why would Kota refuse to let me? And why wouldn't he let the Academy help? Wasn't he part of the Academy, too?

The silence in the room overwhelmed me until I shivered hard against Kota.

"None of you understand what you're doing," Mr. Blackbourne said.

"I don't care," Gabriel said. "Kota's right. We need a little more time. I'll stay with her. Whatever she needs."

"I'll do it," Nathan said.

The others chimed in, too.

Dr. Green nodded. "I will, too. Maybe Kota is right. We need to keep her close. If we involve the Academy, she'll be too exposed and it is far too soon for her. We need a little time, but I bet we could do it on our own." His green eyes flickered at me before he turned to Mr. Blackbourne. "And I can't believe for one second you'd tell us no."

Mr. Blackbourne shifted on his feet, frowning.

"What's the matter, Mr. Blackbourne?" North asked. "Don't think we can keep up with one little girl?"

Mr. Blackbourne adjusted his glasses higher with a forefinger. His eyes closed as he talked. "Fine. If that's what Kota wants, if it's what Miss Sorenson wants, if everyone is sure, we'll do it." He opened his eyes again and pointed a finger at all of them. "But I want your word you'll never take advantage of her, given her situation."

"Who the hell do you think we are?" Victor barked at him. The fire roared to life in his eyes again. "You think we'd ever..."

"I mean it," Mr. Blackbourne snapped back at him. "If I hear one word from her that you have touched her or so much as looked at her in a way she didn't want, any complaint, any rumor, I'll pull you all out of this, and I wouldn't hesitate to drop you from the Academy."

The threat hung in the air. Everyone drew quiet under

the weight of what he was suggesting.

I couldn't believe for a moment any of them would hurt me or do anything bad to me. They were my friends. Kota, Gabriel... all of them. I understood Mr. Blackbourne and his need to say it out loud. No one complained.

Mr. Blackbourne turned back to Kota. "And I'm telling you, Mr. Lee," he pointed at this face. "If this happens again, we're calling in the Academy. I won't allow anything like this to continue. Not with us."

Kota's arms squeezed around me, his hands spreading over my stomach and waist as he glared back at Mr. Blackbourne over my head. I didn't fully understand what was going on, but I did know they were granting my request. In what way they were going to allow it, I wasn't sure.

"That's enough for now, I think," Dr. Green said. He waved a hand in the air. "Let me examine her and we'll clean her up. We'll eat and we'll figure out what our next step is."

Inner Sanctum

Two hours later, I was wearing the shorts and blouse I had on the day before, clean and fresh from Nathan's laundry room. I stood in my parents' driveway, with Nathan holding my left hand and Luke holding my right. North pulled his black Jeep into the drive, bringing Victor, Mr. Blackbourne and Dr. Green. The others were close behind on foot.

Our orders from Mr. Blackbourne were to check to see if my mother was still sleeping and to stabilize her. If she tried to come after me again, the boys would pull me out of there.

I padded over in my bare feet, my bandages in place. My fingers tingled between the knuckles of both Nathan and Luke. With their palms pressed to mine, it eased my trembling. I didn't quite know what to expect. I was bringing them into my world. This was way further than I ever expected them to be. Despite what we'd already been through together, was I ready for this?

We walked in to the garage together. At the steps, I let go of them both so I could open the door.

Once I cracked open the door, I stuck my head in and waited. The house was quiet. I looked back at the guys, stepped inside and out of the way.

My heart was in my throat as Nathan and Luke entered. Both of them scanned the room. Nathan did a second and third glance at the nearly barren family room, with a single, barely touched couch and not much else. Like my bedroom, the house had just enough and not a piece more.

While they both had been inside before, it was strange to me to have them walking in the side door. I felt like at any moment my mother might come around the corner and find them.

I knew if that happened, they were supposed to pull me out of the house. I'd been told repeatedly by all of them what was expected of me. If they couldn't ensure my safety inside the house, I wouldn't be allowed to stay.

I led the way through the kitchen and to the hallway on the other side. I stepped quietly in places where I knew the house wouldn't creak. When I turned to the wall to slide over toward my mom's room, I smelled Luke's vanilla scent and felt his warmth. He was so close that his arm warmed mine. When I looked back, Nathan stationed himself at the other end of the hall, closer to the kitchen, standing by and ready to charge in or fetch the others as needed.

I willed myself to keep moving. I was scared. I was worried my appearance would alert my mother and she'd come after me again. I was worried for the guys, who would be at risk if they were exposed. I was stuck between these two worlds and unsure how to break them apart again.

Did I want to?

I sucked in a deep breath and held it. I tilted away from the wall, so I could peek inside my mother's room.

My mother was in her bed, in a deep sleep. She was snoring loudly this time, too. I moved quickly, pushing the door back to bump against the wall to see if she woke up. No response.

I stepped into view, shuffling forward along the beige carpet toward her bed.

She wasn't sweating anymore. There was a pill bottle spilled over on the comforter. I recognized the morphine pills. The heavy curtains were drawn tight.

She'd blocked herself from the world she imagined was cruel and out to get her. How strange I felt about it now. Despite her efforts that she thought would keep me safe from being raped and murdered, I was now standing over her with a team determined to keep me safe from her crazy punishments. She feared people entering her sanctuary, and instead of warding people away, she drew Kota and the others in as they tried to protect me.

It felt wrong, even as I wished for my friends to remain with me more than anything. I had made excuses for her behavior in the past for punishments and lectures. Her illness made her confused and unable to control herself. My mother didn't want anyone in her world. It felt wrong because she was sick, and her only request was to keep everyone out. Your family should come before friends or anyone else. You should always protect them. Why were principles such as loyalty and blood bonds such cruel, twisted things?

Luke stepped into the room. He crossed as quietly as I had, using the same spots I had picked out as my path. His lean, strong body moved with care and he hovered over my mother, his head tilted as he frowned. His blond hair fell in the way of his dark eyes. If my mother only knew, she would die right then. Despite how kind and affectionate Luke could be, she would only see a stranger, one of the scary monsters she feared.

Luke reached into his back pocket, pulling a tiny brown bottle out. He uncorked the top, and held it out toward my mother's mouth and nose. My mother breathed in deeply as she slept. A moment later, the snoring softened, and her head tilted to the side.

"This should keep her out for a couple of hours," Luke said quietly. He corked the bottle again and slipped it into his pocket.

"Where did you get that?" I whispered. I swallowed, knowing my voice was probably too soft for him to hear anyway. "Do you carry things like that all the time?"

He looked up at me, flashing a smile, his brown eyes catching a spark from the light streaming in through the windows. "Don't ask those questions."

I sighed, twisting my mouth. By saying he couldn't tell me, he just answered both of my questions. Academy secrets.

Nathan popped his head in. His mouth opened like he wanted to say something, but he caught on my mother sleeping in the bed. His blue eyes darkened. "It's hard to believe that's the same person who..."

"I know," Luke said. "It doesn't seem possible."

My eyes hunted out Luke's. I wanted to get this over with.

He nodded to me. "Let's get the others."

♥♥♥

Moments later, Dr. Green sat on the edge of my mother's bed, checking her pulse, listening to her breathing with a stethoscope and taking other vitals. Mr. Blackbourne sorted through the collection of pill bottles on her nightstand.

"There's more in her drawer," I whispered to them, sitting on the other side of the bed. I scooped up the spilled pills across the blanket and dropped them back into the open container. The boys were in the hallway, looking in on us and waiting for orders.

Mr. Blackbourne held out his phone, flashing a picture of the labels. "There's at least five different doctors. Some of these prescriptions are repeats. She's taking them irregularly and getting double the dose of the narcotics if these refill dates are right. Duplicates."

"I'll call their offices," Dr. Green said. "I'll get copies of her medical history faxed over." He sighed, pulling himself away from my mother to sit up and rubbing a finger at his temple. "I'll need to know more before making a decision. I need to get an IV in her, though. Sang's right, she's desperately dehydrated. I might have to order an ambulance. That'll be complicated to do without the Academy."

Mr. Blackbourne nodded. He handed the pill bottles over to Dr. Green. "Do your best to avoid it. Collect what you need." He crossed the room, curling his fingers at me so I'd follow. I crawled off the bed, feeling unsure about leaving my mother alone with Dr. Green. What if she woke up and had a strange person so close to her?

Out in the hallway again, Mr. Blackbourne closed the door, leaving Dr. Green alone with my mother. He turned to us. "Okay, Luke, I want a map of this house, every exit point, every nook covered. Silas and North, go fix that bathroom upstairs. When Dr. Green is done, Nathan and Victor, I want you to get in there and look for any more ropes. Anything that can be used as a restraint, I want it gone." He focused on me. "Show me your room."

I blushed but turned at his command, guiding the way to the stairs. The others followed behind me, with Victor and Nathan staying behind for Dr. Green.

Silas pointed the upstairs bathroom door out to North. The frame was split. They collected near it, scanning the damage.

North's face contorted, eyes going to the floor where the stool remained, fractured into pieces. His fists clenched.

Silas touched his forearm quickly, bringing him back to the job they were told to do.

Marie's door was open and I could see the usual mess in her room. She was probably still over at Danielle's. I hoped she wouldn't pop over right now. I didn't want her to know the guys were here. I didn't want her to know what happened.

At my own bedroom door, I twisted the handle to open it and stepped in.

I stopped short, mortified by the mess. The window was open, probably where Nathan got in when he came to look for me. The bookshelf was smashed down across the carpet. The books were scattered across the floor and torn. My trunk was open, the contents completely dumped out.

My school books were ripped through, the notebooks and papers spilled out. The contents from the closet were emptied across the carpet. The sheets were pulled from the bed. The mattress was slumped over, half hanging on the floor.

Mr. Blackbourne materialized next to me, frowning. Gabriel appeared beside me on the other side. He pressed his palm to mine, his fingers covering mine.

Kota tiptoed around the mess, his eyes seeking out answers to silent questions.

Mr. Blackbourne studied the room. "Was it like this before?"

I shook my head. "I had my school books on the bed but..." My whispering stopped. My voice wasn't going to let me explain.

Victor emerged from the hallway looking curious. He remained quiet, his fire eyes moving over the contents of the room.

"She was looking for something," Kota said. He knelt, picking up the edge of the bookshelf. Mr. Blackbourne crouched with him and helped pick up the bookshelf, putting it back against the wall. Kota looked over at me. "What would she want?"

I shook my head, blushing. I had no idea. I looked at Gabriel. He leaned his head in and I whispered. He spoke for me. "She said her mom found the notes from the boys at school and the detention slip; that's when she flipped out. But the room was intact mostly then. She must have come back looking for more."

"If she found more," Mr. Blackbourne said, "this might have been much worse."

North appeared in the doorway. His eyes, like the others, searching the destroyed room. He held up the pink cell phone. The face was cracked and blank. "It was in the tub," he said. "I don't think it's working."

I leaned in to whisper to Gabriel. "She says she's sorry, Victor." Gabriel smirked, chopping me on the head. "Shut up."

Victor took the phone from North and pocketed it. "I'll get her another one." He flashed me a look and I tried shaking my head, but he pointed a lean finger in my direction. "Don't even start with me."

North disappeared again. I moved away to start sorting out the mess near the trunk. Gabriel went through my closet. Mr. Blackbourne and Kota stuffed books onto the shelves. Victor hung back near the door, watching.

Mr. Blackbourne picked up the stereo, putting it back on the top of the bookshelf. He turned it on, hitting play on the CD player. My guess was he wanted to test it to see if it still worked. A piano piece started. He blinked at it, tilting his head as he listened.

"What song is that?" Victor asked. He had his arms crossed over his chest and was leaning against the wall.

I looked at him, not sure if he could hear me across the room. He frowned when he realized it and came forward, kneeling next to me. I leaned to him, hanging on to his arm as I did to whisper in his ear. "Mysterious by Yuko Ohigashi."

"Who?" Mr. Blackbourne asked him.

Victor repeated the name. "I don't recognize it." I tugged on his arm so he'd lean in again and I could whisper. He repeated out loud this time. "It's one of her favorites."

He reached out to me, brushing a finger across my cheek. He stood up, moving to the door and disappearing.

I went back to folding the old clothes and putting them back into the trunk. Mr. Blackbourne collected my school books. Kota started organizing the books on the shelves by author and title name. I didn't have the heart to tell him he didn't have to. Some of the books were torn. He collected the pages across the floor, finding where the missing pages went and tucked them neatly inside. He stacked the torn ones on the floor beside him.

He pulled out one that didn't have a title, my journal, and absentmindedly thumbed it open, looking at the pages.

His eyebrows shot up and he turned to me. "Sang? What's this?"

Did he expect me to answer? Frustrated that they kept forgetting, I used sign language to quickly spell out, "Journal." If Luke knew it, the others probably did, too. They were smart Academy guys.

Gabriel turned when I was making the last two letters. "Did she just flip you off?"

Kota laughed. "No. She's using sign language. She spelled out journal." He looked back at me. "What language is this?"

I spelled again. It frustrated me because it felt like I was taking forever to communicate something that would have taken a second to say out loud. My sign language skills were rusty.

He repeated what I spelled for him, "Korean lettering, and English words."

"Let me see that." Mr. Blackbourne held his hand out to Kota.

I sighed, exasperated. I shot a look at Gabriel. He completely understood. "You can't go reading her journal," he said. "That's private chick stuff."

"I can't read it," Mr. Blackbourne said. He took the book from Kota and flipped through the pages, checking it. "Is there a key to this puzzle?" he asked.

Kota watched as I signed "She doesn't need one." He smiled, catching on. He slid a finger up to the bridge of his glasses, pressing to his nose. "I get it. She used Korean lettering so she wouldn't need a key. If she ever forgot, she could just check a book to translate." I signed to him again and he relayed the message. "So her family couldn't read it."

Mr. Blackbourne checked the floor, found a pencil and brought it and the journal to me. "I want to see you write in it."

I lifted an eyebrow. *Why?*

"Write: The five boxing wizards jump quickly."

I twisted my lips, confused that he picked such an

awkward sentence. I opened to a random blank page, scratching in the lines and circles. When I was done, I passed it to him.

"You've done this for a while," Mr. Blackbourne said. "You did it too fast to be a new trick." He checked my work.

"Sang's full of little secrets," Gabriel said.

"Tell me about it," Kota beamed at me. "When were you going to tell me about the sign language?"

I shrugged.

"One of these days," Mr. Blackbourne said as he snapped the journal shut and passed it back to Kota, "Miss Sorenson, you and I are going to have a conversation to catch up on what you can actually do. You have some very unique talents."

Kota shot him a look but Mr. Blackbourne turned away, ignoring it.

I was finishing up the trunk and closing the lid when Silas poked his head in.

"Sang, where does your dad keep his tools? Are there any spare wood scraps?"

I blew out a sigh, spilling onto the carpet on my back and rolling my eyes. I looked up at him from my upside down position, smirking. Was everyone going to forget I couldn't talk?

He laughed, shaking his head. "Can you please show me?"

I looked over at Kota, wordlessly asking him if he needed me.

"Go help," he said.

"Kota," Mr. Blackbourne said. "Grab the other end of her bed, will you?" He bent over, his tie swinging free from his blazer as he pushed my bed away from the wall.

I got up, confused at what they were doing, but Silas tugged me out of the room. His large, strong hand enveloped mine and I let him guide me down the hallway. I glanced into the bathroom on our way. North was pulling the loose bit of frame out with a pocket knife. The stool was gone. The shower behind him was in pieces, the plumbing pulled from the wall and spread on the floor. Did Silas do that?

I followed Silas down the back stairs and out into the garage. I lead the way across the drive to the shed in the back, opening the side door and stepping out of the way so Silas could enter.

I was hitting the switch as Silas shut the door behind us. We were cast into darkness. The old fluorescent lights above our heads crackled, needing time to heat up.

My skin tingled and my heart thundered. I was alone with Silas.

Silas's hands found me in the dark. He hugged me close, tightly enough that my breath escaped my lungs. I froze, too stunned to move. His chin dropped to the top of my head, and the warm breath from his nose mixed into my hair.

With trembling fingers, I slipped my arms around him to hug him back. Was this what he needed?

His right arm went under my butt to hold me up and his other tightened at my back to press me to him. He scooped me up off the floor. My feet dangled on either side of his legs.

I buried my face into his shoulder, too breathless and consumed by his embrace. It was too close and everything I wanted right then. How did he know?

"*Aggele mou,*" he whispered, and he moved his face until his cheek was next to mine. "Sang, don't ever do that to me again. Don't you ever fucking wait..." His breath was hot against my ear.

I couldn't speak. Tears stung my eyes. I hadn't realized until that moment that Silas had been holding back something from everyone, waiting until we were alone to tell me this. I swallowed heavily, tightening my arms around his neck. My fingers slipped into his hair, feeling the smooth black locks. I felt so bad. I'd scared him.

"Don't you ever wait to call me," he said. "I don't care

if you stubbed your toe or you're just lonely. You don't even have to wait until then. You call, I'll be here." He sighed, pressing his lips close to my ear and whispered. "If it were up to me, you wouldn't be here at all. I'd take you home with me now."

"Silas," I croaked out a whisper. My mind whirled and I sucked back a sob. I didn't want to cry. If I cried now, I wouldn't be able to hold it in any more. Silas's hug felt good, but I was trying my best to be brave around the guys and not show how scared I was. Monsters. Demons. All the scary things my dreams held and my mother whispered to me over the years. I could handle anything she threw me into. I couldn't handle this. I couldn't see Silas so freaked out.

Silas shuddered against me. His large hand smoothed across my back. "When you called my name on the phone, I knew. Your voice squeaked, but I heard you. The line cut out and I couldn't get here fast enough. I came as quick as I could. Kota and the others were across town and couldn't get back sooner. I called Nathan and stayed on the line with him when I couldn't get back in touch with you. I knew something was wrong. When he couldn't find you, I thought maybe we were too late." He growled softly in my ear. "*Aggele mou*, Sang. We were almost too late."

"Silas," I whispered. "You came for me. I'm here. It's okay."

He pulled back enough until he could press his forehead to mine. The light above finished warming and flickered to life. I was caught up in those soft brown eyes of his, dark and soothing, glistening. "Promise me," he demanded. "Say it."

"I won't wait," I whispered. I swallowed hard. "Silas, I promise. I'll call."

He grunted, pulled me in close against him once again and sighed into my shoulder. "I hate this," he said. "I don't want you here with them."

Where else did I have to go? I couldn't go home with

him or anyone else. I couldn't join the Academy, if I'd wanted and even if Kota said it was fine. My parents wouldn't allow it. The only way to leave would be to call the cops but the results wouldn't be what any of us wanted. "It's not for forever," I whispered. "If I ran away with you, they'd come after me. Won't everyone else get into trouble?"

He grunted again and lowered me to the ground, keeping a hand on me to make sure I was stable. He pulled away to rub at his face. "Fine. Let's fix your damn shower."

"Was it broken?" I asked. I turned from him, my head buzzing after all the emotions. I sucked in some air and looked for the toolbox on the shelves.

"I felt like breaking it," he said. His eyes moved to the collection of boxes that took up the majority of the floor in the garage. It was a mess and I was embarrassed by it but he didn't seem put off. "So I just took it apart. I'm going to put a timer on it, though. If she even attempts to do it again, it'll only be on for a half hour before it cuts off. You can flip it off and turn it back on again, but it'll stop it from being run for hours on end like that."

"Where'd you learn how to do that?" I wasn't sure he heard me. I found the toolbox and pulled it off the shelf.

He took the box away from me. "My dad's a plumber," he said.

I'd half expected him to say the Academy. I smiled to myself. For friends, we still hardly knew each other. I wondered how many other secrets the guys had, and was sure they had many more than I did. I felt as if they were helping a near complete stranger, which was so messed up because my heart was telling me I was much closer to them than my own family that I'd known all my life.

♥♥♥

When we got back upstairs, North had the door off of the hinges.

Silas held up the tool box. “No wood,” he said.

“Damn,” North said. He blew out a sigh. “Okay, I’m going to make a new door and a new frame. Silas, you beat the shit out of it.”

“Yup,” Silas said, beaming.

“Sang Baby? Could you fetch me a pen?” North took the toolbox from Silas’s hands and opened the lid, pulling out a measuring tape and evaluating the other contents.

I sourced a pen and paper and gave them to North and headed down to my bedroom again. Mr. Blackbourne and Kota were next to the far wall, talking. The bed had been moved. Now instead of against the wall, the bed was sticking out lengthwise into the room, with the head of it under the window. The bookshelf was moved near the half door to the attic. It created another barrier, making a square space in front of the attic door.

“It creates an entry way,” Kota was saying, “but it makes it kind of obvious that she might be trying to mask that attic door.”

Mr. Blackbourne rubbed his palm against his cheek. “There’s no other furniture to work with. Unless they demand she move it, leave it there. We’re not prepared to escalate.”

Escalate? What did that mean? I moved further into the room, trying to figure out why they wanted to block the view of the attic door from the entryway. I looked at Kota, asking silent questions.

He smiled. “Gabriel,” he called.

The attic door opened and Gabriel popped his head out. “Yeah?”

“Show Sang.”

Gabriel crawled out of the space, with his two locks of dyed blond hair hanging across his forehead. The rest of his rich, russet brown hair was mussed in the back. He left the door to the attic open. He dropped on top of my bed and spread out a little.

“Go,” Mr. Blackbourne said.

Gabriel leapt from the bed, dropped behind the bookshelf, slid across the floor and quietly shut the attic door behind himself as he crawled in.

"Horrible," Mr. Blackbourne said. "You're not fast enough."

"Oy," Gabriel called from the attic. He opened the door again, letting it swing across the carpet until it stopped. "You try it."

"You still need a security signal," Kota said.

"We could just put a better lock on her door. One they can't open with a push pin," Gabriel said, crawling out of the space again.

I shook my head. Kota seemed to read my mind and knew the answer to this. "It'd be ideal but it probably won't happen. They'd notice a new lock."

Victor appeared in the doorway, his eyebrow going up at the rearranged furniture. "Mr. Blackbourne," he said. "You should come see."

I shot a questioning look at Victor but he held up his palm at me. I wasn't supposed to go along.

Mr. Blackbourne crossed the room, passing me closer than he really needed to. I could smell his spring soap scent. "Stay here," he commanded of me in a low voice.

I rubbed at my eyebrow, feeling awkward. Mr. Blackbourne temporarily grounded me to my room.

"Trouble," Gabriel said. He leaned off the bed so he could grab my hand. "Come show me the platform in the back."

I sighed. "We need a flashlight."

Kota pulled a set of keys from his pocket, Attached was a metallic green flashlight. He unhooked the light from the keychain and handed it to me. "Don't hurt yourself in there."

"Hey," Gabriel said, pouting his lips in a way that made my heart melt. "You didn't say that to me."

Kota waved him off and strolled out of the room and down the stairs.

I walked around the bed toward the open attic door.

Gabriel got on his knees behind me, ready to follow. I flicked on the flashlight and crawled on my knees through the attic space. Gabriel left the door open, shuffling behind me. He had another flashlight on, attached to his own keys and was shining it around the space, looking at the exposed beams and the insulation.

I crawled inside about ten feet and found the platform in the back. I pointed the flashlight back to him to get his attention, swinging the light so he could see the one beam of wood that cut through the middle of the opening. I slipped between the beam and the wall, angling myself in. The platform space was as big as a closet, with enough room above our heads to stand up fully if we wanted.

Gabriel put his flashlight between his teeth and angled himself in. He got in on his knees, and sat down, crossing his legs. He sought my hand in the dark and tugged until I nearly fell into his lap. He held me with one arm around my waist, while he shined the flashlight around, checking how high the ceiling went. "You call us from here?"

"Yes," I whispered. "I think it's above the laundry room." I swallowed, the air was so dry and hot, I felt my throat getting scratchy again. My hands were pressed against his chest as he held me close. I squirmed, twisting to see where he was looking.

A playful chop landed on my head. "Stop wriggling." He pulled his cellphone out. "We need Luke."

"Why?"

Gabriel ignored me, pressing the phone to his ear. "Oy Luke, get up here to Sang's attic. Have you been back here? Come check this out."

A moment later, there was scuffling on the other side of the attic. I swung the flashlight around to help Luke find his way along. Gabriel did the same, casting us into darkness. I sensed his face getting close to mine and I held my breath, unsure of what he was doing. His tongue met my skin and he licked from my jaw to my cheek. I choked out a squeal, poking him in the stomach out of surprise. He lurched forward, laughing.

Luke popped his head up between the beam and the wall of the platform. "What's so funny?"

I tilted the flashlight around to hold it like a candle between us, lighting up the area with a gentle glow. "Gabriel," I whispered, "he..."

"Is a fucking handsome guy. He already knows, Trouble." Gabriel smirked. "Luke, tell me we can take out that beam right there." Gabriel swung his flashlight at the exposed 4x4 that split the opening. I had to go around it to crawl into the platform.

"Hm," Luke said. He borrowed the flashlight from my hands. He checked out the beam and the surrounding wood. "Maybe." He started to rise, putting a hand on my shoulder to steady himself as he crawled onto the platform. Luke leaned into me, and kept himself close. His chest was pressed at my back. His breath tickled my neck.

I pressed myself against Gabriel to give Luke more room. My insides flipped around. Being so close and in near darkness with these two left me blushing.

Gabriel rocked back, leaning up against one of the other beams surrounding the platform. His strong arms around my waist dragged me along. "Yes? No? What?"

"It doesn't look important," Luke said. He stood, finding where the wood disappeared further into the roof structure. He swung the beam of light around, reaching up above his head, trying to touch the ceiling above us. "Probably can take it out," he said. "Not today though. It'll take some work and we're running out of time." He crouched down again, his chest again close to my back and his face close to mine. "The space is small."

"Good enough for her," Gabriel said. I felt his lips moving against my forehead. It was way too crowded with three people. "You should walk the house and see if anyone can hear us."

"You go," Luke said.

"Call North."

Luke pulled out his phone and dialed a number. "I'll

call Nathan. North's run off to our house to grab another door." He paused with the phone to his ear. He leaned his head forward, bumping his nose into my cheek. I twisted my head to smirk at him and he was grinning. "Nathan?" he asked, looking right at me as he talked. "Walk the house, see if you can hear me talking to you. Well, stop being busy, we need to test this attic space." He pulled the phone from his face a little. "Start talking so he can hear."

I twisted my lips, rolling my eyes. "Luke," I whispered.

Behind my head, Gabriel started singing the theme song to *Friends*. Luke started laughing, joining in. Gabriel's voice was golden, but Luke's voice was polished, too. I was giggling so hard, I pressed my forehead against Gabriel's shoulder, smothering myself and breathing in the scent of a light fruity and spice musk. My shoulders shook as I laughed.

"What?" Luke stopped singing to talk on the phone. "Well I mean how much? Where?" Luke motioned to Gabriel, spinning his finger like he wanted him to keep going.

Gabriel started singing again, repeating the chorus as Luke rattled questions off to Nathan.

Luke hung up. "Okay, he can hear us on the back stairs and in the laundry room. We need to soundproof."

"We should do that to her room, too," Gabriel said.

"But then she couldn't hear anyone coming," Luke said.

"God damn it," Gabriel said. He shifted his legs, moving me in the process until my body was tucked neatly into his chest, his hands against my back. "Fuck all this. Let's just take her."

"Gabriel," I whispered.

A chop landed on my head again. "Shush," Gabriel said. "Men are talking."

I laughed, and I poked him in the ribs. He was always picking on me, but I secretly loved it. He was fun and amazing.

"Ow," Gabriel said, letting go of me with one hand to rub at his ribs, feigning hurt and grinning.

"Hey," Nathan called from the attic door. "You've got Sang back there?"

"Maybe," Luke called back.

"Get her out of there. Dr. Green said it's not good for her throat to get all that dry air."

"God damn it, Luke, why did you let her come back here?" Gabriel shifted, pushing me off of his lap and onto Luke's.

Luke wrapped his arms around my waist, holding me as we knelt together on the platform. Being passed around like that was making my stomach flip again.

Gabriel had to angle strangely around the beam to weave his way out. He let go of the beam too soon, and fell on his back. He grunted, picked himself up and turned around, reaching back for me. I took his hand, stepping out next to him, crouching again under the short part of the attic space. He crept ahead of me toward the door. I shadowed him on my hands and knees. Luke angled himself around the beam to follow.

"Oy, Trouble," Gabriel called from ahead of me. "Like my butt?" He stopped and wriggled it at me.

"I like Sang's butt," Luke said.

"Hey now," Nathan said. "Stop talking about her butt."

I stopped and crouched low, laughing against the floor. It was a mistake as I sucked in a lung full of super dry dust and I started coughing again.

Luke's arms grabbed me around the waist and Gabriel gripped my arms. They pushed and pulled at the same time to get me out of the attic. I spilled out against the carpet next to Nathan and Gabriel. I coughed a few times. Nathan put a hand on my back, massaging.

I sucked in the cooler air. "I'm okay," I whispered.

"You keep coughing like that," Gabriel said, "your voice will never heal and we'll never get to sing together."

"That's probably a good thing," I choked out. "I can't

sing."

I escaped the boys for a moment to find water from the bathroom across the hallway. Silas was still working on the shower. He was cursing at the pipes in the wall, smacking a wrench against one. I stood quietly to watch him work, lost in the smoothness of his strong muscles in his arms and the curve of his firm jaw. He sensed me and turned, his dark eyes focusing on my face. "Need something?"

I picked up a tiny paper cup from the counter, taking a sip of water from the sink. I held the cup to him. "Did you want some?" I was whispering and he probably couldn't hear me, but he seemed to understand.

His smile returned. He reached out from the tub and I stepped in to hand the cup to him. Our fingers touched. A spark ignited in my stomach. His eyes held mine. "Thank you," he said.

The moment was too intense for me and I turned from him, walking slowly back to my room. Why were my feelings so confusing? I felt the same flicker of excitement and fear whenever I touched any of them or any of them touched me. I couldn't understand how anyone got used to those feelings. Part of me was afraid Silas would freak out on me again. Part of me wanted him to. I missed his arms. I missed Kota who was only downstairs. I wanted to crawl into their laps and remain there forever. I didn't want to be here in this house anymore. I didn't want them to leave me. How incredibly lonely I felt in that moment and they were all right there in front of me. I didn't have the guts to ask for what I wanted.

I sucked in a breath, giving myself some control before I reentered my bedroom. Gabriel was on my bed, spread out on his back. Luke and Nathan were spilled out on the floor, staring up at the ceiling. I sank onto the foot of my bed next to Gabriel's legs. He shifted slightly to give me more room, bending his knees until his feet were hanging off of the bed. I sat cross legged near him. I wanted to hide in the attic with him again and sit in his lap. I couldn't find the words or the right way to touch him. I couldn't reach out to him.

"What's going on?" I asked. They were quiet enough that I thought one of them would be able to hear me.

Gabriel turned his crystal eyes to me. He heard. "Hm?"

"What are they talking about downstairs?"

"We're trying to listen," Luke said. He put a finger to his lips as he gazed up at me from the floor. He pressed his ear to the carpet.

I slid off the bed, crawling between Luke and Nathan. I put my ear to the carpet, too, and held my breath to hear better.

Kota and Mr. Blackbourne talked over each other. Victor and Dr. Green occasionally cut in. I couldn't really understand what anyone was saying because of distance and how everyone was talking at once.

I caught one phrase from Kota, "Sang isn't ever going to know."

My hand fluttered up to my mouth, and I shoved my lower lip into my teeth. More Academy secrets?

I realized as I was listening that I was staring at Nathan's chest while on my side. I looked up, catching his blue eyes gazing back at me. He caught my hand at my mouth and brought it to his chest, warming it. He pressed his palm over the back of my hand as he looked at me. "Don't listen anymore," he said softly.

"But is it about me?" I asked. "Did I do something wrong?"

Nathan's face darkened and he reached out to me, pulling me across the floor to him. His arm wrapped around my waist, his fingers spread across my lower back. He held up his head with his other arm as he looked down at me. "We're listening to conversations not meant for us. They'll tell us when they want us to know."

I swallowed. The secrets hung in the air like spider webs. They tickled across my skin but I couldn't collect them to examine them.

"Sang should know," Luke said. He rolled across the

floor, bumping into me, pressing me back up against Nathan and smashing me between them. I smirked, trying to roll back into him and push him back. He kept coming at me, grinning.

"We're not making that decision," Nathan said.

Luke shoved me into Nathan again.

Nathan grunted, pushing at my back so I rolled against Luke.

"Hey, what the hell?" North called to us from the doorway.

I sat up on my knees to look at him, confused. Nathan propped himself up on his elbows.

"I leave for a minute and you're all fucking around with Sang on the floor."

Luke sat up. "We were just..."

"I don't care," North growled at him. "Stop it. Mr. Blackbourne's going to come up here and kick the shit out of you and then we'll all get it." He pointed a finger at Nathan. "You come with me and help me haul this shit up. The rest of you find her homework and help her with it."

There was a collection of groans. I blushed.

North caught my look and he pursed his lips. "Sang, keep these boys in line, will you?" He disappeared down the hallway. Nathan jumped up, following him down the hall.

Luke fell on his back against the carpet again. "Nag."

"I don't feel like doing homework," I whispered.

Gabriel slid off of my bed, dropping in a heap on the floor. The glint from the light above caught in the three black rings in his ear, and the green stones in his lobes sparked to life.

"Let's pretend we're doing it," he said.

My heart tripped. "Okay."

Gabriel smirked and shook his head.

Luke picked up my textbooks off of the bookshelf. I grabbed my book bag sitting on top of my trunk against the wall. I sorted through the books, pulling notebooks out of my bag. Of all the things to worry about right now, homework and school were far from my mind. Still, with the work spread out in front of me, I thought if we were going to waste time anyway, I might as well actually do the work. I found a pencil and a sheet of geometry problems.

Gabriel randomly opened a notebook, thumbing through it. "What's this?" Gabriel asked, holding on to some folded notes.

I blinked at him, sitting up again from the floor. "I thought my mom got all those," I whispered.

Gabriel unfolded the notes, his lips moving as he read it over. "Goddamn. They're nasty."

"What's that?" Mr. Blackbourne asked, walking in, frowning.

Kota trailed behind him; his eyes sought out mine. His skin bunched around his eyes, a pained stare. His fingers curled into fists.

I dragged myself to my knees, sitting back on my heels. Something was wrong. I sensed it from him. I stared at him with unspoken questions, asking in silence what was wrong. His eyes darted away toward the wall. Whatever it was, he couldn't tell me.

"Notes from stupid kids from school," Gabriel said. "A few that Sang's mom missed, I guess."

Mr. Blackbourne collected the notes from Gabriel's hand. He selected one, flipping it around and read it. He frowned. "Can't take her anywhere."

"What does it say?" I asked.

Mr. Blackbourne scrunched his eyebrows at me. "You don't know?"

"She doesn't read them," Gabriel said. "North told her not to."

"North is right," Mr. Blackbourne said. He folded the note and put it in his blazer pocket. "Gabriel, Luke and Kota, go hunt the house for any more notes that her mother might have found. I want every last one of them. If she gets any more, take them from her and hand them to me or North. We can't risk her mother seeing them and setting her off in a frenzy again. Go and find them now." He wasn't just asking them to find notes. He was ordering them to leave the room.

Kota shot a glare to Mr. Blackbourne that made me shiver. I never saw Kota so cold before. Luke rose from the floor and put a hand on Kota's arm, tugging him along. Kota gazed quietly at me once and stalked out after the others, closing the door behind him.

♥

Secret Plans

I was alone with Mr. Blackbourne. I'd been alone with him before, but not in my own bedroom, and not under such strange circumstances. It felt worse than the first time I'd been alone with him. I felt naked, vulnerable. He knew so much about me now. Did he regret drawing me further into their circle?

"Would you sit down?" He stretched his hand toward the bed.

I rose from the floor, the dull pain in my tailbone intensifying. I'd been ignoring it before now, crawling around in the attic and playing with the boys, but it was starting to get to me. I sat delicately on the edge of bed.

Mr. Blackbourne planted himself next to me, his feet flat on the floor. He propped himself up with his elbows on his knees, his face buried in his hands. He rubbed at his tired cheeks. Was this the same strong and confident Mr. Blackbourne I'd come to know at school? He felt so out of place here with me, younger and looking for answers like I was. "Miss Sorenson," he said. "Did you know your mother has cancer?"

My heart dropped. My mind solidified into a blank, shapeless mass. I shook my head. Cancer? What was that? I knew what it was, but in my mind, it was like I forgot what it meant for a moment. I was numb. I was hopeless. "I knew she was really ill," I whispered. "My dad never told us the details."

"It's why she's on so many medications," he said.

"When they did the biopsy, she almost died. They're not sure if they want to do surgery because they think it might kill her." He sat up again, twisting his body to put his palm on the bed, leaning against it to nearly hover over me. "If they don't, it'll spread and it might get worse. It might become untreatable."

My eyes dropped to his hand, noting the smooth skin, and the trace of a scar across a knuckle. My mind, however, was a million miles away. How long had my parents known and never told me? Was this what Kota didn't want me to know about?

"I hate to ask you this now," he said softly. "Do you know anything about your mom's past? About her parents?"

I shook my head. "I've never met them. They're still alive, I think. She mentioned them a couple of times before she got sick. She never talks to them and they never call."

His hand moved from the bed to my face. He dropped a forefinger against the tip of my chin, catching it and tilting it up. His fingertip was smooth and warm. He lifted until I was caught up in his soft gray eyes, leaving me breathless. "Have either of your parents ever touched you in a way that wasn't appropriate?"

My cheeks enflamed. "No," I insisted, as loud as I could with what little voice I had. "They've never beat me. I mean, they never..."

"I don't mean in that way," he said.

"Mr. Blackbourne," I said, my eyes narrowing on his. I thought my heart was thumping so loud that he could hear it. "The most she's ever done was to pull me by the arm to get me to sit or stand somewhere. I can't remember the last time my father touched me at all. He's never here." I swallowed. "We're not the closest family. We don't touch." How did he do that? All he had to do was get me to look into his eyes, and I was pouring my heart out, sharing secrets with him about things I never imagined I would tell anyone, not even Kota.

He searched my eyes as if looking for answers to questions he hadn't asked out loud. His hand lifted from my chin and he traced a fingertip over my cheek. My body released a shiver. Didn't he understand? I didn't understand touching at all. Up until a couple of weeks ago, no one ever did touch me and suddenly there's been an onslaught of boys all holding my hand, hugging me, wrapping arms around me. I've never in my life had anyone do that. While I was slowly beginning to not cower at every little touch, deep inside I was craving more than ever, because it was everything I had been missing out on. Maybe it was wrong of me to feel that way. I didn't know what was normal any more. Everything I'd read in books or saw on TV didn't match up to what I felt with them. All I knew was that every time one of the boys let go of me, I was desperate to reach back, to pull them back to me. I just didn't know how.

And I tried to tell him this, to say with my eyes everything I wanted to tell them all but didn't have the courage to. My tongue danced behind my teeth with the words that tasted almost right, but I knew I could never say it out loud. They would think I was crazy. They wouldn't understand.

Mr. Blackbourne released me. "Miss Sorenson," he said softly. "I promise you. If you give me a chance, if you'll trust me, I'll do everything I can to make sure you make it out of this situation safely."

"What do you mean?" I whispered, confused by his overwhelming concern. He still hardly knew me. He and the others helped me set the stage to face off with my mother when she woke up. What more could they do?

The air stilled around us. There were only his steel eyes that seemed to swallow me up like a wave of water.

I forced my lips to part. "Mr. Blackbourne..."

He sighed, pulled back. "Until we get a better system together, one of the boys will stay with you here in your house."

My eyes widened. "How? They'll get caught."

"Your mother needs to be monitored," he said. "You'll talk to Dr. Green and he'll tell you what you need to do. If she wakes up within the next 24 hours, she can stay at home, but if she doesn't wake up, she needs to be taken to the hospital. We've set up an IV for her. Whoever stays with you will be able to replace it as needed but I want them to show you how to do it, too. If she keeps it in while she's awake, you should replace it."

My mind was still whirling about what he said a moment ago. I swallowed back questions. "I'll do my best."

"I know you will," he said. He stood up. "North and Silas should be about done. Victor will get you a new phone. The rest of us still have work to do before Monday."

"I'm sorry," I said softly. My eyes closed to force back the warmth of tears. I felt so badly about everything. I felt responsible for dragging them into this. I was a distraction when they were all so busy with trying to save the school and with whatever other Academy work they had to do. It seemed more important than my problems. They didn't ask to be in the middle. "I'm sorry for all the trouble I've caused."

I was going to say more but his fingers sought out my mouth, closing my lips. "You were unexpected," he said softly. "But you're far from a burden. North was right. What kind of group would we be if we couldn't look after one little girl?" His eyes told me more than he was saying. This wasn't something I could take back. They made a plan. This was what was going to happen. I didn't have a choice in the matter. They were determined to intervene. He swallowed and stepped back, releasing my lips from his touch. "Let's call everyone in. We need to make final plans."

He turned away from me and toward the door, his commanding presence returning as he squared off his shoulders.

I pushed a palm to my cheek, trying to calm myself from the intensity of his words and touches.

Mr. Blackbourne twisted the handle and swung the door open. Kota was leaning against the doorframe with his arms folded over his chest. His face was grim. He wasn't hiding that he had been trying to listen in the entire time.

"Get the others," Mr. Blackbourne ordered. "All of them."

Kota glanced at me, silently asking me if I was okay. I nodded to him, trying to reassure him I was fine. My mother was dying. I'd silently known that for years, only I've never known why. Putting a name to what was killing her didn't change things. It only confirmed what I already knew. This wasn't something she was going to recover from and be better. She was never going to go back to the mother that I had already mostly forgotten.

I may never again live in her house without the fear of what she might do next.

Kota reluctantly moved away from the doorframe. Mr. Blackbourne turned down the hallway to collect Silas and North. Within moments, they were all in my bedroom. Silas sat on the bed next to me. His hand sought out mine, covering my fingers with his against the bed. I wanted to pick my hand up to let him hold it but my nerves were rattling. I wanted to crawl into his lap, but with everyone there, it felt like too much. I didn't have the guts to do it anyway.

Gabriel, Luke, Nathan and the other boys sat together on the floor. Dr. Green and Mr. Blackbourne stood and addressed us.

"Here's what's going to happen," Mr. Blackbourne said in his stern voice. "Gabriel and Luke are staying here tonight."

There was a commotion of protest. None of the boys wanted to leave.

"I'm not going to argue about this," Mr. Blackbourne commanded. "We've all got things we need to do, and they don't all involve Miss Sorenson. We've got to prepare for school on Monday. Victor, get Miss Sorenson a new phone, but bring it to me first. Kota, you've already got a job to do. Silas, North, I need you on Academy business. Nathan, you're going with Dr. Green to the hospital for information." He pointed to Gabriel and Luke. "You two will wait here until Kota comes for her tomorrow. I don't care if you have to sleep in the attic, but don't leave this room unless Miss Sorenson thinks it's okay and don't leave this place at all until Kota comes back. Call if anything happens. Call if *nothing* happens. I want updates."

I pulled my knees up until they were pressing to my chest, wrapping my arms around my knees. When I did, everyone stopped to watch me. I had no idea why and I felt my cheeks starting to heat up, unsure of if I was looking stupid or what. I slid a glance to Silas next to me, questioning with my eyes what they were looking at. He gave me a soft smirk, shaking his head and rolling his eyes. Somehow I sensed it was just that I moved at all and they were super in tune to what I was doing in the moment. I could only guess that they expected me to say something about all this. I couldn't think of anything to add.

Mr. Blackbourne cleared his throat and continued. "We'll have to tighten the schedule. I'll work one out and will send it to everyone's phones. Luke, I still want that map of this house so make one tonight. Someone will bring you a laptop." He pointed at me. "Miss Sorenson, I want you to stay out of the attic tonight and rest your voice. We've got school ahead and we can't have you squeaking like a mouse. If anything else happens, you call me directly."

I nodded to him, clamping my lips shut. His eyes communicated unspoken orders: *stay out of trouble*.

"Let's go," he said.

With that, everyone moved at once. I stood up with Silas. Mr. Blackbourne left the room. His footsteps echoed in the hallway as he marched down the stairs.

When he was gone, Silas turned to me, wrapping his arms loosely around my shoulders for a quick hug. "Call me when you get the new phone," he said.

I hugged him back, smiling. I loved his hugs.

He let me go and turned away. Victor materialized in his place and gave me a hug. His fingertips traced my back, smoothing over a couple of ribs. "I'll be back soon," he whispered in my ear.

I hugged him, too. When he pulled back, Nathan replaced him, and gave me a tight hug without saying anything at all.

When Nathan left, North came forward. He reached around, holding me tight and nearly lifting me off of the ground, hugging. His fingers threaded through my hair. "I don't care that your mother is sick," he said. "If she touches you again, I'm coming back for you."

"North," I whispered. I wanted to say more, but I was stunned and breathless.

He placed me carefully on the ground and stormed out.

Kota strode toward me. His arms encircled my waist and his face buried into my shoulder. I hugged him in return.

"I'll be back tomorrow morning," he whispered in my ear. "Listen to Gabe and Luke. Stay out of trouble. Call me if you want." He pulled back and put his forehead against mine. "You're with us now."

I felt my heart breaking. As much as I loved that Gabriel and Luke would be staying with me, Kota looked so determined and yet so lost at the same time. I wasn't sure how to answer him. I wanted to tell him I'd be okay. He'd be back tomorrow. Right now it seemed like forever. I wanted them all to come back. I changed my mind. I didn't want to stay. I wanted to run away with them, even if it meant hiding with the Academy. Despite what we'd been through, and how they'd come to save me, I didn't feel like one of them at all. I desperately needed to be. I wanted that confidence, knowing I belonged. Would I ever feel as strongly as he did, so assured of my place among them?

"Miss Sang," Dr. Green said from behind Kota. Kota moved away from me. Dr. Green held out a hand to me. "Let me show you how to take care of that mother of yours," he said. "Then we should go. I don't want to have to give her something else to make her sleep and we shouldn't be here if she comes out of this quickly."

I glanced back once at Kota as Dr. Green took my hand and pulled me out of the room and down the stairs. Kota looked not entirely happy about the situation, but resolved that this was what had to be done. I could only hope they were right.

In my mother's room again, Dr. Green guided me to the bed. An IV stand was in place, holding a bag of fluid connected to the needle set in her arm by a clear tube. The liquid dripped slowly from the bag. It actually made me feel better to see it; at least she was getting fluids.

Dr. Green pointed to the three prescription bottles on her nightstand. "These are the only ones she should be taking," he warned. "It's what she's currently prescribed. I think she's been getting confused because she talks to so many doctors and she hangs on to old medicine. I'm going with Nathan to the hospital to dig up information and we'll talk to some doctors about better treatment options. Stressing herself out so much that she comes after you is not an option."

I swallowed, nodding.

"If she wakes up, make her some soup and ensure she eats. Don't let her stress out. If she starts to, do whatever she says as long as it isn't dangerous. Lie if you have to. Luke and Gabriel will be right here, so no matter what happens, they'll pull you out if and when needed. Get her to rest as much as possible. When does your father get back?"

I shrugged. "I'm not sure. And I don't know how to reach him. He didn't mention when he'd be back."

He pointed to the IV stand. "If your mother asks you

about that, say you called a doctor to check her out while she slept. She may not like that but don't worry if she pulls out the IV. I'm more worried about her waking up and if she gets that far, we can take it from there. Gabriel's on watch to make sure she wakes up and if she doesn't, you should use the house phone to call for an ambulance. We can't get any closer."

I sucked in a deep breath, letting it out slowly. I understood what he meant. It was too close now. I knew he meant they didn't want to expose themselves to my family, and possibly they weren't prepared, as they'd said, to do much more. I wondered at what point they would call in the Academy. I wondered what difference it would make.

With his green eyes on mine, he closed the space between us, wrapping his arms around me in a looser hug than the others. The movement surprised me at first. He was my teacher. A doctor. I often forgot, like with Mr. Blackbourne, that he was young, maybe only a few years older than I was. He was also friends with Kota and the others. Nine guys in all when I sometimes just counted the seven. I weakly wrapped my arms around his chest to make this friendly gesture mean something.

"Cheer up, buttercup," he said.

I had no idea how to respond, but my heart warmed at his words. If my mother could see us now, she'd claim he was raping me. I blushed at both his touch and the idea of my mother waking at any moment, along with the guilt that weighed me down like bricks when I thought of how she would look at me.

He let go, moving away from the bed. I followed. There was nothing for us to do now but wait.

♥

Apples

Gabriel, Luke and I stood in the garage as we watched the others get in various cars and move on to do what they needed to do. The bathroom was done. The house was back to what it was before. North took the fractured wood of the stool with him. No one talked about replacing it, but I worried that my mother would assume I hid it or had gotten rid of it and would punish me more when she noticed.

When we were alone, I relaxed. Having fewer people there meant I'd have less chances of my mother waking and catching us. Also, everyone else was so somber and tense. Maybe Mr. Blackbourne was right to keep them busy and away from here. Everyone needed a break to calm down a little and try to get back to the almost-normal that we were.

Luke, Gabriel and I gathered up in my room. Luke settled into drawing out a map of the house on notebook paper and occasionally left the room to go measure something with the tape. Gabriel kicked his shoes off, dropped into my bed, pulled the blanket up and fell asleep.

With nothing else to do, I sat on the floor and finished up my homework.

About an hour later, Luke crawled over to where I was sitting in the corner of the room on the carpet. I was finishing the reading assignment for English.

"Sang," he said, his eyes big and his hand on his stomach. "Will you make something to eat? I'm starving."

I found a pencil and wrote to him so I wouldn't have to

talk. "What would you like?"

"Anything," he said. He tugged a band from his blond hair. Locks tumbled across his face. He raked his fingers through the strands, pulling them back to redo the ponytail. "I'll eat bread and water."

I smirked at him. I could do a little better than that.

A phone ringing cut through the quiet. Gabriel's outline shifted on the bed. "Yeah?" he said in a groggy voice. "No, she's right here. Fuck, yes, I'm sleeping. Shut up. Luke's here. Stop yelling at me. We're supposed to be up all night watching her, so I'm trying to sleep now. Fuck you." Gabriel's hand appeared from under the blanket and he dropped the phone onto the carpet with a thud. "Sang," he called. "Phone's for you." He flipped over. The top of his hair appeared as the blanket shifted but he settled, going back to sleep again.

I looked at Luke. Who expected me to talk to them now?

Luke laughed. He walked over and scooped up the phone. "Yes? Yeah, she's right here." His eyes flickered to me. "No, he's just napping. You know how he is when you wake him up. Yes, she's still asleep. Yes, tell North Sang finished her homework." Luke made a face at me. I smiled at him. "What? No." He held his hand over the end of the phone. "Silas wants to know your favorite color."

"Pink," Gabriel mumbled from under the blanket.

Luke checked with me to confirm and I nodded. "She said pink. Well if they don't have it in pink, go to another store."

I tugged on Luke's shirt sleeve, silently asking him what in the world he was talking about. He waved me off, holding me back with his hand and tilting the phone away. I could hear Silas talking but I couldn't figure out what he was saying. I blew out a breath, shaking my head. I got up and crossed the room. If there was nothing else they needed, I was going to make food.

I padded down the stairs and popped my head into my mother's room. She was still in a deep sleep, but the color in her cheeks looked better. I was going to try to get her to take a bath when she woke up so I could wash her sheets. Usually my dad did it, but now that I knew how bad her illness was, I thought maybe if I helped out more, she wouldn't be so crazy when she was awake.

I meandered into the kitchen. I checked the fridge and started collecting ingredients to make bacon and grilled cheese sandwiches with apples.

Butter melted in the frying pan when I sensed someone behind me. I spun around, nearly knocking into Gabriel.

"Watch yourself, Trouble," he said. He yawned, rubbed a palm against his eye. He combed the lock of blond back to mix in with the rest of his brown hair behind his ears. "What's for breakfast?"

"Grilled cheese," I whispered. I slipped bread into the pan, layered it with cooked bacon and cheese. I thinly sliced Granny Smith apples to add on top, plus another slice of cheese and another piece of bread.

"What's with the apple?" he asked. "That's weird."

"It's good," I whispered.

"Whatever you say." He folded his arms across his stomach and leaned against the counter.

"Gabriel," Luke said softly as he walked into the kitchen. "We're not supposed to leave her room."

"Who the hell is going to tattle on us? Her mom's still passed out. We'd hear her coming if she came through here."

Luke made a face but his head turned as he spotted me cooking. "Oh thank goodness."

"She puts apples in her grilled cheese."

"Cool."

"Do you not want apples?" I whispered to Gabriel.

Gabriel slipped next to me, dropping a hand on my hip and pressed his cheek to my shoulder. "Is it good?"

"Try a bite of this when it's done," I said. "If you don't want it, I'll eat the rest."

Gabriel's phone went off again. He let me go and

stepped away from us to answer it. "What? Yes, she's here, would I be all calm if she wasn't?" He held the phone away from his head. "Sang, Victor's outside. Run out there."

I passed the spatula to Luke. He took it and flipped over the grilled cheese. Gabriel followed me to the side door, opening it for me. He hung out in the doorway as I ran through the garage.

The gray BMW was parked at the end of the driveway. Victor was leaning against the side door. Black slacks. White Armani shirt. The fire in his eyes was lit to a cozy setting. "Hi," he said.

I smiled at him.

"Are they driving you crazy yet?"

I shook my head.

He straightened and turned to open the back seat of his car. He lifted out a brown leather messenger bag. "There's two laptops in here. One is for you to play with. The other is for Luke to work on."

He handed it to me. The leather bag was stiff. It appeared brand new.

He dipped his hand into his back pocket and pulled out an iPhone with a pink case attached. "This is yours."

The cell phone was identical to the old one. "Did you fix it?"

"Sweetheart, you demolished the other one. This is new."

Heat teased my cheeks. "I didn't… I don't really need…"

He dropped a finger to my lips, squishing my mouth closed. "Just say thank you."

I smiled and mouthed a thank you around his finger.

He pulled me in another hug. "I've got to get some things done. I may not see you tomorrow. Text me."

"I will," I whispered, mashing myself into him. I didn't want to let go.

He released me and stepped away. I held back and watched as he started his car and backed out of the drive. I waved as he drove off. How normal was that? Why couldn't that happen all the time? Why couldn't my mother accept that people weren't all that bad? I was making lunch for Luke and Gabriel. We'd been hanging out all afternoon. No death. No raping. Just friends.

I collected the mail, since I was outside. Back inside, burning bread and butter met me at the door. I dropped the leather bag and the mail on the floor, sprinting to the kitchen.

The kitchen was empty. Grilled cheese smoked in the pan. I snatched up the spatula to plate the sandwich. Two additional sandwiches were sitting on the plate, too. Where did the guys go?

"Sang!" My mother's voice clattered through my ears. Thudding footsteps sounded from the hallway.

My heart stopped. I dropped the pan on the stove and shut off the heat.

My mother appeared from the hallway, hair mangled against her head. She tugged the IV pole with her. It was on wheels so she could roll it along. "There you are," she said. "What's burning?"

"Sorry," I whispered. "I left it on when... when I went to go check the mail. I thought I would get back quickly enough."

My mother blinked at me. "Why are you whispering?"

She didn't remember. The worst experience she'd put me through and she didn't know. If I had never called Silas and if they never saved me, I'd still be there now, or dead. "Sore throat," I whispered. I coughed softly once but swallowed hard so I wouldn't go into a fit.

She staggered backward. "Don't come near me," she said. "I can't get sick." She paused. "When did the doctor come?"

I assumed she meant the IV. "I called him," I lied. "You weren't waking up so I called. They set you up with that. I hope that was okay."

She shuffled on her feet, putting her weight on one leg

and then the other. She didn't look happy about it, and I knew it was because there had been strangers in the house, but to her they were doctors. They were who she saw in the hospital. I wondered how she rationalized it. She was okay with doctors but not anyone else? I wonder if she'd like Dr. Green.

She settled finally, as if accepting this answer. "Make sure you call your father if you need to do that again. Let him call."

"Okay."

"Where's the mail?"

I retraced my steps to the side door. She followed me and I was worried she'd ask about the leather bag.

But the messenger bag wasn't on the floor where I'd left it. Luke or Gabriel must have used the back steps to collect the bag. My heart fluttered, hoping they could remain quiet. I scooped up the mail from the floor and carried it over to my mother.

She took it from me. "You made three sandwiches?" she asked me, pointing to the plate I had made.

"I'm really hungry," I said. She noticed that but she didn't notice the bandages on my wrists and ankles?

Now that I was focused on her, I realized she hardly looked at me. Her eyes darted around me, occasionally looking at my knees or something similar but always out of focus until she looked at something else. Did I not notice before? Being around the others, they often touched my face to bring my eyes to theirs. Did I divert my eyes too much without realizing it? Was I looking around others but not really at them?

"You'll get fat," she said.

"Do you need anything? Water? I can make you grilled cheese or some soup."

She considered this. "Bring me water and some yogurt." She rolled her IV pole back to her bedroom.

I collected what she wanted quickly and raced to her room. I was there before she made it to the bed. I gave her a plastic spoon and her water bottle and nudged the plastic trash can closer to her bed. "If you'll take a bath, I can change your sheets."

She narrowed her eyes at me. "What do you want?"

"Huh?" I meant to ask more, but dry air caught in my throat and I started coughing.

She reeled her head back, taking the top off of her water. "Go away. You'll make me sick."

I swallowed and rushed out of her room. I went back to the kitchen, grabbing the plate of grilled cheese and three bottles of water from the fridge and a bag of potato chips, taking them upstairs.

My door was closed, locked. I had to put the water and chips down to find the pushpin in the wall, opening the door one-handed.

When I peeked into the room, the boys weren't there. I replaced the push pin and picked up the water and chips. I put everything on top of the trunk by the wall and closed the door again. "Gabriel?" I whispered.

Scuffling noises broke out from the attic and a moment later, Gabriel and Luke peeked out from around the bookshelf. They looked relieved.

"I thought it might have been your mom," Gabriel whispered.

I pressed a button on the stereo, turning the volume up on the music to help mask our noises. I picked up the plate of sandwiches and passed it to them.

Behind the bookshelf, we sat on the floor to eat together. Since my mother was awake, it meant we had to be extra quiet now. I took the burnt sandwich and pulled the burned side off to eat it open-faced. Gabriel liked the apples.

When we were done, Gabriel sat cross-legged on the bed near the window and I curled up on the other end with the pillow. Luke remained behind the bookshelf on the carpet. Gabriel checked fashion blogs with the extra laptop. Luke was doing his work. I started texting everyone with the new phone.

Sang: Silas! What are you doing?

Silas: North's giving me a lecture about spark plugs. Save me.

Sang: North.

North: What?

Sang: Just checking. Tell Silas I said hi and that I think spark plugs are interesting.

North: You're still full of shit.

Sang: Do you still like me?

North: Yes. Do you still like me?

Sang: Yes.

Sang: Kota, I made grilled cheese. My mom woke up.

Kota: Did she notice anything?

Sang: She doesn't remember. She asked when I called the doctor for the IV but she didn't seem too surprised by it. She did ask about my throat but I lied and said I was sick.

Kota: If she forgets what happened, don't remind her. Keep me updated.

Sang: Nathan, are you awake?

Nathan: Nope.

Sang: Sleep texting?

Nathan: Yes.

Sang: That's a talent.

Nathan: I want to come hang out.

Sang: Will everyone take turns?

Nathan: Yup. I think that's the plan. Don't get caught before it's my turn. If you get into trouble, run over here.

Sang: Thank you, Victor.

Victor: You're very welcome. Keep it close.

♥

Sign Language

After another hour, I slid off the bed onto the floor to go back downstairs. I collected the plate and the empty water bottles.

Downstairs, my mom was asleep again. The yogurt remained unopened. I slipped in quietly to take it back. I didn't want it to spoil and have her eat it. I found some crackers and left them for her.

When I cleaned up the mess in the kitchen and rambled back upstairs, Gabriel was sleeping in my bed again. Luke was still behind the bookshelf. With the door to the attic open, it made the room warmer. I hit the ceiling fan to help cool things off a little.

I angled my way behind the bookshelf and sat next to Luke on the floor. He was putting together some final touches to his map of the second floor. He wasn't just doing exit points and a basic outline. He had images of furniture around the house as well. He tapped in the size of the platform in the attic. I had my cheek nearly pressed to his shoulder as I watched him work.

"I didn't know the platform of the attic space met with the upstairs closet," I whispered.

"It's really convenient for us," Luke whispered back.

"Why?"

He turned his head, pressing his nose to the top of my head. "It's a secret."

"Will you tell me?"

His nose rubbed against my hair. "Not this time."

I pouted. "Is it bad?"

"No." He shifted until he could thread an arm around my shoulder. His fingertips traced along my collarbone. He worked one-handed with the laptop. "I shouldn't say secret. It's more like a surprise."

"You guys are full of secrets."

"You are, too. Hidden hearts. I heard you know how to read Korean. Plus the sign language."

"I only know the alphabet," I reminded him.

"I could show you more, if you want."

"Where did you learn how to do it?"

His fingers rested at the curve of my throat. "When I first met North, he wouldn't talk to me. He wouldn't talk to Uncle, either. I'd say good morning, and he'd walk by me like he didn't hear me. I thought maybe he was deaf. I learned sign language because I thought he'd know it if he was. I spent two weeks practicing with Kota."

"You didn't just ask him if he was deaf?" I asked.

"He wouldn't talk at all," Luke said. "I'd ask him a question and it was like he'd drift and wouldn't answer."

I sat up and his arm fell away. I was sorry I did it because it was cozy. "You had a brother you didn't know anything about?"

"I didn't know he existed. One day when I was eleven, he showed up in the middle of the night. My uncle said we were step-brothers but he wouldn't tell me why or where he came from. That was it. North moved in."

I couldn't imagine an 11 or 12-year-old North, quiet and alone. How did he go from traveling around Europe with his father to ending up on Luke's and their uncle's doorstep? And he was so vocal now. "What happened when you tried to talk to him using sign language?"

"He glared at me like I was an idiot." Luke grinned. "So it didn't work, but I picked up something new. I used to practice with Kota for a while just for fun, but it's been a few years since I've actually used it." He placed the laptop on the floor. He sat cross-legged in front of me. "Let me show you."

I wanted to ask him how he got North to talk, but the

topic seemed out of place now. I sat in front of him and he wrapped his hands around my thighs, dragging me across the floor until our knees were touching. I hid a wince as my tailbone struck funny and pain crept up my lower spine. Thankfully, he was so focused on where he wanted to place me that he didn't notice.

When he was satisfied with where I was, he started signing. "This is asking what your favorite color is."

He showed me the motions and I mimicked as best as I could. When I did one incorrectly, he repeated the motion again and repositioned my hands. He started with some easier things, like asking about music and movies and showing me how to answer.

When he signed the word for 'cute', Gabriel flipped over on the bed. He shoved the blanket away from his face, watching through sleepy eyes.

"So when you do this," Luke said, motioning with his hands, "you're saying, 'You are really cute.'"

I mimicked.

"Why thank you," he said, winking at me.

I smirked at him.

"Try to guess what this is." He made different gestures with his hands, but at the end he shook his hands in front of himself to indicate it was a question.

I tilted my head at him. "What are you asking?"

He grinned, but his eyes sparked something mischievous. "Say yes."

"Yes?" I whispered carefully, making hand signs to say it.

"What did you just get her to do?" Gabriel said, yawning.

Luke smirked. He held up five fingers. Since it was out of context, I didn't quite understand. It took a few moments before I remembered he kept score any time someone at school asked me to marry them.

"God damn it," Gabriel said, and he must have realized the same thing. He grabbed at my arm, pulling me toward the bed. "You can't do that shit to her."

Luke laughed, tugging at my other arm. "Hey, you can't pull on my fiancée like that."

"It doesn't count. You tricked her."

"Guys?" I whispered, grinning.

Luke let go of my arm. "She's gotten a bunch of proposals already."

"That makes you as bad as Rocky and that other idiot," Gabriel said, pulling me onto the bed with him. I crawled up until I was sitting on the edge. Gabriel stuffed the blanket around his shoulders as he sat next to me. He rubbed a palm at his sleepy eyes. "Which reminds me, we need to figure out how we're going to stop this stupid obsession. If this catches on, it'll turn into guys bullying her instead."

The house creaked. I froze, trying to pinpoint the sound. Was it a normal house-settling creak or something else?

Gabriel was oblivious. "And Rocky's on the football team. We don't need the whole team doing that to her."

I leaned over, hovering above him, as I pushed a fingertip to his mouth to get his attention. His eyes widened and his lips closed. My cheeks heated. It was like he was kissing my finger.

A distinctive creak of the pushpin being pulled from the wall sent me falling to the floor in a panic. I meant to get out of the way for Gabriel to get past me to get inside the attic. Instead, he shoved the cover over his head.

Luke seized me by the waist, dragging me into the attic with him. I spilled out onto my back. My shirt got shoved up, exposing my stomach and my back scratched against the wood. My bad ankle locked into an odd position, and I bit at my tongue against the pain. Luke hovered on all fours over me, closing the door behind us.

The door to my bedroom crashed open against the wall.

"What are you doing in bed?" Marie's voice filtered through to us. I heaved a sigh. While it wouldn't be good for Marie to catch Gabriel here, it wasn't as bad as my mother.

Through the attic door, I heard as Gabriel groaned, girly, muffled.

"Sick?" Marie asked. "Why'd you move your stuff around?"

More mumbling.

Dry air clamped down on my throat. I started coughing. Luke shifted above me, drawing himself down against my body and covering me with his frame. His hand found the back of my head and he stuffed my face into his chest. I tried to swallow and breathe, but it felt like the more I breathed in, the more I needed to cough.

Outside in the bedroom, Gabriel started coughing, too, masking my noise.

"You're not going to puke, are you?" Marie asked. "I came to check in. I'm going back out. She's asleep again."

Tears threatened my eyes. My body shuttered against Luke's as I tried to swallow back a cough. His lips found my ear.

"Hang on, sugar," he whispered. "One more minute."

I pressed my face to his chest and smashed my mouth against his shirt.

"You should get some water," Marie said.

Silence lasted for a few minutes. I swallowed over and over again to hold back another cough.

The attic door burst open. Gabriel lunged inside and Luke pushed me out. Coughing spasms took over. I scrambled for the bed.

The door was still wide open but Marie was gone. I gasped for air, got up from the bed and crept to the door.

Marie was in her bedroom, digging through clothes on her floor. I crossed the hallway to the bathroom, tucking my head under the sink to drink from the tap.

Marie entered and nudged my body while I was upside down and I ended up with some water up my nose. I pulled back, pushing a palm to my face as I coughed and sneezed out water. Beautiful.

Marie yanked open a drawer and dug through the back for some makeup. She shoved some into her book bag. "I'll be back tomorrow," she said. She walked down the hallway and down the back stairs.

Did she really check in with mom? She didn't even notice the IV. She also didn't notice the bandages on my wrists and around my ankles. How often did my family walk by each other and never really see? The guys noticed bandages, bruises, my hair pulled back in my clip, the way I moved... How blind was I to their movements and the small things? I vowed to myself to start noticing everything. It mattered to me. I wanted to notice those things because it touched me when they noticed them about me.

I found a washcloth and cleaned my face. I selected a bottle of over-the-counter pain medications. I was tired of my ankle throbbing and my tailbone aching.

When I got back to my room, the boys were still behind the attic door. Did they not hear her leaving? I closed and locked the door again, moving to the attic door and pulling it open.

It was dark and I didn't see them at first. "Luke?" I whispered.

His head popped out from the back. He crawled forward. "How did you hear her coming?"

I shrugged. "I'm used to it."

"Yeah, but Gabriel was talking," he said. He knelt on all fours just inside the door as if hesitating.

"Oy," Gabriel called from behind him. "Get out."

"We should stay in here," Luke said. "That was close enough."

"We won't go far," Gabriel said. "We'll stay behind the bookshelf. It's too hot in here."

I backed away as the two of them slinked out onto the mauve carpet behind the bookshelf. Luke did look relieved.

Gabriel sprawled out on his stomach, breathing in the air. "Oh god," he said. "I was flipping out. I thought for sure she was going to look under the blanket when I started coughing."

"How's your throat?" Luke asked me.

I smiled. "It's fine now. Are you guys okay?"

"Yeah," Gabriel said. "Where did she go?"

"She went back to Danielle's."

He smirked. "Those two deserve each other. She didn't even care you were sick."

I twisted my lips. "There wasn't much she could do if I was."

"Sure she could," he said, getting up on his knees. "She could have offered to get you medicine or at least checked your temperature. Something. Anything."

I rattled the bottle of medicine in my hands. "I'm not five," I said, grinning. "I can take my own temperature."

"That's not the point," Gabriel said. "You're family and everything."

My eyes drifted and I realized I was looking at the wall, the carpet, the open attic door, Gabriel's black sneaker. I forced my eyes to look at his crystal blue ones. "Is that what your family does?" I didn't want to challenge him. I was curious. I'd read different things in books and watched how people responded to family in movies.

Was it real that a mother would make a kid chicken soup and tuck him into bed? If I was sick, my mother told me what to do for myself. Maybe when I was really young, around six or so and before my mother got sick, I could remember her hovering over me. It was a distant, hazy memory that didn't match who she was now.

Was it even real or was I just hoping that once upon a time, my parents might have been normal?

Gabriel's lips pursed and he shrugged. "All families should do it."

He didn't directly answer the question. It had me curious, but Luke leaned forward, reaching around me for the laptop that was still on the floor. It distracted me and the question was lost.

Gabriel's eyes latched onto the bottle of medicine again. "What's wrong?" he asked.

What *wasn't* wrong? I was sore, my tailbone hurt and my throat was itching. "My ankle," I said, reaching for the easiest thing. "I don't think sitting on that stool helped the bruised bones."

Gabriel shook his head. "Trouble, you should say something when you're hurt." He snatched the bottle from me. Chucking it across the room, he pulled a prescription bottle without a label from his back pocket. He twisted the top and spilled the contents into his palm. It was full of a variation of different pills.

"What are those?" I whispered.

He ignored me, finding two red, slim capsules. "Here. Take these," he said, placing them in my open palm.

I flipped the pills over, looking for markings. "What are they?"

Gabriel rolled his eyes. "Will you just listen to the doctor? Take them."

"You're a doctor?"

Luke laughed, shaking his head. "It's fine, Sang."

I hesitated, but grabbed one of the water bottles still sitting around and swigged down the pills.

Gabriel nodded, beaming. "See? Gotta trust me."

"If I die, I'm coming back to haunt you."

They both laughed.

The pills he gave me worked, and I wasn't feeling sore or even the crack in my tailbone. I learned later they were muscle relaxers, given to him by Dr. Green just for me. That evening, I made a quick dinner for the guys and afterward, sought out extra pillows and blankets. They set up a cubby space for the two of them in the attic. The floor of the attic left just enough space so they could sleep side by side with their heads near the door.

Gabriel complained about the heat. I found a fan in the shed and plugged it in, pointing it in their direction. That seemed to help.

I checked on my mom and tried to wake her up. I offered her some soup and put the cup near her bed. She grumbled through half open eyes and drifted off again. I wondered if whatever Luke gave her to breathe in might still be lingering in her system. I sent a text to Dr. Green. His reply said if she didn't wake up again and actually eat something by the next morning to call him.

By nine, I was curled up on the bed, pretending to read, but my eyes were drooping. The boys were preoccupied in the attic with the laptops.

I meant to get up and brush my teeth and do other things to stay awake. With the boys there, I felt awkward falling asleep so early. I turned over on the bed, putting the book down for only a minute to let my eyes rest.

♥

What A Family Is

I dreamed of being swallowed up by a dragon. His fire breath licked at my feet on my way down into his belly.

I shot upright in my bed. Two bodies were tucked one on either side of me. In the darkness I caught Luke's blond head to my left and Gabriel on his side on the right. Did I not feel them crawling into bed with me? Was I okay with this?

I couldn't kick them out. They looked exhausted. I secretly didn't want them to go away, either. I was terrified we would get caught, but my sleepy head desired their closeness. I felt less lonely with them beside me.

I shifted onto my side to try to give them more room. I relaxed against the pillow, listening to the noises in the house.

When I woke up again, Luke's arm was draped over my side, his nose pressed to my shoulder. Gabriel leaned against me, his foot on top of my ankle. I was hot and uncomfortable but didn't want to move, didn't want to wake them. Squished, I forced myself to go back to sleep.

The air shifted around us, causing a draft against the wisps of hair across my forehead. My eyes fluttered, but I closed them again promptly. I dismissed it because the attic door was open and I thought I was sensing changes to the weather outside through it. Sleep was dragging me back in before I could think of *why* it was open.

Dual smacking sounds shattered the silence. Gabriel stiffened next to me and jolted up until he was sitting. Luke tumbled away in a shot and fell out of the bed.

I leapt up, scrambling on my knees until I was upright, afraid. I held my hands up, wary of monsters from my dreams suddenly come to life.

"Ow," Gabriel grumbled. "What the fuck?" He sat on the edge of the bed, a hand shoved against his face. Luke was on his knees on the floor, covering his forehead with a palm.

"At least Sang is paying attention." Kota's voice sounded through the dark. The window was open behind him and a gentle breeze picked up the back of his hair. "What are you two doing sleeping?"

Why didn't he ask why they were sleeping next to me? Didn't it bother him that they stayed so close with me? My insides shook at fully realizing they had slept in the bed with me. While I was half asleep, I appreciated that they were close by. Now that I was fully aware, it felt strange and especially awkward that Kota knew about it.

"The attic sucks," Gabriel whined. "And we were right here with Sang. Nothing happened."

"Mr. Blackbourne left you both here so you'd take shifts. Do I have to explain it?" He turned to me. "How are you?"

I swallowed thickly. "Fine, I think."

"Nathan's outside," Kota said. "He's going to take you both over to Silas's apartment. Victor's there already."

Nathan had a car? I didn't know he could drive.

Gabriel grumbled, feeling around in the dark for his shoes. "What time is it?"

"Four a.m.," Kota said. "Welcome to it." He removed the pillow from the head of the bed so he could sit on the edge near me. "Gabriel, go with Victor to finalize some things. Make sure you check in with Mr. Blackbourne. Luke, you've got homework duty."

"I hate homework duty," Luke said, but he stood up, rubbing at his eyes. He stumbled forward, bending over and wrapping his arms around my shoulders. "Bye, Sang."

An arm hooked around my neck from behind me. I was pulled back and Gabriel dropped his nose to the top of my hair. "Oy, Trouble," he said. "Don't let Kota boss you around."

"Get out of here, guys," Kota said. "Nathan's waiting."

Luke crawled through the window, followed by Gabriel. Kota got off the bed to close the window behind them.

"I thought we were supposed to stay off of the roof," I said.

Kota pointed a finger at me. "*You* are supposed to stay off the roof. But no. We're not ready to start sneaking in the back door yet."

"We're going to be ready for that?" I asked, moving to kneel on the bed, grabbing the blanket and wrapping it around my body. Now that the surprise was over, I was chilled. The ceiling fan and the fan pointed at the attic stirred the cool night air seeping in.

"We have to be ready for lots of things," he replied. He dropped on the bed next to me, his arm moving behind my back. He leaned against me, his shoulder pressing to mine. "You knew I was in the room before the other two. I saw you open up your eyes. How did you know?"

"I felt the air shift," I said. "Probably from when you opened the window."

"You're a light sleeper?"

I nodded. I normally was. That's what surprised me about waking up with the guys next to me. I blamed the red pills Gabriel had given me.

I breathed in deeply in a half yawn, smelling fresh soap and his spice. How early in the morning did he get up?

"You should still be more careful," he said. "I had time

to get in and thunk those two in the head. It would have been enough time for your mom or Marie to open that door and catch us."

"I thought they were going to sleep in the attic," I said. "They snuck into the bed after I passed out last night." I shifted on the bed, pushing back the blanket from my shoulders to rub at my cheek and yawn.

"If they try that again, tell them to get back in the attic. Someone is supposed to stay awake and they aren't fast enough to get into the attic from the bed in a dead sleep."

I nodded. The skin around the bandages itched. I lifted the corner of one on my wrist, to peek at the wound. It wasn't a cut, but the skin had been rubbed raw, enough to make the skin scab over. I ripped off the other one from my wrist and the two on my ankles.

Kota stood and grabbed his book bag that was by the window. He plopped the bag onto the bed and dug through the contents. "Silas got these for you." He handed over a small plastic bag with a sports store logo on the outside.

Inside the bag were two hot pink sport wrist bands. I smiled. "He was asking about my favorite color."

"Gabriel would have a fit," Kota said, putting the bag aside and sitting next to me again. "I agree with Silas, though. We'll need to hide those scabs on Monday."

"I like them."

The corner of his mouth jerked up briefly. "Good. He'll be glad to hear it from you." He brushed his fingertips across my wrist, tugging my hand close to him so he could examine my skin. "God, Sang... it's awful."

I pressed my fingers into my palm and withdrew my hand away from him. "It's fine. It'll heal," I said softly.

Kota's gaze fixed on me, his glasses glinting a little from the street lights outside. His face came close to mine. "Stop doing that to yourself," he said. His hand drifted to my cheek, curling a lock of my hair between his fingers. "You're dismissing what's been done to you."

I scrunched my eyebrows together. "I remember

everything," I said.

"But you're not angry. You're not complaining. Would you even tell me if your head hurt, or if your stomach hurt, if you thought I wouldn't notice? Would you have told me about the rice on the floor or even about the shower if no one knew?"

I bit my lip, glancing away. I didn't know the answer to that. Was I supposed to tell people about every little ache and problem? No one else needed to deal with it.

"What else hurts?" he asked me. His fingers sought out my chin and he brought my face around so I was looking at his eyes again. "Sang, when you're friends with someone, you're honest with them. Tell me what hurts."

I swallowed again, feeling my lips tremble. Why did I find it so difficult to talk now? As soon as he asked me the question though, I really didn't feel anything hurting at all. Most of it was my tailbone, but at the moment since I wasn't moving, it didn't hurt. My wrists were tender and he already knew that. The pain in my ankle wasn't bothering me yet.

"Sang," he whispered, but the power in his voice was taking over, commanding an answer.

"I am a little sore," I offered.

"Is that it?"

"And my wrists and ankles..."

His eyebrow arched.

"My, um... I think I might have cracked my tailbone."

His head tilted. "How?"

My cheeks heated. "When Nathan and Silas were looking for me in the house and I was in the shower. I could hear them talking. I was trying to make noise so I jumped with the stool to try to get the wood to bang against the tub."

He sighed. He shifted, wrapping his arms around my waist. He sat cross legged on the bed and I let him pull me into his lap. He pressed his cheek to the top of my head, keeping his arms around me. "Is that it?"

"I think so. I mean the ankle you know about, but it

isn't so bad right now," I said. My fingertips pressed to his chest and I rested my head against his shoulder. I couldn't believe how easily I'd let him pick me up into his lap. When he'd done it at Nathan's house in front of everyone, I was too in need of wanting to feel him, or anyone, that I didn't give it a second thought. Here and now, when he didn't need to but did it anyway, I didn't know what to think. He called me his friend. Do friends do this?

"Why didn't you tell me about your tailbone yesterday?"

"We were kind of busy," I whispered.

His cheek rubbed against my hair. "Sang, you need to speak up for yourself more."

"I'm not used to talking."

His hand lifted, brushing at the hair against my face. He curled a lock behind my ear. "I like it when you talk to me," he whispered.

"I like when you talk to me, too."

The corner of his mouth curled up. "Then we have to talk together a lot more."

The way he said it made my heart flutter. I did enjoy talking with him, and lately I rarely got to spend time alone with him like this. Did he mean to say he wanted more like this or something else? "What happens today?" I asked, not sure how to approach what I'd been really thinking about.

"Well," he said, dropping his hand against my leg, his wrist hanging loosely over my knee. His other hand rubbed my back. "You and I are going to have a nice, quiet Sunday. We'll keep an eye on your mother. Nathan should be back soon and he wanted to hang out."

"I didn't know he drove," I said.

Kota grinned. "Sweetie, we all drive."

"He has a car?"

"He took mine."

"You let him borrow yours?"

"He can use it when he needs it," Kota said. "We all have copies of each other's keys."

"To your cars?"

"To everything."

I twisted my lips. Something in his eyes let me in on a secret I wasn't sure he wanted to tell me. "Do you have a copy of the key to my house?"

He tilted forward, pulling his set of keys from his pocket. There was a house key with a pink cover near the top of the ring.

"Kota," I said. I thought I should be shocked or angry about it, but I wasn't. I wasn't hurt that he'd done it, just that he didn't tell me. If he had asked me for one, I would have given it to him. North must have made copies when he'd made them for me and Marie. Was Kota not going to tell me they had those?

"It was convenient of you to bring us one," he said, stuffing the keys back into his pocket.

"So everyone has one?"

He seemed hesitant to respond, but he nodded. "If they didn't before, they do now."

I made a face. "Do I get your keys?" It only seemed fair.

He laughed softly. "I suppose you should get mine. Maybe Nathan's. I don't know how you'd get to anyone else's house to use a key."

Wasn't that a big deal to have copies of someone's key? Did friends keep copies of house keys and car keys? "Maybe I'll learn how to drive."

"You still need a car."

"Maybe I'll borrow your car," I said, giggling.

He grinned and his hand brushed over my side, tickling. "If you ask nicely."

I gasped, laughing and playfully patted his hand. "Could I please borrow your car, Kota?"

"Nope."

"Aw."

"I have to teach you how to drive, first."

I perked up. "You'll teach me?"

"Who else was going to?"

I didn't have the answer to that. Outside of the guys, who else would ever teach me how to drive? Marie was old enough now but we knew better than to ask our parents. It wasn't an option open to us.

"Anyway," he said. "You've done your homework, right?"

I nodded.

"It might be a good idea to start working ahead when you can." He reached for his book bag and dragged it closer. "If it gets busier in the next couple of weeks, we won't have to study so hard to keep up."

"Are we going to be busy?"

He was quiet for a moment, his fingers tracing over the zipper of his book bag. "Sang..."

The silence hung in the air, thick with secrets. "Does the Academy keep you busy?"

His fingers curled into a fist. "There's a lot that needs to be done."

"Do you have the time to sit here with me?" I asked.

His eyes darkened and his expression turned serious. "Of course," he insisted.

"But I make things complicated."

He shook his head, but a little too quickly. "It's nothing."

I chuffed. "Friends are honest with each other, Kota. If there's important work to do, the last thing you need is me getting in the way."

"I'm not leaving you alone," he said.

"I'm not afraid of being alone," I said. I didn't want to be, though. I didn't want him to leave. I just needed to be sure I wasn't being totally selfish. If I got them to stay when they needed to be somewhere else, would they come to resent me? "I've been fine."

He frowned. "You weren't fine yesterday."

"I'm fine now. I didn't realize she would do that."

"What happens the next time you think it's not going to be that bad and it ends up killing you?"

"What if that never happens?"

"Then we're lucky," he said. "But we're not taking the risk."

I blew out a breath. "Why?"

His head reeled back, an eyebrow going up. "What do you mean?"

"Why me?"

"God, Sang," he pulled me back into his arms. I wanted to push him away because I was feeling confused. When he hugged me against him, the warmth in his body melted my rigid composure. He buried his face into my hair at the top of my head. "What happened to you? You're intelligent, sweet, considerate. You're too nice to speak up for yourself, even when you're in trouble. If one of us isn't right on top of you, you end up stuck inside a tree, or you're tied up in the shower, or hanging off the arm of some goon at school. And you're asking me if I'm inconvenienced?" He nuzzled his cheek against my head. "You're a beautiful wreck."

I swallowed hard, my head pressed up against his chest. Was that horrible? Was that supposed to make me feel better? "There are a lot of girls in trouble out there, Kota. There's many who have it much worse than I do."

His breath warmed my skin through my hair. His fingers rubbed at my back and side, massaging. I thought he wasn't going to answer. It was true. There were girls kidnapped and tortured every day. My mother said so.

"When I first started at the Academy," Kota whispered to me, "I thought the same thing. You might have noticed the Academy helps when it can. I wondered how they picked who they helped and why. There's so much that needs to be done. Why didn't we try helping everyone we came across?" His cheek brushed against my head again. "But we can't help everyone, Sang. We can't do it all. We have to trust that there's other people doing their best for those they love and hope it works out. We start with friends and family. That's our priority. If that's in order, we move on to helping others where we can. Family first,

Sang. Always."

"But I'm not family," I whispered.

"You're one of us," he said, the command in his voice returning. His fingertip traced the tip of my chin, drawing my head up so I could look into his eyes. His forehead hovered over mine, warming. "I know you don't feel it yet. You've got a family that doesn't act like one. It takes time to get used to someone caring about you when you've never had it. You might not know this, but Nathan and the others know exactly what you're going through."

My lips parted. "What do you mean?"

The corner of his mouth lifted. "They should tell you about it, but none of their families are very close."

"Your mother is," I said. "And your sister."

"We are," he said. "The others' families aren't. It wasn't very hard for them to recognize how lost you were. It's part of the reason why they wanted you."

I thought about Nathan's dad, who I'd yet to see. Nathan said he flew helicopters and was gone a lot. North and Luke lived with an uncle, and hadn't even known each other existed for a long time. I wondered about Gabriel and Silas and Victor. They were all caring and affectionate around me, something I never really experienced with my own family. How did they figure it out?

Maybe I'd been wrong. Maybe they were having just as hard a time figuring this out as I was. "I feel like I don't know what I'm doing," I said. "I don't understand how. Or why."

"I know." He pulled his head back, bringing a palm to my cheek, but still looking into my eyes. I forced mine to remain looking at his, but it was difficult. It felt like he could look inside, see everything. "We had a feeling and we made a decision. When you accepted us, we accepted you. It's how we work. You're one of us, Sang. So we're here for you. Family first."

Family. They were already my friends, but now I was family? I couldn't understand. We weren't related and they still hardly knew me. I was one of them. I sighed. I wanted to believe it. A few weeks ago I was alone. Now here I was in Kota's lap. My heart still raced. I wanted desperately to stay. I couldn't find the words to say it. Tears brimmed in my eyes and I tucked my head down, pushing my forehead against his shoulder because I didn't want him to see how unsure I was.

"I know you don't feel it, yet," he whispered, his hand seeking out mine. He slipped a thumb across my palm, holding on to my hand. "You will. It'll happen. If you want it to. You'll always have the choice. Family is a choice."

"It is?"

His thumb pressed into my palm firmly. "It's your choice. Parents and siblings are your relations. Family takes care of one another and helps each other. When each side is working together, when everyone wants it, that makes the difference."

I did want it. Did I want it with Kota and the others? It was hard to trust them when I was still getting used to them, wondering if one day they'd leave or not knowing what to expect. It was one thing to be a friend. This was different, wasn't it? I sighed, pressing my cheek against his chest and settling into him. I couldn't find the words to respond. I did want it, though I didn't know what it was enough yet to understand it.

He seemed to understand. He held me against him, his thumb tracing along my palm and his other hand massaging my back. It felt good. Awkward. Warm. Confusing. Would I ever be able to relax and simply enjoy his touch without worrying? Was I supposed to enjoy this at all?

A soft buzzing broke the silence. He grunted. The hand holding mine pulled away and he reached into his back pocket for his phone. I pulled my head back from his chest to give him room. He glanced at the screen and pushed a button to answer it. "North? Yes, she's here. No, don't use the D2-28. There's a reference bar." He paused. "The screen should say 'repeat' or 'replay'. It doesn't? Call

Victor. Let him know to take a look at it."

He continued to talk in codes and riddles I didn't understand. North was already awake working on secret Academy projects. Victor was either awake or was about to be woken up if North actually called him. What had the boys up so early? Or was this normal for them?

Creaking sounded on the stairs, heavy and irregular. I gasped, sitting upright, trying to make sure I heard correctly. Yes.

Crap, not now.

My fingers sought out Kota's mouth as he was telling North another code. I closed his lips, getting off his lap and pushing him toward the attic. It took only a fraction of a second for him to realize what was happening. He smashed his phone to his chest and did a back roll off the bed, opening the attic door and disappearing.

The door handle rattled. Knocking followed. "Sang," my mother called from the door.

My hands shook and I checked the room for anything out of place. I kicked Kota's book bag under my bed. I crossed the room, unlocking the door and peeking out.

My mother leaned against the frame. The IV had been taken out. She had replaced her robe with a clean one, but she was sweating again. Her eyes were wild. "Who are you talking to?"

I rubbed at my eyes, faking a yawn. "Talking?"

"I heard a man speaking."

I tilted my head. "The radio?"

She narrowed her eyes at me. Her shoulders heaved as she breathed heavily. It must have been an effort to walk up the stairs. Was she in pain? "Your radio isn't on now."

"I flicked it off when you knocked."

She frowned. "Why do you lie to me?"

My eyes widened. "I'm not."

"I can tell when you lie," she said. She pressed her palm against her cheek. "Sang, you lie and you lie. That's all you've done this week."

My heart tripped to a stop. Did she remember the stool and the shower now?

She entered the room and out of years of habit, I backed away against the wall. Her eyes scanned the room. "Why did you move things around?"

"I was trying something different," I said, my voice catching at the end as I trembled. I was embarrassed that Kota was listening to this. "Are you hungry? I'll make breakfast."

She stumbled to the bookshelf, her face contorting. "What's behind here?" she asked.

"The attic door," I said. "It's kind of ugly and I was trying to think of something..."

She grasped the top of the shelves and heaved it. The shelf slanted back, teetered for a brief second, before it crashed against the wall. The radio cracked between the shelf and the floor. The books flew and scattered. The fan that was behind the shelf smashed against the attic door and held the bookshelf crookedly, blocking the half door.

"Don't lie to me," she howled.

I forced myself against the wall to remain standing, wrapping my arms around myself as I was shaking so bad.

There was another creak. The attic door was opening, but stopped short because of the bookshelf in the way. Kota was going to come for me if I didn't find a way to stop him, or was he trapped?

"We should go downstairs and get something to eat," I said as loud as I could. The rattling at the attic door stopped. He understood. I wasn't hurt. "I'll make eggs and toast."

"Stop deflecting," she said. Her fingers flexed against her palms. She swayed on her feet. "You've moved your room around. There's voices coming from your room. You're lying to me. Something's going on and you're going to tell me right now."

I didn't know how to respond. My mouth opened, but words didn't come out. I couldn't think of another lie.

She stomped across the floor. "Downstairs," she said,

her tone cold. "Now."

I moaned softly but stepped into the hallway, obeying and padding my way downstairs. This was better. I was leading her away from Kota.

I wasn't hurt and I wasn't being told to sit in the bathroom, so this was a good thing, right?

My mother clutched the bannister as she stepped slowly down and into the foyer. She snapped her fingers at me. "Stay right here," she said.

I sighed, relieved. Rice. Or the stool. The stool! She'd find out it wasn't here. I'd be in trouble.

Luckily, she came back a moment later with the bag of rice. She dropped a handful near the door and pointed at it. "Kneel," she said.

I dropped to my knees, kowtowing with my face close to the floor to show compliance.

"When your father gets here…" she said, but never finished her sentence. She stepped down the hallway to her bedroom. The sound of the news droning on filtered through the air. She wasn't going to go back to sleep now.

I remained in the bowed position, trying to ensure she didn't step out to check on me as she used to do. Minutes passed. Was Kota still stuck in the attic? I thought at some point I could at least get up and help him get out before she discovered I was gone and then get back.

"Psst."

The sound rattled through me. I sat up in a rush, the movement making me temporarily dizzy. The rice bit into my knees.

Kota and Nathan sat together at the top of the stairs. Stony faces. Frowning. They gazed down at me.

Not both of them. It was humiliating enough with just Kota.

Kota signed to me, "Are you okay?"

I nodded.

He signed again. "Get up."

My mouth popped open.

The command he normally voiced was in his eyes as he signed. “Get up or I’m coming down to you.”

I crossed my arms in front of my body, trying to hold up my palm to tell him to stop, and then sign for him to go.

His eyes intensified. He nudged at his glasses and reached to pull his Converse shoes off of his feet. Nathan did the same with his Nikes. Then they yanked their socks off.

I couldn’t move. I trembled. I kept signing, begging with my eyes when I couldn’t sign fast enough. *Stop! Don’t do it. If I get up, she’ll hear. If you come down, she’ll hear.* If she caught us, I knew it would be over. Two boys in the house. She would have a heart attack, and call the police. The boys would be arrested.

The Academy would get involved.

Despite my warnings, the boys padded down the steps, tiptoeing at the edge of the stairs to mask their footfalls and to guard against creaking. Kota was risking everything. Nathan stepped where Kota did, always right behind him, a shadow in everything.

Kota crossed the foyer and knelt next to me. He was wearing jeans but I could tell even through the material he didn’t like it. “Sang,” he whispered. “Get up.”

“You should go,” I whispered. “She’ll come back.”

“You can’t kneel in rice, Sang,” he whispered. “That’s not normal.”

Nathan fell to his knees. His shorts slid up so his bare knees were exposed. His face contorted as his bones hit the rice against the hard floor. He mouthed a curse.

I shook my head at Kota, wrapping my arms around myself, shaking. “If she comes back and I’m not here...”

“If you don’t get up, we’re going to kneel here until you do,” Kota whispered.

Why was he doing this? A couple of hours kneeling in rice was nothing. I could deal with it. “You don’t have to do that,” I whispered.

“You’re one of us, Sang,” he commanded in his

whisper. "We're in this together. We're family."

He meant it. He was going to stay until I got up. One look at Nathan's face, and I could tell he was just as determined. He gritted his teeth, and his fists clenched to his thighs. I got the feeling the only thing keeping him still was Kota. Like North, Silas and the others, he would make good on the promise to drag me out of here if they saw fit.

Tears burned in my eyes and I swallowed hard to keep them back. It wasn't the pain from the rice. Would Marie ever kneel with me? Did my mother ever consider what she did? What did family mean? Marie left when she thought I was sick to go back to Danielle's house. She never noticed anything wrong. My mother ignored the bandages. She forgot she left me in the tub, tied and mute. Kneeling in rice wasn't normal.

Here was Kota. Here was Nathan. The loyalty on their faces was stronger than I ever felt from anyone. It made me ache in my core. Nathan shifted on his knees, and I knew he was feeling it. I did, too, but I had thicker skin at the knees now. Would I subject them any longer to this when it was clear I couldn't convince them to leave?

Family was a choice. I had to learn to trust them. If Kota said move, I moved. If Nathan said he'd pull me out of here if I didn't listen, I had to trust that. Whatever happened after this, I had to follow through. Was I going to be part of them or not?

I slid a knee up, my foot gliding until I stepped solidly on the floor. Rice not embedded into my knees bounced against the wood. I froze, scared my mother could hear it and would come for me.

Nathan brushed a palm over my knee to flick away the rest of the stuck rice. Kota grasped my elbow to lift me up with him. I held a hand out to get them to stop. They rose up next to me, waiting.

I put weight on my foot to stand. Once I was up, I was still shaking, but I'd made the decision. My mom was my mother. Kota and Nathan were family. I didn't feel it yet, but I wanted to. If they were willing to face off with my family like this, to risk everything for me, I wouldn't let them down. I needed this. I needed them. Is this what family did? I wanted to know more than anything. I would take the risk with them.

Kota crept to the stairs. Nathan followed.

I was about to move when the sound of the side door opening froze me. Keys rattled. Something heavy dropped to the floor in the family room. A low hum from a deep voice filled the space.

My father was home.

Kota and Nathan twisted to gaze back at me. With wide eyes, I made motions for them to get up the stairs. Kota half turned to me, ready to run back down the stairs. I shook my head, stood up straighter. He told me to get up. He told me to not kneel in rice. I wouldn't kneel again, but I would protect them. I'd be the distraction until they were safe. I could face my father. He was barely more than a stranger to me these days. He didn't matter.

I remained still. The other two slipped to the upstairs hallway. I caught the edge of Kota's toes still sticking out. In his own quiet way, he was reminding me he was right there and waiting.

My father's tall figure appeared at the edge of the living room. He crossed it and stopped when he spotted me in the foyer. His dark eyes were tired, and his gruff, unshaven face was drained. An eyebrow shifted up. "Sang," he said. "Why are you standing there?"

"The rice hurts," I said softly, my voice cracking.

He frowned. "What's wrong with your voice? And what happened to your wrists?"

I blinked. He noticed? I couldn't answer him. My eyes slid to his bedroom where my mother's television droned.

His eyes followed. "Go to your room," he said quietly.

I remained on the rice as he crossed in front of me and went to the bedroom. He shut the door behind himself.

I brushed some rice still sticking to my knees away and started to tiptoe toward the wall near my parents' bedroom. I wanted to hear. I didn't want to be in the dark. Kota waving to me at the top of the stairs stopped me. He motioned for me to come up. I held back the urge to disobey to satisfy my curiosity.

Kota commanded, I listened.

Lies

I tiptoed up the stairs. Kota caught me by the waist, lugging me into the bedroom. When I was inside, he let go to close and lock the door.

Nathan stood by, running fingers through his red brown hair. I turned to him and he wrapped his arms around me, hugging me close. I breathed in the cypress, weakly hugging him back, unsure how to tell him thank you for it.

"Crazy girl," he whispered. "I told you not to get into trouble before it was my turn."

"What's going on down there?" Kota asked behind me.

Nathan let go of me and I wobbled on my feet next to him. "He's talking to her. I don't know what about. He'll probably sleep off this business trip today and will go back to work tomorrow. He'll get her to eat, though. She'll probably feel better then."

Kota's face darkened. "I'm going to go listen."

"You just told me not to," I said. "I was going to hear at the door. And you can't do it, you'll get caught."

"I'm going to Marie's room," he said. "Her bedroom is right above theirs. I should be able to hear."

"I'm coming, too," I said.

Nathan grabbed my hand, drawing me to stand closer. "Nu uh. You're staying right here."

"But shouldn't I listen?"

Kota shook his head. "I'll listen. You stay."

I frowned. I didn't understand but was shaking and too emotionally drained to fight them on this.

Nathan held onto my hand as Kota left. I heard him creep across the hallway to Marie's room and then get quiet again as he stepped on her carpet.

Nathan pulled away and sat on the edge of the bed. "Come here. Let me check your knees."

I sat on the bed next to him. He hooked an arm under my thighs and slid my legs over until they were on his lap. He bent over, his fingertips tracing over the little indentations in my kneecaps. His breath drifted across my skin.

I shivered.

"Why did she make you kneel this time?"

"She knew I was lying to her. She heard Kota's voice. I claimed it was the radio."

"You're not a very good liar," he said. He glanced up, his blue eyes meeting mine. "We'll have to train you."

"I need to be trained to lie?"

He placed a warm palm on the outside of my knee. "Maybe not lie. Maybe just twisting the truth. I don't want you to lie if you can help it. You shouldn't have to, but if it means lying or being punished by kneeling in rice or being tied up in the shower again, I'd rather you lie. Sometimes you just have to."

"Do you have to lie?"

The corner of his mouth lifted. "Most of the time, I don't have to."

"So how do I tell if you're lying?"

"I don't lie to you."

I made a face. "Never?"

"Friends don't lie to each other."

I bit my lower lip. I didn't want to lie to him, either, and didn't plan on it. I felt guilty, though, because of how many times I kept things to myself, like my tailbone and how long I'd stalled before calling them the night before. Maybe I was lying to them by keeping it all to myself. Did I have to tell them everything?

He patted my thigh and pushed my legs off of his lap.

"Let's pick up your bookshelf."

The bookshelf had been tilted against the wall at an odd angle, the books scattered along the floor. We moved the shelf back to the other side of the room against the wall and picked the books up, even though so many were now damaged. The fan was cracked at the base. Nathan picked up the radio, plugged it in and hit the CD play button, but nothing happened. He flipped it over, checking the damage.

"Can I fix it?" I asked.

"Sang, sweetie, I think it's dead." He unplugged it.

I frowned softly. I had so few things that belonged to me. Now half of my books were torn and the radio was busted. There was little reason to keep the bookshelf at all.

A laptop had been left behind the bookshelf, too. I opened it, pushing the button to turn it on. The screen flashed. The keyboard started sparking like a fire cracker. I fell back on the carpet in surprise.

Nathan lunged over me, picking up the laptop, slapping the top down. He flipped it over and pulled out the battery. The sparks stopped.

"You broke everything." He grinned.

I knew he was teasing me, trying to make me feel better. It was my fault, though. "Victor's going to kill me," I said, pushing a finger to my lip.

Nathan frowned. He put the laptop down on the ground. He sat cross-legged on the carpet and pulled me into his lap. How easily he did so. My heart fluttered. He held me in his lap as Kota had done, as Gabriel had done. How did they seem to know what I needed? "Victor would never lay a finger on you," he said. His broad shoulders made me feel even smaller than I'd felt with Kota. The muscles in his arms were hard against my body. "You have to stop worrying so much."

My finger pinched my lip to my teeth. "He's not going to be happy."

Nathan pulled my hand away from my mouth. "Sang, Victor doesn't give a shit about a laptop. We have more important things to deal with."

I sucked in a breath and let it out slowly. "Like helping Ashley Waters get more funding."

He squeezed my hand, pressing my palm against his chest, his pressing on top of mine. "And making sure you're safe."

My cheeks heated. I wanted to look in his eyes, but he was too close and I felt too shy. I kept looking at his hand pressed to mine against his chest. I felt his heart beating. I wished I could be as comfortable as they seemed to be with all the touching. Kota promised it would happen eventually. I wondered how long it would take.

Kota crept back from across the hallway, opened the door and peeked his head in. Nathan tensed at the noise, but when I didn't move, he didn't move, either.

Kota spied the laptop on the floor and looked at us. "Something wrong?"

"The laptop is broken," I said.

"So is her stereo. And I think that fan is, too."

Kota frowned, glancing at the torn books stacked on the shelves. He pressed a palm to his forehead, rubbing his fingers across his eyebrow and putting his other hand on his hip. "The stereo will be hard to replace. It's old."

"I don't need a new one," I said.

A chop landed on my head. "Shut up," Nathan grinned at me.

"So what was said downstairs?" I asked.

Kota sighed and knelt on the floor next to us. "He's making her eat. That's a good thing."

I slipped out of Nathan's lap, to sit between them on the floor. "What else?"

Kota pursed his lips.

"Kota," Nathan said. "If it's about her, she should know."

Kota rubbed his palm against his jeans, smoothing out the material. "Her mother's denying knowledge of what happened yesterday. She claims she doesn't know what happen to Sang at all. She's lying and saying Sang was on her knees this morning for stealing money."

My breath caught in my throat. "Stealing?"

"She said there's money missing from her purse."

I blinked, shaking my head. "She has a purse?"

Kota and Nathan focused on me, eyebrows raised.

I shrugged. "She never goes out. I don't think I've seen her with a purse since... I don't know. I can't remember."

"Regardless," Kota said, "she's lying to cover up why. I don't really understand her motivation." He turned to me. "Would he believe her?"

I shrugged. "I never talk to him. I never see him. I don't know what he thinks."

Nathan frowned. He reached for my hand, squeezing it. "It might be why he turns a blind eye to everything going on. He really doesn't know because he isn't here."

Kota nodded. "You're probably right. So if she lies about any injuries he happens to notice, or sees you kneeling, he's going to take her side because... well... she's his wife."

We all grew silent. I sighed, letting go of Nathan's hand to rub both palms across my face. "It's conjecture. It isn't helpful. He'll go back to work tomorrow and I'll not see him for a while. We'll go to school. Things will cool down."

Kota shifted, his lips pursed as if he wanted to say something, but wasn't sure how to approach it.

Nathan blew out a puff of air. "What now?"

"Let's get ready for the day," Kota said. He stood up, lowering a hand out to me. I slid my palm into his. It was easier to touch them when they reached for me first. My heart still fluttered. I was still nervous. In the back of my mind, I worried one day they wouldn't want me to touch them or I'd go too far.

I stood up. "I guess I'll go wash up and get dressed," I said. "Are we staying in or heading out?"

Kota hesitated, shifting on his feet while he held my

hand, intertwining our fingers. "I don't want to cause any more trouble, but if your father's here, maybe we should take advantage of it. If you're sure they won't come looking for you."

"They haven't even asked about Marie," Nathan said.

"Right," Kota said. "We'll fall back to Nathan's house. No offense, Sang, but I don't want to scare my mom or my sister with those wounds on your wrists. I'm not sure they'll understand."

I didn't want to worry them anymore, either. I wondered how much Kota told them about what happens over here. How far did this inner circle of friends go? I moved away from them to open my closet. I started to pull out a skirt and a blouse.

Nathan grunted behind me. "Wear shorts," he said. "And a t-shirt. We'll start some training."

"Maybe we should give that a rest," Kota suggested.

"You're the one that gave the order, remember? Self-defense this weekend."

"I think she's had enough. We need to let her heal," he said, looking pointedly at me.

I knew what he was asking me to say. I swallowed. "I cracked my tailbone yesterday," I told Nathan. "It kind of hurts."

Nathan's blue eyes widened. "What? When?"

"When I was knocking the stool around in the tub to get your attention."

Nathan looked confused for a moment. "Oh," he said. "Was that what it was? Well shit. How do you fix a broken tailbone?"

"You don't. It's like her ankle," Kota said. "You wait for it to heal. That means no rigorous training for a while, though." His mouth twisted. "We may need to take her in for another X-Ray."

"Why didn't anyone tell me?" he pushed his palm into his eye.

"We've been busy," I said. I still traded the skirt for

shorts, thinking I should save the skirts for school.

Kota and Nathan withdrew to the attic, so quietly that if I wasn't watching, I probably wouldn't have heard them. Music started and I guessed the other laptop was okay. It would mask their noises and my parents might think it was from my stereo.

I crossed the hallway and locked the bathroom door. I put down the clothes I was going to wear on the counter by the sink. I moved to the tub. My fingers lingered on the faucet. Silas had fixed it. That meant something to me.

I flicked the water on. The shower spray crashed into the basin. At first, I stared at the light sparkling in the water before it touched down to swirl toward the drain.

My knees wobbled as I thought about stepping into the shower. My stomach churned, my hands started to sweat. I had to sit down.

Flashes came over my eyes. Water streaming into my face. Screaming with no one listening. Nathan's confused, horror struck face. Silas's contorted rage.

The thought of stepping into it made me lose my breath and my stomach twist.

I swallowed, shifting the water from the shower to the faucet to fill up the tub instead. The shaking and the sweating subsided. I breathed some mild relief.

At least I wasn't afraid of a bath. My heart was still thundering, but I didn't feel so lightheaded like before.

How embarrassing. When the bath filled up with warm water, I slid into the tub. I tucked my knees against my chest and I rested my head on my left one. The warm water surrounding me felt better, anyway.

I'd been lucky I hadn't collapsed. It was one thing they didn't have to know about. They had enough to do and most of it was involving me now.

Kota had to be mistaken. You couldn't tell everyone all of your secrets. You couldn't burden someone else with every little thing. You took care of yourself and tried not to be in the way and help others as best as you could.

I didn't need to worry them about how I felt about

showers.

♥♥♥

By Monday, the marks on my wrists were still obvious, but Gabriel permitted the pink bands Silas had given me. Gabriel did, however, spend the night again Monday evening to determine what I should wear that would go along with wearing them.

My father was home in the evenings and my mother was subdued, in a gentle routine of sleeping most of the day and eating regularly. A doctor called, conveniently, on Tuesday afternoon to 'verify' which pills she was taking and to schedule an appointment in a month. She complained about doctors telling her what to do and tried to get them to put the appointment off, but they said the next available date would be in three months.

Part of me wondered if it was Dr. Green on the phone, but I would never know.

Someone spent the night with me every evening. After the first night, the others slept only in the attic under Kota's command. I would stay out at Kota's or Nathan's as late as I could risk it, usually until a half hour before my father got home. There was less of a chance for us to get caught together in my room if we weren't there in the first place. One of the guys followed me home, climbed the roof and waited for me to open the window. They'd slip into the attic. I spent a lot of time next to them as they huddled inside the attic door to finish up homework or to play on some electronic device they brought with them or just to talk. If there was Academy business to deal with, they closed the attic door, disappearing to the platform in the back to make phone calls. In the morning, I had to get up early to give whoever it was time to run to Nathan's to shower and change for school.

We tiptoed around eggshells in my hollow house. The Academy became my shadow.

ESCAPE

I dreamed of being chased on foot through the woods. I was weaving through the trees, but no matter how hard I tried to run faster, my legs felt clumsy and sluggish.

Growling emanated from behind me.

"*Aggele mou*," Silas pressed a hand to my back, shaking me.

I was sleeping on my stomach. I twisted to look at him and pressed my palms to my face to rub out the sleep. "Hm?"

Silas was kneeling on the floor near my bed. His dark eyes softened with concern. "You were shaking. Are you okay?"

I sucked in a deep breath, my cheek rubbing against the cotton of the pillow case. "Yeah," I said. "I was just dreaming."

He nudged me and I flipped over onto my back, making room so he could sit on the edge of the bed. He leaned over me. "What about?"

"Running," I whispered and yawned, pushing a finger over my eyebrow. "Too slowly, in my opinion."

He chuckled, his deep voice reverberating through my bones. "Tell your dream self to exercise more."

"Did you sleep?" It was Silas's first night staying in the attic.

"No," he said. He lifted a finger to my cheek and slid a

lock of hair away from my face.

"You're on the football team," I reminded him. They'd gotten the official word the day before. Silas and North were first string for the varsity team, no surprise considering their size and sheer power. For sophomores, I supposed it was pretty good. Neither of them seemed too excited. "You should sleep. You can't stay up all night and then go to school and practice."

"I can't sleep in that thing," he said, nodding his head toward the attic. "It's like a coffin. And I should be listening for trouble."

"We can't do this forever, Silas," I whispered. "You guys can't come over every night and stay awake all the time. And we'll get caught one day. We've been lucky so far." Every night, I was scared my sister would pop in at the wrong moment, or I would go to the bathroom and come back to find my mother peeking inside the attic door, or my father would overhear our early morning shuffle to get out of the house before anyone woke up. I snoozed more than I actually slept because of how terrified I was. I wouldn't be able to hide how tired I was for much longer.

His lips pursed. He leaned closer to me, his face inches from mine. "I know. We're working on it."

I blinked at him. "How? On what?"

The corner of his mouth drifted up. The finger returned, coarse and strong, and it slid across my cheek again. "You'll see. Soon."

I pouted. Secrets.

"Don't give me that face," he warned. He nudged me, tucking an arm around my body. "Come here."

I kicked the blanket away, blushing because I was wearing Nathan's blue shirt and really short shorts. The shirt was long enough to make it look like I wasn't wearing anything on the bottom.

Silas didn't hesitate, but picked me up, placing me in his lap. It'd become almost a tradition for all of them. They woke me up and the next thing I knew, I was in someone's lap. It was like if one of them did it, the others followed. How they knew, if they told each other, I wasn't sure. I didn't complain, but it did confuse me why they did it. I could only trust it was because they were my friends and they were doing their best to make me feel better.

I buried my face into his chest, inhaling the faint scent of the ocean mixed with attic dust. He dropped his chin to the top of my head. His strong hands rubbed my back and side. "I can't stand when you pout."

I smiled against his chest. "Gabriel said it doesn't work."

"He's full of shit," Silas said. "It totally works on him. He just tells you that so you don't try it or to get you to stop. Watch. Next time do it and keep doing it. Just not to me. And don't tell him I told you."

I giggled, shaking my head. "He'll be mad that you gave away his secret."

"If he gives you a hard time, tell me. I'll beat him up."

I stuffed my hand to my mouth, smothering a laugh.

He dropped his face, pressing his nose to my hair. "Ready to get going? I want to stay, but I can't sit here with you like this."

I sighed, nodding and wriggling to get up. He was right. The longer we were there, we were more likely going to get caught.

He squeezed me once more before his hands slid away from me. I stumbled to my feet and a wave of shivers swept through me.

"Will you stop shaking?" he begged quietly. His hand smoothed over my back. "What's wrong?"

"Nothing," I said, being honest. "It's just early and I'm still waking up."

"You shake all the time. That's going to drive me crazy."

The tease of a smirk touched my face but I turned away to hide it. I went to my closet to figure out what I was going to wear today.

Silas followed, standing behind me. I fingered over the

blouse and skirt Gabriel had picked out for me.

"Wear this one," he said, pointing to a thin dark blue hoodie. "You look good in it."

I smiled softly. Having the boys pick out my clothes was peculiar, but I appreciated their opinion and it gave me a small surge of confidence that the clothes I wore weren't too weird. "Gabriel..."

"Yeah, I know," he said. He turned to me, bowing his head closer to my face. "It'll drive him crazy."

We shared a conspiratorial smile and I took the hoodie along with a matching sporty skirt. "It won't match the pink wristbands."

"I don't care," he said. He turned away, heading back to the attic. "Knock when you're done."

♥♥♥

Twenty minutes later, I was out of the bath, with my hair still wet but smoothed out and twisted into a clip. I dressed in the skirt and hoodie and went back to my room. I knocked at the door to the attic. Silas emerged, crawling out on his hands and knees. I collected my book bag and he took it from my hands, along with my violin case and his own overnight bag. I crept to the window to open it for him.

He hefted the bags and crawled out onto the roof. My heart thundered in my throat as he did. I did it now every time they started to leave. I don't know where it came from, but the five minutes between being upstairs with them and then downstairs in the yard was by far the scariest for me. I wondered if they'd fall or if someone would hear their footsteps on the roof or someone in the neighborhood would notice.

I grabbed my shoes and slipped down the stairs, stopping short when I spotted my father in the foyer. His head tilted up and he was looking puzzled.

"Up early?" he asked. He was dressed in an oversized

shirt and pajama pants, looking sleepy.

I felt the blood draining from my face but nodded quickly. "Yes."

"It's too early for the bus, isn't it?"

"I... like going for a walk before it's time. Clears my head a little before I have to study inside all day."

He raked a hand through the curls on top of his head as if considering this. "Oh." He moved on to the laundry room.

Were we late getting up? That was close. If he'd been listening earlier, he might have heard Silas's deep voice through the walls. Maybe that's what woke him.

I chewed on my lower lip, pondering my next move. It seemed obvious, I should do just what I said, pretending to go for a walk.

I slipped my sandals on and cut through the house to the back door. By the time I got there, my father was leaving the laundry room with folded clothes.

"Maybe you shouldn't go," he said. "You know how your mother feels when you go out. It's still dark."

He had an opinion? I stuffed my fingers into the front pocket of the hoodie to hide how they trembled. Nathan was right, I needed to learn how to lie better. "I just go to the woods behind the house. No one is ever out there."

He frowned but shrugged me off and headed back to his bedroom. I hesitated, waiting for him to relay what was going on to my mother and my mother to punish me. I couldn't spare another minute. If I wasn't outside now, Silas would come back for me. If I ended up kneeling in rice again, I wasn't sure what I could do. He'd pull me out for sure.

I opened the side door and slipped out into the early morning. It was the risk I had to take right now. Maybe by that afternoon when I got home from school, she'd have forgotten or I'd get lucky and he wouldn't think to mention it to her at all.

Silas stood, ready to go in the drive. He turned to me when I rushed out, his eyebrows going up. "What took you?"

"My dad's awake," I said, frowning. I grabbed his arm, tugging him toward the back yard. "Let's hurry. I don't want him looking out and spotting you."

He frowned, shaking his head. "Forget the long way." He jerked his head toward the neighbor's yard. "Come on."

I followed on his heels behind him as he cut through the neighbor's front lawn, taking the shortest distance possible and one where we wouldn't be seen through any windows by my parents. If anyone else was awake, I wondered what they would have thought of two teenagers sneaking off together before dawn. Would they think we were running away together? Would they assume we were off to have sex or get high? Would they believe that he was helping me to escape my mother's crazy punishments and I was helping him avoid being discovered?

I yearned for a time we didn't have to slip out into the shadows of the night in order to find some peace. How long did we have to sneak around like the bad people my mother thought Silas and the others to be? Would they ever get tired of having to deal with this? Would the boys eventually hate that they made this decision to include me? It took a lot of work to survive around my parents. How could it be worth it to them?

When we got to Nathan's, I reached the door first and started to knock but Silas nudged me aside and opened the door without warning. He pushed me through, entered behind me and shut the door.

He dropped our things onto the floor, pressing his back to the doorframe. My fingers fluttered to the base of my throat as he scanned out the glass panes on either side of Nathan's front door, waiting. My breath caught. Did my father see us at any point? Would he go out looking for me? Would my mother demand for my return?

"What are you doing?" Nathan's voice cut through our silence. Silas and I jumped and spun around. Nathan was wearing only shorts, rubbing the back of his mussed, rusty hair and yawning. A shiver of guilt slid down my spine as I admired the muscles in his chest and arms. It wasn't the time to stare, I knew, but I couldn't help it. He was incredible.

"Her dad woke up," Silas said. He stepped away from the door.

Nathan frowned, looking to me. "What happened?"

I relayed the events from the moment I spotted my father in the foyer until we were running through the yards. "I had to go," I said. "If he told my mother, she's yelling for me right now. But if I stayed, I don't know what she'd do and Silas was outside waiting and..." I swallowed, rubbing a finger across my lip. Maybe it was the wrong move. I'd panicked, worried about Silas and my own selfish desire to escape. Maybe I should have told my dad I was going to stay and sent a text to Silas that I was going to be delayed and to go to Nathan's without me.

Nathan took my hand from my mouth, squeezing. His blue eyes darkened. "Wait here with Silas."

My eyes popped open at his words. "What are you doing?"

"I'm going back to check."

"You can't!"

"We have to make sure," Nathan said. "I'll go listen and see. If she's calling for you, I'll call Silas and let you go back, but we'll be there if she tries one of her punishments. We just need to make sure she isn't calling the cops on you or anything. We'll try not to let this get out of hand."

I turned to Silas. "Don't let him. He'll get caught."

Silas sighed, looking conflicted. "He's right, *aggele*."

There was nothing I could say. Nathan ran to his room, coming back out to the foyer where we were still standing as he pulled a t-shirt over his head. Silas stepped out of the way and opened the door as Nathan walked back out into the early morning, disappearing across the lawns that we'd come from.

Silas repositioned himself into the kitchen, watching

from where he could see out the front windows toward my front lawn. He dug his cell phone from his pocket to keep in hand.

I wanted to curl up in his lap again. I wanted to go back and change my decisions. I wished I had fought them on this harder. If Nathan got caught, it would be my fault. If I had to go back for a punishment, and Silas and Nathan had to pull me out, it'd be my fault.

I clutched a hand over my heart, and leaned against the wall, counting off my heartbeats for every moment Nathan was gone.

Silas glanced over at me, frowning. He held his arms out to me. I crossed to him and he wrapped an arm around me, his hand moving behind my head to hold me against his chest. I hugged him, my fingers rubbing absently at his back.

He separated the blinds with his other hand to keep a look out as he held on to me. I didn't mean to be in the way. I didn't have the courage to let go.

"I'm sorry," I whispered against his chest.

He bowed his head, breathing against my hair. "What for?"

"I should have been more careful," I said, pressing my face to his chest to avoid his eyes.

His hand shifted, petting my hair. "It isn't your fault."

"But I..."

"No," he said. He pushed me away from him until my back was against the wall. He held his fingers to my lips to stop me from speaking. "No more blaming yourself. You're doing your best. If you had normal parents, we wouldn't have to sneak around and do all this. If you want to blame anyone, blame them." He bowed his head closer to my face, his deep brown eyes gazing into mine. How they treat you isn't your fault. Anyone with half a brain would never neglect you like they do."

"Silas," I mumbled against his fingers.

He grunted, pressing his nose to my forehead. His

breath warmed my face.

I closed my eyes.

"You shouldn't have to do this at all," he whispered. "You're too sweet to be stuck there. Say the word, Sang. Tell me to take you. I'll do it. I'll do whatever you want."

I couldn't find my voice to reply. Was he serious? Was he just trying to make me feel better? Part of me wanted to say something, to ask him just to see how far he took this. What did he mean? Where would he take me?

His fingers clutched my chin, lifting. It forced my eyelids open and I was lost in the concern and yearning in his face.

"Say it," he commanded.

"Silas..." I whispered. My mind was in a frenzy. The words teased my tongue. How easy would it be to tell him, but how was I going to? How could I do that to him? I didn't even understand what he meant. Those dark brown eyes were begging me to just tell him anything but I didn't know how.

What scared me the most was how badly I was tempted to say what he wanted.

The sound of the front door opening had me stiffening against the wall. Silas grunted, turning with his hands clenched into fists. I could only pray it was Nathan and not my father or the police having snuck up on us. It frightened me to think of what Silas might be preparing himself for if it were the latter.

Nathan popped his head in from around the corner. His eyes caught mine and he seemed confused, tilting his head. "He's packing a suitcase," he said. "He left a note on your door." He held out a neon yellow paper stuck to his fingertips. "I checked in on your mom after he left the bedroom. She's asleep and doesn't know anything."

Silas crossed the room before I could, taking the note from Nathan's fingers. He glanced over the writing before frowning and slowly passing it back to me.

Business trip.

"Another one?" I wondered. I swallowed, taking the note from Silas's fingers. I folded the paper. Relief flooded through me. I wasn't in trouble. He'd gotten up early because he had to leave. "Thank goodness. We're not caught."

Silas continued to frown, and Nathan joined him, shaking his head.

I didn't understand. Wasn't this a good thing that we weren't discovered or that she wasn't calling for me? "What?" I asked.

"Not even a fucking goodbye," Nathan mumbled.

Silas grunted again in agreement. He marched off, grabbing his bag and heading to Nathan's bathroom.

It scared me that I still didn't understand.

Thick In The Nettles

It was Thursday. School was quiet. No fights. Notes passed to me in class were intercepted by North or the others, or I handed them over the moment I got them. I wondered when the people sending them would ever learn that I didn't get them or read them and I wasn't interested. Part of me wondered if it was some sort of joke now. Pass the strange girl a note and watch her not read them. Maybe it was a game.

That afternoon, Kota said he was going to the Academy with Victor. Silas and North had their first football practice. Luke and Gabriel joined Nathan and I on the bus for the ride home. I was under orders from Nathan to check in at home with Luke as my shadow. After that, we were going to hole up at Nathan's house for the evening.

Marie walked with me to our house. The sweltering heat made the thin hoodie I wore feel heavy against my skin. Luke took the back trail around Nathan's house. He'd wait for Marie and me to enter before he scaled the house to my bedroom window.

I waited until Marie went into her room before closing and locking my door. Luke slipped quietly into my room, dashing into the attic. This was a critical point. Marie could barge in any minute and I didn't yet know what kind of day my mom was having.

When the attic door closed behind Luke, I thumped down the stairs louder than necessary to give Luke an idea of where I was. I peeked in at my mom. She was awake but her eyes drooped as she gazed at the television blaring the news. She didn't notice I was standing there, so I pushed the door against the wall to make some noise.

She turned her head to me, her dull eyes focusing on my elbow, my shoes, at the frame of the doorway above my head. "What?" she grumbled.

"Just letting you know I was home," I said.

"Go clean your room," she demanded. "I don't want to hear a peep out of you today."

"Can I bring you something to eat?"

She picked up a cup of soup from her night stand to show to me. "Get out of here."

I ran back upstairs. I tapped on the attic door before crossing the room to pick out a pair of short blue shorts and a thin t-shirt. I checked on Marie before I got to the bathroom to change. She was gone. I suspected she was on her way to Danielle's house. It occurred to me that our mother hadn't asked about her. I dismissed it. Maybe she would never have asked for me at all today. Popping in to check on her just set back the unseen timer on when my mother thought to actually check on us.

After I dressed, I poked my head into my room. Luke was ready at the window. He shuffled out onto the roof and I took the back stairs. We met in the garage and took off for Nathan's house.

I knocked because it was awkward to me to just walk in.

Luke held my hand, grinning at me and shaking his head. "You're too nice."

Gabriel answered the door wearing a pair of jeans and a bright neon green tank shirt. He smirked at me, crossed his arms over his chest and leaned against the frame of the door. "Oy," he said. "Hey there, Trouble." His eyes went to my hair. "Nope, nuh uh." He held out his hand. "Give it up."

I felt my eyebrows pop up. "Why?"

"Pay the toll. You can come in if you give me the clip."

I sighed. "It's too hot to have my hair down."

"Stop it," Luke said. He slipped off the blazer he was still wearing, undoing the tie at his neck.

Gabriel rubbed his head. "I've been looking at that thing all week and I haven't said anything. I hate it. I want it back. I was gonna do her hair anyway."

Nathan appeared at the door. He was in running pants, sneakers and a red Nike shirt. "Oh good, you're here." He held a few water bottles in his hands. "Come on, we're going out."

"Let me get this stupid uniform off first," Luke said, pulling off his shirt as he trailed into the house.

Ten minutes later, Luke had changed into a pair of jeans and sneakers, but remained shirtless. I followed Nathan through Kota's backyard. Gabriel and Luke trailed behind us. We all carried water bottles. Bees buzzed around the dandelions in the grass. It felt more like a summer day and I had mostly forgotten about school and homework already.

"Why are we going into the woods?" Gabriel asked, sounding more curious than concerned. He had his arms up over his head, resting his forearms on top of his hair. With his arms up, his shirt lifted to reveal the red edge of his boxers above the hem of his jeans and a little bit of tanned skin at his hip.

"I promised to take Sang," Nathan said. He leaned into me to whisper close to my ear. "I really needed to get out of the house."

"No worries," I whispered back. I didn't mind. We'd been cooped up at school and with hiding from my parents at home.

"Stop talking about me," Gabriel whined. When I looked back, he was pouting, but as he caught my eyes he winked and smiled.

We stood at the edge of Kota's yard. The trees behind his house thinned out at one spot and there was a brown dirt path between two palm trees. The palm trees seemed out of place to me. I forgot how far south my family had moved sometimes.

Nathan led the way under the two trees. There was a broad, cleared path just behind the tree line, the ground flattened wide enough to perhaps make a paved road in the future. Or maybe someone had wanted to but changed their minds and left the spot abandoned. The grass was overgrown, up to our mid-calves.

Nathan headed east and was lifting his knees high to flatten down the grass as he walked. I wished I had worn jeans this time, but I fell behind him so I could follow along in his trail. Luke shadowed me. Gabriel blazed his own trail to my right.

"Hey wait up!" A girl's voice shouted from behind us. My heart stopped in my chest. For a moment I was worried it was Marie.

Instead, Kota's sister Jessica was running up, following Gabriel's trail in. The edge of her glasses had fogged a little and her cheeks were flushed.

"What's she doing?" Nathan asked, wiping his hand against his cheek.

"Maybe she wanted to come along," I said.

"I don't know about that," Nathan said. "I didn't think she was the outdoor type."

"She can, can't she? Let her come." I had a warm spot for anyone in Kota's family. They were always so friendly to me. "Hey," I called to her. "You wanted to come with us?"

She slowed when she got close. She was wearing khaki pants and a rose colored blouse that suited her shoulder-length dark hair. She glanced at the guys, hesitating.

I wondered if she was as intimidated as I felt when I was around them. I smiled to her and stretched my hand out. I had to make an effort to be friendlier and it felt a lot easier with Jessica. Maybe because she looked like Kota and she was younger. "Come on," I said.

She reached out to take my hand and I helped her over the tall grass until she was standing behind me.

We set off again, letting Nathan lead the way. At certain points the grass was up to our thighs. With Nathan's persistence, we weaved our way through.

We soon got to a part where the grass had thinned out considerably. The main path curved northward. There was a small dirt road to the right that twisted away, shaded in an archway of walnut trees.

Nathan pointed to the dirt road. "Don't go back there," he warned. "There's a big pile of sawdust they never came back to clear. It's dangerous so stay out of it." He glanced back at me, making his point clear. He was specifically telling me. I hid an eye roll at his assumption that I would do anything dangerous on purpose.

Since the grass was short here, it was easier to walk beside each other. The boys moved ahead of us and Jessica and I tailed them. They hovered at the entryway to the dirt road, talking about a good way to post a sign or block it so no one would go in there. Academy boys were always working.

I struggled with something to talk to Jessica about. There was little I actually knew about her other than being related to Kota. I forced my lips apart to start talking. "How do you like your school, Jessica?"

"It's okay," she said. "I wish we didn't have to wear uniforms."

I blinked at her. "Do you go to a private school?"

"Yes," she said. "Not to the Academy though."

"Why not the Academy?"

"Kota won't let me."

I perked up. He didn't want his own sister going, just like he didn't want me going. "Why not?"

She shrugged. "I don't think I want to go anyway. They are always working and always at the school. They never get a real break. They're there during the summer, too. I like school, but not that much."

I struggled with the idea of Kota not allowing his own little sister to go to the school he went to. Was it because of the things they were doing now? Was getting beaten up and being subjected to crazy situations like helping Ashley Waters a requirement? I wondered how the others felt. They hadn't objected to Kota's request.

Crunching sounds and voices reached my ears, noises that didn't come from us. I wasn't quite sure where it was coming from. The guys continued to argue about what to do and didn't seem to have noticed.

"Guys," I said softly.

Luke was saying something about a barn. "Let's show it to her."

"There could be wasps," Nathan said. "I don't want to take her there until I've had a chance to clear it out."

"Guys..." The sound of footfalls was getting closer, but I still couldn't locate the direction.

"Sang doesn't want to see some old barn," Gabriel said. He splashed some of his water in his face. "Let's go swim."

"Guys!"

They all turned to me. I held a finger to my lips to indicate they should be quiet.

Once they stopped talking, they caught on to what I was hearing. Their heads turned, but it was Nathan who turned fully around, looking down the dirt path.

We watched as Derrick emerged from further down the dirt path. He was wearing jean shorts and Converse high tops, but was shirtless. Following him were two boys who looked to be about Jessica's age. One had straight blond hair cut to his shoulders, was gangly, and shorter than Jessica. The other one had dark curly hair, was thin but taller than her and deeply tan.

We stared at each other for a moment. Both groups seemed surprised the other one was there.

"Hey," Derrick said, waving.

"Hey," Nathan said. "What are you doing back there? It's dangerous."

"We were checking the surrounding woods to see if there was more than one sawdust pile," said the blond. His face was pale, his eyes dark and he wore jean cutoff shorts and a white t-shirt and glasses. I couldn't be sure but it looked like he was scowling.

"Who's that?" the curly-haired kid asked, pointing to me. He was shirtless and wearing camo shorts were ripped and old. His ribs stuck out. He wasn't sickly, just thin.

"That's Sang," Nathan said. "She's with the family that moved into the new house."

"Yeah," Derrick said, his dark eyes lighting up. "Are we allowed to come over and play basketball yet?"

I blushed. I glanced at the others. Little did he know he couldn't ever come over.

"We're working on it," Nathan said, his hand finding mine and squeezing gently. "Her mom's a little shy."

Relief washed over me. At least they weren't going to tell everyone about what happened.

"I know. Her sister mentioned it," he said. He pointed toward where we had come from. "You all heading this way?"

"We were thinking of seeing where this main path ends," Nathan said, nodding his head in the opposite direction.

"There's nothing out there," Derrick said. "It goes on for about two miles and then cuts off against a line of trees."

Nathan looked disappointed. "Why build this thing in the middle of nowhere?"

"Why clear out the trees and leave that sawdust hazard?" Derrick asked and shrugged. "Who knows? They probably meant to make more developments but ran out of money."

We started heading back the way we came. I wondered why Derrick wasn't part of their circle. They seemed friendly enough with each other and he was our age.

The younger boys were talking to each other in hushed voices.

"Who are the other two," I asked Jessica quietly.

"The blond is Micah and the dark-haired guy is Tom," she said. "They live in the houses across the highway."

"Do they go to your school?"

"No, they go to the public school." Her eyes kept drifting to them. "They don't really like me, though."

"Why not?"

"I'm a girl."

I laughed. "I'm a girl, too."

"They might not like you either, then."

We followed the guys to the trail with the higher grass. We stood together in a big circle. I felt the eyes of the new guys on me as if trying to weigh out who I was and if they could trust me.

"How old are you?" Derrick asked me.

I blushed, looking at Nathan. Nathan shrugged, his face suggesting it was okay to talk. Why was I turning to him as if he was going to answer for me?

"We're in the same grade," I replied. Maybe it wasn't a direct answer, but I thought it should be obvious.

"I know," he said. "I wasn't sure. You look younger. I thought maybe you skipped a grade."

"It's those clothes," Micah said. "You look like you belong in third grade."

"Hey," Gabriel said loudly. He hooked an arm around my neck and half leaned against me. "What's wrong with her clothes?"

"They're all..." Micah started, but he fumbled his words and pointed his hand toward me as if just looking at them was enough to explain it.

"Like girl clothes?" Gabriel snapped at him. "Sue her. She is a girl."

"Stop it, Micah," Derrick said. Micah shot him a look but Derrick had turned to Nathan. "Did you show her the barn yet?"

"I wanted to make sure there weren't any wasps," Nathan said. "I haven't been back there in a while."

"We were just there," piped in Tom. He seemed happier than his friend. He smiled at us. "There weren't any."

"Let's go through the woods instead of taking the long way," Derrick said. "We've been trying to see if there's anything else through this mess here. Like any more secret barns in the middle of nowhere."

Micah grunted and started walking toward the trees. "Let's get this over with."

Micah led the way. I looked at Nathan, awaiting confirmation that this was a good idea. He shrugged, hesitating, but Gabriel and Luke were already following Derrick and Tom into the woods. I did a short sprint to catch up with Gabriel. Nathan fell in behind me, Jessica behind him.

We walked in a line because it was really the only way to make it through. The woods were thick and there wasn't a specific trail. The underbrush swiped at my legs. The heat and humidity seemed to intensify as the trees enclosed around us.

The sunlight filtered down to us thinly through the crest of leaves overhead. The area took on a heavy haze of green.

Micah wound his way through the trees with Derrick occasionally pointing a direction out to him.

"Why do you keep telling me where to go?" Micah asked. "If we take a straight line we'll get there faster."

"Just cut through here," Derrick said. He pointed to where there was a break in the trees. "There's a big open space there. I want to check it out."

We spilled out into a natural circular clearing. The canopy of leaves above us appeared thicker and blocked out the light. It was almost like a dome over our heads. Two huge oaks sat in the middle, gnarled into each other as if in an ongoing battle for dominance of the space. The roots twisted above the ground surrounding them.

We moved forward as a group. The trees were really beautiful, with thick branches dripping with moss. The air was thick with the smell of green and pollen and I let it fill my lungs.

My legs itched and I lifted one high for a moment to scratch. I wondered if I was getting bit by mosquitos.

"You okay?" Nathan asked, his eyes on my fingers scratching.

"Just a bug bite," I said. I continued to try to scratch at it. I felt one on my other calf, too but I ignored it while he was watching so he wouldn't worry. "Remind me to spray for bugs before we do this again."

"Welcome to the south," he said. "The bugs will eat you alive."

We were halfway toward the two trees when Jessica shouted behind us.

"Stop!" she said. I turned around to see her waving her hands in the air. "Don't move!"

"What?" I asked.

"She's just going to tell us there's some rare bug or some crazy wild flower," Micah complained. "Who cares?"

"No," she cried out. "There's stinging nettle here."

We all froze, eyes surveying the ground around us.

"What's stinging nettle?" I asked. In my mind flashed images of tiny wasps. More southern bugs?

"It's the plants," she said. She carefully stood on one leg, bringing her other foot up high so she could unfold the hem of her khaki pants over her shoes to make sure her socks at her ankles were covered. "If you touch it, it'll sting your skin."

I looked down. In the underbrush were some prickly looking plants about up to our knees.

The whole area around the two oak trees was covered in the same sticky little plants. The leaves swayed in the breeze that picked up around us.

"It's all over," I said.

"If you have pants, you should be okay," Jessica said. "Sang's already been stung."

She was right. The outside of my legs were red and splotchy. I could have mistaken them for a hundred tiny mosquito bites. I hadn't really looked at them before, but now that I knew, my legs itched like crazy.

"What do we do?" I asked, squeezing my legs together in an effort to subdue the itching and become as thin as possible to get away from the plants around us.

Nathan stepped forward as if testing out the area. When it seemed like he wasn't getting stung, he marched toward me. He turned around and crouched. "Get on my back," he said.

My heart pounded against my rib cage. I wrapped my arms around his neck. He scooped up my legs under the knees and hauled me up. His back muscles flexed against my chest and stomach as he stood.

Once I was safe in the air, Nathan turned to talk to Derrick and the others. "Micah, take your shirt off and give it to Derrick. You, too, Gabriel. Luke, grab Micah. Gabe, get Tom. Let's go back."

"I'm not getting carried out," Micah said. He backed up but I could see from my position that his legs were already red.

"Derrick, tie the shirts to your legs," Nathan ordered.

Derrick caught the shirts in the air that were tossed to him and bent over to tie them at his knees. When he was finished, he grabbed Micah by his belly and hoisted him over his shoulder.

"Put me down," Micah said, squirming. Since he had his shirt off and was sweating, Derrick nearly slipped trying to hang on to him.

"If you don't stop wiggling, I'm going to drop you into the nettles," Derrick hoisted him again.

"Fine. Just don't drop me."

Tom hopped on Luke's back without question.

"Jessica," Nathan turned around to face her. She was

standing by, watching us. Her face flushed. "Take us out of here. Shortest path."

Jessica nodded, took one look around and then started heading toward the tree line again. Nathan followed close behind her. I did my best to try to hold on by my legs on to his back. I shifted my arms so I wasn't strangling his neck, my palms pressing against his chest.

Nathan didn't seem to notice me wriggling. His hands gripped my thighs to the point where I thought it would cause bruising, but I didn't want to tell him it might be a little too tight.

Jessica was a pro. She threaded her way through the trees and picked the easiest paths that would allow those carrying people to get through without too much trouble.

"Still think it was a bad idea to bring Jessica?" I whispered to Nathan as he marched forward.

He glanced back at me over his shoulder. I noticed where he hadn't shaved for a few days. With his tan skin and his reddish hair, it was nearly undetectable until I got so close. It was unbelievably appealing.

"Don't you ever tell her I said that," he said.

Soon Jessica had us back to the long grass path that was behind Kota's house.

"Put me down," Micah said. "I can walk from here."

Derrick dropped Micah into the grass on his back. He grumbled but stood up. Tom jumped off of Luke's back, giving an appreciative nod. At least one of them was polite.

"We made it," Tom said. "I thought for sure we'd gotten turned around and we were lost again."

"Want to put me down?" I asked Nathan.

He retucked his arms under my thighs and hoisted me higher on his back. "I've got you. Let's get home."

We made it to the two palm trees in Kota's backyard. Max, Kota's golden retriever, was tethered but barked when we approached, sniffing at our legs when we got close.

Nathan was still carrying me through the backyard and

onto the driveway when a familiar green sedan pulled into the drive. Through her windshield, Erica took one look at our faces and at Nathan carrying me and parked her car in front of the garage doors. She jumped out, her mouth open in surprise. "What happened to you all?"

"Stinging nettle," Jessica said. "Sang's legs were stung. And so were the boys'."

"I'm okay," Derrick said. "They didn't get me that bad." He stood on the concrete and untied the makeshift pants made from shirts, handing them back to Gabriel and Micah.

"I'm out of here," Micah said. He sprinted off toward the road.

Tom shrugged, waved goodbye and followed along, nearly sprinting on his way.

"I'm going to make sure they cross the road without getting run over," Derrick said. "See you guys later."

"Bye," Luke said.

"Well, get Sang inside," Erica said, a sympathetic smile on her face. She unclipped her nametags off of her nurse's uniform and tucked them into the purse on her arm. "We'll put some lotion on her."

Nathan carried me into the house. Jessica headed into her bedroom to change. Erica dropped her purse on the dining table and disappeared to the downstairs bathroom to grab the first aid kit. Gabriel pulled out a seat at the table and Nathan knelt so I could slide off his back.

After I sat in the chair, Nathan took the seat next to me, scooting his chair over. He lifted my foot up into his lap so he could inspect my leg.

There were tiny blotches covering my skin from the tops of my feet to my knees. His warm breath fell over my calf. I twitched, the intense itching returning. I reached down to rub at them but Nathan smacked my hand when I tried. "You scratch at it now, you'll just keep scratching until it bleeds."

Erica reappeared with the kit. "Luke," she said. "Could you get Sang a glass of water?"

It made me smile. She was taking charge a lot like how Kota did.

Luke disappeared into the kitchen. Erica checked the kit and selected a pink bottle of lotion. "This should work." She twisted open the plastic top and handed the bottle to Nathan.

Nathan spilled the calamine lotion into his palm and started rubbing it onto my legs. He focused intently on the task. From the serious look on his face, I wanted to tell him it was okay, but I was embarrassed as it was. Erica was witnessing this and I couldn't imagine what she was thinking. I knew my own mom would have plenty to say about something like this.

Only she didn't seem fazed by this, either. Maybe their touches with me were normal and I was still super sensitive. My mother's constant fear had me still paranoid and unsure.

Gabriel slumped into a chair behind me. His bright blue eyes had contrasting dark circles underneath. I hadn't realized he looked so tired before. Was it the sun and heat that got to him or was staying up at night with me earlier that week getting to him? Or was it the Academy? "Kota's going to kill us," he said.

"Kota won't kill anyone," Erica said. "It was an accident. I'm just glad you boys got her out safely. You should be more careful when you go into those woods." Luke came back with the glass of water and Erica held out a couple of pills to me. "You're not allergic to anything, are you?" she asked.

I shook my head, taking the glass of water from Luke. "Not that I know of."

"Those antihistamine pills should take care of the inflammation. If it gets worse or if you start running a fever, we'll take you to the doctor."

I swallowed some water and took the pills. Nathan gently dropped one of my legs from his lap, reaching to pick up the other. My heart was racing at how sweet Erica was and how nice the boys were. This was normal. I was sure of it. People took care of one another. I should do this for them. I couldn't help but think of how lucky I had been to run into them. Erica, Jessica and everyone seemed worried about me. Kota's mom barely knew me and she was doing more, hovering over me more than my own mother did when I was sick or hurt.

Jessica returned wearing shorts and a loose t-shirt. Her face was washed and looking refreshed.

"We're lucky we had Jessica," I said, wanting to be as kind as they had been. The best I could do was offer a compliment.

"Yeah," Nathan said, seeming to understand my thoughts. He beamed at Jessica, nodding to her. "She picked up that we were in nettle. Otherwise I think we would have gotten it worse."

Jessica's cheeks turned as pink as the primrose still in her hair. "It wasn't a big deal."

Erica shared a pleased smile and pulled in her daughter by the shoulders for a hug. "I'm glad you were with them."

My heart swelled. Was that good? I was envious of how easily Erica hugged her daughter. I wanted a hug, too, but I quelled my desires by focusing on Nathan's touch on my leg.

Luke fell into another chair, wiping his brow. "Let's not let Micah lead the way next time. I bet those nettles grew around our ankles just to bite him."

Erica popped him on the hand with her palm. "Don't say things like that. You all should get along."

"It'd be easier if he was trying," Luke complained. "You should have heard the fuss he made about Sang."

Nathan finished up my legs, but kept my foot in his lap as he sat back and replaced the lid on the lotion bottle. "Well, he can complain all he wants. Sang lives on this street now, too. If he doesn't want to hang out, he can go home."

"He'll miss out," Gabriel said, scratching at his ear behind the black rings, "When we play basketball at

Sang's."

Like that was a possibility. Why did he even suggest it?

Erica smiled. "That sounds like fun. What are you all doing tonight? Are you guys staying for dinner?"

"No," Nathan said. I was grateful he answered because I wasn't sure how to say no to her after being so nice. I didn't want to bother her any more, either. He patted my foot. I dropped it to the floor and he stood up. "We should get home. Homework."

Erica laughed. "I love you guys. I never have to remind you." She hugged Nathan, wrapping her arms around his neck and dropping a kiss on his cheek. Nathan's cheeks tinted red but he seemed used to this attention, patting at her arm in an awkward way to hug her back. "Make sure Sang gets home safe." She turned to me. "You should come over this weekend. We'll have a fun night together."

I felt my heart racing with happiness. "Really?" I asked. I wondered what exactly she meant. She wanted me over for dinner?

She smiled and nodded. "And we may let the boys come, too," she said, glancing at the others. "If you will all behave and keep her out of trouble."

"We'll see if Trouble can keep herself out of trouble," Gabriel said, hooking an arm around my neck.

I pulled a face at him. How much worse trouble could I get into now?

♥

NAKED

That evening, I got back later than I normally did since my dad was gone. Luke followed me home and climbed up the back wall to the roof to get to my window and wait.

I walked in and paused when I spotted Marie in the kitchen. She was huddled over a pot of macaroni, stirring in cheese mix and milk. She looked different with the makeup she was wearing. Wasn't she worried about wearing makeup in the house? Our mother would see it and she'd be on her knees for sure. I wasn't sure if the guys would pull her out, too.

There was something else off about Marie, but I couldn't put my finger on it. She ignored me as she stirred, so I didn't stop to ask. I wasn't sure what to say, anyway.

I padded my way up the stairs and pushed the door open. The door caught on something behind it and stopped short. I had to shove to squeeze myself inside.

A clump of clothes was on the floor right behind the door. I hurriedly shut the door and locked it. When I turned, Luke was already inside, the window open behind him. My heart thundered, worried because of the concerned look over his face.

He stepped to the open closet door and looked in. I closed the window behind him. I came back to puzzle over the haphazard pile of clothes on the floor. Did Marie go through my things again? It wouldn't have been the first time.

My heart stopped. I went for the attic door. It was

closed but I peeked in, checking for the cell phone. It was still there where I'd hidden it in the wall.

I breathed out a sigh of relief.

"Your clothes are gone," Luke whispered to me, still standing inside the closet door.

My eyes widened. "What?" I shifted away from the attic, closing it and came up behind him.

The closet had been emptied out, some remnants piled on the floor at the bottom; mostly underwear and bras that had been piled up on the shelf.

Luke helped me as I picked up the spilled clothes on the floor, dumping them on my bed. It looked like Marie's clothes but there were some others mixed in that I didn't recognize. I separated the t-shirts and jeans in an effort to shuffle through them. My blouses and skirts were missing. Nathan's and Luke's shirts that they'd given me were gone.

Luke shifted on his feet, rubbing the back of his head. "Did your mother do this?"

I bit my lip, my brain churning, but shook my head. "No," I said. It didn't feel like something my mother would do. My mother wasn't usually interested in what we wore. My father bought clothes in bulk once or twice a year, from places I didn't know, but I had guessed were garage sales. He bought a variety of sizes and Marie and I would sort out what we could wear between us.

Luke leaned into me, finding my hand and squeezing it. "Who?"

I shook my head again, blinking. "Marie, I guess," I said. "I don't know. She doesn't really like the clothes I wear and they don't fit her. She's downstairs. I'll go talk to her." It surprised me. She once in a while borrowed a shirt, but it seemed odd she would take out all of my own clothes and leave hers in my room.

He nodded. "I'll wait in the attic," he said. "But come get me as soon as you figure out what's going on. Don't bother your mom about this, even if this was her."

I thumped my way back down the stairs to the kitchen. Marie had her brown hair pulled back in a ponytail away from her narrow eyes. She sat on the counter, swinging her legs as she ate her macaroni and cheese. I realized she was now wearing a pair of jeans and a t-shirt I'd never seen her wear before and that was what was bugging me earlier. The t-shirt was a simple soft green, with a low scooped neck and looked too small on her frame and the jeans were tight.

"Where's my clothes?" I asked her. "Why are your clothes on my bed?"

"I traded you," she said. "You can have the stuff I left you."

"You can't trade clothes if I don't want yours. Yours won't fit. Where are mine?"

"You have to trade," Marie said. "It's not your clothes. It's our clothes. Mom said..."

I left the kitchen, not willing to hear what she was saying.

"Don't go through my stuff," she called after me.

I ran back up the stairs and used the push pin to unlock her door and enter her bedroom. This was really weird. She snapped at me about my nerdy clothes all the time. Why the sudden interest in what I was wearing? And the clothes she was wearing now I didn't recognize at all. So where did she get them?

Inside her bedroom, I yanked open the closet door. A collection of more t-shirts and jeans were hung up. There were small piles on the floor, underwear, crumpled t-shirts and unwashed jeans. Nothing inside looked like mine.

Marie marched in behind me. "I said don't come in here."

"I thought you said you traded me." I reached into the closet floor and pulled one of the t-shirts out. "Where did this come from? And where are my blouses?"

"I traded them."

Something in the way she said that made me angry. "Marie, who did you trade with?"

"Danielle and I went through each other's closets."

My jaw dropped. "And mine?"

"They're mine too. We went through and sorted them. She..."

"Has my clothes." I finished for her, dropping the t-shirt in my hand to the floor. I pressed my palm to my forehead. "Why would you do that?"

"Just get out," she said, her mouth twisting into a horrible frown. "It's none of your business. Why do you care?"

"You can't give away things that don't belong to you. Why would Danielle want my skirts?" My voice rose. I couldn't help it. And Nathan's shirt! And Luke's! Where were they? "How did she get into the house?"

"I let her come in," she said. Her sharp nose crinkled. "You always wear the same nerdy clothes in the wrong way. Everyone thinks you're a dork. Just wear the jeans."

I pursed my lips. I didn't have a way to argue with her further. I stalked out of her room and across the hallway.

Marie knew I couldn't go to our mother to complain. It would break the pact we'd managed to forge between us, shaky as it was. She could easily tell our mother I was out with the boys today, or that I had a key to the house, or a few other things that would get me into trouble. Did she know the boys came into the house? Is that why she thought it was okay if Danielle showed up? Her bedroom was right above our parents' room. How could she get away with Danielle talking with her? The only way I thought the boys and I got away with it was because I was on the other side of the house.

There was no one to turn to. Our dad was gone with no way to reach him on his business trip. I couldn't tell my mom without starting a fight and risk getting a strange punishment. With Luke there, he would pull me out and it would be a complete mess. I was stuck without recourse against this. If I fought Marie on it too hard, she'd go to our mom and I'd end up in a punishment anyway.

I retreated back to my room, closing the door and

locking it. I pressed my back to the frame. I swallowed, frustrated and biting my tongue to restrain the words burning behind my lips. Nothing I could say would help. I didn't even know Danielle and she had my clothes. It creeped me out.

I knocked gently on the attic door. Luke emerged, pushing his blond locks behind his ear. "What happened?"

"Danielle was here," I said. "Her and Marie 'traded' clothes with me." I went to my bed to go through the assortment again, hoping the boys' things were at least there and I'd missed them the first time through. No luck. "Danielle took my clothes. Marie has hers and gave me whatever they didn't want for themselves, I guess."

Luke frowned, approaching the bed and tracing a finger over a pair of jeans. "Can't you get them back?"

"I don't know how," I said. "I can't complain to my mother." I picked through the pile, holding up a pair of jeans to my waist and then another. It wasn't much use; each one was too big for me. The bottom hems pooled around my feet.

Luke sat on the bed. "You can't go to school naked," he said. "We should get your clothes back. Let's go to Danielle's. We'll confront her."

"We can't. We're supposed to stay out of trouble, remember?"

Luke blew out a breath. He shifted, wrapping an arm around my waist and tugging me into his lap. He pressed his cheek to my forehead. "Sang, you can't let yourself get walked over like this. They stole your clothes."

"What choice do I have?" I whispered to him, staring absently at my knees.

He sighed, brushing his fingertips over the outside of my thigh as he held me. "I wish I knew. She can't do this to you. She's taking advantage of you."

"If I went to our mom, she'd get into trouble, too," I said.

"Would she?" he asked. He drew his head back, gazing down into my face. "Do you remember the last time your mother even talked to your sister? Or even asked about her?"

I blinked, unsure. "I don't know. She does that sometimes."

"When is the last time you saw your sister on her knees?"

I tried to recall, but my mind was hazy. After learning my clothes were gone and the crazy day we'd had, it was hard to concentrate. "I don't remember."

"Or maybe it's been a really long time, long enough for your memory to fade?" he asked. "Sweetie, you've gotten so much done to you in the few weeks that I've known you, and Marie hasn't once been called out for anything. You thought you went unnoticed at school before? Your sister is invisible here."

Was that true? If it was, how did that happen? How did I not notice? I thought perhaps maybe she did get punished and I wasn't around when it happened. She never looked surprised when she saw me on my knees or on the stool or in any of the other punishments over the years. My father was never there to acknowledge either of us... but then he told *me* about going on his business trips, didn't he? And my mother shouted for *me* instead of Marie when she needed something or wanted to check on us. Did they forget about her?

"She might not get the punishments you get," Luke continued, smoothing a fingertip over my knee. "But that's no excuse to take advantage of her own sister. I want to feel sorry for her, but I can't right now."

I made a small noise from my throat, frustrated, confused. "There's nothing else to do," I said. "She got what she wanted, I guess. She traded with Danielle for clothes, and I've got the leftovers." I wanted to stop talking about problems I couldn't fix. The lingering questions about why Marie was invisible in the house and why I was sought out for punishments wasn't something I was ready to look at. "I'll find something I can work with."

Luke sighed and let me go. I crawled off of his lap, returning my attention to the pile on the bed. I chose the smallest pair of jeans I could find and measured out the length cutting them into shorts.

I picked out the smallest t-shirt. It looked like a boy's shirt. Other jeans and shirts looked like old boy clothes; maybe some of these belonged to Derrick.

I thought about washing the clothes I was wearing, but the shorts were too short for school regulations. The shirt, maybe. What else would I wear later? I couldn't go to school wearing the same two pairs of shorts and shirts.

Luke remained quiet on the bed as I fiddled with the clothes. I discarded items that were too big for me. He folded those pieces carefully and set them aside. "I could go get your clothes," he said softly.

I blinked at him, my eyes tracing over the gentle angles of his face, the way his smooth lips twitched down at the corners. "How?"

His dark eyes met mine. His normal, happy disposition was gone, replaced by something hard and cold. "I'll take them back."

The way he said it made my heart stop. I envisioned Luke sneaking into Danielle's house and stealing the clothes. He was quiet on his feet, sneaking around my own house. Did he think he could do it at Danielle's without anyone noticing? Was that what he meant?

The clothing I held slipped from my fingers to the floor. I stepped toward him, closing the distance between us. I reached my arms around his neck and buried my face into his shoulder. He leaned back, as if surprised at my sudden hug.

I couldn't stand to see his eyes like that. I couldn't take it if he got caught stealing from Danielle's house. Then he'd really get into trouble. "Don't do it," I begged him. "Please."

His palm pressed into the small of my back. "I want to. You can't wear these to school, Sang."

I squeezed my arms around his neck. "No," I

whispered. "Don't. Please."

"I really should. She deserves it."

Was he asking or was he telling me he was going to and wanted me to tell him I was okay with it? My mind searched for something to say to him, anything to get him to change his mind. "I'll... I'll never talk to you again if you try." It was a weak threat and I would never mean it. How immature was I? Only I didn't have anything else. What could I really do if he did run off and attempted to steal them back?

The moment the words slipped from my mouth, he stiffened against me. His other hand clutched my back and he pulled me against him harder than ever before. "Sang, don't you dare."

I realized my mistake. North didn't talk to him when he arrived at their doorstep years ago. I was threatening him with almost the same thing, with not talking to him. He didn't know I couldn't really stop. Could I ever really stop talking to someone so sweet?

"I'm sorry," I whispered. "No more trouble. Okay? I'll wear what I have. We'll figure it out. Let's get through Friday."

He pushed his forehead down to my shoulder, breathing against me. Locks of his hair tickled my neck. "If you don't want me to, I won't."

"Don't," I said.

He nodded against my shoulder and then pulled back, frowning. "Maybe we should call Gabriel," he said.

"Let's not worry about it tonight," I said. I reflected on how tired Gabriel had looked. The last thing he needed was to stress out about what I was wearing to school and maybe lose more sleep over it. "We'll go to school, we'll tell them all about it and we'll figure it out. Maybe we can talk to Danielle. We'll do it tomorrow when we're calmer. Maybe she didn't realize the clothes she took were mine or the ones she gave me would be too big."

Luke's eyes became lost in shadows. "I don't think she

was thinking of you at all."

I sighed, letting go of him to push the collection of clothes off of my bed. I padded over to the light switch to turn the overhead lights off. I didn't want to think about it anymore.

He seemed to understand. He fell into the bed on top of the blanket, kicking his shoes off. I crawled in next to him. He wrapped his arms around me, hugging me close and pressing his face to my hair; my silent guardian for the night. I knew we weren't supposed to. He was supposed to sleep in the attic. That night, I didn't care. I hid my face in his chest.

We dared anyone to walk in on us, discover us and cause a scene. If my mother only knew, if she ever came after me when she learned the truth, everything would change. Now my sister could easily tip over this delicate facade to expose me and the boys. And Danielle, a girl that I'd never once said a word to, was leading the way to our own destruction in a silent war she could never understand.

Luke knew. I knew. This was no longer us waiting things out until it calmed over. This was us counting down the moments, waiting for the time bomb to go off.

How To Dress A Girl

I dreamed of tiny green bugs slipping into my window. Thousands of them crept into my bed, smothering me.

A buzz shocked me out of the dream. Luke grumbled next to me in the bed, his head against my shoulder. He pulled his arm from around me, reached into his back pocket and put the phone to his ear. "What?" he asked without looking at who was calling. A second later, he yanked himself away from me, sitting up on the bed and rubbed his face. "Sorry," he said. "Sorry. We'll be right there." He jabbed his thumb at the phone and turned to me. "Sang, we're late."

I jolted out of bed. Late! How late? What was late? I tried to pull myself together and figure out what I was supposed to do next.

Luke was on top of it. He grabbed the clothes I'd picked out and tossed them to me. "Wash up, but don't take a full shower," he said. "Get dressed and meet me outside. Don't worry about your bags. I've got it."

I dashed to the bathroom to wash, especially my legs, and they looked better. I put on the newly made shorts. They were beige jeans, and at least they were clean. The baggy t-shirt, a faded blue and advertising a band I didn't know covered my butt.

When I opened the bathroom door, my sandals were in the hallway. I wanted to scold Luke later for risking sneaking out to leave them there for me but knew I would forget. I slipped them onto my feet and took the back stairs, dashing out into the garage.

Luke was waiting in the drive, a clean white shirt on and he was tugging his blazer on. I took my violin case from him as he grabbed our book bags and we ran for Kota's.

I kept having to hike up the shorts as they felt like they were about to fall off. I was hanging my head, watching my feet. Luke jogged ahead of me. It was already warm and sticky. How did we sleep in?

Nathan and Kota were already waiting out in front of Kota's drive. Derrick stood talking with them. I was just opening my mouth to say hello when I noticed Marie and Danielle standing together and my mouth dropped open. Luke slowed down to fall in next to me, his eyes catching where mine went.

Danielle was wearing one of my own dark skirts and Luke's blue button up shirt on top. Since she was long-legged and her hips were wider than mine, the skirt looked more like a mini-skirt, barely covering her hips. The shirt was unbuttoned at her stomach, so as the breeze picked it up, it fluttered open to reveal her pale belly. She had the buttons at her chest undone until her cleavage was exposed. She was smirking as she chatted with Marie, wearing large sunglasses that covered half of her face.

Marie was in jeans again, but wore Nathan's shirt.

Kota's eyes fell on me. "What's wrong, Sang?" he asked.

"What are you wearing?" Nathan asked, his head tilting. "What's with the t-shirt?"

Derrick gazed at my shirt, looking puzzled. "I have a shirt like that."

"I think it *is* your shirt," I said, closing the gap between us to stand closer so I wouldn't be overheard by Danielle or Marie. "My sister traded clothes with Danielle last night."

Derrick's tanned cheeks tinted. "I was wondering where she got the skirt. I told her it's too small."

"Danielle's going to get into trouble at school," Kota said, touching the bridge of his glasses with his finger. A displeased frown formed on his face. "There's no way the teachers will let her stay. She's way out of regulation."

"She took all of Sang's clothes," Luke said. "All those blouses and skirts, leaving Sang with barely anything. She tried on all of it. What's she's wearing now was the closest in size and it barely fits."

"Hey," Nathan said, his blue eyes fixed on Marie. "Isn't that my..." He turned, squaring off his shoulders.

I grabbed Nathan by his arm. The girls had started to notice we were looking at them. "Yes," I said through my teeth. "And that blue shirt Danielle's wearing is Luke's. Don't say anything. If we make a big deal about it..."

"I don't give a fuck," Nathan said. "I didn't give that to her." His fists clenched and he started across the drive.

"I'll get it back," I said, stepping in front of him. Out of desperation, I pressed a hand to his chest. This seemed to distract him and he looked down at me. "Give me time. If we tell her it's yours, or if we try to force this, Marie could tell my mother things we don't want her to know."

He narrowed his eyes at the two of them, but they seemed disinterested. His jaw set, his glare crushing. He grabbed my hand from his chest, holding on to it as he turned away. It felt like his squeezing my hand held back the fury bubbling under the surface. Did he feel so strongly about that shirt? I didn't realize. I vowed to steal it back and hide it the first chance I had. If he liked it, I'd give it back. I wouldn't want it ruined or held over our heads by Marie.

Kota stepped up next to us. "They didn't leave you anything?"

"Just a bunch of jeans and t-shirts," I said.

Luke followed, dropping our things at his feet and

straightening out his hurriedly put together outfit. Derrick stepped up next to him, looking uncomfortable and out of place.

"I'll try to bring them back so you can go through them," I told Derrick. "I'm sorry about this."

He shrugged. "That shirt was old anyway. I don't think it fits any more."

"Can't you do something about her?" Nathan asked. "She's your sister."

"I don't know. I'll try talking to her." He kept looking over at his sister, maybe wishing he had stuck with talking to them. I hooked my fingers into the jean shorts and readjusted them on my hips. "We'll get through today and figure it out later."

"Do we have time to change?" Nathan asked. He looked to Kota. "Can't we get something for her? Does Jessica have...?"

The school bus turned the corner, heading in our direction.

"No time," Kota said. He fished his cell phone out of his pocket. "Maybe if we catch the guys before they leave."

When the bus got there, I fell into the seat next to Kota and Nathan slid in next to me. Luke fell into the seat next to us. Derrick trailed to the back, not sitting near his sister and not sitting close enough to us to be considered 'with' us. I found it strange. The guys may not have been openly popular, but they were good-looking and nice and dressed well. They seemed to get along well with one another. Why did it feel like Derrick didn't really want to be associated with them in public?

At the school, Kota, Nathan, Luke and I were the last to get off the bus. We trailed Marie and Danielle out of curiosity. Boys hooted the moment Danielle walked into the crowded cafeteria. She stared ahead with a scowling smirk and swinging her hips a little more. Marie crushed her books to her chest, looking out of place next to

Danielle in her t-shirt and jeans.

"Oh yeah," Nathan mumbled next to me. "Holler at the girl who doesn't know what dress size she is."

Kota checked his phone again. "Let's get out to the parking lot," he said. "Gabriel says to meet them at Victor's car."

Nathan took the violin case from me. I followed after Kota, putting my hand on my hip so I wouldn't lose the shorts on the way out. When I was falling behind them because of how I had to walk to keep the shorts up, Kota came back for me. Blushing, he wrapped an arm around my waist, hooking his thumb into the belt loop and hanging his hand on my hip. We walked together like this, trying to look casual. I think I was blushing more at feeling his hand on my waist than I was about the clothes. Still, I felt so out of place next to them in their nice slacks and shirts with ties.

Cars were still pulling into the lot and we had to make a slow crawl toward the back where Victor had parked his BMW. Victor and Gabriel were leaning against the car's trunk waiting for us as we approached. Gabriel looked intense but the shadows under his eyes were gone. I was happy Luke and I hadn't bugged him last night. At least he got some sleep.

"Oh my god," Gabriel said, his bright blue eyes sliding down my clothes. "You weren't kidding."

"Can you help?" Kota asked.

He nodded. He curled his fingers at me and then had me spin a little in front of him. "Motherfucker. All right, hang on."

He opened the passenger side door and took a seat with his legs stretched out. He pulled me by the hips until my waist was eye level with him. "Okay, you guys make a barrier. I don't want anyone thinking I'm molesting her."

I blushed and watched the guys crowd themselves together to make a wall. With the car door open, I was blocked on the other side, too. Gabriel reached for his book bag and pulled out a pair of scissors. He started cutting the shorts, hooking his fingers up into them, pulling at the crotch a little to straighten it out.

A wave of heat washed over me. "Gabriel..."

"Just give me a minute," he said. "I'm going to make this into a skirt. It'll still look like shit but it'll be less shit. And why the hell did Danielle steal your clothes?"

"Attention," Kota said. "And she got it."

"Fucking ugly," Nathan said.

Luke's lips twisted into a frown as he stared out into the parking lot.

Victor stood sentinel with his arms crossed over his chest. His fire eyes blazed. "Why don't I just go get her something?"

"We don't have time," Kota said. "The closest store is a Wal-Mart and you won't make it back by the first bell."

"That's what we're doing this weekend," Victor said. "I'm taking her for clothes."

The definitive way he said it made it sound like they were planning something to do with me that weekend and this was the confirmation. "No, guys," I said softly. "Don't..."

"You need clothes, Sang," Victor said in a sharp tone. "You're going."

I was turning a little to say something to him but Gabriel slapped me on the thigh. "Stop wriggling," he said. "I'm going to cut you by accident if you do that."

I stood still hoping anyone passing by wouldn't notice. Gabriel worked at cutting out the shorts. He folded them to make a hem and he used some tape inside his makeshift cuff. He also managed to tape up the inside of the skirt at the waist so it hung tighter. "Nothing a little duct tape can't solve," he said. "Now we need a shirt."

Victor went to the trunk of his car, pulling out a clean white shirt. "Always carry a spare."

"I can go put it on in the restroom," I said.

"Put it on here," Gabriel said. "No one's watching."

"I can't..."

"Just do it quickly."

My cheeks lit on fire. I accepted the shirt. Victor stepped back into place, his back turned to me. Gabriel hung his arms over the open door, blocking the window with his frame. The boys focused on cars around us, distracted.

I ripped the big t-shirt off. The warm, moist air of the south touched bare skin that had never before been exposed. I slipped my hands through the sleeves of the shirt, catching the Armani label. The shirt probably cost more than all of my old clothes combined.

While it was still big, it was far nicer than the t-shirt. I buttoned it up to my neck. "Okay," I said.

The guys all turned around, checking out the finished product. The hem of the shirt stretched over the top of the shorts-turned-skirt. It was enough and hid the wrinkle where Gabriel had used duct tape to correct the size.

Victor's fire eyes lit up to a smolder. "It's not bad. You look pretty good in my clothes."

"It'll do for now," Gabriel said. He picked up my wrist, unbuttoning the sleeve and rolling it up my arm to make a cuff above my wrist. "At least you won't be tripping over your shorts today."

Relief washed over me. Gabriel approved for now. The guys had come to the rescue again. "Thank you. Really, I mean... thank you," I said, fumbling over my words. There was no way to express the feelings I had for them at that moment. How many times have they gone out of their way to help me? I was starting to lose count. It made me wonder why they bothered to be around me when I really was so much trouble.

Gabriel's eyes fell on my face. He stared at me for a moment, his lips moving but nothing was coming out.

Nathan took my wrist. "Let's get out of here before anyone thinks we're taking turns."

I had no idea what he meant but the others followed close behind.

♥♥♥

Danielle never got on the bus that afternoon.

"She got sent home around third period," Derrick said on his way to the back seats.

"Karma's a bitch, isn't it?" Nathan said under his breath, the corner of his mouth lifting.

♥

Weekend

I dreamed of a hovering dark ghost that wanted to devour anyone who did wrong. Thieves, murderers, rapists, it enveloped them in darkness and they disappeared.
And I was the thing it wanted the most.

"Sang," Victor's smooth baritone voice drew me from the depths of my dream. My forehead was on his arm stretched out underneath my head and I'd been curled into him. His free hand swept over my cheek, brushing my hair from my skin. "Wake up."

I half remembered Luke saying we were late the morning before, and I sat up quickly, afraid I'd slept in again. "What's wrong?"

Victor rolled onto his back and looked up at me. "I was going to ask you that. You were shaking."

I sucked in a slow breath through my nose, stretching my back and pushing a palm to my face. "I was?" Did I always shake when I was sleeping? No wonder I scared Silas so much.

It was dawn. I realized it was Saturday. We weren't late for anything.

"Were you dreaming?" he asked. He sat up, the blanket falling away from his chest. He'd taken off his Armani shirt he'd worn the night before and was left in the ribbed tank he'd worn underneath. It was fitted to his chest and stomach. My eyes refused to stop staring at his lean, strong physique. It was the most undressed I'd ever seen him.

I barely remembered him crawling into bed. After letting Luke sleep in the bed with me the night before, it felt wrong to chase him back to the attic.

I blushed when I realized he was staring at me with the same intensity.

"Mmm... maybe. I don't remember," I said, the fib dripping from my lips, positive my lie was obvious.

Victor's fire eyes sparked. "Are you sure?"

A finger wandered to my lip, and I nodded, afraid to admit to lying and afraid to tell him the truth about the dream. His fire eyes forced me to put extra effort into not shaking in front of him. The dream seemed too small and unimportant.

Victor's head tilted and he looked uncertain. "Okay... well do you want to get going?"

I nodded. Not that I really wanted to go, but it gave me an excuse to escape his questioning and a chance for him to forget, or so I hoped.

He got out of the bed. "Go shower and dress. I'll call Nathan, and let him know we're heading over."

I started to move and then paused. Something felt out of sync to me. I was still half asleep, uncertain exactly what it was.

"What's wrong? Do you hear something?" he asked. He was standing by the attic door, looking back at me.

My cheeks warmed again when I realized what I was missing was sitting in someone's lap. They'd done it so often that now when it didn't happen, I felt out of place. It was Victor's first night with me. He didn't do it like the others. Maybe he didn't want to.

"Sang," Victor stared at me for an answer.

I shook my head. "Sorry," I said as I drifted to the closet, pulling out some clothes to wear.

He frowned, waiting until I was at the door before he opened the attic and crawled inside.

I drew a bath, taking a little extra time to wash, shave

and take care of my hair. Victor had warned me we were going out today and I didn't want to look as shaggy and worn as I felt. I wanted to soak but I knew Victor was waiting for me.

The bath drained as I dried off. I slipped on the pair of blue shorts I'd worn into the woods and a light gray shirt Kota gave me after we got home from school.

I opened the bathroom door and leapt backward. Victor was leaning against the doorframe in the hallway. My hand fluttered to my chest. "Victor?"

His fire eyes locked on mine again. "Do you always take baths in the morning?"

What was he doing in the hallway? He could tell I was taking a bath? If he'd been listening at all, he must have known. How long was he out there?

"I... well I felt like one," I said, which was mostly true. "Did I take too long?"

He shook his head slowly, the fire dimming. "No," he said, the soft frown remaining on his face. He turned away from me. "Check on your mom and let's get out of here." His voice dripped with something heavy, sad.

It broke my heart. Maybe there was a reason he didn't like me. I'd been lying to him all morning. I summoned some courage and pressed forward, vowing to try to be honest with him the rest of the day.

♥♥♥

My mom was asleep in her bed; I left her a banana, a box of raisins and a bottle of water. Marie was in her room, her music playing, and would sleep until late in the afternoon. I was surprised she was home, but I suppose she couldn't go out to Danielle's house every evening. Her parents might notice. Maybe I should have been worried that my mother or Marie would check on me, but according to Victor, we had too much to do and he didn't seem too concerned if we were caught out.

We met with Nathan in the woods behind my house. He was kicking at some leaves near the wood slab bridge. When he heard us coming, he looked up, smiling.

"Got everything?" he asked me.

I nodded, hiking my book bag up on my shoulders. They'd warned me to bring anything I'd need as we might swim at some point. There wasn't much in my bag except for a change of underwear and the charger for my phone, which was tucked into my bra.

Kota, Silas, North and Luke would be gone for most of the day at the diner.

Nathan reached for my hand, wrapping his fingers around mine. "Let's get going. I left Gabriel at my house."

Victor trailed behind us, and my heart weighed heavily with the guilt of the morning we'd had. I wanted to take it all back. I was worried he didn't like me now.

We walked through the woods to Nathan's backyard. Nathan led the way to his back porch and opened the sliding glass door for me and Victor.

Victor walked around us, collapsing onto the leather couch. Gabriel was sitting on one end. He handed off a controller to Victor. I recognized Soul Caliber, a fighting game, on the wide-screen TV. The couch was big enough that all four of us could sit. Victor scooted closer to Gabriel and let go of the controller long enough to pat the seat next to him, his eyes expectant on mine.

Relief flooded through me. He wasn't going to stay mad at me, at least.

I dropped my bag on the floor by the foot of the couch and sat down next to Victor. Nathan sat on the edge, putting one arm on the armrest and stretching to put his other arm on the couch over my shoulders, his fingers on my collarbone.

I willed my heart to stop fluttering so much.

"When are we going?" Gabriel asked, clicking buttons on the controller. I wasn't able to tell which fighter he was. They were both about half drained of health according to the screen.

"When the stores open, I guess," Victor said. "Around nine or ten or so."

I squinted at them. It was barely dawn now. "You guys wanted me come over this early?"

Victor shrugged. "Have something else to do today?"

"No," I said. "I was just wondering."

Victor cursed under his breath as Gabriel's fighter kicked his hard enough to knock him out and end the battle. The big screen flashed with blood and gore from Victor's fighter. Victor patted my knee, grinning. "You can come over when you want, you know," he said. "You don't have to wait for an invitation all the time."

I blushed; if it were up to me, I'd never leave. "Meh, you guys will get sick of me eventually." I meant it to be funny and cracked a smile.

Nathan's hand lifted from my shoulder and chopped me on the head. "Shut up," he said.

"What did I tell you?" Gabriel said. "See what I mean? She does do that girl shit. I knew it."

I blinked in surprise, unsure what they meant. "I'm sorry," I said quietly, blushing.

"You were doing that thing where a girl disses herself to get more compliments," he said.

"That's not why she said it," Nathan said. "She doesn't like attention."

"What do you mean?" Gabriel asked, resetting the game.

"Don't you see her at school? She practically hides behind us. She's totally oblivious when the guys are trying to make eye contact in class."

My eyes widened. "What? When do they do that?"

"See?"

Gabriel pointed a finger in my direction. "Just don't say shit like that. That stuff drives me crazy. I can't stand it when I'm telling a girl she's pretty and she's just giving me a load of insecure bullshit."

I wondered if this was similar to what Silas was saying

about the pouting and Gabriel asking me not to do it, but I didn't know what to say to test it. I also wondered what girls he was telling such things to.

Victor sighed heavily, sitting back against the cushion of the couch. "Stop it. Sang's not like that."

"Gotta stop that stuff before it becomes a habit," he said.

Victor passed the controller to me. "Your turn," he said. He patted my leg and got up, walking around the couch and disappearing down a hallway.

I picked up the controller, rubbing my thumbs over the buttons, feeling the warmth of Victor's hands still on the smooth plastic. He didn't hate me.

"You know how to play?" Gabriel asked.

I sat back on the couch, pulling my feet off the floor. "A little." Total lie. The closest I got to a video game was watching one on television or on the rare occasions I could get on the home computer. Most of the time though I was so busy downloading new music that I didn't waste time with games. The Soul Caliber logo splashed across the screen. I wasn't familiar with the game and had no idea which character was better. I picked a scary looking one that resembled a zombie pirate.

Gabriel picked one of the girls in a skimpy outfit and half of her breasts hanging out. He pushed the button for the game to start.

"Kick his ass, Sang," Nathan said. He lifted his hand from around my shoulder, folded his arms at his chest and leaned back to watch.

I pushed the buttons for my character to move across the screen, smashing buttons to get him to jump and do random attacks. I really wasn't fighting as much as I was trying to figure out what the different buttons did. Still, I was scoring some hits against Gabriel.

We were halfway through when Victor came back with a bottle of Starbucks Frappuccino in his hands. He snapped the top open and stood over his old spot. He bent over, putting his fingers on my stretched-out leg. "Move for a second."

"Sorry," I said, lifting my knee out of the way.

"No, hang on." He sat down again, holding his drink up. He reached out for my knee guiding it until it was pressing against his thigh, his hand resting on my leg. "There," he said.

Victor had distracted me badly and now it was even worse as my leg was in his lap and his hand was on my inside knee. My heart thumped and I wasn't even watching the game anymore. My eyes kept going to his hand.

"Hang in there, Sang," Nathan said, bringing my attention back to the game.

"I'm trying." I started smashing all of the buttons at the same time. My zombie pirate did some special move and I managed to unlock and drove a sword into the girl. It was enough to get Gabriel's girl to die and the game ended.

"Ha!" Victor laughed. He held up his coffee in salute.

"How'd you do that?" Gabriel asked, pushing a button to skip the replay of the fight.

I shrugged, blushing. "Don't know. Smash all the buttons?" I passed the controller over to Nathan, looking at him. "Playing?"

Nathan's fingers brushed against mine as he took the controller from me. He scooted until he was sitting at the edge of the couch, putting his elbows on his knees as he played.

Victor held out his half-finished coffee to me. "Want some?"

I shook my head. "I've never had coffee. It's bitter, isn't it?"

They all laughed. Victor pushed the edge of the glass bottle to my hand. "Try a sip." I hesitated and he grinned at me. "It's sweet. There's chocolate in this. It's a mocha."

I took it, wrapping my fingers around the chilled bottle. The condensation on the outside of the bottle wet my hands. I held it to my lips, letting the coffee wash over my tongue. It was almost like milk with a unique additional taste in it and a hint of chocolate. I licked my upper lip after. "It's not bad," I said.

"Want one?" Victor asked. "There's more."

"I'll get her one," Gabriel said, tossing the controller onto the couch after he'd already been knocked out by Nathan in the game. "I want one, too."

We spent a good portion of the morning taking turns playing the game. I won a couple more times. Smashing buttons only worked for so long, though. Still, it was nice just to be included with them and with something where I wasn't causing them any trouble.

The coffee, however, made my insides shake like crazy.

♥♥♥

Around nine-thirty, we headed out to Victor's BMW parked in the driveway.

"Shotgun," Gabriel called as we all approached.

"Sang gets shotgun," Victor said.

"Aw," Gabriel said. "She didn't call it."

"I drive, I get final say."

I blushed again, trying to look sympathetic to Gabriel. Gabriel sauntered forward, opening the passenger door for me.

"Maybe on the way back?" I asked him.

He smirked and shook his head. "Just get your pretty ass in the car."

I got in quickly, trying to mask how hot my face felt. He shut the door for me and got in behind me. I slipped my seatbelt on so Victor wouldn't get after me about it.

A thrilling sensation swept through me as we started out of the neighborhood. I was leaving my family behind to go hang out with my friends. It was hard to fully enjoy it knowing I had to escape my parents' house.

In the back of my mind I was worried my sister would sneak into my room and maybe take something else. What if my mother went looking for me in one of her crazy rampages? One of these days, I hoped I could get permission so I could feel more confident and fully enjoy going out. It was a fantasy I knew wouldn't ever happen.

As it was, I had to settle for knowing that for the moment there was nothing to do but enjoy the day as best I could. There wouldn't be very many opportunities like this.

I kicked my sandals off, putting my feet on the seat and drawing my knees up to my chest.

"What's wrong?" Victor asked, his fire eyes catching mine again, the same intensity from this morning returning. "Are you cold?"

I blinked at him and shook my head. "No, I'm fine." It was another warm day. I didn't understand why he would ask. The car was cooling quickly with the air conditioner on full blast but it was far from chilly.

He eyeballed me for a moment, a lock of his wavy hair falling across his forehead. It was stunning against his beautiful face. He flicked the air conditioning lower on the dash. "You tell me if you're cold."

"Really, it's okay. I'll tell you if something's wrong."

"Will you?" he asked quietly, but before I could answer, he was skimming through radio stations.

♥♥♥

We got to the mall a little after ten. The parking lot was nearly empty, but I guessed it was still early for some people on a Saturday.

When Victor had parked, Gabriel jumped out and opened my door for me. I thanked him and he seemed pleased. As we approached the mall together, Victor strolled ahead and held the door open for me. I thanked him, too, wondering how much longer they would continue to open doors for me. Was I still the new friend they were being nice to?

"Where are we going?" Victor asked me as we gathered inside.

I blinked at him, pushing a finger to my lip and feeling nervous now. I knew he intended to buy a couple pieces of clothing for me. I thought about what Mr. Blackbourne had told me about how the boys handled any situation, helping each other. I tried to swallow down my pride. "I don't know where to start. Any department store ought to have..."

"We're starting with underwear," Gabriel said. He grabbed my hand and tugged me down the hallway of the mall.

"Gabe!" Nathan called after us. He jogged until he was on the other side of me, taking hold of my arm. "We can't take her for that."

Gabriel rubbed at his temple, looking confused. "Of course we can," he said. He pointed to a Victoria's Secret store a couple of shops down. "It's right there."

"I mean," Nathan said in a lower tone, "We can't buy her underwear. Come on."

"What the fuck?" Gabriel blinked at him. "She's a fucking girl. She needs underwear. And bras that are the right size. Have you seen her bras?"

Nathan narrowed his eyes at him. "I don't expect you to have..."

Gabriel twisted his lips. He hooked a couple of fingers in the neck of Kota's shirt that I was wearing and tugged it down over my shoulder to reveal my bra strap. He dug a finger under it, pulled and let it snap back against my skin. I winced, reaching up to rub the spot.

"They don't fit her right," Gabriel said.

"How would you know?" Victor asked, standing by with his hands in his pockets. His tone was more curious than trying to challenge him.

"It's my job," he said. "What do I do? What the hell am I here for?"

"Okay, shit," Nathan said. "We'll get her some underwear."

"That's what I thought."

"Guys," I said. "I don't think..."

Gabriel hung his arm over my neck and led me toward the store. "If you say something stupid like you don't deserve new things or try to tell me to shut up, I'm going to spank you in front of everyone here. Now let's get busy." He seemed much happier now that he was directing the way the shopping trip was going.

My face was radiating heat as Gabriel hung onto me as we walked through the open doors of the shop. Tables of underwear were out on display and mannequins modeled in suggestive poses wearing sheer lingerie.

"Go ahead," Gabriel said. "Pick out what you like."

I pushed my finger to my lower lip as my head tilted from side to side. Where did I start? My fingers traced over the lace of a pink bikini. My eyes flitted to the different pairs. I'd never been shopping before. What did I do?

Nathan stuffed his hands in the pockets of his jeans. His cheeks were red enough to match his hair as he stared at the displays on the walls. To me it seemed like he was trying to avoid eye contact with everyone in the store. Victor merely looked curiously at some of the racks, fingering the material of a couple of the shirts.

Gabriel snapped his fingers close to my face. "Come on, Trouble. Pay attention."

I flinched at him, blowing out a puff of air. "I'm nervous."

"Stop being nervous," he said. He pointed to a pair of pink boy-cut panties. "There. You love pink and that style is in fashion."

Victor materialized next to me. "She doesn't need her underwear to be in fashion." He nodded to some of the more frilly pairs of panties. "Get what you think you'd like."

"Do y'all need any help?" An attendant in a black dress suit and a heavy gold necklace came up beside us. She was in her late forties, with red hair piled high on her head. Her skin was heavily tanned and her lips were buried under a thick layer of deep red lipstick. She studied my face and the guys standing next to me.

"Our friend," Gabriel said, elbowing me, "needs a bra fitting and new underwear. Can you take her measurements and help her pick out some stuff?"

The woman smiled. She reached out her hands to me, wrapping one around my arm. "Come with me, honey. I know exactly what you need," she said. "You boys want to wait by the registers? How many does she need?"

"Ten of each, at least," Victor said, the fire in his eyes subdued. "And whatever else she wants. Don't let her come back until she has enough."

The attendant smiled a toothy grin and took up my hand to stick it through her arm. "I'll take care of her."

I swallowed, allowing the woman to guide me to the back of the store and out of sight from the boys. I kind of felt relieved to be out from under their curious faces. Was Victor serious? Why did he say so many?

"Don't worry," the attendant said. "I know it's tough shopping with boys when you need stuff. They all have their own opinions."

I wondered why she didn't consider it strange for someone like me to be buying underwear with boys. Was this normal?

Within a few minutes, she had me measured and helped me to select a variety of bras to try on. She showed me into the fitting rooms and instructed me on how to ensure the bras were fitting correctly.

She asked my preference on color, and I told her I liked pink. She made sure that every piece of underwear had some bit of pink attached. She would hold up something and I simply nodded at her suggestion. I was too timid to interject an opinion. She had me pick a couple of different styles; sporty, vivid, elegant and cute.

I finally had to tell her to stop. I had lost count of how many items she had given me. "I think this is enough," I said.

"Make sure you get what you like," she said. "Your friend said whatever you wanted."

I nodded. "It's nice of him, but I'd like to keep it simple."

She smiled, knowingly. "Honey, you've got to take advantage of it while you can."

I wasn't exactly sure what she meant, but she laughed softly at me, removing the collection from my arms and walked ahead of me to the registers.

Victor was standing by the counter. He caught my eye as we approached. The attendant held up the pile. "Is this enough?"

Victor nodded quietly in approval.

I slid next to him, my cheek hovering close to his shoulder to hide my blushing.

"Where are the others?" I asked him quietly.

"I made them wait outside," he said. "They wanted to buy half the store for you."

I turned my face away, rolling my eyes and pressing a palm to my warm cheek. He took my hand and held it, his thumb smoothed over my skin; it calmed me a little.

"Add that pile, too," Victor said to the attendant. He pointed to a small collection of shorts and shirts that were folded nearby on the counter. Most of it looked like clothes one would sleep in or made for exercising.

The attendant beamed. "Would you like to open a line of credit?"

"No," Victor said. He let go of my hand to take out his wallet. He slapped a black credit card on the countertop.

"You have some very nice friends," the attendant said as she finished up the order.

Victor sighed, removing his cell phone from his back pocket. As he tapped the screen, the attendant finished ringing up the order and the final price glowed green on the display.

Over eight-hundred dollars.

"Victor..." I said nervously, touching his elbow. I hadn't looked at the tags and I was floored. Was this how much clothes cost? He had to be out of his mind. I felt sure the moment he saw it, he'd refuse and want to send back most of it

He glanced at the screen. His eyebrow lifted but he seemed unaffected and went back to typing in his phone as the attendant swiped his card.

"Vic..."

"Just say thank you," he said calmly.

I sighed. "Thank you, Victor," I said in a small voice.

He did a half smile, tucked his phone into his pocket, signed the slip and put his card back into his wallet. "You're getting the hang of it."

♥♥♥

I had two pink bags dangling off my arm when we left the store. Gabriel and Nathan were waiting just outside the doors. They had their heads tucked close to each other as they talked. When they spotted Victor and me, the conversation ceased abruptly. I half worried for a moment if there was some Academy business that was about to call them off.

"Okay," Gabriel said, slapping his hands together and rubbing them. "Go put on a new bra and pair of panties and we'll get started.""Right now?" I asked. I was already feeling overwhelmed.

"Yes," he said. "If we're going to get clothes that fit you right, you need to be in a bra that fits you. Just slip into the girls' restroom and go put something on."

We found the restrooms and I went in to change in the stall. I put on a pair of pink and black striped underwear. Confidence started to thread its way through my skin. I felt daring. I found a white bra and put that on, too. It did feel much more comfortable than my old one. I wondered how Gabriel knew mine didn't fit. I didn't even notice.

I stuffed my old things into the bottom of the bag and tossed the tags in the garbage. I met with the others out in the hallway. They all turned to me. Gabriel nodded his head in approval.

"Yes," he said. "Much better. Shit, you do have boobs."

Nathan smacked him in the arm.

"Ow, hey." Gabriel rubbed at the new red mark on his skin. "I was complimenting her. Jeez, I can't tease her. I can't compliment her."

Nathan narrowed his eyes at him but said nothing.

I followed the guys into a Macy's. Gabriel floated to the racks with the newest clothes on display. "Stand still over here," he said. He directed me with a finger until I was beside him.

One by one, he held up blouses, skirts, shorts, pants and everything else hanging on display. He would tuck the hanger into my neck or to my waist and flatten the material over my stomach or thighs to get an idea of how it would look. I think he pulled down nearly one of everything. When he didn't like something, he'd hang it backward on the rack. When he did like something, he passed it off to Nathan to hold onto.

Victor had mysteriously disappeared.

"Nathan?" I asked while Gabriel had drifted away toward the jeans. "Where did Victor get that black credit card?"

Nathan juggled the collection of clothes in his arms. "Don't you know? Victor's parents are loaded. They gave him that thing when he was still in diapers."

"Won't they notice all this?" I held up my arms where the pink underwear bags were still hanging.

"Probably not," he said. His lips curved in the corners. "If they did, they wouldn't care. They only get interested in what he does when he's about to play the piano at one of his fancy concerts."

My eyes widened. I knew he played piano, but I hadn't heard about this. "He plays for other people?"

"Well, yeah. He's really good. He hates the concerts though. His parents are usually the ones that sign him up for that. They like showing him off."

I sighed, thinking about what it must be like to have parents that were rich. A warm spot fluttered in my heart for Victor. I reminded myself to thank him again for everything later. It was important to me to let him know.

My insides rattled thinking of the eight-hundred dollars he'd already spent so far.

Gabriel snapped his fingers in the air at the two of us. "Are we ready for fitting?"

I slid my eyes over to look at Nathan, pleading silently with him to help me.

He shook his head, grinning. "Nu uh," he said to me. "We've all gone through this. It's your turn to get poked and prodded by him."

Gabriel led the way to where the fitting rooms were. They were unattended and the fitting area was empty.

The boys joined me inside. Nathan dropped the clothes onto a bench outside the individual rooms and collapsed into the seat next to the pile. Gabriel picked out a couple of shirts and shorts and handed them to me. "Get in there and do it."

I locked the latch on the door to the fitting room and froze nervously in front of the mirror. My fingers traced over the buttons at the neck of Kota's shirt. Cotton fibers kissed my fingertips in return. His shirt didn't look terrible on me, even if it wasn't the best fitting thing. It felt far different than when I was wearing Derrick's shirt. Just like when I had worn Victor's shirt at school, I felt comfortable. It was like wearing a piece of the boys with me, and I felt protected. My heart warmed at the thought of all of them and I wondered what they thought when they saw me wearing something that belonged to them. Did they feel this same connection with me that I did?

I undressed and put on the new clothes. I sucked down some courage and opened the door again. My chin dipped to my neck and I shuffled forward in my bare feet.

Gabriel and Nathan had been talking and they stopped and turned their eyes toward me. Nathan's eyes lit up. Gabriel, however, lifted his fist, thumb down.

"No," he said. "It's awful."

I looked down at the pink cotton t-shirt and the jean shorts he had given me. "What's wrong with them?"

"They don't fit." He picked up another set of clothes from the pile. "Try these."

I slid my eyes to Nathan.

"Your turn," he mouthed to me from behind Gabriel's back.

I sighed, locking myself back into the room. According to the mirror, the shirt appeared to fit just fine. The shorts looked a little weird on me but they sat on my hips. What did he mean?

I tried on the next pair of black cotton shorts. They sat low on my hips and were too short. They almost felt like underwear. I pulled on a green t-shirt with quarter sleeves.

This time I just stood inside the doorway. I didn't want to step forward and let other people who might be around see these shorts on me.

When the boys turned to me, both of their mouths dropped.

My cheeks flashed with heat. "Too short," I said.

Gabriel nodded. "I like that shirt, though. Keep that." He picked out a skirt from the pile and tossed it to me. "Keep the shirt on but put this on with it."

I spent an hour in Macy's trying on several dozen items of clothes and in different combinations. Gabriel nitpicked his way through the collection, discarding the unwanted clothes into a bin and created a separate pile for anything that met his approval.

He was relentless with his opinion. "Too tight. Too short. Doesn't fit."

"What do you mean when you say it doesn't fit?" I asked when he rejected what seemed like a perfectly good shirt. "It's the right size."

"No," he said. "It doesn't fit *you.* Your personality. Your style. It's not what we want."

"What do we want?"

"Clothes are telling everyone who you are in one glance. What do you want to say?"

"What am I supposed to be saying?" It was confusing. How can people know what you are like by your clothes?

He laughed, his bright blue eyes lighting up. "You know it when you feel it. Don't worry. I've got this. Just trust me."

When I was done and back in Kota's shirt, I slumped onto the bench next to Nathan while Gabriel went out to find a smaller size in a pair of shorts he liked. "I'm exhausted," I said.

Nathan laughed. He dropped his palm onto my back. "Sweetie, you just started."

"Tell me that after we're done here, they'll be happy," I said.

The corner of his mouth lifted and he shook his head at me. "They're busting their asses to make you happy."

"I'm fine!" My voice strained as my tone rose. It probably sounded like I was complaining but I was tired and stressed. "I keep telling them that. I'm happy."

"Your sister just gave all your clothes to the bratty girl next door and your parents never let you out of the house and you've had all kinds of crazy things going on, and you're happy?"

"It's not that bad," I said. "I'm here with you."

He nodded slowly. His blue eyes appeared to glow. "What do you want to do?"

"I... I want them to know they don't have to do this for me. It's just a little overwhelming."

"You're not used to the attention," he confirmed.

"Maybe."

He chuckled again. "You've landed yourself in the wrong group of friends. We're always up in each other's business."

"Is this what it's always like?" I asked. I turned my head to face him. "Is this normal?"

His jaw set and that serious look returned. "It's been different with you here."

I raised my eyebrow at him, confused by his comment. "In a bad way?"

He flinched like he was bringing himself out of his deep thoughts. "No. I mean with us," he said. "We've been together for so long. I guess we just worked out this system. We do our part."

"What's your part?"

He half smiled again. "Right now I'm holding clothes while Vic's run off to play and Gabriel's probably getting a one-over by the salesladies as he's picking out girl clothes."

I laughed at how silly and simply he put it. He seemed pleased with this. "So what's my part?" I asked. "I mean am I just throwing everything out of whack, or what?"

He shrugged, nudging me with his arm. "We're figuring it out. Don't worry about it."

It was easy for him to say. I thought about how Kota was out with the others right now at the diner. I could easily picture him relaying orders and the others falling into line. Silas and North were probably trading swings with sledgehammers, with Luke busting in to give them a break with his antics. Would they have done all that last weekend if I hadn't gotten into trouble? I felt like I was the weak link in this otherwise very put-together Academy troop.

Nathan stared at me while I was thinking and I blushed. He parted his lips as if he wanted to say something, but before he could, Gabriel returned, a more clothes tucked under his arm.

"Last load," he said. "Then we'll go somewhere else. I think I've looked at everything here."

I sucked in a breath. "Round two," I whispered to Nathan under my breath.

"Go get 'em, tiger," Nathan said, nudging me in the back as I stood.

♥♥♥

After Gabriel had seen everything on me and made his choices, he chased me off to go find Victor while he and Nathan carried the approved set of clothes toward the registers.

Grateful for the breather, I took a walk around the store, glancing in different sections for Victor. I headed toward the men's section, thinking maybe he was getting things for himself. Something caught my eye as I crossed the walkway.

Victor hovered over a glass case. He was signing a credit card receipt. The attendant slipped a black box across the glass toward him. She leaned on her elbows as she watched Victor's penmanship. She was pretty, with black hair and dark eyes. She batted her eyelashes at him and said something.

My feet were moving of their own accord and I stepped closer just in time to hear Victor say as he put his credit card back in his wallet, "...just some crazy beautiful girl I met at school."

The words gave me pause. The attendant continued to smile sweetly at him. His eyes drifted to her, an eyebrow arching in confusion. She slipped away from the counter to take care of another customer.

Victor turned, and spotted me. "Sang?" His hand went to the counter and the tiny black box disappeared into his pocket. "Is Gabe finished?"

I was suddenly struck with trepidation. He didn't want me to see what he bought. Had he met another girl at school? Why was he buying jewelry? Was it for her? Was he going to try to win her over with a gift? The thought of it made my heart burn. Why should it concern me, though? We're friends. He could like whoever he wanted.

In response to his question, I simply nodded. I was surprised to find my finger at my lip, pushing it to my teeth.

His head tilted and he came closer to me. "Why do you look like that? Are you okay?"

I blinked, trying to draw up a smile. "It's um... Gabriel," I said. "I think I've tried on everything in the store."

He laughed and shook his head. The fire in his eyes smoldered. "I'm sorry I left. I was just browsing. I'll stick nearby so he's not driving you crazy."

He found my hand and held it. The move confused me. Would the girl he liked think it was okay we were holding hands? Was the real reason he didn't hold me in his lap this morning because he was conscious of how the other girl would feel? What would she think of him sleeping in the bed with me?

My heart fluttered as his thumb traced over my hand. I was so conscious of every fiery look he gave me, the way he drifted as he walked beside me, and the way his lips curled gently up in the corner as he lead me toward the registers.

Gabriel and Nathan stood in line as the attendant was ringing up items. She eyeballed them curiously. When Victor and I stepped up beside them, she seemed even more confused.

Victor surveyed everything on the counter and nodded in approval to Gabriel. He let go of me so he could take care of the purchase. I stood behind him, my cheek pressed to his shoulder, smelling his smooth berry and moss fragrance.

"Say it," he said over his shoulder to me.

"Thank you, Victor."

"You're welcome, Sang."

Nervous

At the fifth store, Victor bellowed at Gabriel for wanting me to try on yet another skirt in a different color when I had already tried on twenty. I was slumping against Nathan as we sat on a bench together. My stomach growled.

"You're speaking my language," Nathan said. He stood up with the handful of items Gabriel put into the yes pile. "We need food."

"I agree," Victor said, looking pleased with this distraction. "Let's go."

"Aw," Gabriel said, but he relented. I wondered if he was hungry, too.

My arms were overloaded with bags as we left the store. Shoes were now included with everything. I had boots that were meant for skirts and sandals meant for jeans. Gabriel rattled fashion advice off his tongue so quickly that I was dizzy with what I was supposed to do with it all. Nathan took half of the bags from me but insisted I keep the pink Victoria's Secret bags. "People are going to think I'm a pervert," he said.

We were trailing back down the walkway toward the entrance we had come from when Gabriel stopped short in front of a sporting goods store. His eyes squinted as he scanned the racks.

"No," Victor said to him.

"But I just realized she doesn't have a bathing suit," he said. "She's got to have one. Just one. I swear."

Victor's eyebrows rose together and his fire gaze fell

on me. "Do you have one?"

I really wanted to lie in that moment. For one thing, I didn't want to spend another hour trying on bathing suits in front of the boys. Another reason was I had lost track of how much Victor had spent and I didn't want to spend another dime. But the way his eyes were so intense on mine, I couldn't think and lying was impossible. I simply shook my head, my finger at my lower lip. "But I don't need it," I insisted. "I mean, it's September. There can't be too many opportunities to swim before winter."

They laughed together. Victor reluctantly nodded at Gabe. "One swimsuit. And she's not trying on all of them."

This time Gabriel insisted Victor and Nathan wait toward the front part of the store. I didn't want to be left alone with Gabriel and I pleaded silently with Victor for him to come with us.

"If you're not back in a half-hour, I'm taking Sang back and leaving you here, Gabe," Victor said.

"Don't worry," Gabriel said. He hooked an arm around my neck. "I'm getting the hang of her style."

I dropped the bags at Victor's feet with a sigh. Nathan merely grinned, looking somewhat smug about the idea of me getting another round with Gabriel.

I followed Gabriel to the section of women's bathing suits. Despite what the guys seemed to imply, swimming was out of season. There were only a couple of racks.

Gabriel thumbed through different suits. He completely skipped over the one-piece suits and mumbled something about the possibility of mixing and matching tops and bottoms.

"What do you think?" he asked me, holding up a blue halter top and a skimpy bikini bottom.

My cheeks heated. "It's... um... pretty." There wasn't an easy way to reject his selection without saying that I thought it wasn't to my taste.

"Hm," he said, taking another look at it. "The color isn't good."

Gabriel selected a variety of suits and we headed further into the back of the store so I could try them on. "Pick your favorites first," he said. "We're limited on colors and sizes, so we'll just go down the line."

This time there was only a crinkly curtain separating me from the rest of the store. I realized at that moment that I would have to get almost naked to try on the bathing suit. My eyes drifted to the corners of the curtain next to the walls. Could there be cracks where people could look in?

I shoved the thought to the back of my head. I removed my clothes and I tossed them carefully to the floor, except for Kota's shirt, which I hung on the wall to keep it clean and also wanting something nearby so I could shield myself if I needed.

I started with the most modest two-piece Gabriel had picked out. It was a black pair of shorts and matching halter top that barely left any skin revealed along my midsection. If I pulled the hem of the halter down, it completely covered the area.

When I was finished, I wasn't exactly sure if I wanted to open the curtain. I didn't want to step out and be seen. "Gabriel?" I called softly.

The curtain slid to the side and Gabriel appeared. His eyes swept over me. "No," he said, shaking his head. "That's just ugly. I thought I said pick your favorite."

I blushed. "I was just..."

"Nervous?"

I nodded.

He sighed, reaching out and tugging at a lock of my hair. "Your next choice better be a pink one." He closed the curtain again.

I went through the choices carefully. There was a black, white and hot pink plaid suit. It had a moderate bra top and the bottoms were plain black, but there was some pink plaid material designed to look like a miniskirt. While it wouldn't cover my mid-section, it was flirty without being too much like a string bikini that I had worried Gabriel would insist on. I thought maybe it would be a little too bold, but I really liked the color, and if I was completely honest with myself, I thought it would surprise Gabriel.

After I put it on, I checked myself out in the mirror. It fit perfectly. The miniskirt hem covered my butt just enough but when I swung my hips, I could see the black suit part underneath covering me. It sat a little lower on my hips than I wanted but I couldn't deny how it made my hips look nicer.

The top felt like one of the bras I had just bought and curved around my breasts snugly. I picked at the cups and the straps, trying to see if I could swim in it without it falling apart. It seemed to be solid.

I called for Gabriel again. I folded my arms around my stomach, waiting for him to appear.

He opened the curtain quickly as if he'd been standing by, waiting. His critical eyes started to sweep over me. His face changed, his eyes started shining, his lips parted slowly and his cheeks tinted red. He blinked, stumbled through the opening and closed the curtain behind himself.

I stepped back a little to allow him room. He whirled on me. I bit back a shiver, feeling intimidated that he was seeing me in this.

His eyes drank me in, his head tilting back and forth. "Move your arms?" His tone was gentle, the softest I've ever heard it.

I dropped my hands to push my palms against my thighs. My eyes sank to the dingy utility carpet below his Converse shoes.

"Turn around."

I turned in a slow circle.

"Now do it once more and bend over."

My head shot up, my mouth parting as I looked into his intense blue eyes. "Gabriel..." I felt myself tremble again, surprised by his request.

He jerked his head back, looking as shocked at me as I felt. He stepped forward, closing the gap between us. His palms found my cheeks and he held my face up until I was looking into his eyes. "Sang," he said. "Will you please trust me?"

I parted my lips to say something but the words eluded me.

His eyes darkened. "I would never hurt you," he said with an intensity that matched his eyes. "I handle the clothes. Okay? I know every inch of the guys' bodies because I've dressed them all since I was little. If you stick with us, if you let me, I'll know yours, too. Not in a perverted way. It's just what happens."

I still couldn't answer him. My cheeks were on fire. It wasn't me being embarrassed anymore; it was his words and those crystal eyes.

He leaned his forehead against mine. "Please, god," he breathed. "Don't look so scared. I swear it on my dead momma's grave that I'll never lay a hand on you. Never."

"Gabriel," I whispered, surprised. "You... your mother..."

His ears turned red. He lifted his forehead away from mine and nodded. "Yeah. When I was little." He pressed his palm again to my cheek. "But I'm talking about you, now. If I'm asking you to do something, there's a reason, okay? I just wanted to make sure it doesn't slip around when you move. That's all."

I sucked in a deep breath, trying to swallow back the emotion in my throat.

He backed away from me. I turned around. I bent over at the hips until my fingers were touching the floor. I couldn't see behind me but I sensed his eyes.

"Remain bent over and lift one foot at the knee."

I did.

"Other one."

I put my leg down and lifted the other one.

"Now put your leg down but just kind of... shake or something."

I blushed again, but I put my leg down and I wriggled my hips at him.

"Oh god, okay. Yes. It's fine," he said quickly. I stood up. He turned partially away from me and his ears were still red. "Okay, we're good."

"This is the one?" I asked, curious as to why he had turned around.

"Yeah, yeah," he mumbled. "You're perfect." He shoved the curtain out of the way without looking at me again, walking out.

The moment he did, a loud voice sounded right outside the curtain. "Sir," said a burly male voice, "you can't do that. There can't be two people in the dressing room."

"Who says?" Gabriel asked. "There's no sign."

"I'm the manager," the man said.

My heart jumped and I lunged for my clothes to pull them back on.

"Don't you know who that girl is?" Gabriel said in a low tone.

"I don't care who she is," the voice said, though softer.

"This girl has a shoot tomorrow and we're here to get her a bathing suit because that's what they want her in and I need to make sure it doesn't look like shit."

"Who are you?"

"I'm her photographer."

I smothered a giggle as I put Kota's shirt back on.

The manager huffed. "You still can't just..."

"Get over it," Gabriel said. "This isn't the pervert show, okay? I was just giving her my opinion. Besides, you need to let boyfriends have opinions about their girls' in their suits. Girls get it all wrong."

I wanted to toss my shoe at him. Instead I finished up, opening the curtain with the pink bathing suit hanging over my arm.

The manager was a husky man in a blue dress shirt and khakis. He took one look at me and started to mumble. "I… just...um..."

Gabriel smirked haughtily and grabbed the bathing suit from me, tossing it at the guy. "Will you ring this up for us?" Gabriel turned to me. "Can you go fetch your agent, please? Let him pay for it if he wants it so bad."

I dashed off to fetch Victor. By the time he followed me back into the store to the registers, the manager had already bagged the bathing suit and was waiting for the payment.

"Don't I get to see it?" Victor asked.

Gabriel leaned against the counter with his arms folded against his chest. He looked distracted, distant. "Later."

♥♥♥

When we got back to Victor's car, Gabriel opened the front passenger side door for me.

"You can sit up front if you'd like," I said to him. "I really don't mind." I was trying to be nicer since I spent a good part of that morning complaining about him. I felt badly about it now. He'd worked hard today to do all this stuff for me and I wanted to let him know I appreciated it.

He seemed confused by my response and tilted his head at me. He glanced at the others, but they had already gotten into the car. He tucked his head closer to me. "Okay, but only because I hate Victor's music and I can't switch the stereo from the back."

I shared a conspiratorial smile with him and he opened the back passenger door for me. I slid in next to Nathan, who beamed. Victor flicked a confused glance at us.

"Where do we want to go?" Victor asked. He readjusted his rearview mirror until he could catch my eye. "What are you hungry for?"

My eyes flashed to Nathan. He mouthed: *Italian*.

"Italian," I said out loud for him, pleased that someone else made this choice.

Victor rolled his eyes. "What's your favorite food, Sang?"

"Pancakes."

He laughed, shaking his head. "All right, we'll get Italian. Only because Erica makes the best pancakes and we're not asking her right now."

Victor drove to a nearby Italian place. When we got inside, he said something to the hostess and she guided us to a table.

Victor held a hand toward the booth and gazed back at me. I slid in on one side and he slid in next to me. Gabriel sat across from me and Nathan sat next to him.

"Good afternoon, gentlemen," said a tall waiter with slicked back, dark hair and a nametag that read "Cody" as he handed us menus. His eyes caught mine and he grinned. "And lady. Can I interest you in our specials or the wine menu?" The last part sounded more like a joke. He had to know we were underage.

"No, thank you," Victor said.

"May I get you something to drink?"

"Coke," said Gabriel.

"I want one of those strawberry smoothies," Nathan said.

"Sprite," Victor said.

Cody looked at me, an eyebrow raising. "And for you, sweetie?"

Victor flinched but said nothing.

"Water, please," I said.

"You can get more than water," Victor said to me.

I blushed. I wasn't sure what else to get. "Um, a strawberry smoothie, too, please?" I checked with Victor who nodded.

Cody shot glances between Victor and I. He gave us a small smile that was oddly curious. When he left, we opened our menus. The prices were more than I expected for spaghetti and other pasta dishes. I tried to calm my heart. After all, Victor just spent several thousand dollars on clothes. Thinking of it made my stomach twist and I started to rattle again.

"What are you getting?" Gabriel asked. His foot nudged mine under the table, pulling me from my thoughts.

"I was thinking of the chicken salad," I said.

"Get what you really want, Sang," Victor said coolly without looking up from the menu.

"How do you know that's not what she wants?" Nathan asked, closing his menu and dropping it on the table.

"She's conveniently picked the lowest priced item on the menu that isn't an appetizer." He lifted his head. The fire in his eyes seemed amused as he faced me. "Sang?"

I blushed and scanned the menu. "Tortellini?"

"Better," he said. He folded his menu, placing it on the table.

The waiter came back with our drinks. The smoothies were served in big green glasses with strawberry wedges around the rim. Nathan's had two. Mine had six. Nathan's eyes narrowed on my glass but he said nothing.

"Have you decided?" Cody asked. He looked intently at my face. I was confused and felt a finger fluttering up to my lip.

"We'll start with the zucchini fritté," Victor said. "I'll have the veal marsala. She'll have the tortellini." He paused, gazing at the others across the table.

Nathan and Gabriel put in their orders, but Cody kept glancing at me. "Anything else?" he asked, seemingly to the table in general but his gaze never left mine.

"That's it," Victor said.

Cody's smile teased his lips in an almost smirk. "Call on me if you need anything. I'll get these right out."

The air pressure around the table seemed to lift when he left.

"I don't like our waiter," Gabriel said.

The others mumbled in agreement.

"Did he do something wrong?" I asked, not completely understanding their displeasure.

None of them seemed to want to answer, so I focused on the strawberry smoothie. I picked up one of the strawberries from the rim and took a bite.

Gabriel stretched in his seat. "Mmm... long morning," he said. "We got a lot done, though. And Sang's got a new wardrobe." He wriggled his eyebrows at me. "Enough room in your closet?"

"I don't know how I'm going to get it all up to my room." I absentmindedly rubbed at the collar of Kota's shirt at my neck. "And I'm worried. I mean, what if Danielle comes back? And my parents might wonder..."

"We're taking care of that," Nathan said. He snagged one of the strawberries off of my glass and popped it into his mouth. He'd already eaten his.

"How?"

He glanced at Victor. Victor only shrugged. Nathan turned back to me with a smile. "Don't worry so much."

"Besides," Gabriel said, "Danielle won't be able to get her ass in your clothes now that you've got shit that fits. I saw her in your skirt. I'm surprised she didn't rip it."

"I don't understand why she wanted my things, anyway," I said. "They weren't exactly expensive or new."

"She was trying to get attention by wearing what you wear," Victor said. His fingers slipped through the condensation on his drink. "A lot of the girls are doing that."

"Doing what?" I blushed.

"They're all wearing nicer things. I've seen the girls starting to wear skirts." Victor's eyes lifted to settle on my face. "Apparently you're a trendsetter."

"Yeah well," Gabriel said, sitting back and hanging an elbow over the back edge of the booth. His foot slid next to mine again, this time staying pressed against me. "They're about to get their minds blown. She's got a whole new look now."

"I don't know, guys. I don't want to stand out."

They all laughed.

"You're wearing skirts to school in the first place," Gabriel said. "You started it."

I shrugged. "It was what everyone wore at my old school."

Under the table, Victor found my hand. His fingers

interlocked mine, his thumb smoothed over my skin. I tried to feel calm about it, but it set my heart speeding along.

"What were they like? The kids at your old school? What did they wear?" he asked.

"The clothes were a little nicer than what kids wear here, I suppose," I said quietly. "They were a lot calmer. Quieter. There wasn't as much fighting. The girls wore skirts and blouses most of the time. During the winter they might trade for nicer jeans."

His eyebrow rose and his thumb stopped. "Were you that different from them?"

"Who?"

"The other kids."

"Their clothes were nicer. Newer."

"You didn't look like a monster in yours, so I don't understand. And they still didn't talk to you?"

I shrugged, feeling cornered. "They weren't mean to me. They just never said anything to me. After a while, I settled into a routine. I was usually reading at my own table. It wasn't as crowded at my old school, so I could find space for myself."

Gabriel smirked. "I think Kota was right. They were probably blown away by you and didn't know how to approach you."

Heat radiated my face again.

Nathan cleared his throat. "Anyway," he said, his blue eyes on me. "Do we want to go help the guys when we get back or are we doing something else?"

"Else," Gabriel said. "We're going to get roped into working at the diner soon enough. Might as well take the time off while we can get away with it."

"Want to swim, Sang?" Nathan asked.

I brightened, nodding. I was grateful he was interrupting the others and redirecting the attention. "Sure."

"We'll tell the guys when we get back that Sang wanted to swim so we have to stay behind."

After we had eaten the appetizer and the meals were delivered, Cody took special care to place the boys' plates first.

When he got to mine, he stopped halfway as if he was feeling awkward about reaching over everyone else. His eyes fell on me. I caught something in what he wanted and without thinking, I reached out to help, taking the plate from him. His rough hands traced over mine as he let go.

"Thank you," I said to be polite, even though I was confused. Why was he touching me?

He flashed an amused grin. "Need anything else?" he asked, though his eyes were on me alone.

"No," Victor said shortly.

Cody shot him a glare. He bowed his head at us and left the table.

As we ate, the conversation turned to school. They started talking about the teachers, the homework we had and expectations about upcoming tests. It wasn't long before I was feeling full and finally had to push my plate away.

"Left room for dessert?" Victor asked me.

I shook my head, covering my stomach with my hand and rubbing. "It's too much."

"They've got a nice tiramisu here."

I slid over in the booth until I was leaning my shoulder against his. "What's tiramisu?"

He smiled, amused. "You'll see."

"I like the strawberry cheesecake," Nathan said, pushing his empty plate away.

"I want chocolate," Gabriel said. He speared some pasta from my plate and ate it. "There's a chocolate cake thing here, right?"

Cody came back and took our plates. Nathan ordered the strawberry cheesecake, chocolate cake and the tiramisu for the table.

"And bring four spoons," he said.

Cody's eyes once again landed on me. "Would you like anything else, sweetheart?"

I flinched, not understanding why he kept asking me.

"I'm fine."

He flashed another smile my way and turned from us, carrying the dishes back to the kitchen.

"What the hell is he doing?" Gabriel said. "It's like he's waiting for us to punch him or something."

"What do you mean?" I asked.

"He hasn't stopped flirting with you since we got here," he said.

My mouth popped open and my hand fluttered to the base of my throat. "I thought he was just being nice."

"He's being an ass," Victor said.

I sighed, swallowed, and sat back again with my arms around my stomach. I didn't understand flirting at all.

Cody returned, and he placed the desserts in the middle of the table, spoons placed beside each one.

He had a small bowl of vanilla ice cream, too, and positioned it in front of me. He held the spoon out for me to take from him. "Thought you might like some," he said. "It'll cleanse your palette."

I glanced quickly at the guys, who were glaring at Cody. He ignored them, intent on me. I slowly reached for the spoon. He turned his fingers to lightly brush at my hand, lingering longer than necessary for me to collect the spoon.

"Thank you," I said quietly, unsure of how to respond otherwise.

He brightened, flashing a satisfied grin and walked away.

"His tip is standing in the negative," Victor said. "One more thing and I'm talking to the manager."

"What are you going to tell him?" Gabriel asked. "That he's being too polite to a girl we're with? It makes us look like jealous freaks."

Victor grabbed the spoon on the tiramisu plate.

Nathan scooped at his cheesecake. "Don't make it look like we're bothered by it," he said. He held his spoon filled with red swirled cheesecake out toward me. "Have a taste," Nathan said.

I steadied his hand with mine, bringing the spoon to my mouth. The cheesecake was heady with strawberries and something tangy I couldn't place. I let go of him to put my fingers over my mouth as I swallowed, licking my lips. "It's good."

Victor nudged the plate of tiramisu toward me. "Try this."

I picked up my spoon, taking a bite of the fluffy, creamy dessert. It tasted like cinnamon or chocolate and there was a soft after-bite. "What's in this?"

"Rum, I think," Victor said, taking a bite of it himself and grinning. "It's not bad."

"Okay now this one," Gabriel said. He positioned his plate until it was between both of us.

I took a spoonful of his cake and ate it. "Okay," I said. "I can't pick. They're all really good."

Gabriel's eyes lit up. He dabbed his spoon into the ice cream cup, scooped up a little and then dug out a corner of cake to eat both together. "I have to admit, the ice cream is perfect for this."

I took a bite of ice cream, too. Within minutes, the plates were empty. I felt ready to roll out the door.

Cody returned, dropping off the check and taking our plates. As Victor pulled his wallet out again, I pressed my cheek to his shoulder.

He turned his head slightly to me and parted his lips to say something, but I beat him to it.

"Thank you, Victor," I said softly.

"You're welcome, Sang."

When he signed the receipt, he scooted out of the booth. The others followed. I trailed behind them through the crowded restaurant.

Cody materialized ahead of us and made his way along the same path, thanking us for coming.

When he got to me, he held his hand out in a strange way like he wanted to shake my hand. Out of instinct to be polite more than anything else, my hand drifted up and he grasped it. I felt a piece of paper being pressed to my hand.

He leaned in to me to whisper. "When you get tired of being bossed around by those losers, call me."

My eyes widened and I blushed. I shoved the paper back to him, without checking to see what it was. "My friends," I said loud enough to draw the attention of the boys to turn and look, "are way nicer than you are."

Cody's face reddened. He let the paper drop to the floor between us and turned away quickly, sulking.

The guys laughed. Gabriel hooked an arm around my neck, his head touching mine as he walked beside me the rest of the way out the door. "That's our girl."

♥♥♥

Out in the car, I was leaning back in the back seat, my head against the door. Now, in the warmth of the day and with the drone of the car and a super-full belly, I was feeling sleepy.

Nathan popped my seat belt undone. He tugged lightly at my arm. "Come here."

I was confused, but he pulled me over until my head was pillowed by his thigh. I stiffened, nervous. He rested his arm against my shoulder as he moved his fingers to my ear. He smoothed his thumb over my lobe.

I was asleep in a minute.

♥

Sang The Cheater

I woke up as Victor made the turn onto Sunnyvale Court. I yawned, rubbing at my eyes, surprised I had actually fallen asleep.

Nathan smiled at me as I sat up. "Are you going to want a nap or swim?"

"Swim."

His face brightened in a way that made me blush.

Victor parked in Nathan's driveway. We got out and took armloads of the bags into the house. Nathan pointed to the square kitchen table in the dining room and we dropped the bags on top of it. Collected together on the table, the pile was overwhelming.

"I don't think it will all fit in my closet," I said.

"Will you quit worrying?" Gabriel asked. He chopped me on the head and fished out the bag that had the bathing suit in it. "Go put this on."

I started to second-guess my choice in bathing suits. I hadn't thought ahead enough to think of the guys seeing me in a bikini.

Gabriel sensed my hesitation and shoved me toward the bathroom.

When I was locked inside, I washed my face to refresh myself after sleeping in the car and borrowed some of Nathan's toothpaste, brushing my teeth with my finger. I folded the clothes I had worn, taking extra care with Kota's shirt.

When I finished dressing, I stared at myself in the mirror. The suit appeared just as daring as it had in the store. Was this me?

A gentle knock sounded at the door. "Sang," Gabriel called to me. "Stop being nervous."

With my cheeks flushed, I unlocked the door and opened it. Gabriel leaned on the doorway, his arm up on the frame and his head resting against his bicep. He was already in his swimming shorts. His slim frame was cut, his abs defined, and a line of brown hair came up from his groin, through his abs above his belly button before the trail faded. How did I miss this part the day before yesterday in the woods? Maybe I was too distracted by my stung legs to notice. He was easily one of the slimmest guys in the group, but he was exquisite.

His eyes drank me in again and the side of his mouth curled up. "Knockout," he said quietly. He grabbed my hand, his slim fingers folding over my palm. He tugged me back into the kitchen.

Nathan wore red swim trunks. Victor was still dressed, his arms crossed over his chest as he leaned against the gray granite kitchen island. They talked in hushed voices. Gabriel stepped out of the way so they could see me. Their eyes widened and mouths popped open.

This was worse than if they had said they didn't like it. Heat tickled my cheeks.

Gabriel lifted my hand above my head and twisted it slightly so I would spin. The hem of the miniskirt flew up around my waist.

"Can I dress or what?" Gabriel asked.

Nathan's cheeks reddened, his eyes bouncing back and forth from my face to my legs to my breasts and everywhere. Victor's fire eyes were blazing. His eyes slid very slowly to my legs and back up across my body.

"Come on, Trouble," Gabriel said, as he clasped my hand tight and led me toward the living room. "Let's go try it out."

As we walked through the living room, Nathan's voice floated to us. "That was so worth every penny."

Victor replied, "I don't think I spent enough..."

♥♥♥

Outside, Gabriel insisted on spreading a thick layer of suntan lotion on my back and stomach.

"Sunburns are not for you," he said, as he dabbed my nose with a little lotion.

It was Nathan who finally pulled me away from him. He picked me up into his arms. I laughed, wriggling against him as I knew what was coming. He didn't stop at the pool's edge. He simply continued walking and we splashed together into the water.

The clouds were wisps in the sky. Freshly mowed grass and an ocean breeze tickled my nose along with the chlorine. The day was perfect for this.

Gabriel took a shallow dive from the edge, and popped up on the other side of the pool. He shook his head, his blond locks scrambled into the mix of his dark hair.

Victor emerged from the house. He wore plain gray swimming shorts. The silver medallion still hung around his neck. His shoulders and chest were just as toned as Gabriel's. While Nathan beat them both in definition and mass, they were all fit, and prime examples of Academy students.

Victor squatted down to sit on the edge of the pool and slipped into the water without a splash. He did a quick lap across the pool under the water and surfaced. Water slid across his trim abdomen. He raked his wavy brown hair out of his eyes. I couldn't believe how beautiful he looked.

"You know what this means now that we have Sang," Nathan said, distracting me from watching Victor. "We've finally got even teams."

"For what?" I asked. I untangled my clip from my hair, twisting my hair against my head and putting the clip back to keep it out of my eyes.

"Everything," Nathan said. "There's been seven of us for so long, we've always had uneven teams unless someone bowed out."

"So I am useful," I said, grinning. The water energized me. I didn't realize how down I'd been until that moment when my blood was pumping through my veins again. How long had I been sleepwalking through life?

He smirked, splashing water at me. I laughed, pulling away to swim under the water to the other side of the pool. When I got there, Nathan was right behind me. He bumped into me on purpose and broke the surface, slapping the beige concrete patio. "Another race?"

I nodded, flicking water away from my brow. "What do I get when I win?"

He laughed, his hand pressed against his chest. "I guess you don't want one of my shirts now that you've got your own."

"Maybe I do," I said, as I fixed a teasing stare at him. "I will steal all your clothes and then you'll have to go out with Gabriel."

"You have to beat me first."

I took off under the water, holding my breath and racing toward the other end. There was no point in waiting for him to say go.

It didn't take him long to break my lead and he touched the other side quickly enough to straighten up out of the water and lean against the edge on his elbows as if he'd been waiting for me for hours. When I came up on the other side, I made sure to splash him more.

Victor was in the corner, leaning against the wall. He tilted his head at us. "What's this?"

"Racing," Nathan said. He turned to me. "And I get all the strawberries off your smoothie when we go out next."

Victor's eyebrows shot up. "Betting?"

"Hell, yeah," Gabriel said, coming up next to us. He held his arms above his head and stretched. I got a better view of his abs. His shorts slid down his hips, stopping at the curve of his butt. "What's the winner get?"

I laughed, shaking my head. "It's whatever you want."

"You better watch that," Victor warned, but he smiled

and got into a racing position against the wall. "Asking for whatever we want might be more than you're willing to give up."

"Hey," Nathan said, a warning tone in his voice.

This seemed to confuse Victor, but he shook his head dismissively. "Are we going?"

I kicked off with my legs. The others shot off but it was Nathan who won again.

"Ha!" he said, his laugh cutting through the air. He pointed at my face. "I get shotgun next time."

I smirked and stuck my tongue out at him.

"Well this will suck a lot if Nathan wins every time," Gabriel said, pouting.

"He might not," I said, slipping him a wink. He caught it and made a devilish grin.

This time I took off again, but I didn't swim my fastest. Instead I waited for Nathan to get close and I grabbed him around the waist, using what little power I had to push him out of his projected forward motion. He grinned at me under the water, catching me around the hips and stood up, breaking the surface.

I struggled and pushed against his arms. I laughed, breathless.

"You little cheater," he said as Gabriel tagged the other side, winning.

"It's not cheating if you don't set the rules," I said.

"I won," Gabriel shouted at us from the other side of the pool. He pointed in my direction. "And I get your damn clip for an entire week."

I gaped at him. "And I bothered to help you! I want it while we're swimming."

"After," he said.

"And why does everyone want my stuff?" I asked, pushing against Nathan again who was still holding on to me.

They all laughed at me.

Nathan hefted me up over his head. "Get ready for it,"

he said.

I held my breath as he tossed me easily across the pool. I landed with a splash, catching Victor in the face with water.

I swam to the surface, laughing. Victor had his arm raised to ward off the splashing. His fire eyes smoldered and a pleased smile played across his face.

Gabriel cannonballed into the water and popped up next to me. "Okay, I have to see you do one of those."

I splashed at him, thinking he was joking. He came after me with a wicked grin. I scrambled to get out of the way, running against the resistance of the pool.

Victor stepped in front of me, and we collided. My hands pressed to his chest in an effort to keep myself from falling over. "Tell him I don't have to?"

Victor laughed; his arms encircled my bare middle and nearly lifted me out of the water as he tugged me toward the wall. "No," he said. "I want to see it, too."

Gabriel climbed out of the water. I wriggled against Victor, who held onto me easily with a strength I wasn't expecting. Gabriel took me from Victor.

Gabriel carried me until we were standing at the edge of the middle of the pool where the water was the deepest. Nathan and Victor sat together on the deck at the other end, their feet in the water.

Nathan cupped his hands together and shouted, "Make a bigger splash than Gabriel, and you get your clip back."

I brightened.

"No fucking way," Gabriel said.

"What if you win?" I asked him.

His blue eyes glowed at this. He leaned into me to whisper in my ear. "I get that clip forever."

My heart stopped and my breath escaped. "Hmm," I said, pretending to ponder it. "And it's whoever does an awesome cannonball splash, right?"

He nodded, his crystal eyes still intense on me. His back was to the pool. I placed a casual hand on his chest. His eyes lit up again.

"You're on," I said.

And I pushed at him as hard as I could.

His face popped in surprise and he grappled for my arm. It was too slippery to hold onto and he fell back into the water in a mess.

I did a sloppy cannonball next to him, but used the momentum to swim to the other end of the pool under the water before Gabriel could grab on to me.

Nathan stood up on the edge of the pool, laughing. Gabriel was catching up to me. I reached out for Nathan. He snagged my hands and hauled me from the water until I was on my feet next to him.

"No fair," Gabriel said. "She fucking cheats."

"Yup," Nathan said, beaming proudly as he kept a hand on my back, fingers spread over my bare skin. It warmed me and yet my insides were doing flips.

Gabriel swiped his hands at my ankles. "Get back here."

I laughed, squealing and leaping out of reach. Nathan looped an arm under my knees and carried me. I threaded my arms around his neck to hang on. He started running from the pool. Gabriel flew onto the patio, giving chase.

"Hey!" A voice boomed over the sound of our laughter. "Don't run with her like that."

Nathan stopped cold and stiffened. He let go of my legs to let me stand but still held my waist.

We turned together to see North coming through the front gate near the side of the house. His black tank shirt and his dark blue jeans were dusty. He carried a couple of overstuffed book bags on his back.

Behind him from the gate stepped Silas, Luke and Kota, similarly dusty. As they looked at us, shyness sparked through my core. I slipped a finger to my lower lip, blushing as their eyes fell on the pink plaid miniskirt bathing suit.

"Sang baby, don't let them do that to you," North said. "He's going to slip and crack your head."

"Well look who all decided to show up," Gabriel said behind us. He hooked his arm around my neck even as Nathan still held onto my hip. Gabriel pressed his side against mine, which in turn made me lean against Nathan. Skin on skin.

My core vibrated.

"We came to make sure you weren't dead," Kota said. His eyes hadn't left my body but he smiled as he touched a forefinger to the corner of his glasses. "No one checked in but I can see why."

My cheeks heated again. "Sorry."

Gabriel chopped at my head. "Shut up. You're not sorry."

"I'm not?"

He smirked, and tugged at my arm. "Let's do it, Nathan."

Nathan seized me around the stomach and Gabriel snatched up my legs. They held me tightly so that even as I squealed and laughed and tried to break free, they hauled me up over their heads. They walked over to the pool and shifted until I was hanging above the ground. Nathan had a hold of my wrists and Gabriel had my ankles and they started swinging me like I was a hammock between them.

"One," Nathan shouted.

I drifted precariously over the water.

"Don't..." North bellowed at them.

"Two," Gabriel said.

There was no three. I flew, splashing into the water sprawled out on my back. I twisted under the surface and swam for the other end of the pool. I pulled my body hard against the water resistance, using an arm motion Nathan had showed me before to get to the end. I slapped the deck with my hand. Nathan had been on my heels but he was too late.

"I win," I said, making a face at him. It wasn't a real race, I knew. I just wanted to say it.

"Shit," he said, but he didn't look at all disappointed.

The new arrivals disappeared into Nathan's house.

When they came back out, I was up in Nathan's arms about to get flung across the pool. I only caught a glance of them all in bathing suits before I started flying. I hit the water, letting myself sink to touch bottom.

I felt the water shift. Silas came at me, wrapped his arms around my stomach and hauled me up until I was cradled in his arms.

"Hi Silas," I said in a soft voice, oddly shy again as his big hands held me, hugging me. My bare, soft stomach met with his hard muscles.

"Hi *aggele mou*," he said. His wet black hair stuck to his forehead. A droplet slid down against his cheek. "Miss us?"

I brightened. "Yup."

"Well, we've got all night."

My fingers traced my parted lips. "What do you mean?"

"Don't you know? Erica said to come over and we're all hanging out tonight."

Was that what she meant? "You mean sleeping over?"

He laughed, nodding.

My heart beat wildly at the thought of spending the entire night out with all of the guys. Were they sure we could? I was having so much fun now that I was completely forgetting my parents and everything that had happened. I checked the others to see if they had been listening and looking for confirmation.

North, Luke and Kota stood in the pool. They were talking together at one end with Victor, Nathan and Gabriel.

At first I was distracted because it was the first time I had seen Kota without a shirt. I was thrown into near shock. He seemed just as well-built as the others. Why had I thought before that he was weaker or was it just the almost geek-like stereotype he resembled? He was almost as defined as Nathan, but slightly slimmer, smoother.

Then it was seeing them altogether with their shirts

off. I felt myself taking in a slow breath, in awe of their bodies, their striking handsomeness. How in the world did I end up friends with them? It felt like an eternity had passed since the first day and I had forgotten where this started. I felt so out of place compared to their shocking good looks and various talents. Plain Sang didn't belong.

After I had gotten my eyeful of them, I overheard my name being mentioned and I strained to hear.

Silas lifted me a little higher in his arms. "So do you really want to fly?"

My eyes popped open and I grinned wickedly. I knew this was a distraction, but I was too excited to care. "How?"

He let go of me until I was standing next to him. He backed up until he could stand waist-deep in the water and positioned his hands out in front of himself as if he wanted to give me a boost. "Put both of your feet in my hands," he said.

I dropped my hands onto his broad shoulders. My fingertips tingled at the touch of his bare skin. I slipped a foot into his hands, and pushed myself up until I could get the other one next to it. He wrapped his fingers around my feet.

"Bend your knees a little," he said as he lifted me slightly out of the water.

I wobbled, mostly due to nerves, and my hands gripped at his shoulders.

"I've got you," he said. His face floated close to my belly. I sucked in my stomach but steadied as he used his shoulder to bolster me at my thighs. "I'm going to move down into the water and push you up and out. You should get ready to jump from my hands at the same time. Push yourself off."

I let out a slow breath as he grasped my feet. He slipped into the water until it was up to his shoulders.

I bent my knees slightly, waiting.

"Ready?"

"No," I said in a tiny voice. I shut my eyes and

squealed. “Do it.”

He grunted as he lifted, shoving me up to boost me into the air.

“God damn it, Silas,” North yelled as I put my full energy into jumping from Silas’s hands.

I was flying. I somersaulted, flipping over until I hit the water with my knees, almost upright.

I surfaced and could hear Gabriel hooting. The others laughed. North tried to give me an angry eyeball, but he was grinning.

Gabriel backed away from the others and stepped to the edge of the pool. He jumped, doing a full front flip and shallow dive, zooming under the water toward me.

I scrambled to get behind Silas thinking Gabriel was after me again. Gabriel surfaced, nodded at Silas and they did that silent communication.

“Watch this,” Gabriel said. He positioned himself like I had done in Silas’s hands. In a flash he was up in the air, light as a feather, flipped twice and landed smoothly into the middle of the pool.

My mouth was open; I was impressed by the acrobatics.

“I can do better,” Luke shouted. “Let’s do it at the same time, Sang. Gabriel, you push her in the air.”

“Shit, make them stop, Kota,” North said.

“I think there’s enough of us around to make sure they aren’t going to drown,” Kota said calmly.

North huffed but slipped into the water. He eyed me intently and swam toward me.

His wide shoulders parted the water in a wave. The line of coarse hair starting from his black bathing suit and ending above his belly had me hypnotized.

He hooked an arm out, and grabbed my waist to drag me with him in the water until we were next to Silas. “If anyone’s going to, I’ll do it. Make sure you don’t break your head.”

North boosted me in his hands like Silas had done.

Again I sucked in my stomach as North's warm breath teased my belly button. Silas lifted his hands again for Luke. Luke grabbed Silas's shoulders and hauled himself out of the water.

"Ready?" North asked. His dark eyes focused on my face.

I squealed a little. "Okay."

North counted off with Silas and I was flung into the air. Luke did a double flip and I managed simply to twist and flip almost completely over. I crashed into the water, bobbing up and laughing.

North swam up to me, catching me by the hips. My arms instinctively wrapped around his neck and he held me against his body. "You okay?"

I started to nod, trying to assure him I was fine, but my eyes caught on something over his head.

A face was looking in at us over the fence.

North caught where I was looking. He pulled me down again into the water, turning to block me from view of whoever it was, covering the side of my head with his big hand to pull me closer to him.

Gabriel shot out of the water and raced toward the fence. The face disappeared. Gabriel caught the edge of the fence and scaled it, hanging off of the top to look over. His head twisted to watch whoever it was and then he dropped down again, walking back toward the pool.

"It was Danielle," he said. "She ran off."

North grunted near my ear and his arm tightened around my hips. "I'm getting really tired of her."

♥♥♥

Kota was insistent that we not worry about Danielle. I wondered why she was spying on us or how she knew we were there. Was Marie with her? Would she tell our mom?

Despite my questions, everyone obeyed Kota. It wasn't mentioned again.

It was easy to lose track of time swimming with the

others. Silas, North and Nathan took turns flipping us and each other. Victor and Kota chose to stay out of the water most of the time, watching us with their feet dangling into the pool. On occasion they gave instructions to us on how to do it better or offered a challenge.

When I was exhausted, I swam up next to Kota, pulling myself up to sit next to him. Without his glasses, his green eyes sparkled.

"Hi," he said, the friendly smile warm and inviting. "Having fun?"

I nodded, breathless. "I can't flip as high as the others."

"It's practice," he said. "You have to work at it."

I laughed, shaking my head. "When am I ever going to get to practice?"

He brought his face close until his forehead was touching mine. "You ask nicely."

I blushed. "Are you going to swim?"

"I thought you were flipping."

"I haven't raced you yet," I said. "I've been flipping so much I'm dizzy. Let's just swim."

He chuckled. "Are you sure you want to race me?"

Victor nudge Kota's arm. "It's a trap. If you win, you get a favor or something and she totally cheats."

"Shhh," I said. "Don't tattle."

Victor smirked back at me. "You're lucky I haven't won yet."

"Let's go," I said. "You can't win if you don't race." I splashed into the water again, reaching a hand out for his.

His fire eyes ignited. His hand drifted out toward mine. I grabbed it and tugged lightly. He slipped into the water.

I glanced over at Kota. "Ready?" I stretched my free hand out to him.

His smile looked strange to me and I didn't quite understand it. He clutched my hand, his fingers enveloping mine. He pushed himself off into the water and kept hold on to my hand.

I was holding both of their hands at the same time. I laughed, trying to deflect feeling awkward. Friends touch, I kept repeating in my head.

We positioned ourselves at one end of the pool. Gabriel and the others backed out of the way, giving us room.

I was in the middle, Kota to my left and Victor to my right. From what I remembered, Victor was slower than the others. I was questioning how fast Kota was. I bent my knees against the side of the pool and readied myself.

“On your mark,” Nathan shouted over the buzz of voices surrounding him.

I shot off before he finished what he was saying. I accidentally started laughing at the same time, which wasted a whole bunch of air. It felt so wrong to be cheating against Kota.

Kota started to pass me and out of desperation, I grabbed at his leg, trying to pull him backward in the water as Nathan had done to me before. I meant to distract him long enough to breeze past him. I wasn’t as strong as Nathan and my effort only caused Kota to look back at me, confused. He turned mid-stroke. He swam after me, picked me up in his arms and lifted me out of the water.

I gasped as we surfaced, squirming against him. “Hey,” I said. “We’re supposed to be racing.”

“No way,” he said. “If I’m going down, you’re going with me.” He re-gripped my waist and splashed backward into the water, sinking.

I fidgeted to get out of his grip. Those green eyes sparked, locking on me and I stilled. I didn’t completely understand the look we shared together in that moment but it was the happiest I could ever remember being. Under the water with him, my parents had faded away from my mind. The Academy’s heavy secrets disappeared. All of the worries about school and stress melted away. Here was Kota. My friend. Holding me. Laughing with me. The other guys were close by and watching over us and blocked out the rest of the world from our own little place here in

Nathan's backyard. I didn't want to be anywhere else.

Kota beeped my nose with a forefinger and released me, floating to the surface. I drifted up next to him.

When he broke out of the water, my breath caught at how the water rippled away from his broad shoulders and down his long, defined torso. Droplets traced along his high cheekbones, curving under the angle of his jaw.

His head tilted, as if he didn't understand why I was staring. I released a laugh to break the tension. He laughed with me, shaking his head.

"I told you she cheats," Victor called to us from the other side of the pool. "But that's awesome. I get the favor, now."

I sighed, grinning. "What do you want?"

His fire eyes lit up. "I'll tell you later."

♥♥♥

There were several more races. The final count: Victor's one favor plus a promise to wash his car for him, Gabriel won my clip for three months, Luke wanted to go shopping with me next time we were going and I was shocked he fully expected there to be a next time. North won one day where I was to work alongside him at the diner, Nathan won every strawberry from my smoothies for the rest of my life, Silas wanted a hug, and Kota made me promise to sit next to him at lunch for the next three weeks. I won squat, but I did like the hug.

The last race was who was going to make dinner that night. We all gathered on one side of the pool. By now they all knew I openly cheated and they all worked together to stop me. This time I simply had to not be last. The last person was chef for the evening.

Somehow I ended up in the middle. They forced me to wait until someone actually shouted "go" before we took off. Little did they know I was going to play fair. It was part of the strategy. I expected to throw them all off thinking I was getting ready to tackle them and instead would zip across the water.

North counted off and when he shouted "go", I ducked under the water, putting my full effort into the strokes. Several bodies pulled ahead but Nathan and Kota kept pace with me. It confused me because I knew out of all the swimmers there, those two were the fastest. Kota was the only one who could match Nathan for speed.

When we crossed the halfway point and we were almost at the end. Kota flung himself sideways and snatched me around the waist. This caught me off-guard and I sputtered, losing the air I had in my lungs. He quickly hauled me out of the water.

"Ugh!" I shouted at him, smacking at his arms around my stomach. "Cheat... cheat..."

"Yup," he said.

Nathan stopped, too. He gathered my legs, holding them as I tried to kick to break free. "Ready?" he said.

"On three," Kota said.

"Wha--" I gasped but I was already in the air as they held me over their heads.

"One, two, three," Kota spit out.

They tossed me into the air. I splashed back into the starting end of the pool on my side. I cleanly touched bottom and drifted to the surface. I swished my legs to keep afloat, laughing.

All of the boys perched themselves on the edge of the pool, wearing matching grins.

They had chosen who was going to cook dinner.

♥♥♥

After I managed to crawl out of the pool, I was handed a towel. They gathered on Nathan's back porch. There was a collection of outdoor benches and poolside chairs clustered into a circle under the overhanging roof. A wicker fan squeaked as it worked, spinning over our heads.

I sat between Nathan and Kota on one of the benchess.

Gabriel was telling Kota and the others about the day.

I buried my face behind Nathan's shoulder when Gabriel mentioned the waiter who had openly flirted with me and how I had reacted at the end.

"What did he say to you anyway?" Gabriel asked.

I blushed, and picked my head up. "He said you were all nice and wanted us to come back soon," I said sarcastically.

They all laughed but Kota dropped an arm around my neck, tugging me to lean against him. "No really," he said. "What did he say?"

I sighed. "He said when I get over being told what to do by..." I hesitated because I didn't want to say it out loud, "by losers to call him."

"Huh," Victor said, grunting. He readjusted himself in a green lawn chair across from us. His fire eyes flickered.

"I don't know what he meant," I said. How could some stranger ever understand me or what the others were doing for me and continued to do for me?

"I do," Victor said. He folded his arms across his chest as he sat back in the chair. "It's partially my fault, I guess. I was pushing you to get things you really wanted."

"Naw," Nathan said. "He was flirting with her from the start."

"He only got persistent after I ordered for her. It doesn't excuse his behavior. I wasn't beating her or belittling her so he should have backed off."

"Did you tip him?" Kota asked.

Victor frowned. "Yes."

There was a collective tilting of heads, eyebrows going up.

"Why would you do that?" Kota asked.

"I left him an exact fifteen percent," he said simply. "He was probably expecting nothing. Instead I wanted to let him know he was just the help, and nothing more to us." His smoldering fire eyes met mine, and it rattled me. "I've never done that to anyone in my life."

♥

RUNWAY

When we had dried off enough that we weren't going to drip all over Nathan's house, we went inside so we could change. I stood near the table in the kitchen with the others as Gabriel and Victor snuck off to change first.

My limbs were tired and I started to lean my cheek against Silas's bicep as I was feeling drowsy. He dropped his arm around my shoulders, pulling me so I could lean my head against his chest.

"I can't believe you got her all this," Kota said, scanning the bags on the table. "I thought Victor said you would take her shopping. I didn't know he meant buy her the mall."

My face flamed. It was too much! Why hadn't Victor or the others stopped?

"She didn't have anything," Nathan said. "We weren't adding to stuff she already had. She was starting over. Besides, Gabriel picked it all out."

North's eyes fell on the Victoria's Secret bags. "All of it?"

There was a rattling at the bathroom door and Gabriel strolled out wearing dark blue Levi's jeans and a green V-neck shirt. There were new green studs in his lobes, the usual three black rings remained at the upper part of his ear. He clapped his hands together and tugged one of the bags closer to peek inside. "In this pile somewhere is what Sang is wearing tonight."

I blinked at him, blushing. "Tonight?"

He laughed. “You’ve gotta show off, Trouble. They’re going to want to see it.” He shifted through the bags. “Find yourself some underwear.”

The others left to go change. Victor came out wearing a pair of Calvin Klein jeans and a red Polo shirt. He raided Nathan’s fridge for another coffee and snapped it open. He slid up next to me, handing me the bottle. I took a couple of sips and passed it back for him to finish. I reveled in the idea that he knew what I needed before I knew.

Gabriel found what he wanted and gathered the bags. “Ready?” he asked me.

I picked up a Victoria's Secret bag and waited with him outside the bathroom. Luke strolled out, wearing a fresh pair of jeans and a towel twisted around his blond hair, no shirt. He smiled at me as Gabriel went into the bathroom to put the bags down on the counter.

“Going to let him dress you?” Luke asked. “Can I help?”

“Get out of here,” Gabriel barked at him.

Luke winked at me and poked me in the stomach, making me jump. I smirked, swatting at his hand. He laughed and walked off, rubbing the towel at his head.

Gabriel dragged me inside the bathroom and shut the door. He dug out one of the shorter black skirts from the bags and splayed it out on the counter. It had lace layers on the outside. I remembered it because he had asked me to spin when I tried it on and the lace material feathered up as I moved.

He hung up a more modest black t-shirt with quarter sleeves and a hot pink stripe across the stomach. “Okay,” he said. “Put on the underwear and the skirt and shirt. Call me back in here when you’re done. I’ll wait outside.”

“What are we doing?” I asked. Couldn’t I just put it on and throw some shoes on and go?

“It’s runway time,” he said. He patted me on the cheek. “We’re going to show the guys your new look.”

I bit my lip as he left. I made sure to lock the door

behind him just in case he decided to pop his head in.

I picked out a pair of black boy-cut panties with hot pink hearts all over them and one of the black bras. I squeezed on the skirt and tried my best to slip the shirt on without getting it too wet; my hair was still damp.

When I had it on, I unlocked the door and opened it a crack, calling out for Gabriel. He filled the doorway, blocking Luke and Victor as they peered in from over his shoulder. Gabriel shut the door in their faces and cursed at them before turning on me. His eyes glided over my body and his face lit up.

"Yeah," he said. "That's hot."

"Are you sure I should wear this over to Kota's?" I asked. It seemed a little more dressed up than I was expecting for the evening.

"It's perfect," he said. "Stop worrying." He dropping a small duffle bag onto the counter and he searched it for a hairbrush and blow dryer. The blue plastic of the dryer had "Coleman" written on it in black permanent ink and looked ancient. "Sit," he said, snapping his fingers at the toilet.

I perched on the closed toilet seat and let him brush out and dry my hair. He applied some leave-in conditioner with a heady scent that made me want to sneeze. He added volume to my hair, brushed it straight, and removed what little wavy curls I had. He dug out a single black bobby pin to tuck locks of hair behind my ear and out of my eyes on one side. When he was satisfied, he backed away, head tilting as he considered his work.

"Stand up," he commanded.

I stood and he had me perch on top of the cabinet this time. He fished out a pair of thigh high socks from one of the clothing bags and opened the box. He tenderly lifted my foot, placing my heel on his thigh as he rolled and readied the sock and slipped it over my foot. I was blushing, embarrassed that it really felt like he was dressing me.

He smoothed his palms over my thighs when the socks were on, as if testing if they might unroll or slide down. I watched his face as he did it, looking so serious like he had a vision of what this would look like in the end and he was working so hard to make sure it happened. I was breathless, not wanting to disappoint him.

A soft knocking rattled the door in the frame. "Hurry up, you all," Luke said. "We want to see."

"Fuck off," Gabriel said. He opened a box of high heeled boots. He unzipped the side of one, tucking fingers around my ankles to push my toes into the shoes.

I gripped the side of the counter to hang on as he angled my feet in and zipped up.

When they were on, he planted a palm on either side of my hips. "Hop down," he said.

I let him pick me up and place me on the floor. I wobbled in the heels.

"Step back," he said.

I did with my palms pressed to my thighs, fingering the lace of the skirt and trying not to sway in the boots.

His lips parted, his eyes losing the determined look, and brightened into that crystal blue. He made a low whistle. "Perfect."

"Gabriel..."

He went to his bag, pulling out a tube of lip gloss and a small, brown, unidentifiable bottle. He placed the bottle on the counter and opened up the lip gloss. He pointed the brush tip toward my lips. "Pretend you're kissing me," he said, smirking.

A giggle escaped my mouth but I tried to pout my lips at him.

He laughed. "Fuck me, you've never kissed shit."

"Hey!"

He squeezed my cheeks together until I was making a fish face. He applied the lip gloss. He mimicked a move with his lips as if I should press my lips together, so I did. He rewarded me with a pleased smile. "One more thing." He threw the lip gloss back into the bag and picked up the bottle of liquid on the counter. He held it up for me. "I think this is you."

I lifted an eyebrow at him, unsure of what he was talking about.

He uncorked the bottle and held it close to my face. "What do you think?"

I blinked in surprise at him but he held it up toward my nose. I breathed in the fragrance; a soft musk with a fruit and sweet undertone. Just the scent of it left me feeling excited and soothed at the same time. "I love it."

He beamed, picking up my wrist to get me to hold it up. He dabbed the perfume onto his fingers, dropping some on each of my wrists and then at my neck.

"Forgive me," he said. He leaned in to me close enough to put his nose to my neck and breathed in. When he drew back, his eyes rolled in his head and he sighed. "Oh yeah. That's it."

"Where did you get it?" I asked quietly.

"I made it."

I tilted my head at him. "You? You make perfume?" Is that why he often smelled different every time I came near him? Did he experiment?

He smiled. "Sang, you don't know the half of it." He brushed his fingers through my hair again, nearly combing the new fragrance into it. He made me twirl once more. When I finished, he nodded, satisfied. "I'm going to step out and close the door. I'm going to pull those bozos in into the kitchen. Don't come out until I come to get you. Okay?"

"Okay."

He winked at me and had me stand behind the door so the others couldn't peek in. He stepped outside, cursing at Luke who tried to wriggle past him.

As I waited for Gabriel, I checked myself in the mirror. The girl that stared back was a surreal look-a-like from what I'd looked this morning. My hair was the same chameleon color, straighter and silky. I had the same small nose and the same green eyes. The lip gloss was a tea rose pink, and matched the blush that swept over my cheeks and nose. The skirt's lace swayed when I wobbled on the heels. Still, it was moderately conservative. With the socks high on my thighs, I was only showing maybe four inches of my skin. The style was playful and cute. There was something else in the black as well, and the boots. I wanted to say dangerous. Was that who I was?

Gabriel popped his head back in. "You ready?"

I released a puff of air. "No," I said, but moved forward anyway. I wanted to get this over with.

Gabriel walked ahead of me, blocking my entrance into the kitchen. I spotted North and Silas first from over Gabriel's shoulder. They were leaning against the far wall, heads tucked together as they talked. They turned their eyes on us, and they smirked in a way that told me they had seen this a hundred times before; Gabriel liked to make an entrance with his live dolls.

Gabriel side stepped.

I tiptoed forward to stand next to him, my eyes on the gray tiled kitchen floor. No matter how I tried, the smile wouldn't leave my face. I resisted the urge to touch my lip, afraid of smudging the lip gloss.

A gasp drew my curiosity and I glanced up.

Heads were tilted, eyes were wide, mouths were open, all except Gabriel, who grinned like a madman.

At first I was worried they were horror struck that such a plain girl was all dressed up and that I looked ridiculous. Silas swallowed, his Adam's apple bobbing and his lips parting again, his eyes narrowing on my boots and up again to the clothes and my face. Victor's eyes erupted into a wildfire, sweeping over and over again along my body. Nathan whistled in a low tone. Luke's head tilted in the other direction, and remained perfectly still as he stared. North roughed his fingers through his hair and away from his forehead. Kota's cheeks were red and he mumbled something, but with my heart thundering in my ears I couldn't catch it.

Gabriel was beaming. He hooked an arm around my

neck to pull me close. "That's the best reaction I've gotten out of them yet," he said. "We should have picked you up a long time ago."

Kota swallowed. "I'm not sure she should wear that to school. If Danielle wanted your clothes before, she'll rip them from your body, now."

"School?" North asked. "I don't know if I want her leaving this house."

♥

Time Off For Good Behavior

The guys collected our bags to walk over to Kota's house. The new clothes were to remain on Nathan's table for now. Gabriel only took out pajamas for that evening and a set of shorts and a t-shirt for the next morning. I wasn't sure how Gabriel took over the decision of what I wore, but it seemed so important to him and I didn't have the heart to question it. Part of me was grateful. I was always unsure of the right thing to wear and Gabriel's decisions lightened my burdened mind. I already felt guilty that Victor bought the clothes. Letting Gabriel make decisions about them eased that. They weren't my clothes. They were ours. Sort of.

The skirt did feel amazing. The lace tickled my thighs when I walked.

Gabriel wanted to walk over in front of Danielle's house to parade me like a model in case she was watching. Kota and the others didn't want to egg her on.

I was beside Nathan as we trailed behind the others. I stopped in the street, and glimpsed at my home down the road. Nathan paused, following my gaze to the two story gray house.

"I already checked on your mom," he said, reading my thoughts. He wrapped his hand around mine, and tugged me toward Kota's. "There was an empty soup cup by her bed. She was asleep. I made sure to leave some crackers for her. Marie wasn't there."

My eyebrows popped up. "You did all that?"

He nodded. "Luke checked on her while we were at the mall, too. She's fine."

"Maybe I shouldn't sleep over," I said softly, unsure if I wanted the others to hear. "My dad isn't there. Should she be alone?" It felt wrong to abandon her. A couple of hours out, that was different. Usually my father came home in the evening and was there on the weekends to watch out for her. Now he wouldn't be. Despite her mood swings, she was still sick, dying. What if she needed something in the middle of the night and no one was there?

Nathan's blue eyes darkened and he squeezed my hand. "I'll check on her again tonight. I promise. Okay? Try not to worry about it."

"If you're sure," I relented. She wasn't his responsibility. Was it selfish to let him so I could enjoy the night out?

His serious face lightened. "You're too sweet for your own damn good."

My cheeks warmed again as he tugged my hand, holding it.

We were almost to Kota's drive when North paused, turned around and faced the opposite side of the road. He cupped his hands around his eyes against the sun's glare.

I turned, as did Nathan. Everyone stopped.

Micah and Tom were headed down the road together behind us. Tom was waving. Micah looked annoyed. Behind them trailed Jessica. I wondered if they were actually friends, but I realized that on this small street, those boys might be the only kids her age within walking distance. Or maybe she was friends with Tom. He seemed nice.

Their group caught up with us. "What are you guys doing?" Tom asked, and he eyeballed me. "Is there a school dance or something?"

Gabriel smirked. "Not tonight."

Jessica shared a look with me, and a small smile. I

took it to mean she liked the clothes. It made me feel a little more comfortable in them. "You're staying the night?" she asked.

"Yes, I think so. Aren't you?"

She shook her head. "I'm waiting on a ride to my other friend's house. I'd stay but I promised her two weeks ago I'd go to her sleepover."

She didn't think anything was wrong with me sleeping with the guys at her house. That made me feel better, too.

Micah blew a raspberry. "That's it? You're sleeping at Kota's? She made it sound like you were doing something kinky."

Kota lifted an eyebrow. "She who?"

"Danielle," Micah said. "She was going to pay us twenty dollars to come take a photograph of Sang and you all being stupid."

Silent communication flew between faces of the boys. A photo?

"I think she meant to put her on Facebook," Tom said. "Or maybe Photoshop her face onto a pig or something. I wasn't going to take a horrible one."

"You guys are the worst spies," Luke said. "Don't you know if you're going to take secret photos that you're not supposed to tell?"

"I don't care," Micah said. "I was going to take one picture. It's all high school drama to me. Personally, I couldn't care less. Danielle's stupid."

I looked at the guys, but it was Nathan who caught my glance. His expression mimicked my own concern. This wasn't just stealing my clothes. This sounded more like she didn't like me at all and was trying to get… revenge? I didn't understand why.

"Jessica," Kota said, disappointment dripping from his tone. "I can't believe you'd agree to this."

"I wasn't there," Jessica said. "I was leaving the church and when I walked past on my way home, she stopped talking to them. She wouldn't talk to me."

"Here," Luke said. He pulled out a wallet from his back pocket, unfolded four twenties, and passed two to Micah and two to Tom. "I'll pay you both double to take a picture of someone's butt and tag Danielle on Facebook."

Tom brightened, taking the money. "I bet I can get Derrick to post it on a day she isn't able to log in. Maximum exposure."

"Then it'll be your butt on her page," Micah said. "But fine. We'll do that." He turned around, heading back down the road. Tom followed. Jessica stayed with us.

"Should we be pranking her like this?" Victor asked.

"Probably not," Kota said, but he turned, heading back toward his house. "But I let her get away with stealing Sang's clothes. This will show her we're not going to sit by idly any more. If she wants to humiliate Sang in some way, she'll have to take on all of us, too."

The others muttered in agreement.

My heart thumped, and I tried to smother the feeling that I was very happy about this decision.

Kota led the way to his front door, pulling his keys out of his pocket and unlocking it. He entered and held it open for us to join him in the foyer. Jessica floated past all of us, heading down the hallway to her room.

"Kota?" his mother called from deep in the house. "Is that you guys?"

Nathan released my hand. My fingertips tingled as he had held on so tightly, but I wondered why he let go as soon as Kota's mother sounded close. Was it bad we were holding hands?

"It's us," Luke called to her. "We're home."

I smiled at the thought of him saying it as if we all lived there together.

Erica came out from a hallway. Her green eyes lit up and she smiled. She reached out and wrapped her arms around Luke's neck, who was the closest, and kissed his cheek. He air kissed hers and stood back. She did the same with everyone, lastly me.

When she finished hugging me, she stepped back, still

holding on to my hands and looking over the clothes I was wearing.

"Oh my goodness," she said. "You are adorable."

"Gabriel," I tried to explain, but it felt awkward to finish the sentence. He helped me buy the clothes? He dressed me?

Erica shook her head and pressed fingers to her lips quickly. "Oh yeah, he's good. This is gorgeous." She hugged me again and whispered in my ear. "I'm so glad you're here."

I blinked rapidly, trying not to tear up. Did she mean it? Was I really wanted?

She stepped back and we moved into the living room together. Our bags were dropped against the far wall. Silas and North sunk into the couch. The others took the floor with Kota and Luke disappearing. Loud thudding thundered from Kota's stairwell. They returned with huge bean bag chairs.

"All right," Gabriel said. "It's about f... time." He glanced at Erica, but relaxed when she didn't appear to notice the slight slip.

The beanbags were all the same dark blue color, big enough to sit two people and they were about as high up off the ground as the couch. It took a couple of trips to get all four downstairs. The coffee table was moved against another wall beside the bookshelves to make room.

I wasn't quite sure where to sit until Silas scooted over on the couch and patted the seat next to him. I sat down between him and North, feeling oddly tiny next to them.

"Okay, kids," Erica said over the chatter. Everyone else collapsed into the bean bag chairs and quieted. "Quick rule check. Since Sang's here, we have to change it up slightly."

"Aw man," Gabriel said, but he was grinning.

"Everyone sleeps downstairs tonight," she said, pointing to the blue carpet. "Not that I don't trust you boys, but I want Sang to be comfortable. Besides, I don't know if all eight of you will fit upstairs together."

I leaned into Silas. "Do you all do this often?"

Silas nodded. "Either here or at Victor's house. The rest of us have small rooms in our houses so it's kind of tough with all of us."

"Also," Erica continued. "If I hear from Sang you guys are picking on her, I'll beat you senseless. She's a girl so treat her like a lady."

There was a collection of giggles.

"Other than that, the house is yours. I know it is still kind of early but what do we want for dinner?"

"Sang has to make it," Nathan said. "She lost."

"They cheated," I said, but they all laughed. I did, too.

"That's good," Erica said and she winked at me. "Since you have to cook, you get to pick. We'll worry about it later." She waved her hand in the air as if dismissing us. "Other than that, try not to break anything expensive and..."

"Don't set the house on fire," they all chorused.

My eyes widened and I looked at Silas.

"Long story," he said.

Maybe I was a little jealous that they had spent all these years together and I was just starting to get to know them all. Would I ever know these tiny secrets they shared?

Erica said she'd be in her room and to call on her if she was needed. She disappeared down the hallway. Jessica appeared a second later and barely waved to us as she headed out the front door. She had an overnight bag attached to her shoulder, so I guessed she was leaving for her sleepover. I was going to be alone with the boys.

Kota found the remote to the television and the others were trying to decide if they wanted to watch something or play a video game.

North stretched and settled back into the couch, his arm going around my shoulder. Had he waited until Kota's mother was gone to do it?

North sniffed at the air and leaned toward me. He pushed his nose to my neck and he inhaled deeply. "What is that?" he asked, sitting back. His intense dark eyes and the curl of his lips made my insides twist.

"Something Gabriel made."

"What is it?" Silas asked. He put his nose to my neck and breathed in. "It's sweet. Soft." He straightened again. "It's a good match."

My cheeks tingled with heat. "How's the diner going?" I asked, deflecting.

"It's missing a couple of walls now," North said. "The freezer is installed. We're waiting on the delivery of some little things and we need an inspection. Needs new paint. We should be up and running in a couple of weeks."

"Can I help?"

He turned his head to me, his dark eyes curious. "Willingly?"

I smirked. "I think I can hold a paintbrush better than a sledge hammer."

They both laughed.

"We'll call you if we need help," North said. "Besides, you do owe me a day of work."

"It doesn't have to be a favor. Really. I'll come help. I'm right up the road. I can come when you want."

North's eyes softened. "Just don't get into trouble."

"She is Trouble," Gabriel said. He was on his feet and walked over to me, holding out a hand. "Come on. I want to see that skirt work."

I didn't quite understand what he meant, but I let him take my hand and stood up, wobbling slightly on the heels of the boots. Gabriel guided me until he was at the corner of the room where there was a stereo system. He found the power button and was flicking through CDs to pick out something to play. He found a *Relient K* album and popped it into the player. He hit the play button and twisted the volume up to 'ear ringing'.

My hands started to shake and my heart was thudding. Did he want me to dance?

Gabriel wriggled his hips and bobbed his head to the

beat. He snapped at me and slipped forward, his hands positioned on my hips. I panicked, my hands fluttered on their own to his chest. He smirked and started pushing my hips until I moved with the music at the same pace he did. Once we were dancing together, the anxiety started fading. I just swam in a bikini with these guys. What was dancing now?

Gabriel let go of my hips and I swayed to the music on my own. I bent my knees a little and swung my arms close around my head like he did.

His crystal blue eyes lit up. His lips parted and he sang along as he danced. This caught me off guard and I almost stopped moving. His voice was so smooth and beautiful. He smiled at me as he sang, reached out to put an arm around my waist and started swaying with me again. His cheek met mine; his voice filled my ears until he was the only thing I could hear.

He backed off again and I wondered where he was going. Sensing someone behind me, I spun, and nearly wobbled on my high heels, finding Luke. He grabbed my hands and danced with me, too. Nathan got up on his feet, and the four of us danced and laughed together. Nathan wasn't quite as good a dancer, but it looked like he was having fun. I felt ungraceful and ridiculous, but their smiles were encouraging. I didn't want to stop.

Luke moved away from us and came back with a CD. He popped it into the stereo. I blushed when I recognized the song.

"What's that?" Nathan asked next to me.

"Some Japanese rock," I said. "Luke stole one of my CDs."

Nathan smiled and grabbed for my hand. "Sounds good to me."

We danced to this song, too. I thought they might laugh at my music but they bobbed heads and swayed their hips. I sensed eyes on us but was terrified to look and see if North and the others were watching. I focused on Nathan, Luke and Gabriel dancing so I wouldn't feel so out of place.

The next song was different, a symphonic rock tune, slower in tempo. Nathan backed away from me and I watched him, confused as to why. A hand brushed my arm.

Victor stood behind me, fire eyes ignited.

I stilled, unsure. He took my hand in his and wrapped his arm around my waist. In time with the violins of the music that streamed from the stereo, Victor held me close to his body while he led me in the dance. My heart fluttered and I glanced down to try to avoid stepping on his feet.

"Look at me, Sang," he said in his sweet baritone voice. He let go of my hand, his fingertips tracing my chin until my gaze lifted. My face was on fire, matching the burn in his eyes. The hand touching my chin dropped to my waist. My own trembling fingers pressed to his chest. He guided me through the dance steps. His fingers smoothed across my back, fingertips traced along my ribs. My heart was melting. He was graceful, handsome.

When another song started, Kota got up and crossed the room toward us. His eyes were intent on mine. Victor and Kota shared a look that I didn't quite understand. Victor's eyes blazed, Kota's were determined. Victor let go of me and Kota took his place.

"Ready?" Kota asked.

A drift of his spicy scent filled my nose. I bit my lower lip.

Kota moved with precision. He put his hand to my lower waist, drew me close to him and guided me through the steps.

"One, two..." he counted under his breath. He pulled me to him, pushed me out and twirled me so the skirt flared, and then brought me back. I had no idea what I was doing, just following his lead. He spun me, dipped me. His hands clutched at my waist. It was way too intense. His green eyes swallowed me up. The quiet smile on his lips, the way he held me close at some points until my chest was pressed against his had me floating. I was on the toes of my boots to keep from tripping. My heart was going crazy.

When the song was over, I backed away, fanning a hand before anyone else could step up. "Okay guys," I said to them, breathless. "I can't any more... in these heels."

They all laughed.

I wobbled my way back to the couch, and fell into the seat between Silas and North. The others left the music on but moved to the bean bag chairs and grabbed Xbox controllers.

"Here," North said, patting his leg. "Put your foot up here."

He dropped a hand on my knee and brought my leg up until it was hooked over his. He unzipped the boot and tugged it off. Surprisingly, this didn't bother me in the slightest. Gabriel had dressed me, North was undressing me. Sort of. He was removing my shoes. Was I finally getting used to their touches and the way they did things for me?

While he was doing it, I was leaning against Silas. His stomach growled. I laughed. "Why didn't you tell me you were hungry?" I asked him.

"You were busy," Silas said.

"Should we get started?" North asked. He finished taking off my boots, leaving the socks on. He pushed my legs off of his knee and stood up.

"I thought I was cooking."

"You are," Silas said, standing and reaching back for me. My hand disappeared into his and he pulled me to my feet. "We're helping."

I slipped across the carpet in the socks as I followed them into Kota's kitchen. North opened the fridge, checking the contents. "We've got two pounds of ground beef. So I guess grilling burgers is out. That's not enough for all of us."

I stepped up next to him to inspect the fridge. As I did so, I pressed my cheek against his arm to look inside.

North shifted and his fingers closed around my

shoulder and pulled me in tighter next to him. “Have an idea?”

I glanced at the contents, spotting bacon and onions. “Hmm... could make a big pot of cowboy stew.”

“What’s that?”

I snagged bacon and onions and the ground beef from the fridge. I dropped them on the counter and looked around at the cabinets to try to guess where the pots were.

“What can I do?” Silas asked, his hands stuffed in his pockets as he leaned against the archway. His broad shoulders bulked against the baseball jersey he was wearing.

“Can you cut an onion?”

He smirked. “I think I can handle that.”

Within a few minutes, I had bacon sizzling at the bottom of a big pot. Silas chopped onions next to me on the counter and I was directing North to grab other ingredients.

When the bacon was finished cooking, I scooped it out onto a plate.

“Want me to drain the fat?” North offered. He hovered over me, watching as I worked.

“Nope,” I said. I motioned to Silas to bring his cut onion over and he dumped it in.

“Fat’s not healthy,” North said.

“Your brain is made of fat,” I replied. “You need fat for your brain.”

North smirked, rolling his eyes.

Silas laughed, and massaged my neck and scalp with one hand. “She’s right. She cooks and she’s smart. Let’s keep her.” His big hands were rough and not as precise as Kota’s or as soothing as Gabriel’s, but I enjoyed it.

As I cooked, Silas and North asked what I needed, and found things for me quickly. When I was almost done, I added barbeque sauce to the mix.

“How much are you adding?” North asked. “Are you measuring?”

“Not really,” I said.

"How do you know when it's enough?"

"When it tastes good." I stirred the sauce into the mixture of ground beef, bacon and beans. "There. Let it stew for a while. It'll taste better if you let it sit."

North gripped my hand over the spoon and brought it to his mouth, holding my hand as he took a bite. He let go and licked at his lips. "It's simple, but it's good."

"What are we having?" Erica asked as she came into the kitchen.

"Cowboy stew," Silas replied. "Sang's recipe."

Erica beamed. "We're going to have to get together and swap recipes."

I blushed. "I wasn't sure what else to make. There's so many people here."

Erica waved me off. "Sometimes I just order pizza for them or we grill out. We're flexible." She bent over the pot, smelling deeply. "I think I'll make cookies."

"Should we help?" Silas asked.

"Nope. You've made dinner," she said. "I'll take care of dessert. You three go have fun."

We tried to insist we could help or at least clean up, but she wouldn't allow us to remain in her kitchen.

Back in the living room, North and Silas went back to the couch. The others were playing some car race game on the big screen.

Luke was sitting alone in one of the double bean bag chairs. He waved me over to him. I slipped into the chair beside him. With the way the bean bag chairs worked, we were tilted in together, our hips touching. It felt intimate.

Luke swept a finger across my cheek and brushed a lock of hair from my face. "So how do you like it?"

I blinked at him, confused.

"I mean the chairs," he said. "The ones we got."

I'd only been sitting down for a minute, but it was cozy. "It's comfortable. I bet I could curl up in one and take a nap."

"That's perfect. We'll keep them."

I laughed, dropping my fingers across my mouth.

"Would you have kept them if I said I didn't like them?"

"Nope."

"Is my opinion that important?"

"Yes."

"But..." I hesitated, remembering what Gabriel had said about girls sometimes dissing themselves, but this was different. "I mean, what if you like them? You bought them so you should feel comfortable in them and not worry about my opinion."

"All our opinions matter," he said. "You're one of us now."

"Sang!" Gabriel's voice cut through the chatter and the game music. "Come race the cars."

A controller was tossed at us. I was teamed up with Nathan for the game, racing against Victor and Gabriel.

Nathan took one look at me and mouthed the word: *cheat*.

Easier said than done. Swimming cheating was one thing. How was I going to cheat now?

To start, I climbed away from Luke. Victor's chair was closer to the screen, and I plopped down next to him. Victor beamed. He leaned into me, his side pressed to mine. My arm, because of the way I had to hold the controller, was neatly tucked under his.

The game started and I had plenty of trouble trying to figure out the right controls. As it was, I was dead last from the start. Nathan wasn't doing too badly.

I tried bumping my car into Gabriel's, and taking dangerous cuts across the street just to block Victor, but it wasn't helping. Every move I made just pushed me further behind.

Out of desperation, I nudged my elbow into Victor, hoping to distract him.

"Hey, hey," he said in a low voice. He started nudging me back.

Well, if he's going to do it...

I moved my hand from the controller, poking him in

the stomach. His muscles flexed out of reaction. He laughed, nudging me over with his elbow and practically leaning over me, trapping my arm against my body.

He managed to take the lead in the game. I went for curling my fingers and tickling.

"Sang!" he called out, cracking up. He kept leaning on me, but I had given up trying to beat any of them so I left the controller in my lap.

My hands sought out his sides and I brushed my fingertips against his red polo shirt. "Yes, Victor?"

He grunted and dropped his controller, reaching for my hands and drawing them together until they were over my head. I struggled, but he took both wrists in one hand and his other moved over my stomach and he started to tickle.

"No!" I squealed, laughing and trying to twist and pull away from him. It didn't help. His fingers found my sides and he traced delicately along my stomach. I was howling with laughter and near tears. In order to find any relief, I was pressing myself close to him to trap his arm between us. His breath fell against my ear as he giggled.

"Hell yeah!" Nathan shouted, dropping the controller in his beanbag chair. He pumped his fist in the air. His car spun on the screen, declared the winner.

"God damn it," Gabriel said. He glared over at us. "What the hell are you guys doing?"

"She's cheating," Victor said breathlessly through his laughter. He let me go, but I was still in a fit of sniggering.

"That's my Sang," Nathan said. He leaned over in his bean bag with his hand up in the air. I slapped my palm against his for a loud high five.

"That's it," Gabriel said. "She's on my team now."

"Fine," Nathan said. "Then I get Kota."

"I'll play," Kota said. He was sitting cross-legged on the floor. He patted his palm to the spot next to him. "Sit next to me, Sang."

"Watch out," Nathan said as I pulled myself out of Victor's chair. "She'll get you. She fights dirty."

I crossed the floor and sank to my knees next to Kota,

sitting on my heels. I tried to give Kota my most innocent smile.

"She won't cheat around me," he said, his eyes narrowing at me but there was a slight curl to his lip. "She wouldn't dare."

"You get him, Sang," Gabriel ordered.

I bit my lower lip a little and grasped the controller.

When the game started, I did nothing but play, since I knew more about how the controls worked this time and I wanted to try to win. Unlike swimming where the boys were stronger and faster, video games kept us on an even field.

For a while, I was in the lead. I took a lot of risks, cutting corners with my car and driving on the wrong side of the road for extra speed bonuses. No matter how fast I was going, though, Kota was always right behind me. He was the hunter, I was the hunted.

I leaned into him, nudging my elbow into his ribs, hoping to gain a stronger lead. It made me uncomfortable that he was so close.

"Stop it," he growled at me. A smirk tilted the side of his mouth.

In the middle of the second lap, Kota's car dashed around mine, claiming first place. I thought I could retake the lead by nipping his bumper and cutting around on the opposite side of the road and then take off. He seemed to anticipate this and instead of simply trying to move faster or work around me, he half slammed his car into mine, causing me to spin out of control. My car crashed into a tree and he took off.

"Huh," I groaned at him.

He grinned but kept his eyes on the screen.

I was already far enough behind now that I wasn't going to catch up. I poked Kota in the ribs, trying to tickle him.

"Sang," he said in a warning voice. No matter how lightly I traced against his stomach, he wasn't stopping.

Just grinning.

"Do it," Gabriel said. "Get him."

I wasn't sure exactly what I was supposed to do. Tickling wasn't working. Gabriel's car was right behind Kota's. Out of desperation, I yanked the controller from Kota's hands, tossing it behind me quickly so it rolled across the carpet. I innocently returned to the game, pretending to be totally focused on it.

Silas and North hooted with laughter.

"Oh that's it," Kota said. He grabbed me around the waist and pushed me to the ground until I was on my stomach. I squealed, laughing and trying to wriggle free. He sat square on my butt, pressing my hips to the floor. He snatched my controller and tossed it away. Silas caught it, and took over my car, turning it the opposite way along the road, and purposefully smashing it into trees.

North flung Kota's controller back to him. Kota kept me pinned to the ground as he resumed the race. I tried wriggling underneath him, but as I squirmed, he briefly sunk his full weight into me and it sparked a slight sting to my still healing tailbone. I laughed, giving up and watching the rest of the race with my head propped up in my hand.

"Ugh," Gabriel shouted as Kota took the lead again.

"You have to get him now," I said from the floor.

"Are you kidding? He'll kick my ass."

"I have to do everything," I said, and I half twisted from the floor, reaching back to poke Kota square in the stomach.

"You're already in trouble, missy," Kota said, wriggling on top of me.

My poking seemed to be getting to him. I kept doing it, aiming for different spots.

He tried ignoring it but when the race was almost over, he let go of the controller long enough to reach around and land a deafening slap on my thigh.

I squealed, crying out. The guys laughed. Kota won the race.

"All right, enough," Victor said. He got up to stand by

my side. He nudged Kota with his leg. “Come on, you can’t sit on her like that.”

“She started it,” Kota said. He popped me on the leg again. I squealed again, laughing. Kota hovered over me, standing.

Victor bent over to take my hands in his and assisted me up until I was standing next to him. “Did he hurt you?”

I smiled, blushing. “No, I’m fine.” I squeezed his hand gently, trying to convince him that I was being honest.

Victor dropped a hand on my hip and lured me around so he could take a look at my leg. “She’s got a big red handprint on her now.”

“I didn’t get her that bad,” Kota insisted. “She’s not hurt. Look at her, she’s laughing.”

Gabriel stretched from his chair and poked at Kota’s knee. “You leave a bruise on my model, you’re gonna get it.”

“What’s wrong with you guys?” Kota said, losing his smile. “We’re playing.”

“Well don’t play so rough,” Victor murmured.

The air stilled around us. I glanced between Victor and Kota, not understanding the harsh stare falling between them.

“What the hell, guys?” Nathan stood up next to Kota. “We just spent two hours flinging her across the pool and now you’re all worked up over this? We’re just playing around. She’s having fun.”

“I’m fine guys,” I said softly. I wasn’t sure what was happening, but I maybe I’d taken cheating too far. “Really. Let’s just play another game.”

The silent communication zinged between all of them and I simply couldn’t keep up. I had never seen them so worked up between each other. Was it my fault? Why did I have to take things so far with Kota?

“Hey,” North bellowed. He stood up, stepping between Victor and Kota. “That’s it. Game over. Sang, in the kitchen with me. Everyone else straighten up and pick out a DVD. We're going to eat and we're going to watch a movie." North snagged my hand. He guided me away from the others. I heard some grunting, but everyone broke away to rearrange things.

North just gave orders to Kota! How did that happen?

North held on to my hand until we were in the kitchen again. He let go when we were within view of Erica, who was bent over the counter pouring no-bake chocolate cookies out onto waxed paper. "How's it going in there, guys?"

"The boys are hungry," he said. He crossed to the pot of cowboy stew and gave it a stir. "Is this done?" he asked me.

I nodded, feeling shy again. I wasn't sure where to move or what to do. My mind was whirling as to what had just happened. Were they still mad? And why did North let go of my hand in front of Erica? Why did it feel like he was hiding it? They didn't do that at school.

Erica stopped her cookie making and put the pan in the sink. She dug in a cupboard for some plastic spoons and bowls. She handed them to me. "Here," she said. "I let the boys eat in the living room when they're all here. Should we have anything else?"

"They might like some cheese or sour cream on top," I offered. I was grateful for a job to do. I stood next to North, stacking the bowls on the counter near him and putting the spoons nearby.

Erica ducked into the fridge to collect cheddar cheese and sour cream to place on the counter.

North caught my eye and whispered low enough so only I could hear. "Smile," he said.

I grimaced.

He patted my arm. "They'll be fine. Don't look so scared. Go call the guys in," he said, nodding to the doorway to the living room. "We get them fed, and they'll be in a much better mood."

I sucked in a breath and started back to the living room. Kota was calling out DVD names and the others were yay-or-nay voting.

"Ready guys?" I said, trying to test the mood in the room.

Silas jumped up from the couch, stretching and smiling. "About time," he said.

The others got up as well, but quietly. I sensed an unspoken and tender white flag hovered in the air between them.

"Where's Victor?" I asked, noticing he was missing.

"He went outside," Kota said. "Wanted some fresh air." Something in the way he said it made it sound like there was more to this than he ever wanted to say.

"I'll go get him," I said.

"Not in those socks," Gabriel said. He fell behind the others heading to the kitchen and snapped at me. He bent over, stripping the socks from my legs, balling them up and shoving them into his pocket. He tucked his head close to mine and whispered, "Be gentle with Victor." He caught my eye with his crystal blue gaze and headed toward the kitchen, leaving me puzzled as to what he meant.

The Crazy Beautiful Girl

I tiptoed out into the garage, not wanting to spook Victor. He stood alone in the driveway, half leaning on Kota's car that was parked in the corner. The sun had gone down and he stared toward the sprinkle of stars just over the crests of trees. His hands were stuffed into the pockets of his jeans. He looked so quiet and lost. I almost hated the thought of interrupting him. What happened when I left? Why was everyone being so weird?

I padded across the pavement in my bare feet, wondering where Max was and why he wasn't barking. The concrete was still warm from the day's sunshine. The air was muggy.

I closed the gap between us until I was a couple of feet away from him. "Victor?" I called softly.

He flinched and made a slow turn to face me. His deep brown eyes seem distant, but when his eyes met mine, a spark flickered. There was a tiny curl to his lips, but he lost it and instead stared at me, his face blank perfection.

What should I say? Could I pretend what happened never did? Should I just insist he come inside and eat dinner like everyone else? I remembered what Gabriel had whispered to me.

"Are you okay?" I asked in a small voice.

He huffed. "I'm fine."

Was that not the right thing to say? "Would you tell me if you weren't?"

That seemed to strike him. His eyes blazed again. "Only if you promise to tell me."

I pushed my forefingers and thumbs together in front of me as if I was holding a tiny ball between them, twisting nervously. "I don't know what to say. I feel fine. I'm a little worried about you."

He sighed. He turned away from me and looked back toward the sky.

What now? I wasn't sure if I should leave him. I didn't want to. Instead, I moved up beside him, standing to his right. I glanced up at the twinkling, trying to depict planets from stars.

"What are you thinking?" I asked.

"Mmm," he mumbled.

To lighten the mood, I thought of something I didn't really want to know. Still, Victor needed cheering up. "Maybe about some crazy girl you met at school?"

His eyebrows furrowed as he gazed down at me. "What?"

My lips trembled because I was unsure of how to approach the topic but I forced a smile. "The one you told the lady at the jewelry counter about."

The corner of his mouth lifted. "You heard that?"

"Yup," I said, looking back up at the sky to avoid his stare. I couldn't stand to see them blaze now and I wasn't sure why. "So is she nice?"

"The jewelry woman?"

"No," I said, but laughed. "The girl you like at school."

He chuckled. "She's amazing."

I reflexively looked at him and his eyes were intense on me. My fingers started quaking so I put them behind my back. "Pretty?"

"Of course."

"Have you talked to her? Did you tell her you like

her?"

"I've been trying," he said, shifting on his feet. The waves of his soft brown hair drifted in the gentle breeze that swept around us. "Sometimes I wonder if she notices. She gets a lot of attention from other people."

"Well if she doesn't, then she's an idiot," I said. Suddenly I was very uncomfortable with this. What did I know about giving advice about boys and girls? Anything I knew was from books. Nothing like that could apply to real life; I learned that much from being around them. "I mean, if you have to buy her stuff for her to realize how awesome you are, then she doesn't deserve it."

Victor's head tilted back in surprise. "You think I'm awesome?"

I laughed softly, bringing my fingers around to cover my mouth a little. "Victor," I said, perplexed that he didn't know. "You're generous and strong and look out for me and fun and um..."

"Handsome?"

I giggled, nodding. "So if what's-her-name won't talk to you, then she doesn't deserve you. So next time you see her, go talk to her."

He backed his head up, eyebrows creasing in confusion again. "What do you mean?"

I blushed. Helping out like this made my heart burn. But could I deny him my honesty? How much did I owe him for all the kind things he had done for me? "I said you should talk to her. What class is she in? She's not in Japanese or history, is she? She must not be, or at least I haven't noticed…"

His lips parted and his cheeks tinted. He blew out a sigh, shaking his head as he swept a fingertip across his eyebrow. "God, Sang. I'm such an idiot."

"What did I say wrong? I'm sorry. I was just trying to help."

He laughed, shaking his head again. He dipped his hand into his pocket and removed a square black jewelry box. He opened the lid and held the box out to me.

Inside was a small gold bracelet with a tiny heart charm.

My heart fluttered. “It’s very pretty,” I whispered.

Victor removed the bracelet from the confines of the box, and thrust the box back in his pocket. His eyes were a gentle rolling smolder. “I wanted to give this to you later,” he said. He took my wrist and with graceful fingers, he placed the bracelet on my arm. “I was never good at hanging onto gifts until the appropriate time. Besides, you’ve got all those new clothes. You need something nice to wear with them.”

My face flamed, my lips trembled. “Victor,” I whispered. I understood what he was implying but the reality didn’t want to click in my brain. He couldn’t be serious. “The girl…”

“Is beautiful, funny, and puts up with our wild, reckless group,” he said. He finished locking the bracelet on and held my hand up to let it glitter under the light from the garage. His thumb traced over the skin on the back of my hand. “And she’s the most brilliant and naive girl I’ve ever met. I’d give her anything she ever wanted to let me in. To trust me.”

A thousand words jumbled into my throat, catching just short of my lips. What did this mean? I understood then that he had intended the bracelet for me; he had meant me the whole time. My mind tried to replay the conversation we’d just had. How could I have not realized who he was talking about? I wasn’t at all ready for something like this. The bracelet felt like it was burning against my skin at the same intensity as the fire in his eyes as he begged silently for answers. I didn’t know how to respond. I didn’t know the questions.

“Hey,” a shout shattered through my awkward pause. Nathan hung from the inside garage door. “We’re going to eat it all if you don’t get in here.”

Victor grumbled. “We’re coming,” he called back.

Nathan disappeared back into the house.

I sighed. "We should eat," I said. It wasn't what I really wanted to say. There was a lot I wanted to ask. Did this mean something? Was he still my friend?

He smile softened and he took my hand, our fingers interlocking, his thumb tracing my skin. "Let's go."

As we walked back together, I fingered the bracelet on my wrist. I pressed my cheek to his shoulder.

"You're welcome, Sang."

♥♥♥

After everyone had eaten, I wanted to change into something else other than the skirt. It made it hard to sit in the bean bag chairs or on the floor. I took clothes with me upstairs to Kota's bathroom and changed into the black shorts and a soft pink t-shirt I was going to sleep in.

I leaned against the counter in Kota's bathroom, tracing the bracelet on my wrist and thinking about Victor and worrying about my mother and the thousand other fears I'd pushed to the back of my mind all day. What happens on Monday when my sister and Danielle noticed the new clothes? How would I stop Danielle from taking everything if Marie let her? What would the other students think of my new clothes, mismatched on such a plain girl? What would my mother do to me if she ever learned the truth? And why was Victor so confusing?

Everything was so far out of my control now, on the shoulders of guys from the Academy. That alone was the biggest cause for my fear. Before they invaded my life, I may not have been so free, but my life was predictable. Now I was a shattered mess, and the boys were blowing my tender shards across the floor, toward a destination I wasn't privileged to know. Academy secrets.

Maybe I would have been dead by now if they'd never intervened. I wasn't ungrateful. I really liked them and hoped this family thing was true. I didn't understand how it worked. Would I ever?

I folded the clothes I had taken off and ran back

downstairs to avoid collapsing in on myself from all the overhanging fear and worry.

Downstairs, the guys were waiting with a comedy paused on the title screen.

"Hurry up, Sang," Gabriel said.

I ran over to where our book bags were and put the new clothes on top of mine. Kota, Silas and North were sitting together on the couch so there wasn't any more room there. I scrambled over until I was in front of the bean bag chairs. A couple of them patted the empty seats next to them.

I was about to plop down next to Gabriel since he was the closest when Luke bellowed. "No," he said. "Over here."

I popped up and slid on my feet on the carpet over to Luke's seat.

"Sang Baby," North said. "Will you sit that beautiful ass down, please?"

"I'm trying," I said, ignoring the compliment, assuming he was teasing me. They all laughed at me.

I was lowering myself next to Luke when I felt a pinch on my butt. I yelped and jumped up, rubbing at the spot.

Luke laughed, his hand on his chest. There was a roar of chuckling from everyone.

"That's it," North said. He snapped his fingers at me. "Get over here."

"Uh oh," Nathan said. "You're in trouble now."

"Trouble is who she is," Gabriel smirked at him. "That's what I've been telling you."

I pushed my finger to my lip and crept over. I couldn't believe Luke did that and now I was getting reprimanded. I glanced quickly at Victor, who seemed strangely at ease at the moment. He jerked his head toward North, as if to tell me to go.

North leaned forward on the couch, curling his fingers at me. When I was close enough, he grabbed my hips and dragged me down until I was on his lap. I gasped in surprise, my face heating.

"Looks like the only way we'll get through this movie is to make you sit where I can reach you," he said. He turned me until my back was against the side of the couch. He brought my legs up until my feet were tucked between his legs and Silas'.

Silas shifted, picking my feet up and moving them until my knees were over his lap, his palm rested against my knee. My feet ended up in Kota's lap.

"We want her down here," complained Gabriel. "Let her come back."

"No," North said. "You guys had her all day. It's our turn now."

"Let her come sit by me," Luke said.

"You lost that privilege when you pinched her," he barked at him. "Now shut up and watch the damn movie."

My mind was whirling so much that I missed a good portion of the first part of the movie. All I could feel was North's body against mine, with the fingers from one hand wrapped around my side and almost tickling my stomach. His other hand dropped onto my thigh. Silas had a hand on my knee. Kota's fingers wrapped around my feet, warming my toes.

It was like sitting in all of their laps at once. My heart thundered. My mind whirled. My body stiffened because I wasn't sure if I should enjoy it. I wanted to, but it was overwhelming. Again, I glanced at the other boys, especially at Victor. But no one seemed surprised. Victor shared a sympathetic smile with Luke. Nathan and Gabriel turned back toward the movie.

North adjusted underneath me. He tucked his head until his lips traced my ear. "Relax, Sang baby." He sucked in a deep breath, inhaling my new fragrance before he put his head up again to watch the movie.

I tried to. I leaned against him more, resting my head against his chest as I tried to focus on the movie. I was breathing in the musk of his cologne, catching how it mixed with mine in such a pleasant way. I snuggled into him and stilled. He seemed happy with this, as his palm massaged the small of my back.

Halfway through the movie my butt was asleep. I adjusted so his thigh wasn't pressed up against my tailbone. My shifting woke Kota up. I couldn't see him behind Silas' frame but his fingers started working over my feet. He started massaging my toes with an exquisite precision. I wriggled, forgetting the movie and feeling lost in touches and closeness and aromas.

"Keep still," North whispered to me.

I tried to, snuggling into him. I moved my hands from my stomach and slipped a palm against his chest. My fingers trailed over his shirt against his heart.

His body stiffened as bad as mine had earlier. I thought perhaps it tickled, so I switched from fingertips to the flat of my palm to smooth out the shirt.

He grunted, hooked his arm under my thighs and picked me up. He deposited me into Kota's lap and walked around the couch. I heard Kota's bedroom door open, close again and North's footsteps on the stairs.

"Kota," I whispered. "What..."

He pushed a finger to my lips, stopping me from saying anything. "Don't ask," he whispered back.

I snuggled into Kota's lap, worried that I did something wrong. Kota's hands rubbed my back. He wasn't massaging like before, but tracing his fingers over my shirt. I relaxed, my cheek pressed into his collarbone. I wasn't facing the movie any more. With Kota rubbing me, I closed my eyes and listened to the boys laughing.

♥

First Ever Sleepover

I woke up when the light flicked on. The movie credits rolled on the screen. I rubbed at my eyes, sitting up and yawning.

Kota laughed at me, brushing a lock of hair away from my cheek. "I guess it's time to get some sleep," he said. He picked me up as he stood and deposited me on Silas' lap.

Silas' muscled arms wrapped around me, cradling me. It was almost warm and cozy enough to fall back asleep.

"I'll go get blankets," Kota said.

I blushed, wondering why I was deposited with Silas instead of just being put down on the couch but I was too lazy and comfortable to care. I didn't mind anyway, I was just curious and confused.

"You better keep your eyes on that one," I heard North say behind me to Silas.

"What's the matter, North?" Silas asked. "Scared of a little girl?" There was a thud and Silas flinched but his eyes were laughing. I could only guess that North punched him in the arm.

The others moved into action repositioning the bean bag chairs off to the side by the wall. Some of them left to go change and the others took over laying out blankets. I pushed myself off of Silas' lap so I could help Victor when he came in with an armload of pillows. Silas got up and walked off to change.

Seven makeshift beds were made across the floor, one on the couch. Gabriel wore red pajama bottoms and a fitted black tank shirt. Nathan, Silas and Luke wore shorts, no shirts. Victor had a white t-shirt and gray striped pajama bottoms. North wore black pajama bottoms and his black t-shirt. Kota wore a soft gray t-shirt, green pajama bottoms.

We sat together as a group on top of the blankets in a circle. The others were talking about the movie. I sat between Luke and Nathan. Luke had a glass bottle in his hand and was taking sips from it.

"What's that?" I asked, nodding to his drink, noting the milky dark liquid. "Isn't that coffee?"

His eyes narrowed at me and nudged me in the arm with his elbow. "Maybe."

"Won't that keep you up all night?"

A chop landed on my head and Nathan leaned into me. "Drinks one coffee and she's suddenly an expert."

I laughed. "I was just asking."

"Oy," Gabriel said from across the circle. "All right we've got do some girl shit," he said.

The others laughed at him.

"No," he said. "I mean for Sang." He looked at me. "Girls do something like truth or dare or pillow fighting or something like that, right?"

I blushed, shrugging. "I don't know." Who did he think I was? I'd told them before no one really talked to me and I wasn't close to anyone. Didn't they believe me?

"What did you do..." Gabriel started but he caught on to my confused look and slapped a palm to his head, laughing. "God damn it, Sang. Why didn't you tell me you've never done a sleepover thing? I thought girls did that stuff all the time."

Seven pairs of eyes landed on my face, seeking a million answers, making my cheeks heat. My finger pushed at my lower lip. "I just... I mean... I don't know."

"You all are forgetting her parents," Nathan said, wrapping his fingers around my wrist to pull my hand away from my face. "She's not even supposed to be here right now."

"We are all getting arrested if they figure this out," North warned.

"We're not getting arrested," Kota said. "But let's stop talking about it for now."

"Right," Gabriel said. He clapped his hands and rubbed them together. "Since it's Sang's first time, we've gotta do some girly shit. It's truth or dare time."

"Try to keep the dares to a minimum," Kota begged. "My mom's probably asleep by now."

"Sang," Gabriel said, fixing his crystals on me. "Truth or dare."

I pushed my lip into my lower teeth, tracing my finger across my mouth. "Truth?"

Everyone groaned.

"What?" I asked, and laughed. "I thought I had a choice."

"You're no fun," Gabriel said, as he brushed his palm against his chin. "Okay, I know you haven't kissed anyone but has a guy ever wanted or tried to kiss you?"

Mouths dropped open. Victor was sitting back against the base of the couch and his fire eyes caught mine out quickly. "You've never kissed anyone?"

"Shut up," Gabriel said. "I'm asking the question. I'm telling you, she's never done it."

"We should do it now," Luke said. "Get it over with."

"No," Nathan barked at him. "First kisses are supposed to be all nice and stuff. You're going to scar her for life making her do it now. No kiss dares."

There were arguments about this. Luke and Gabriel were vocal about getting kissing out of the way and one of them should do it. Nathan, Kota and Victor argued a first kiss for a girl had to be special. I brought my knees up to my chest, wrapping my arms around my legs and pressed my cheek to my knee. If I wanted to stop them from fighting again, I had to distract them.

"There was a boy," I said a little loudly to get their attention. When they heard me, they quieted. "I was in third grade," I started, "it was snowing outside for recess and I was supposed to stay in the classroom. I had been sick the day before and my parents didn't want me out in the cold. There was someone else there with me, I don't remember who. He was playing on the computer in the back and I was just kind of watching him. Another boy walked in. He got sent in for being in trouble out on the playground."

"Huh," North said. The others hushed him.

"I don't remember his name," I continued. "He came in and watched whatever the other guy was doing for a moment and then asked me to follow him. I never talked to him before so I guess I was kind of surprised he wanted to. He had me go with him into the coat closet..."

"I don't know if I want to hear the rest of this story," Luke said.

There was a chorus of shushing.

I pulled my cheek away from my knees to look up. "When I was inside, he closed the door and he said he wanted to kiss me. I was so shocked that when he stepped up to me, I pushed him away." I started to smile at the memory, shaking my head. "I don't remember how it happened, but he pushed back and suddenly I was on the ground. He was wrestling me, trying to kiss me. I remember really not wanting to. I think mostly it was because he was trying to make me and I didn't think I needed to be made to kiss anyone."

"What an ass," Gabriel said. "Did you make it out of the coat closet?"

"That's another question," Kota said, grinning. "You only get one."

"It's part of the same... God damn it, Kota." He pulled a pillow out and tossed it at him.

Kota caught the pillow in the air before it hit him. "Besides, if she's never been kissed, then she got out of the closet fine without doing it."

"Oh yeah," Gabriel said. "Good point."

"Your turn, Sang," Nathan said. "Pick someone."

I closed my eyes and let my finger fly around the circle randomly. When I opened my eyes, I was pointing at Victor. "Truth or dare?" I asked.

"Truth."

Everyone groaned again.

I bit my lip trying to think of what to ask him. There were a million questions in my mind right then. What does this bracelet mean? What does opening up to you mean? I didn't think it was the appropriate time, but it was tempting. I settled for something simple. "What did you say to me in Japanese on the first day of school? *The kirei.. um...*"

Victor's face turned red. "I don't want to say it."

"You have to," Gabriel said to him. "It's the rules. You picked truth."

Victor grunted. He curled his fingers at me and leaned into the circle. "Come here. You're asking. You're the only one who gets to know."

"Oy! Cheating!" Gabriel howled.

"Keep it down," Kota said. "He's right. She asked. He only has to tell her."

I crawled over until I was close enough for Victor to whisper in my ear.

"Your eyes are beautiful," he whispered.

I blushed, trying to remember that day. He barely knew me!

The others laughed as Victor pulled away and my cheeks were still red. Victor shared a secret smile with me.

"Your turn to choose, Victor," Kota said.

"Sang," Victor said.

I rolled my eyes. "I just had a turn."

"I get to pick whoever I want," Victor said. "Pick one."

"Truth."

Groans.

Victor was quiet for a moment as if considering his question carefully. "Why did your parents name you

Sang?"

This perked everyone up. Again eyes fell on me.

"My grandmother's name was Sangrida. My mom shortened it to Sang."

"Which grandmother?" he asked.

"My dad's mother. She died when I was eight, I think. I don't really remember her. Marie was named after my mom's mother."

"That was two questions," Gabriel said. "Pick someone, Sang."

"Your turn, Gabriel," I said defiantly.

He smirked. "Dare."

"Crap," I said. Not that I had a truth picked out, but I wasn't sure what to dare him to do. "I don't know what I'm supposed to..."

"Anything," he said. His crystal eyes sparkled. "Just don't make me burn the house down."

"Make him kiss something," Luke said.

"Make him drink from the toilet," Victor said.

I thought about it. "You know the lip gloss in your bag?" I asked him.

"Uh huh," he said, his eyebrow lifting.

I nodded toward his bag. "Go get it for me and I get to put it on you."

The others roared with laughter. Kota had to ask them twice to calm down.

"God damn it," Gabriel said. He stood up, ran over to his bag and dug through it for the tube of gloss. He brought it back and knelt next to me, smacking the tube into my open palm. "You're so fucking mean."

"You said anything," I said. I pulled the brush from the tube and held it out toward him. "Pucker up, sweetie."

He made a kissy face at me, smacking his lips as he kissed the air. I handed the bottom part off to Nathan to hold. I grabbed Gabriel's cheeks and made him do a fish face like he'd had me do. I got the brush close to his lips and he made some strange face and poked his tongue out at me that I stopped, turning my head to laugh.

"Don't mess up," Gabriel said through his squished mouth.

"Then stop making faces," I said. I swiped the brush across his lips. I smeared it pretty well, marking up part of his upper lip just under his nose.

"Hey," he said. He pulled back his head and reached with his palm to rub it off.

"No. You have to leave it on."

"For how long?"

"Forever."

He grunted.

I shrugged. "Until the end of the game."

He growled. A flash went off. We both turned and there was another flash. Luke had his cell phone out, pointing it at us.

"Oh my fucking god," Gabriel said and he lunged after Luke. Luke ducked out of the way, shifting to hide behind North. North took the phone from his brother and sat on it, giving Gabriel a look as if daring him to come get it.

I was leaning against Nathan, laughing way too hard. Nathan wrapped a hand around my waist to hold me up, pressing his cheek to the top of my head.

"Fine, fine," Gabriel said, going back to sit cross-legged in his spot. "Sang's turn."

I was going to say truth again but everyone was looking and waiting for it. I relented. "Dare," I said in a small voice.

Gabriel beamed, his shiny pink lips glinting in the light. "I should make you kiss a toilet."

"Please don't," I begged.

He smiled and curled his fingers at me. "All right, come here. You have to sit on my lap until the end of the game."

My mouth popped open but what could I say? I sat on laps all night. No one argued his dare. I smirked, crawling over to him. He opened his arms and pulled me in to sit in the middle of his crossed legs, my back pressed to his chest. He put his cheek next to the side of my head. His arms threaded around my waist.

"Nathan?" I said, hoping he might be able to save me.

"Dare," he said.

Gabriel's lips traced my ear as he whispered. I started repeating what he was saying. "You have to... get three pieces of ice... and... oh man that's so mean!" I said to Gabriel.

"You aren't supposed to help her," Nathan said.

"She wants you to put ice in your underwear," he said. "That's tame shit. I just did you a favor."

Nathan turned to me. "Is that what you want?"

I blushed, putting my fingers to my lips, but I couldn't hide my smile. I didn't have a better idea and Gabriel's suggestion was funny.

"Fuck," he said and he got up to go to the kitchen. He came back with three pieces of ice which he held out to me so I could see. He sat down in his spot, yanked out the elastic to his shorts and dropped the ice inside. "Christ," he barked, and he closed up his legs, shoving his face into his knees. "Sang!"

"Dare!" I called out, still hoping he'd have pity on me.

"Bite Gabe," he said through his teeth, seething. "Hard enough to leave a mark."

"Hey," Gabriel said.

I started a giggle fit. Gabriel shifted his legs so I bounced in his lap. I grabbed his arm, brought it to my mouth, and stopped short to laugh again.

Nathan's head lifted. They all stared in silence as I opened my mouth and sank my teeth into Gabriel's skin. I tasted salt, felt the hair on the back of his arm tickle my tongue.

"Good girl," Gabriel said, nearly purring.

"I said hard, Sang," Nathan said.

I bit down.

"Ow, fuck," he said, yanking his arm from my mouth.

His forearm had my teeth marks indented into his skin.

"Silas?" I asked.

"Truth."

I knew exactly what I wanted to ask him. "What did you say..."

"You have a beautiful laugh," he said. His brown eyes zeroed in on me. "That's what I said to you outside of class in the hallway. I'm not ashamed to say it out loud."

The others giggled.

"He's right about that," Gabriel whispered in my ear. He bounced me on his lap again.

"Sang," Silas said.

"Dare," I said.

He was quiet for a minute, looking at my face as if weighing in on what he could ask me. "I want another hug."

The guys laughed again. I crawled out of Gabriel's lap and knee walked over. Silas held open his arms for me, catching me. He wrapped his strong arms around me and squeezed me against his chest. My cheek pressed against his bare shoulder and chest. His nose pressed to my neck, and he inhaled deeply. I wrapped my arms around his neck, my fingers curled into his hair, breathing in his ocean scent.

When he let go, Gabriel called out to me, "Get back here."

"Luke," I said as I crawled back into Gabriel's lap.

"Dare," he said.

"I want the damn photo deleted," Gabriel said.

"That's not what I want," I said, laughing. "I want... um..."

North caught my eye. He made a kissing motion with his lips.

"I want you to kiss..." I started to say.

North wiggled his toes.

"My foot," I said, getting another round of giggle fits.

"I said no kiss dares," Nathan growled.

"It's her foot. That doesn't mean anything," North

said, shrugging. "I actually meant to get her to say her shoe but close enough."

Luke laughed, pushing blond hair away from his face. "I've got the easy one." He crawled over. I held out a leg. He grabbed at it, and puckered, pressing his lips against the top of my toes.

A spark slipped from my foot to my stomach.

The others were laughing.

Luke gazed up at me and we locked eyes. He winked. "Sang," he said.

"Tru...," I said, but I got a jab in the ribs from Gabriel. "Ugh, dare."

Luke's brown eyes flickered. He stood up and held out his hand to me. "Come with me for a minute."

I dropped my hand into his and he hauled me to my feet. He tugged and I followed him to Kota's bedroom door. He opened it and pulled me up the carpeted stairs. The others trailed behind us.

We clustered together in Kota's room. Luke went to the closet and then held the door open. "In," he said, jerking his head toward the dark space.

I blushed. He wanted me to stand in the closet?

"I don't think so," North said.

"She said dare," Luke said. "She gets to sit with me in the closet for two minutes."

"No way," Victor said. "That's too far."

"You guys don't trust me," he said. "I slept in her room all night and you won't trust me in the closet for a minute. I'm not going to hurt her."

"No kissing, either," Nathan warned.

Luke pouted. "You guys ruin everything." He grabbed at my arm and yanked me into the closet, closing the door.

We stood in the dark.

Luke pressed himself close to me, enough to where I could inhale his vanilla scent. His fingers brushed against my chin.

"Luke," I whispered. "They said no."

"I know," he said. He felt for my cheeks. "Trust me." He traced his hand over my mouth, his fingers covering my lips. "Now, I'm going to let go for one second, okay? When I do, yell at me about something. Tell me to stop. When they open the door, I'm going to make it look like I am kissing you."

I smothered a giggle. I should have known. He was trying to prank them all.

Luke uncovered his fingers over my mouth.

In my best distressed voice, I cried out. "Luke! Stop it! No, they said not to!"

Luke's hand flew back over my mouth. The door was opened quickly and Luke bent his head down and kissed the back of his fingers, tilting his head in a way that made it look like we were making out.

I still felt the warmth of his face so close to mine. His fingers were pressed to my lips. Was this what a kiss felt like? I was too flustered and my heart was thundering from being exposed.

The guys gasped together in surprise. Luke lifted his head away to reveal his hand had been there all along.

"You little shit," North said. His brown eyes shot bullets at his brother. He reached into the closet and yanked Luke out by the shoulder. "I should take you home right now."

"I didn't kiss her," he cried out. "We were just kidding."

My face was radiating as I stepped out of the closet. Maybe that was too far. How was I going to lighten the mood again? "North? Want to go next?"

"I don't want to play," he said, letting his brother go with a glare.

"You have to," Gabriel said. "It's Sang's game."

North huffed. "Dare."

Gabriel stood behind him and tugged at his shirt and tried to mouth something to me but I wasn't understanding.

"Take off your shirt?" I asked out loud.

Everyone laughed. North shook his head with a smirk but pulled his shirt off of his body, hanging it over his shoulder. His muscles flexed, my eyes lingered for much too long on his abs and the trail of hair below his navel.

Gabriel laughed, shaking his head. "I was trying to tell you to get him to strip."

"That's too far, Gabriel," Kota said.

"It's truth or dare. It's what girls do."

"He knows so well," Luke said.

"Sang," North said, looking at me intently.

"Tru..." Nathan tagged me in the ribs. "Ugh, dare," I said quietly, sighing. Of all the people to dare, North was scariest. His eyes were intimidating.

He curled his fingers at me. "Come here. Get on my back."

I bit my lip, crossing the room. He turned and lowered to the ground so I could wrap my arms around his neck. His hands clutched my thighs to pick me up off the ground. He dug a cell phone from his pocket and flicked the camera on.

"Smile, Sang Baby," he said. I grinned and he snapped the picture. He kept me on his back as he turned the phone around to look at it. His face was almost grumpy, tough and serious and I had a crazy face while I smiled. Night and day. "Not bad."

"Kota!" I called.

"Dare," he said.

North put me down on the floor. My eyes flitted around the room for an idea. I was trying to ignore Gabriel since he picked so many. Luke popped into view. I did my best to mimic what he was trying to pantomime.

"Rub your nose... against mine?"

The others laughed. My heart seemed to stop when I realized how close he'd get if he did that.

"As you wish," Kota said. He closed the distance between us. His fingers found my shoulders, drawing me closer. His face hovered a breath away from mine. I had to close my eyes as it made me feel cross-eyed. Kota slipped the tip of his nose down to meet mine. He glided his nose back and forth.

Our lips were close enough that he only needed to tilt his head a tiny bit to kiss me.

A shiver, like a whirlwind, danced up my spine. Our noses touching felt like gentle spring breeze against my skin. I secretly wanted it to continue.

He drew away, cheeks red and his lips twisted up. I wondered why I felt odd now. I realized it was because no one was laughing.

"Sang?" Kota asked.

I sighed. "Dare?"

He seemed pleased. "Come with me," he said.

He padded into his bathroom and flicked the light on. He took my hand and guided me inside.

"Hey now," Luke said. "You all made a fuss when I did that."

"You guys can come watch," Kota said. He pushed the door open wider in invitation.

The others followed us, crowding into the doorway of the bathroom. I smothered my shaking, nervous as to what Kota was coming up with. It was exciting and scary at the same time.

Kota pulled me until I was in front of the sink. "Sit up here," he said, patting the counter. He put his hands on my waist to assist me so I could hop up and sit on the counter in front of him.

"Close your eyes," he said.

My heart did flips in my chest, my stomach tightened. I let my eyelids fall. The air shifted in front of me and imagined it was Kota waving his hand at my face to make sure I wasn't peeking.

I heard the water from the sink behind me turn on for a second and Kota shifting around on the floor. Some of the others started giggling.

"Open your mouth," Kota said.

I gaped at him. "What are you..."

"You said dare," he said, the command slipping into his voice but in a happy tone. "Don't you trust me?"

How much did I trust him? I took a deep breath, letting it out and opened my mouth.

A tender touch brushed up against my tongue and I flinched, pulling back. The object was removed from my mouth.

"Sang," he said in a sharper tone. "Open your mouth."

I opened my mouth again and steeled myself. Pressure fell against my teeth as he applied the object again. I tasted mint. I realized it was a toothbrush and he was brushing my teeth. I started giggling as the way he was brushing was ticklish against my gums.

"Don't laugh," he said. "I don't want you to choke."

I was going to say something, but I mumbled around the toothbrush. He reached up for my jaw, tugging at it with his fingers so I'd open up further. I opened my eyes. He was focused on my mouth, with a determined grin on his face. A flash appeared, causing me to jerk back again in surprise. North had his phone back out and he snapped a picture. I squinted my eyes at him, trying to send him a mean glare, but he only grinned.

"The best part is," Gabriel said, "he could have put that thing in the toilet first and you wouldn't know."

My eyes widened and I choked a little.

"You know I didn't do that. Calm down," Kota said. He pulled the toothbrush from my mouth. "Okay, you're done. Go ahead and rinse. Let's get back downstairs. You guys get out."

It sounded like thunder as the guys ran down the stairs. Kota remained behind with me as I bent over the sink to swish my mouth and spit. I pulled back and he had a towel ready for me.

"Having fun?" he asked, crossing his arms over his chest and leaning back against the sink.

"Yup," I said, smiling as I wiped my mouth dry with the towel. The toothbrush was beside the sink. "Is this yours?"

"Yeah," he said.

I pushed the toothbrush under the running water to clean it. "Aren't you worried about girl cooties?"

"Are you worried about boy cooties?" he asked, smirking.

I didn't know the right answer for that. Did that mean something?

"I'm glad you're having fun," he said as he leaned against the sink and watched me. "The guys are doing their best."

I knocked the toothbrush against the sink. Water droplets flicked back into the basin. "What do you mean?"

"We did this for you," he said. "It's been a tough week. A tough several weeks, actually."

I blushed, dropping the brush back onto the counter and shutting the water off. "You guys didn't have to go through any trouble."

"We wanted to," he said. He turned slightly so he was facing me.

"Why?" I asked, focusing on the basin. I started folding the towel. Did I really want to know this answer?

Kota wrapped his hands around mine holding the towel, forcing me to look up. His green eyes sparkled against the light. "When I first met you, you were this little haunted girl, and I just didn't know why. Next thing I know, you're neck deep in trouble, with us at school and at home. Despite all those problems, you're positive and hopeful. Every time you've been knocked down, you've gotten right back up. But there was always some ghost hanging over your shoulder. You'd come up for air for a split second and then slip right back into that distant stare. Now look at you."

I tilted my head at him, confused. Ghosts? Haunted? Is that how he saw me? I wasn't sure. I just wanted to stop feeling so kept apart from everything. He'd said I'd eventually feel a part of their group, and I wasn't sure if I felt that way at all, or if it would ever happen. "I haven't changed," I said. "I'm still me."

"You have changed," he said. He dropped the towel to the floor at our feet. His arms wrapped around my shoulders and he pulled me into his chest, hugging me. My breath escaped at the suddenness and my arms froze at my sides. "I think today was the first time I saw you smile without those shadows in your eyes. I knew you were different."

"Different?" I asked.

"Special," he said. His palm brushed against the small of my back. A soft tingling swept through my core. "You've got a sweet disposition. At first I was worried you were dismissive, like I said before. Now I'm wondering if it's because you forgive and forget because of that big heart you have. You're too good for the family you've been stuck with. The other guys know it, too. So we thought maybe you needed some time away from worrying about so much stuff."

"I feel like I haven't done much for you guys," I said. "You all do so much for me. I don't know how to thank you."

He tightened the hug. "You've been good for us, Sang," he said.

My hands drifted up to his back, pressing my fingertips against his muscles. "How?"

He sighed pleasantly. "We've been kind of listless the past few years, going through the motions without thinking." His fingers started to rub in circles along my spine. "You woke us up somehow. I think it's because now we've got something to fight for again... to fight over."

I withdrew from the hug, gazing up at him. "Fight over?"

He smiled down at me. "It's not a bad thing. We're only human," he said. "It's good to argue once in a while. Just a little. It shows you care." He pulled away from me, grabbing my hand. "Come on," he said. "Let's go to sleep."

My free hand pushed at my lower lip as I thought about what he'd said. He was happy they were fighting? I wasn't sure I understood it. I wasn't sure I wanted them to fight. I didn't like fighting and I didn't like to think they were angry with each other because of me. And why would they fight over me, anyway? I've done barely anything for them. Do families and friends fight?

Downstairs, Victor was on the couch. The others were dispersed around the room. North was sitting on top of a blanket near the end and patted the free spot between him and Silas. "Come on, Sang. I don't think anyone will get to sleep unless you're over here."

"Hey," Gabriel said. The lip gloss had disappeared from his mouth. "We're not going to mess with her."

"Uh huh," North said.

I stepped over some of the guys and nearly crawled over Silas lying down on his side and plopped down on the blankets where I was supposed to sleep. North still had his shirt off. He plumped my pillow for me as I tucked my legs under the blanket. When I was on my back, with the pillow under my head, Silas blocked my view of the other guys. A hand dropped on my forehead and I looked up to see Victor above me. He had a sleepy smile and brushed my hair away from my face.

I wriggled in my spot, unsure of how to sleep. On one side I had Silas looking at me and the other North was there. Above me was Victor. I was going to sleep in a room full of boys. My skin tingled. Would I be able to sleep at all?

Kota turned off the light and I started giggling. I couldn't help it. I was nervous and didn't know another way to release the tension. It set off a few of the others. Someone snorted and we all started laughing.

North leaned over me. "See what you started?"

"Yeah, yeah," I said. "It's always the girl's fault."

"That's true!" Gabriel said.

When my eyes adjusted to the dark, I caught the

outline of Silas's face. He was still on his side, looking down at me. His tongue shot out, his eyes and lips contorting as he made a face. It set me off with giggles again.

The others started laughing.

"Sang," North grumbled.

"It was Silas!"

"Silas doesn't giggle like that, I'm pretty sure."

Silas's eyes nearly glowed in the dark and I could tell he was grinning. There was no way I could sleep with him looking at me. I pulled a face at him as I flipped around and he chuckled. He moved closer to me, enough to where I could feel his breath on the back of my head. North had turned around so I could see his back and the outline of his cheek and ear.

My heart raced. My blood surged through me. My ears strained to hear any little noise of the house and of the guys. Breathing slowed around me. I sensed Silas behind me. I admired North's back muscles and his arm. I wondered if Victor was asleep on the couch yet but I was too nervous to check. If he was looking back at me, it would be impossible to sleep thinking he might be watching.

I willed myself to keep my eyes closed and to remain still.

♥

The Truth About Dreams

I dreamed I was drowning.

Someone was shaking me. No matter how strongly I wanted to open my eyes, I sank deeper. My limbs were numb, un-cooperating.

A voice spoke and in my confusion, I didn't recognize it. "Sang Baby, wake up."

"Ti eínai láthos?"

"I don't know what's wrong. It sounded like she stopped breathing."

Shivers rattled through me but I couldn't draw myself up out of wherever I was.

"Sweetheart. Baby. Sang. Sang!"

My eyelids fluttered, my lungs opened up. It was like I was discovering I could breathe for the first time. My hands drifted up and landed on something soft and warm.

The world stilled and when it did, I was falling asleep again, descending back into the shadows.

"Sang!" The shaking started again.

Flashes of light swept across my brain, memories and consciousness slipped in all at once. Something's wrong! Who's got me? Someone has me! I needed to stop it.

My hands were on someone who had grabbed me. My heart jumped to life in a panic. My hands flexed out of instinct and my fingernails tore into softness.

"Fuck... shit ow."

I was dropped and it shook me enough that my lungs opened up again and I was coughing. There was a dim lamp on somewhere, and I barely made out Kota's living room through my sleep-blurred eyes. I rubbed at my face to clear my vision.

North was sitting back on his heels as he hovered above me, his arms crossed. His dark eyes shot questions and confusion like spitting fireballs at my face. "What the fuck?"

My poor brain couldn't piece together what happened quickly enough. I gripped someone. That someone was North. "Oh god. Did I do that? I'm sorry," I cried out. My body started quivering so hard that my bones rattled together. "Oh please, I'm so sorry."

I pulled myself up to my knees, backing away from North's intensity. I sensed someone behind me, and felt a big hand on my back, a calm warmth against my quaking. Silas.

North re-folded his arms. "What the hell was that about, Sang?" he shouted at me.

I didn't know. I couldn't think. I hurt North. I felt so bad. "I'm sorry, I'm so sorry."

North growled, letting go of his arms. He crossed toward me on his knees, grabbing me by the elbows. I felt something warm and wet pressing to my skin and knew he must have been bleeding. "Why did you claw me?" he shouted again.

"Whoa, hey," Silas barked at him. He hooked an arm around my waist and dragged me away from North. "Stop it." Silas pushed me behind his back, blocking my view of North's rage.

I started shaking again, tears clouding my eyes so I couldn't see. I'd hurt North. He was bleeding. I pressed my hands to my face to hide myself, my shame.

Someone came up next to me, wrapping arms around my waist and hugging me close. I smelled Victor's opulent berry cologne. I pressed my head against his shoulder, my tears wetting his t-shirt. I felt so terrible, that I didn't deserve his comfort.

"I'm sorry," I whispered.

"She stopped breathing and she clawed my arms. I want to know why," North growled.

"It wasn't her fault," Silas said. "She didn't mean it."

"I know she didn't fucking mean it," North shouted.

"You can't yell at her like that," Victor said. His hand found the back of my head, his long thin fingers massaged at the base of my scalp. "Sweetie, calm down. It's okay."

"What's going on?" Kota's voice shot through the dark, full of command. Where had he been? Where was everyone else? Victor held my face so close that I couldn't see.

"Sang clawed the shit out of me," North shouted.

"Stop yelling," Kota said.

North's voice boomed, "I'm not fucking yelling. I'm asking. Fucking Sang--"

The air electrified as shouting erupted at once. Silas boomed something in Greek that I didn't catch and North was shouting back, in what sounded like the same language.

There was quick movement next to us and Victor yanked me up until I was standing. He swept me away from where the shuffling was going on. I turned my head enough and through my tears it looked like Silas had lunged himself at North. North was on his back, with Silas holding down his chest to keep him on the floor. North's fist sailed and made contact with Silas's shoulder.

"That's it," Kota said. He marched over to the two of them and pushed at Silas's back with a foot. "Silas get off of him. Now. Everyone gets an hour tomorrow."

Silas backed off of North. His fists clenched and his shoulders heaved. North growled, jumping up to his feet.

"I'll make it two hours," Kota said in a voice darker than I'd heard him use before.

The room quieted. I shook, terrified, confused. What did he mean? Two hours of what?

Victor moved his hand from the back of my head to my face, pressing my cheek with his palm. His thumb smoothed at a spot under my eye, wiping my tears away. "Shh, darling," he cooed under his breath. "Don't cry. God please, don't."

"This is what's going to happen," Kota said, "Sang and North upstairs. You two stay down here."

"You can't do that to her," Victor said.

"Now." Kota's command rang out in the single syllable. There would be no compromise.

Victor grunted. Before his hands slipped away, I felt something that later I would wonder was his lips against my forehead. I would never know for sure.

My body rattled where I stood. I crossed my arms under my breasts, sinking into myself. I couldn't do this. I should go home. I should stay there forever. I didn't deserve them.

Kota hooked his arm under my legs and lifted me off the ground. I pressed my cheek to his chest, exhausted, confused, scared to death. I hadn't meant to be such a blubbering mess but I was still a mush brain after sleeping.

I'd hurt North.

Kota marched me up to his bedroom. I heard North following behind us. I wanted to jump from Kota and run home. I couldn't face North. He was so angry with me for clawing at him. I didn't even have a good reason. I didn't know why I'd done it. I had that dream. He'd tried waking me and for some reason I reacted so badly. No one had ever tried to wake me like that before. I didn't know where I was or who he was. My explanation was inexcusable. He would hate me.

Kota carried me into the bathroom. North flicked on the light. Kota set me to perch on the counter. "Lock the door, North," he said.

There was a click. I focused my eyes on the chrome towel rack hanging on wall. I couldn't face anyone. I sucked in a deep breath, but another typhoon of shaking swept over me as I sensed their eyes on me. I felt so tiny and lost and sorry all over again.

"Sang," Kota said softly. "Stop crying." He snatched tissues from a dispenser, bundling them and pressing them to my cheek. "Please, sweetie, stop crying."

I swallowed, peeling my lips apart to whisper, "I'm sorry. I didn't mean to."

"I know that," North said, his tone immensely softer than it had been downstairs. "Kota, let me have her for a second."

I didn't want this. My heart was pounding so loud and it felt like it was burning. I hiccupped on a sob.

Kota stepped back and in his place came North. North's strong hands slipped around my body. He wrapped his arms around my back and pulled me in close until I was pressed up against his bare chest. My hands were between my breasts, wringing against themselves and now crushed between us. My tears touched his skin.

He dropped a hand on my scalp and his fingers smoothed my hair. "Sang Baby," he said, "I'm not mad, okay? I was upset because there was something wrong with you and I didn't know what. You scared me." His cheek pressed against the top of my head and I felt the gruffness of his unshaven face against my forehead. "I'm sorry I yelled."

"I'm sorry," I said again. I swallowed, and my lips nearly pressed against his chest with the way he was holding me. My hands instinctively went around his stomach, my palms pressed against his back to hug him.

He tightened the hug. "I know, Baby. I know. I forgive you. Just don't cry, okay?"

I tried to stop, sucking in another bit of air and holding it, pulling one hand back to wipe at my face.

"What happened?" Kota said softly next to us.

"She was asleep," North said. "One minute she was breathing and the next, it's like she wasn't. I waited, but when I didn't hear her catch her breath, I started shaking her to wake her up. I think I scared her." He pulled back and brushed the hair out of my face with his rough fingers. "I'm sorry if I scared you," he said.

I shook my head, blushing hotly and mumbling, but I really wasn't sure what to say. He did scare me, but I didn't care. It simply felt wrong that he was apologizing for things that weren't his fault.

"Were you dreaming?"

I blushed more and looked away from them toward the wall. "It's nothing," I said.

I sensed they were exchanging looks. I trembled. North's rough finger caught under my chin and lifted my face around until I was looking at those intense brown eyes. "What did you dream about, Sang?"

My voice cracked while I was talking. "I was, um, dreaming about... I was in an alley and there were three boys chasing me. I don't know who. They grabbed me and took me to a dock by a river and they held me under the water." I bit my lip, recalling the angry looks on their faces. "At first I struggled, trying to get away. I was swallowing water. I was fighting to breathe and then..."

"Then what?" North asked in a quiet voice.

I wasn't sure how to express myself here. "And then I just didn't have to breathe anymore. The need was gone." It was crazy. Being able to breathe one moment and then knowing for sure I didn't need to. In the dream, I was in the water and I simply was without air, without want of it.

North's eyes intensified and his finger released me. "Holy shit."

I closed my eyes, caressing my cheek against his chest. His hand dropped to the top of my head again, sweeping over my hair.

"Do you get nightmares often, Sang?" Kota asked.

I pushed my palm against my other cheek to hide myself. I didn't know how to answer that question without them worrying about me more. How stupid I felt for having nightmares the first time I slept over with them. I didn't want to lie because they would know.

"How often do you have nightmares?" North asked. His fingers stroked over my face. He caught my hands and tugged them away so I couldn't hide anymore. "Every night?"

I blushed. "Not every single night..."

"But often enough?"

I sighed. "Whenever I dream, I guess. Most of the time."

He frowned. Kota did, too.

"It's no big deal," I said quickly. "I usually just wake myself up and I don't even remember later. They're just dreams."

"When did you start having nightmares?" Kota asked.

The question caught me off-guard. I blinked, trying to recall. "I don't know... nine? Ten? It's been so long..."

North muttered a series of curses and collected me in his arms again. He pressed my face to his chest, holding me by the back of the head. "God damn it, Kota."

"It's just dreams," I said. "Everyone gets nightmares."

"Not all the time," North said. "Not like that. God, Sang. You stopped fucking breathing."

"She might have been fine," Kota said calmly. "You don't know if she stopped."

"She was breathing and then she wasn't. I couldn't hear her. I don't know what else to tell you. Did you see what I had to go through to wake her up?"

"She was just in a deep sleep."

"She shouldn't be getting nightmares like that in the first place."

Kota frowned. "We don't know why..."

"There is no why," I insisted. I pulled myself away from North and wiped at my face. "I just get them. It's no big deal. It happens, I wake up, and I'm fine."

"Are you always drowning in them?" Kota asked.

I sighed, flustered and leaned back until my shoulders were against the mirror. "No."

"What happens?"

I shrugged. "I don't know. I'm usually running, trying

to get away from something."

"Someone?"

I shook my head. "Sometimes it's a person, sometimes it's a lot of people, sometimes it's a monster or a dragon or zombies or just something I can't see. They shoot at me. Or they try running me over. It's just crazy, messed up dreams." I was feeling frustrated. What was the big deal? I hated that they worried about me already and here was something that I couldn't help and they couldn't help either and they were making the biggest thing out of it. I'd hurt North and that was what the bad part was.

"Have you ever died before in them?" North asked.

"A few, I think. I fell from a building once. I was shot a couple of times..."

"Shit," North growled.

Kota put a calm hand on his arm. "All right, we'll figure this out, but we can't do it tonight."

"There's nothing to figure out," I said. "You can't do anything about dreams." Suddenly I was desperate for an earthquake or for someone to interrupt. I wanted them to forget about all this. It really didn't matter to me right now about nightmares. They didn't mean anything to me. My eyes fell on North and the blood drying in spots on his forearms. I leaned forward, taking his arm gently. "Oh, North. It is bad."

North drew his arm away from me. "I'll live."

I frowned. "We should clean you up."

"I agree," Kota said. "Sang, find the medical kit, okay? I'm going to go calm the others downstairs and we'll all try to get some sleep. It's late. We'll talk in the morning." He slid his glasses up with a forefinger before turning away, unlocking the door and marching out.

I jumped off of the counter and dug in the drawers for his medical kit.

"I don't need a bandage," North said. "Just let me wash." He nudged me away from searching and made me stand behind him as he turned on the sink and started rubbing his arms under the water. The wounds opened again. Blood dripped into the sink.

"North," I whispered. I ripped tissues from the box on the counter and held one of his arms, pulling it close. I applied pressure against the marks. "I'll sleep on my hands from now on," I promised. "Maybe I shouldn't have done this at all. I should have known better--"

North lifted his other hand out of the water. He pushed two fingers to my lips, drawing my mouth closed. "Stop talking like that."

"But..." I mumbled through his fingers.

"What do you want?" he asked. "Is being locked up by your parents the life you really want? Do you want to leave us?"

My eyes widened. My head started shaking. No! I didn't want to leave them at all. They were all I ever had.

He slipped his fingers away from my mouth. "This is what we are, Sang Baby. You're one of us now. Your problems are our problems. Running away from us isn't going to help. So stop it." He smirked. "Besides, I'm bigger than you. I'll sit on you if I have to."

I closed my eyes, cracking a smile. "North..." I didn't want to laugh. I didn't want to go back to crying either. I didn't know what I wanted. Maybe I did and I was lying to myself. I wanted to feel that connection he did. I wanted to understand.

He took the tissues from my hands. "I think I've stopped bleeding," he said. He tossed the tissues into the trash and clasped his hand around mine. "Let's go."

Friends hold hands. Friends help each other. Friends were there for you when you had nightmares at a sleepover.

It was a lot to get used to.

♥♥♥

Downstairs, the lights were off. North held my hand to guide me back to the makeshift bed. I couldn't see in the dark, but I sensed something wrong. The room felt empty. When my eyes adjusted enough, I realized Nathan, Luke and Gabriel weren't in the room. North ignored this, dragging me down into my spot and commanding I go to sleep.

I wondered if Nathan was keeping his promise to look in on my mother that night. I wondered if Luke and Gabriel went with him. If so, what was taking so long?

Or was the Academy demanding their attention?

♥

In It Together

Cracks of light seeped between my eyelids. My cheek pressed against Silas's bicep.

My eyelashes flickered over his skin each time I would partially open my eyes. His face was close enough to the back of my head that his breath swept at my hair. I was lying on my side facing North, who had both of my hands wrapped up in his as he slept. They were both so close I didn't need the blankets to keep warm. I was so cozy and comfortable. I kept drifting in and out of sleep.

"It's time guys." Kota's voice drifted so softly to us that, for a moment, I wondered if I had dreamt it.

Silas stirred. He leaned over me and I felt his lips at my ear. "*Aggele mou,*" he whispered. "I need my arm back."

I groaned, lifting my head up so he could slide away from me.

When he pulled away, he rolled over and I sensed him sitting up.

North grunted something and released my hands. He wrapped his arms around my waist and drew me close to him, pulling me underneath his blanket. His hand went to the back of my head to press my face against his chest and he yanked the blanket over our heads. His mouth, chin and nose dropped against the top of my head. The gruff feeling of unshaven face scratched at my scalp. His leg hooked over both of mine.

He fell still. I snuggled against him, drifting back to

sleep. Why didn't it bug me that he was holding me so close? Maybe if I had been more awake I would have been flipping out that he was doing this, but for the moment, I was too sleepy and comfortable to care.

"North," Silas said above us.

"Go away." North grunted. His fingers gripped my back against my rib cage to draw me in tighter.

"If Erica comes out here and sees you like that, she'll never let us do this again."

North mumbled something that even I couldn't understand.

"We've got to go," Silas said.

"Where are you guys going?" I whispered to North.

He sighed heavily and spoke against my head. "Nowhere, Sang baby. Go back to sleep." He grunted again and put me down in his spot, slipping away out onto the floor to stand up.

I wanted to wake up more. I wanted to ask where they were going. It should have bothered me. I pressed my cheek to his pillow, smelling the musk. I felt his warmth still around me and the blanket blocked out the light. As much as I willed myself to sit up and ask questions, sleep dragged me down again.

♥♥♥

When I woke again, it was Erica hovering over me, shaking my arm. "Sang? Do you want to get up?"

I sat up quickly, shoving the blanket away and dragged a palm over my eyes to rub away the sleep. Through squinting eyes, I gazed over at the others.

All of the makeshift beds were empty.

Erica smiled. She was dressed in black yoga pants and an oversized gray t-shirt with USMC scrawled in yellow block lettering across the front. "I recommend if you want a shower, you should do it now."

"Where are they?" I asked.

"Outside," she said. She pressed a hand to my knee. I willed myself not to flinch at her touch. Somehow the urge to pull away was stronger when she did that compared to the boys' touches. I wasn't sure why. "Come see." She nodded her head toward the far window.

I crawled out of North's spot and followed behind Erica to the dining room. She stopped at the window where the simple white blinds were closed. She threaded her fingers between two blind slats and separated them with her fingers, peeking out into the yard. She stepped back, motioning with her free hand in the direction of the open space to indicate I should look.

Sunshine blinded me for a moment. I blinked back against it. Familiar voices were shouting and it was enough to wake me fully. I focused.

All seven of the boys were outside. They were lined up, side by side, faces firm, eyes set. They were doing push-ups in the grass. Each one had matching, fitted gray shirts and sweatpants. They were barefoot. As they moved, they counted off together. I could hear Silas's booming voice and Victor's baritone and the others in chorus. Kota's glasses had fogged. They were all sweating, their hair soaked. Gabriel's arms shook, but he kept up with all of them.

After a few minutes, they jumped up together and started doing jumping jacks, starting together in eerie unison.

My heart tightened in my chest. My brain couldn't piece together this puzzle. "What are they doing?" I whispered.

"From what I understand," Erica said, her head moving next to mine to gaze out at the boys, "this is a punishment of some sort."

"Punishment?"

"When they've been misbehaving too much. I probably shouldn't say punishment. It's more like a reminder." Erica sighed, a haunted smile tucked into the corner of her mouth. "My son has been enrolled in the

Academy since he was little. When he was twelve, they sent him, everyone, to something like a boot camp for eight weeks." She paused as there was another change in the boys' routine. They fell to the ground to do sit ups. "When he got back, he had changed so much. I didn't really recognize him. He was stronger, faster. He started giving orders like a sergeant. Now whenever they're together, if there's a scuffle, the next morning they're out there."

"How long will they keep going?"

She shrugged. "An hour. Maybe two. It depends on Kota."

That's what it was yesterday. One hour meant working out together that long. "He tells them to? And he does it too? They do it all together?"

"All in," she said. "If they do it, he does it. They're a team. I don't understand it, really, but they've formed this brotherhood. I used to worry about this. I wondered why a twelve-year-old boy was working so hard and how could he order kids, sometimes twice his size, around like that. Instead, ever since then they've worked together, they've played together. They became each others' world." She laughed softly. "To be honest, I never thought they'd talk to anyone else," she said. She faced me. Her green eyes lit up, familiar like Kota's. "I thought it was those boys for life."

I wanted to share her curious looks. I couldn't get over how this was my fault. I knew it. I stirred them up. Kota said I was giving them something to fight over. "Is it bad that..."

She turned on me, grabbing my hands and looking me in the eye. "Sang," she said. "You're a bright little girl and for some reason, whatever reason, they've picked you to join them. To be honest, I'm rather jealous."

My eyes widened. "But why?"

"I've never seen a group of friends like them before. I wish I had friends like that when I was your age."

My eyes flicked to the window. "What does it mean?"

Her smile warmed. "I don't know what this means. I just have a really good feeling. I've asked Kota a million times about why they did certain things. I made him promise me that if he ever wanted out, he would tell me. He never once indicated he would ever leave those boys. The Academy changed everything."

I reached over to the window to tug one of the blinds up to look back out at them. The boys were now sitting in circle together, cross legged. Kota talked. They listened. They looked exhausted, especially Luke, Nathan and Gabriel. They were hunched over, with dark circles under their eyes.

"They're almost done. This is some pep talk before he dismisses them," Erica said. She patted my arm. "Go get a shower or you'll never get any warm water."

I didn't really care about warm water but I did as she suggested. I didn't want to be there when they came in. I didn't want them to know I knew.

I grabbed my bag and ran upstairs to Kota's room, locking myself into the bathroom just as I heard the back door of the house opening. I couldn't face them, knowing this punishment was all my fault. If I hadn't been there, if I hadn't had that dream, if I hadn't hurt North or made them bicker, they wouldn't have had to do it.

Why was it that no one complained about it? North had resisted at first but he got up and went with them. None of the others said anything about it. They did what Kota said. Kota the boss. Luke and Nathan and Gabriel weren't even there last night.

Despite what North said last night, I wasn't part of them. They didn't tell me their secrets. I wasn't really part of the Academy. I wasn't even included in the punishment when it was my fault in the first place.

So what did Kota and the others mean? Or were they trying to make me feel better when they said I was one of them?

I'd slept with Victor's bracelet on. I removed it, placing it on the counter by the sink. My fingers flicked over the tiny heart attached to it. Victor said he wanted me to open up. Maybe that was what was wrong.

It was too confusing to think about. North was right. What was I going to do? Run off and tell them to go away? I had to stay, behave, try not to cause any more problems, be as helpful as possible and maybe at some point it would all make sense to me.

Maybe I had to do what Nathan suggested. Don't worry about it and eventually they'd figure out where I fit in.

Haircut

I turned on the water in Kota's tub, plugging the hole quickly. I didn't care about hot water. I'd bathe in something lukewarm and save them as much heat as possible. I didn't work out like they did. I didn't need it. Plus if I bathed, I'd use less of the warm water anyway.

When the bath was only a quarter of the way filled, I hopped in, shivering and leaping to my toes at the chill. I cranked up the hot water. I slipped into the tub, kneeling and sitting back on my heels. I forced my chattering teeth closed and powered through, grabbing Kota's soap and washing.

The water warmed, and I settled in more, shutting off the faucet. I was rinsing away the last of the soap from my back and chest when there was a knock. The air shifted around me like the door opened.

"Oy, Trouble," Gabriel called.

My spine tingled from my butt to my neck. I shifted to draw my knees up to my chest, and wrapped my arms around my body. I didn't dare turn around and look at him. I hadn't drawn the curtain. Could he see me? "Gabriel?"

"Did you wash your hair yet?"

Of all things! "No."

"Don't. I'll wash it. I've got something for it."

"Ga..."

"After you put a towel on. Sheesh." The sound of the door closing caused another tingle to sweep up through me. I peered over my shoulder, but I was alone again. Didn't I lock the door?

I was finished with the bath, but I remained for a moment to make sure Gabriel wouldn't pop his head back in. Did he even do that or did he open the door and call in?

I hopped out quickly, dripping over the blue carpet. I opened the closet door and dug out a plush green towel, big enough that I could wrap myself up. Was I really going to open the door with just a towel wrapped around myself? Gabriel said I needed to trust him, right? Maybe this was part of what I needed to do to become closer to this strange family.

I stepped behind the door to use as a barrier and opened it slightly. "Gabriel?"

Gabriel stepped through, with two white unmarked plastic bottles in his hands. There were heavy shadows under his eyes. His hair was wet and combed back. He was wearing a neon orange tank top and Levi's jeans, barefoot. Deep blue crystals sparkled in his lobes, along with the usual three black rings.

His eyes did a sweep across me in the green towel and his cheeks tinted. "Oh."

"You said..." I started. Was he just kidding me? How was I supposed to know? "Do you want me to wash..."

He rolled his eyes. "Shut the fuck up. I'll do it." He jerked his head toward the sink. "Get your head in there, Trouble. We've got work to do."

"I don't want to model today," I said, stepping over to the sink. It'd been a long day yesterday, a long night, and it was already a crazy morning. The last thing I wanted to do was parade in front of the others.

"No. I'm going to cut your hair. I didn't have time to do that yesterday." He dropped the bottles onto the counter and turned the sink faucet on, testing with his fingers to find the right temperature. His eyes were barely open slits as he leaned his body against the sink.

"Do you have to do it today?" I asked. "You look sleepy."

"I'm fine," he said, his eyes on the water.

"Are you really?"

His crystal eyes flashed and settled on my face, puzzled. His smirk shifted and he patted me on the hip. "Come on. I can cut your fucking hair."

I swallowed, moving to bend over and let the water run over my head, mostly to please him. Maybe if I let him cut my hair, he could take a nap and relax.

Gabriel remained quiet as he cupped his hand to change the flow to wet my hair. He pulled back to open one of the bottles he brought in. A dollop chilled a spot on my head, the coolness sending another shiver through my spine. I adjusted the towel against my body.

The smell of the shampoo hit my nose. Acidic, a pang of metallic odor. I held my breath, wondering if it would go away. When I breathed in again, the scent lingered strongly in my nose.

"Gabriel..."

His fingers lathered the shampoo into my hair, massaging against my scalp. "What?"

"It smells."

"It's a special formula. Just let it work."

I swallowed, trying to hold my breath. The scent accosted my nose and mouth every time I breathed in. It was like the air was dripping with fermented fish and pennies.

He rinsed my hair, applied conditioner and had me back my head out of the water so he could work it in. The conditioner was worse than the shampoo, and I moved a hand from the towel to clutch my palm around my nose.

"It's not that bad," Gabriel insisted.

Was his nose broken? "Will it stick to my hair?"

"Will you stop worrying? Fucking shit, let me do my job, please?" He pushed my head into the water again.

He was getting the last of the conditioner rinsed out of the ends of my hair when a knock sounded at the bathroom door.

"Gabe," someone called from Kota's bedroom.

"What?" Gabriel called back.

The door rattled and North's head poked in, his hair messy and dripping water onto his cheeks. His eyes fell on me in the towel then shifted to Gabriel half bent over me with his fingers in my hair, and back to me in the towel.

"Oh hell no," he boomed. The door crashed against the bathroom wall. He had a towel wrapped around his waist, one hand clutched at his hip to hold it in place.

"Get out," Gabriel barked at him. "I'm washing her hair."

"You're not fucking washing her hair."

"Fuck you. I'm already done." He snapped the faucets off and stepped toward North, blocking me as I stood up fully.

I trembled, and my hair dripped around my bare shoulders. Not now! I didn't want any more fighting.

"What are you doing barging in?" Gabriel yelled.

"I thought it was you in here, and I came in to grab a razor. And now you've got Sang naked and you're fucking with her."

"I washed her god damn hair," Gabriel said. "And now I'm about to cut it."

"She can wash her own fucking hair."

"She let me in!" Gabriel snapped. He jabbed a finger back toward my face while staring down North. "Do you think for one minute I'd do anything to her? Have you lost your god damn mind? I didn't force my way in."

North's jaw set and he glared back. "Just go."

Gabriel rolled his eyes and he turned back to me. "Get dressed and meet me in the garage. Don't take too long." He opened the closet to grab another towel and handed it to me. "Wrap your hair in that so you don't drip everywhere, but don't dry it out."

I clutched the extra towel to my body. I didn't trust the towel I was wearing to hang on if I lifted my arms. I was also scared to say anything or move in fear they'd start fighting again. How could Kota be serious to think arguing meant they cared?

North started sniffing the air. He stepped over to me, pressing his nose to my scalp. He jerked his head back. "What the fuck is wrong with her head?"

"It's the shampoo," I whispered, holding the extra towel up close to my mouth to partially hide my face.

"Gabe," North barked. His eyes met mine and held firmly. "Change the formula. It smells like shit."

"It's not there to make her smell pretty."

"I don't care. It stinks. Change it." He smirked and winked at me. "Sang can't smell like a dead rat."

"God damn shit," Gabriel grumbled, marching into Kota's room and down the stairs. "Gabriel, don't wash her hair. Gabriel, change the motherfucking formula. Gabriel, cut off your own ear and eat it." There was more but he'd wandered off into the house and it was lost.

I rattled when I realized I was standing naked in a towel, alone with North, also naked in a towel. His was hanging off of his hips lower, and I saw more of the line of hair below his belly button, and the start of the angle of his hip bones. I focused on the wall.

North's fingers found my chin, lifting. "Don't let him walk over you," he said. "If you're uncomfortable, tell him to back off. If he doesn't listen, come find me."

I nodded. Was this the same North that was yelling a minute ago? His eyes were softer now, his touch gentle.

He stepped back. "Get some clothes on. I'll wait," he said. He closed the door behind himself.

I hurriedly put on my underwear and a pair of jean shorts with the bottom hem made to look like cut strips. Half of the shorts were bleached out at the thighs and covered in hot pink dye. I dropped a form-fitting, black t-shirt over my head. I put the bracelet on my wrist and wrapped the extra towel around my hair, twisting it up on my head to stop from dripping.

When my heart wriggled back down from my throat to my chest, I opened the door, wondering why there was a lock. Did it even work?

North was leaning against the frame. He turned, his eyes falling on my clothes. His lips parted and his palm brushed the side of his neck. "That's a... that looks really good on you."

My cheeks flushed. I squeezed the towel at my head. "Gabriel picked it out."

"He knows his shit." A smirk touched his lips. "Don't tell him I said that."

I shared a quiet smile with him. Black was his favorite color, right? Maybe he liked it when I wore it. I wanted to remember that. It felt like he was pleased and I wanted to do that again. I side-stepped away from the bathroom. "Sorry if I took too long."

He waved his hand in the air. "Go let that bastard cut your hair, will you?" He shut the door behind himself.

In the garage, Silas was sitting in a metal folding chair. Gabriel hovered over his head with a pair of electric clippers. Max was at Silas' feet, rolling over his toes. When I stepped barefoot down the steps, Max hopped up and met me, sniffing at my knees.

"I'll get you in a minute, Trouble," Gabriel mumbled, a black comb dangling from the corner of his pressed lips.

"Okay," I said, squatting to rub Max on the head before stepping around him to cross in front of Silas. I wanted to watch Gabriel cut hair.

Silas had a towel wrapped around his shoulders, wearing jeans and a white tank shirt that made his strong arms look more massive than usual. His eyes lit up when I came into view. "Nice shorts."

"Do you like the pink?" I asked, pulling back my head and holding out a leg so I could look down at the material on my own body.

"I like the blue with the pink," Silas said, pointing to the top half of the shorts where the colors blended together. "They're a good match."

"He likes dark blue," Gabriel said as he made his way around to the front of Silas, bending over slightly around

Silas' knees. He pointed the end of the clippers at Silas' nose. "Okay now for the shitty sideburns you've let grow too far on your face."

Silas' fingers smoothed over the hair in front of his ears. "Leave it midway like it is," he said.

"It's too much," Gabriel said. "I gave it a try. It's not working."

"Sang likes it." Silas peered around at me. "Don't you?"

I didn't recall seeing him with shorter sideburns. He'd always looked the same to me, so I didn't know how to respond. I did like how Gabriel had trimmed the top of his hair a little shorter. It looked like smooth fur on his head. I wanted to thread my fingers through it as it looked soft. "Yeah," I said, wanting to please Silas. "Let him keep it."

"Nu uh," Gabriel said. "They're coming off. They need to be shorter."

"Aw," I pouted. "Please?"

Gabriel turned on me, pointing the clippers in my direction. "Nope, stop that. I want that lip gone."

Silas appeared in my field of view. He made his own pout behind Gabriel's back and pointed to his lips and then to me.

It was difficult not to crack a smile at Silas's pout and his little plot, but I puckered my lower lip out more.

Gabriel scoffed. "Suck that lip back in, Sang. I mean it."

I tilted my head down, casting my eyes to his feet as if defeated, but left my lip out. I wasn't sure if it was working like Silas thought it would.

"Trouble, I'm gonna count to three, and if that god damn lip isn't pulled back in, I swear..."

"Don't be such a meanie," I said, glancing up with my head still tilted.

Gabriel's eyes slitted at me. "Trouble..."

"Meanie," I countered. I twisted the pout. Without intending to, it quivered as I sucked in a breath.

"Shit... fuck," Gabriel clutched his tools to his chest,

stepping away from Silas. The comb dropped from his mouth, rattling to the ground. "Trouble, don't do that to me," he begged. He stepped closer. Since his hands were full, he used his wrists to push my cheeks at my face. His eyes were stressed, his mouth drawn. "Don't do it anymore. God, please, no, please. You can't do that to me."

"You said you would cut them off," I said, with difficulty since he was squishing my cheeks.

"I won't. I won't touch it. Don't look at me like that. He can keep it. As long as you want it."

I stopped the pout, making a half smile against the squishing. "Are you sure?" I asked with enthusiasm, brightening up again quickly.

Gabriel's eyes focused on my face with an unsteady relief. Silas caught my eye. He held up a thumb, mouthing *good job*, and grinning. I grinned back at him without thinking and Gabriel caught it, whipping his head around just as Silas was lowering his hand and smoothing out his face.

"You motherfucker. That's it. You're done." Gabriel stepped back and ripped the towel from Silas' shoulders. "Walk around with uneven sideburns for all I care."

Silas laughed, stood up, and brushed his fingers around his shoulders to sweep away lost bits of hair. "Totally worth it."

"Thank you, Meanie," I said, trying to sound thrilled with his decision. I was pleased with the nickname I'd made up.

Gabriel's mouth fell. "No, not that..." He pointed the clippers at my face. "Don't you dare."

"It's only fitting," Silas said. "You call her Trouble."

"She *is* Trouble," Gabriel groaned. "And you know it."

"Nope, she's *aggele mou*."

"A devil's angel, maybe." Gabriel smirked. He snapped his fingers at me. "All right, now you." He pointed to the chair.

I tiptoed over to the chair, perching carefully. I was worried he would give me a horrible haircut. He'd only done boys' hair before, right? Would mine be cut short? Or would I end up looking like Luke with his longish blond hair hanging around his shoulders?

Silas backed off, sitting on the ground cross-legged, putting his hands behind him to lean back. It comforted me that he was there and might run interference in case Gabriel tried to buzz my hair short. I smiled pleasantly at Silas and he beamed.

Gabriel put aside the clippers on top of his blue duffle bag and out of the way of Max sniffing around our legs. Gabriel put the scissors in his back pocket. He took my towel from my shoulders and readjusted it to cover my body and started combing out my hair. He smoothed out the strands, feeling them between his fingers. "Feels better," he said. "Don't use the stuff you were using at home, okay? Wait for me to bring you a new batch."

Silas started making faces at me. My shoulders shook as I giggled.

"Stop it," Gabriel commanded. "You make her giggle when I'm cutting her hair, I'm likely to fuck up."

"Don't fuck up her hair," Silas said.

Gabriel stepped in front of me and blocked my view of Silas. Gabriel angled his head down to me. "You're too short," he said. He swept a finger across my cheek as he combed the hair close to my face. "I should take you home with me."

"We don't have time for that," Kota's voice floated out to us from beyond where I could see without turning my head. Max greeted him with a yip, leaping to meet him.

"I need her higher," Gabriel said. "It won't look right if I try to do it like this."

"Stand up for a second, Sang," Kota said, his footsteps moving closer.

I stood up, holding the towel in place around my shoulders. Kota was wearing Levi's jeans and a hunter green polo. His brown hair was smoothed back, still slightly damp. His eyes swept over me, a smile catching on his lips. He nudged his glasses up by the bridge and sat on the chair, putting his knees together.

He patted at his lap. "Come sit here," he commanded.

"I can't move around you," Gabriel said.

"She can sit facing me and then sit facing away as you need," he said. "Unless you want to wait."

Gabriel grumbled, shifting on his feet as if considering the options. "Fine."

Kota planted his hands on my hips and I sat on his knees, facing him first. I sat closer to the edge of his knees so Gabriel didn't have to lean around Kota's legs. My palms met with Kota's chest to steady myself. My face felt hot. It was an awkward position. I was forced to look at Kota. His eyes were always so questioning, so invasive. Not for the first time, I felt he could see every little secret buried inside me.

Gabriel combed the back of my head and started snipping the scissors. *Comb, snip. Comb, snip.*

"Is he making spikes in my hair?" I asked Kota.

Kota laughed, his friendly voice echoing in the garage. His palms fell to rest on my thighs just above my knees. "Did you want spikes?"

"No spikes," Silas said.

"I'm not doing spikes," Gabriel mumbled. "Not today at least."

"I didn't know you cut girls' hair," Silas said.

Gabriel shuffled around to the side. *Comb, snip.* "Sang's my first."

My eyes widened at Kota. "Really?"

Kota grinned. "He's kidding."

"Like hell I am," Gabriel said. "What, you think I've got dummy girls in my closet at home to practice on?"

"What about all those girls you woo or break hearts of or what not?" I said, recalling his poem and his singing and all the times he talked about things he knew about girls.

"Mergh," Gabriel said. "Shut up or I'll leave you with

half a haircut."

I rolled my eyes, but pressed my lips together. I didn't want to bug him anymore. We'd been picking on him a lot that morning and he still looked like he was about to fall over from exhaustion.

Gabriel was measuring out my hair just off my shoulder when the side door opened. Erica stepped out, wearing shorts now, and a faded brown t-shirt. She padded out into the garage. The air electrified around me. Silas half coughed. Kota stiffened in the chair at this. Gabriel combed my hair more than he snipped. Silent warning system?

Victor followed behind her, wearing designer jeans, and a short sleeve button up white shirt. Victor's eyes fell on us. His eyes blazed at me in a way that was confusing. I wanted to tilt my head at him to ask silently what he was thinking, but I forced my head to keep still, worried Gabriel might mess up. Victor roughed fingers through his wavy hair and rubbed at the back of his head.

Erica's eyes fell curiously on me in Kota's lap. "How's it going?"

Kota didn't flinch, didn't move his hands from my knees. "So far, so good," he said.

"She's still too short," Gabriel complained.

"I know you can do it," Kota said. "You can't stop now."

Erica moved to her car at the other side of the garage, leaning against it and folding her arms over her chest to watch. "Do we need a stool?"

"No," Silas and Gabriel said at the same time. Victor remained quiet but his eyes ignited and flared.

Erica's head tilted, confusion slipping into her eyes. I knew why the boys refused a stool, but now I knew Erica most likely didn't know anything about what was happening with me. They didn't tell her.

"Or pillows for her to sit on?" she asked. "Phone books?"

"She'll be fine," Kota said. His legs raised up and

dropped out from under me, causing me to bounce.

I gasped, gripping at his legs, half grinning and mouthing a small ouch.

"Hey, hey," Gabriel said. "I'm gonna cut her ear if you do that."

Erica's eyes flickered back and forth between my face and her son's. Gabriel continued to measure and cut but she didn't seem as interested in this. I watched her from behind locks of hair in my face. Her lips twitched. She was eager to ask something or say something, but I thought maybe she wasn't sure how to start. No one else was talking, either. Kota was intently watching Gabriel work. I stiffened, feeling the weight of something floating in the air, left unspoken. I wasn't sure how to move or behave.

"All right," Gabriel said. He nudged my arm. "Turn around so I can do the front."

I slipped back off of Kota's knees, turning around. Again I was facing Silas. Erica was out of view now. Kota's hands felt for my hips again and he pulled me back until I was perched on his knees. In an effort to keep myself stable, I put my hands behind myself on his legs. Kota kept his hands at my waist to steady me.

Gabriel started combing hair in front of my face, closing off my view of nearly everything.

"What are you all going to do today?" Erica asked, finally breaking the lull.

"North and I are going to do some work at the diner," Silas said.

"Oh," Erica's tone lifted, but it lingered in a peculiar way. This wasn't who she was hoping would answer. "Is it almost done?"

"A couple more weeks," Silas said, seeming oblivious to the inflection from Erica. "We're trying to finish it before football games start."

"That'll keep you busy," Erica said. "But football sounds fun." *Pause.* Kota's fingers tensed against my hips, gripping more than just holding me. "Are you going to take

Sang to the football games, Dakota? It'd make a nice date."

There it was. It was what Erica was waiting to hint at the entire time. I couldn't see her face, but her voice tipped higher at the end of her last sentence. Expectation.

Kota's leg shifted underneath me. "I didn't know she liked football."

What did that mean? He would have asked me if he thought I liked it? Did he want to? My mind blazed through a thousand different possibilities. Dating? I'm just trying to get through my sophomore year with my new strange group of friends and a mother insistent on punishments they told me weren't normal. When in the world did I have time to date anyone? When did they? Jessica had been right, we were always busy.

"You didn't ask her. Sang, do you want Kota to take you to the football games?"

I felt a silent pressure from everyone in the room. What was I supposed to say? If I said no, did it mean I didn't like Kota? If I said yes, did it mean we'd be going on a date? What did that mean to everyone else? I couldn't see anyone to confirm how I was supposed to answer.

Gabriel swiped at my hair with his comb, removing a lock from my eyes. His crystal blue eyes stared down at me and he inclined his head a little.

"Yes," I said quickly to recover for the moment I had paused. If Gabriel was telling me to answer positively, I would. "I'd like to." It wasn't a dishonest answer. I'd never been to a football game. It was Kota's hesitation and unease behind me that had me stumped.

"There," Erica said. "That wasn't so hard, was it? You should ask girls about date ideas before you assume."

"I didn't know she was interested in dating," Kota said in a quiet voice. Where was Kota, the confident leader of an elite Academy crew that barked orders?

"Of course she's interested," Erica said. "She's your age. You guys should be dating."

"That's not exactly what I meant," Kota replied.

Gabriel combed the hair in my face, raising the

scissors to my cheeks, shaving off the start of bangs that hung over my eyes. He started layering my hair from my cheeks to an inch from the start of my shoulder.

"Well what do you mean? She's a nice girl and it is obvious she likes you and would date you."

"How do you know?" Kota asked, sounding genuinely curious.

"A girl doesn't sit in your lap unless she's interested in dating you," Erica said in a happy tone.

My eyes widened and my lips parted. Was that true? Is that what the guys meant? Is that what happened when I sat on their laps? Were they all thinking the same thing?

Gabriel combed my hair away from my eyes and winked down at me. When he moved aside to comb my hair, Silas was sitting up on the concrete of the garage, his dark eyes sought out mine, intense.

What have I done? I've sat in most of their laps, and in front of the others. Dating wasn't what I was thinking about at all. I had no idea if that was what they were thinking.

Kota made a guttural grumble with his throat. "Maybe we shouldn't talk about it now."

"All I'm saying is, if you're going to do it, you should ask her outright. If you wait, someone else might and then you'll lose your chance. She's a pretty girl and she's a sweetheart. I'm surprised she's not dating one of the football players."

Silas beamed at me, his eyes brightening. I wasn't sure what he was thinking. Since he played football and I sat in his lap, was I expected to date him?

Did I want to?

Kota's fingers loosened and then gripped at my waist repeatedly, "Well, I'll have to take her out sometime."

"You should take her tonight. She's got that new outfit and now a new haircut."

"We've got school tomorrow," Kota said quietly.

"I think my straight-A son can handle being a little

tired Monday morning after going out with a girl."

"Fine," Kota relented. "I'll take her out."

"Well don't make me pull your arm or anything," Erica said. There was movement just outside of my vision, the sound of footsteps and the side door opened. "You guys come in and have pancakes. North is making them."

The door closed.

Awkward pause. I released the breath I'd been holding since she first started asking so many questions. Dating! Was she serious? My face heated. My core shook. I was ready to run home and hide for a few hours to figure this out. I didn't know what I was supposed to do or say or feel.

"Holy shit," Gabriel said. "The first time Sang gets asked out and it's by Kota's mother."

"Shut up," Kota said.

Gabriel laughed. He curled one of the locks of hair beside my face in his fingers. "Well if you don't want to, I'll take her."

"Sang has to go home," Kota said, the command returning to his voice. "We've already taken enough risks this weekend and we've got enough to worry about before Monday."

I knew Kota was right. A last minute date probably wasn't in the plans for the day. Still, the way he said it made me cringe. It felt like he didn't want to and he would stuff work and school in as an excuse to get out of it. It wasn't fair of me to think of it this way. After all, his mother started it. But the slight of his almost-rejection still stung.

At least Gabriel wanted to. I held onto that thought.

"Okay, I think this is done," Gabriel said. He put down the scissors and chewed on his comb. He picked out a big brush from his bag and started brushing through my hair smoothly. "I should take her back upstairs to do it up nice."

"We should get out of here," Silas said. "Give Erica a break."

"And you have other things to do, Gabe," Kota said.

Gabriel twisted his lips. He beeped my nose and

reached for the towel, freeing it from my shoulders. With his free hand, he took mine. “Stand up, Trouble, so they can see.”

I stood. My hair felt cool and lighter against my head and the freshly cut bangs tickled my face. I lifted a hand to check the length around the back. It was shorter than I expected, maybe an inch below the top of my shoulders.

Gabriel popped my hand with a palm. “Stop. You’ll mess it up.”

I turned around. Kota scrutinized from his chair, smiling. His cheeks tinted red. “Looks good.”

Victor was standing against the back wall, his arms crossed over his chest. He’d been so quiet the entire time that I had thought he had slipped into the house again. His fire eyes simmered when he caught my gaze, almost sad. Was it because of the conversation? Is that what the bracelet meant? That he wanted to date?

Victor shook his head, as if shaking away deep thoughts. His eyes flickered as he examined the new haircut. The corner of his mouth lifted. “Gabriel, you’re such a bastard.”

Gabriel smirked. “Oy, why?”

“You made sure she couldn’t use her clip.”

“She can use it,” Gabriel said. He smoothed his hands through my hair, pulling most of it back into a pony tail that he held between his fingers at the back of my head. A few locks of hair fell across my face. With a free hand, he pushed the locks behind my ears but they wouldn’t hold. The edges tickled my cheeks. “But check it out, even if she does, her bangs frame her face. In a sexy way.”

“Is that how we want her to look at school?” Victor asked. He rubbed at his chin. “We have enough problems already.”

“Fuck those guys,” Gabriel said. “I don’t care what they think. I’ll beat the shit out of them if they touch her.”

“Me, too,” Silas said. He lifted himself to standing, stepped over and swept his fingers through the shorter strands of my face. "I like it."

I smiled, simply happy my hair wasn't in spikes or something weird.

"We've got a lot to do today, guys." Kota said.

"Yeah, yeah," Gabriel said, groaning, and crossing to put his things back into his duffle bag.

"Thank you, Meanie," I said quietly.

Gabriel rolled his eyes, a grin popping onto his face. "Trouble, I swear, if you weren't so damn cute…"

♥

The Academy, Capable

Erica refrained from talking about dating at breakfast, which was both a relief to me and made me sad, too. I almost wanted her to pry more into Kota's thoughts about me. I wanted to understand why he dismissed her request so easily with excuses about work. Did I want to know the truth? Maybe we were just friends. Perhaps he didn't see me as someone he wanted to date.

I didn't want to think like that. It was too soon. Last night was the first time we'd hung out together, outside of school, in a very long time. At least not at my house where we expected my mother or someone else to pop in at any moment. Dating probably didn't even occur to him, like it hadn't occurred to me at all.

Now I was thinking about it, though. It was like Erica had woken up something inside of me. It was the first time I realized that dating was something I could do, and there were guys around me I could possibly do it with. It was an overwhelming thought that I wasn't sure how to take.

Maybe he, too, needed time to register this. Or was I hoping for thoughts that might not exist at all? Did I want to date Kota? What about the others?

My lips were glued together during and after breakfast. I helped Silas collect pillows and Victor with folding blankets to put away in the downstairs closet. North helped Erica clean up dishes and the kitchen. Gabriel, Nathan and Luke disappeared to Nathan's house. Kota said it was for work, but they all looked exhausted. I hoped they were going to take a nap.

Silas and North left after the house was clean. When Erica wasn't looking, they both hugged me.

North brushed his fingers through my hair when he stepped back. "Call me," he said, his intense dark eyes cutting through mine in a silent demand. He wanted me to call him for a reason. He had something to say. Why he didn't say it here?

I promised I would and they both left. Erica escaped to go to the grocery store. Kota went outside to walk Max. I helped Victor drag the new bean chairs back upstairs.

"Ugh." Victor huffed as we tossed the last bag chair on the floor inside Kota's room. He stood back, his hands on his hips. "I like them, but we should've gotten more, some for upstairs and some for downstairs. We wouldn't have to drag them all over. They're hard to navigate up those stairs."

"That'd be a lot of chairs."

He sank into the chair, and stretched. "I told Kota we should just go to my house."

"What's your house like?" I slipped into another chair next to him, curling up to put my cheek against the back of it. From my angle, I could gaze over at him. I admired his long fingers, the lean muscles of his body and the way his jeans framed around his legs.

"It's okay," he said. "A little bigger. More room for all of them. Us." He rocked his head back and flashed a smile at me. "I mean you, too."

I knew what he meant, but I was happy he felt he needed to make sure to include me. "So I'll see it one day?"

"Of course," he said. "Whenever you want."

A smile touched my face as I honestly wouldn't have minded going right in that moment. "Where is it?"

"Downtown."

"In Summerville?"

"In Charleston. On the peninsula."

I blinked at him, tilting my head. "I haven't been there

yet. Not that I've really been anywhere, but you know."

"The next time we get a chance, we should go. There's a lot to see."

Something caught on in my brain about what he'd just said. "You drive in from the city every day for school?"

"I pick up Gabriel on the way, too."

"Isn't it a long drive?"

"Depends on traffic. Sometimes forty minutes, sometimes an hour."

My lips popped open. "You drive that far every morning?"

"Every morning."

I traced the edge of the chair, feeling the smooth softness, the coolness of the material against my skin. "That's a long way to go for a school that doesn't want us there in the first place."

"I can't think of it that way," he said. "We could all quit when we want, but the school would be no better off and we'd feel awkward knowing all we had to do was stick it out for a few months."

"You only have the one year," I said, swinging my head back around to look up at him. "I've got a couple more years left to go after this one."

The fire in his eyes faded a little. "You've got us now."

"You'll still hang out with me after school is over, right?"

He grinned. "Of course. If you're not tired of us by then." He nudged my leg with his toe.

"I think I'm supposed to chop you now," I said, lifting my own leg and nudging him in the thigh.

"You wouldn't do that to me," he said.

"Wouldn't do what?" Kota's voice echoed to us as he thumped his way up the stairs. He grinned when he spotted the two of us. "I'm going to forget these are here and trip over them in the night." He fell into another one across from us. He tilted his head back, staring up at the ceiling.

"Or I could just sleep like this."

"I like them," I said, curling up tighter, hanging my feet off the edge.

"We can't get too comfortable," Kota said, picking his head up.

I rolled my eyes. "We've got work to do, right?"

He smirked. "You'll get the hang of it."

"Then what's my job? What am I doing today?"

Kota opened his mouth to answer, but his face changed and he leaned in the chair, pulling his cell phone out of his pocket. He poked at it, scanning the screen. "Well, I, unfortunately, have to go."

"Where?" I asked.

He typed something into his phone. "Academy."

Should have known. Did it mean there was something about the school? Other Academy business? Was one of the other guys in trouble? I pressed my lips together to hold back the questions. If he could have told me, he probably would have.

Kota released a small grunt, stood up, looking at Victor. "Can you make sure she gets inside?"

"Of course." Victor hauled himself up until he was standing, dropping a hand down close to me, palm up, open and waiting. "I get to take you home."

I twisted my lips. I knew I should go home. I'd been gone for so long that it felt awkward to be going back. Had it only been for a day? It felt much longer and yet it all happened so fast.

I put my hand in Victor's. "So my job is to go home?" I didn't want to sound disappointed, but for some reason I thought there was something else I needed to do. I didn't want to go back yet. I wanted to be with them.

Victor laughed, gripping my hand and tugging me to my feet. "I'll take you anywhere you'd like to go. Name it."

"Take her home, Vic," Kota said, utilizing his commanding tone. "No detours."

Victor rolled his eyes. "But first, we should get you

back home for now."

I caught the feeling that this was the plan in the first place, except perhaps Kota had meant to come along and now he couldn't.

Victor's thumb drifted over the back of my hand. Kota collected his green messenger bag and dug his keys out of his pocket. "I should be back tonight. I'll text to check in, Sang. Okay?"

"Okay," I replied, with my free hand touching my finger to my lower lip. Did I need to be checked in with? Should I be doing something like that?

Kota smiled, catching a lock of my hair between his fingers. He tucked it behind my ear, and it held in place. "Listen to Victor."

"Was I not going to?"

They both laughed. Kota headed to the stairs. "Let's get out of here before my mom gets home and she has to ask why I'm not taking you with me."

He kept secrets from his mother. What would he say later if she asked? Would he lie?

I collected my book bag downstairs as Victor picked up his overnight bag. Now that the house was nearly empty, it felt as if the night before might have only happened in my head. How sad.

I stood with Victor outside in the driveway as Kota started his car and turned onto the street, disappearing around the bend. The sleepover was done. Back to reality.

♥♥♥

I walked in the back door to my house with my heart thundering and my knees shaking. Victor was climbing to the roof and would meet me back in my room. We were back to this secret Academy protection. This time I had the disadvantage of being gone for a day not knowing my mother's condition or location in the house; if she was awake and anywhere other than in her room, I could be in trouble.

My father's car wasn't in the garage so I knew he wasn't home yet. I stood near the back door, listening to movements in the house, trying to reacclimatize myself. Music from a radio drifted toward me. Was Marie home? It had to be hers since mine was broken. No television, but it could mean my mother was asleep. Or awake and roaming the house.

I snuck up the back stairwell, tiptoeing to my room. I didn't want to alert my mother to my presence before letting Victor inside if I could help it.

When I made it to the upstairs hallway, the sound of music drifted not from Marie's room, but from mine. I froze in the hallway. Was Marie in my room? Was my mother? Did something happen? I strained to hear any noise, any movement to confirm the location of either my sister or my mother. The only thing that made me hesitate checking with either of them first was the risk of getting into trouble and leaving Victor on the roof waiting.

My door opened from the inside. I took a step back, pressing myself to the wall as if that would conceal me in some way.

Victor poked his head out. He checked the front stairs and turned, finding me against the wall.

I pressed my hand to my heart to try to calm it. "Victor," I whispered, "you're not supposed to..."

"It's okay," he said. He held out a hand to me and winked. "Come on, princess. You were taking too long. I can't wait to show you."

"Show me what?" I asked, reaching for his hand.

His fire eyes sparked and his long fingers enveloped mine as he lured me into my room. He shut the door behind us and stepped away from me, putting his back to the door frame, his eyes expectant.

I sensed differences in stages. The air wasn't stale, as I expected after a night with the windows closed, but electrified with warmth of recent visitors. The air smelled of cypress and vanilla and berries and spice, familiar. At first glance though, it was all the same. There was still the single bookshelf against the wall, the broken stereo on top. There was still the same bed next to the window, the bed made with the soft green comforter. Or was it?

I tiptoed closer. It wasn't the same comforter. The stitching was different and the color was a couple of shades off. It was a slight difference, but to me, it was noticeable.

It wasn't the same bed, either. It was bigger, about a foot wider and a little longer.

I angled my head to try to get a different perspective, suddenly unsure of my own memory and my own eyes.

A second look at the bookshelf forced me to turn my attention to it. It was the same dark brown color, but it was definitely wider and taller. The torn books had been replaced with new copies, plus additional volumes by the same authors and some other titles I didn't recognize.

The stereo, too, was different. The music playing was a piano piece. I recognized a song by Yuko Ohigashi, who I'd mentioned was one of my favorite composers, but it was a tune I hadn't had the chance to download yet.

With my mouth hanging open in surprise, my hand drifted to the edge of the bookshelf. My fingers hovered over the wood but stopped short. The top was intricately carved.

I was terrified to touch as if touching made it real, or would make it disappear. Either option felt like too much. It was impossible.

"The last time it fell over, the back support was fractured," Victor stage-whispered to me. I gazed back at him. His head rested against the door frame, his eyes on me. "North was pretty sure it would have fallen apart if you put anything more on it. He and Silas made you a new one."

They made it! I forced my fingers to it now, tracing the details of the carving. It was mostly a leaf and vine pattern with roses mixed in, but when I peered closer, I caught hearts replacing a few of the leaves. Hidden hearts.

"And the books?" I asked quietly.

"Kota."

I swallowed the lump in my throat, reading the titles of the books on the shelves. Thick volumes of *Sherlock Holmes*, *Gone with the Wind* and other stories I'd told him I liked but didn't personally own filled the space, in alphabetical order according to author name.

"And the bed?"

"Wasn't sure if you'd notice," Victor said. His footsteps alerted me that he was moving closer. I couldn't make myself face him. I stared at the books. "Gabriel tried to match your blanket. It was thin and needed replacing. There's a spare, too. And new sheets."

"It's bigger," I said, still not turning. I didn't want him seeing me confused, touched, terrified, warmed, a mix of so many emotions at once.

He stepped closer behind me until I could smell the rich moss and berries of his cologne. His palm smoothed over the bare skin of my forearm. "Sweetie, no one liked your bed. Maybe you didn't notice, but there were springs poking out. You really needed a new one."

"The stereo?" I whispered, a tremble spilled down my spine at his touch. I gazed down at his hand on me, staring blankly at his lean, strong arm, and the way the start of his white shirt fell across his bicep.

"Mr. Blackbourne found something similar to what you had. It isn't exact, but I think it's close enough. I was going to get you a new one, a nicer one, but we were taking a lot of risks as it was with the bed and the shelf. I'm willing to bet they won't notice a thing, though."

They replaced everything. I had new clothes thanks to him. I had new bedroom furniture thanks to all of them. I didn't know where to start. I didn't know what I should do. I knew the answer to my next question, but I asked anyway. "How?"

He inched closer. His breath fell on my hair. "Last night."

The admission forced another shiver through me. It

was obvious. Scenes from the night before raced through my mind, suddenly becoming clear, like Nathan pulling me away from checking in on my mother to keep me with them instead of trying to talk myself out of spending the night and going home. There was Silas and North and Victor, my guardians, had placed me next to them so I wouldn't notice the others were gone. Nathan the courageous ninja, Luke the silent thief, and Gabriel the ever-demanding stylist weren't there when I had the nightmare and instead were in my room, putting everything into place. Kota walked in after North had started shouting. Was he observing from his bedroom or was he outside as a lookout?

It was perfect timing, and the perfect night to do it. Marie had been gone. My father wasn't going to be home. I was under their protection. With my mother, another sniff of Luke's brown bottle would ensure they could move everything in without being noticed.

My heart thumped so hard, I wavered where I stood. I forced out the last question I could think to ask. "Why?"

Victor's fingertips traced the soft side of my arm, sliding down to my palm. He took my hand in his, warming. The thumb traced the skin on the back of my hand.

"You belong with us," he breathed against my neck. "And this is who we are. Whatever you need. From now on."

The tear traced my cheek, circling my chin before I realized it'd fallen from my eye. I wrestled with the idea that they shouldn't have. I didn't need a new bed. I didn't need a new shelf. I didn't need new clothes. Part of me wanted to fling my fears back at him, not wanting to accept any of this. I wanted to demand my old things back. The thought of them putting so much effort into me felt like too much. They'd already saved my life. They'd already protected me at school. They stood by me when no one else would. What could I have possibly done to deserve it?

What more could I ask of them?

But they did it without asking. The Academy gave them whatever they needed, like Mr. Blackbourne had explained to me in what felt like an eon ago. I had thought about it since that day, trying to understand what it must be like for them. They lacked nothing they needed so they wouldn't be distracted when they had other things to do. Like saving a school.

Or saving me.

I thought of Gabriel cutting Silas's hair, of Victor driving Gabriel in from downtown to school, and of Kota and the others pitching in at the diner. They took care of each other, and sometimes without asking. They got what they needed and worked together so they could do their job and move forward.

Family first, Kota had said. Family first and when that was in order, we moved on to other things.

And I was now family.

I spun around to face Victor, my arms finding his neck and my cheek tracing the crook of his shoulder. I wanted to say thank you. I wanted to find the words.

I wanted nothing more than to no longer be the one who got help, but to be one of them that fit in, that knew my place where I could give back to them in every way possible. If it meant quietly accepting so they would no longer feel I was in need, so we could move past it and do something else, I would swallow back all the pride forever. But I would always thank them. I would always remember.

My voice caught, and my lips trembled too much to say what I was thinking. I could only rub my cheek against Victor's shoulder, begging silently that he would understand.

Victor's arms wrapped around my body. His fingers traced the spaces between my ribs. His breath tickled the top of my head as he chuckled. "Don't start thanking me yet, princess. There's still a lot to show you."

I pulled back from him, pushing my fingers to my cheeks to wipe at my eye. "What do you mean?" I whispered. How could there be more? There was nothing left in the room.

"First things first," he said, his fire eyes ablaze and the curl of his lips stoking the flames. He took my hand again, guiding me to the closet. He twisted the handle, opening the door.

The old traded clothes from Derrick and Danielle and my sister hung neatly on the rack. My old shoes were at the bottom. Nothing else looked touched.

"Oh," I said, unable to hide my tone of surprise. I assumed he was going to show me the new clothes were in place.

"It's part of the secret," he said. "We wanted to make sure Danielle or your sister wouldn't be able to take your new clothes. So we're leaving these here. They won't be able to steal your new things if they can't access them."

"Where did they go?"

"We've been after Nathan to clean that closet of his out for a while. You make the perfect incentive, I guess."

"They're in his closet?"

Victor nodded, a gentle wave of his brown hair falling across his forehead. "I'm sorry. It means more effort on your part. You can keep a handful of things in the attic. The rest you can keep at his house. You can trade off as you need and do your laundry at his house. If they happen to discover the attic, there won't be much there to take. It'll limit the damage if they try." He hovered his face over mine. "But if they do try it again, we won't hesitate to make them stop and return everything. They got away with it this time. Next time won't be the same."

I had to agree with this. I didn't like the idea of a confrontation. It could easily escalate with my parents, or with Danielle's parents perhaps. It might turn into something bigger that no one would want to deal with. "I guess I could have gone over and asked for my old things back. Now that she probably realizes she can't wear them to school. Maybe she wouldn't have made a big deal about it."

Victor rolled his eyes. "Gabriel's been dying to take you shopping for weeks. I haven't had a conversation with him since school started that didn't involve him asking about taking you out."

I pressed a palm against my heated cheek. "Gabriel would have done it anyway."

"Gabriel likes having a new doll to play with," he said, gently squeezing my hand. "And you're a lot more appreciative and patient with him than we are."

I couldn't help but smile. "You're kidding."

"When he goes shopping with me, I barely last through two rounds of trying on clothes before I'm yelling at him."

I giggled at the thought of Victor and Gabriel shopping together, or from that thought, of Silas or North shopping with him. I couldn't imagine them accepting Gabriel's demands.

"A couple more things," he said, his fire eyes cooling to a simmer. "I don't know if you'll like this part, though."

"What?" Was there a catch? Of course. There had to be. Maybe I had to work off the expense. Maybe it meant working hours at the diner or doing favors for them at school.

He closed the closet door and slanted his head toward a vent in the wall. "Look close."

My eyes drifted to the vent. The grate was standard, painted white. It didn't need replacing. It still looked the same.

Victor stepped away from me, pointing. "Right here," he said.

I followed him, squinting. Light reflected against a peculiar spot behind the grate's blades. My eyes adjusted enough to catch the hint of a lens. "A camera?"

"Mr. Blackbourne's orders," he said. "I'm sorry. There was no talking him out of it. It was the condition to let you stay."

"You'll be watching?" I asked, but I knew this answer. There was no way the boys could stay here with me every night. The risk was too great to get caught, something else had to be done.

I had assumed when my mother calmed down and didn't dispense punishments as often, they would realize it wasn't that bad. I thought we were waiting for that moment and they would back off.

Instead, they were ten steps ahead of me, only thinking the opposite direction. They were going to keep their promise to ensure I would never again end up tied to a chair or something worse.

"It's not recording," Victor said. "It's not even on right now. The cameras will only turn on if for some reason we can't reach you on the cell phone. There's one in every major room and the hallways."

"And the bathroom," I realized, feeling the thread of a shiver starting at the base of my spine.

Victor breathed a sigh. "Yes, but also not on right now. The procedure is to text you if you're not with us and we haven't heard from you within an hour or so. We'll text three times within ten minutes. It gives you an opportunity to reach us in case you didn't hear your phone the first time. No text or call back, we start with your bedroom, and then all other major rooms before checking something like the bathroom."

I wasn't sure I liked this new plan. They could look in on me at any time. But would they? Did I trust them?

I swallowed back the fears. I had promised I would do what they asked in order to remain here. Otherwise Mr. Blackbourne would remove me from the house. They weren't ready for that sort of thing, not without involving the Academy. I wasn't sure what it meant, but wasn't sure I was willing to find out just now. I wanted to know about the Academy, but didn't want to do it at such a high risk. I had to trust them.

"What about at night?" I asked. "Am I supposed to check in every hour?"

"No. You can sleep. Keep your phone with you." He

shifted on his feet, putting weight from one foot to the other. "I can't promise they won't check on you while you sleep."

My fingers fluttered to the base of my throat. It was surreal, but perhaps since they'd already slept in the room with me, some even in the same bed, it didn't feel intrusive. It felt almost lonely.

Did I prefer to have them with me?

"You're not mad, are you?" Victor asked, stepping closer to my side.

I glanced over at him. "Mad?"

"I know it feels... invasive. I felt the same way when it happened to me."

This surprised me. "Is your house rigged up like this?"

"Yes. We all have cameras."

My eyebrows flew up and my eyes widened. "And you get checked up on?"

He shrugged. "Only if no one can reach me by my phone. It's a security precaution. We're not at risk due to our families so much now, so we're not required to check in. Your situation is a little unique to us."

He didn't have to say it. His tone did it for him. My parents were a high risk. Theirs weren't.

But how could I be mad about something they lived through already? Maybe I had been wrong. If they all went through it, maybe the cameras would have been something they would have eventually done. Maybe I was wrong about not being a part of them because they didn't include me in the morning workout or a few of the other things they had to do. Maybe they were getting around to it, working it in slowly as they thought to do so.

"I'm not mad," I said. "It's... surprising. But I understand. You can't sleep here all the time."

"I wouldn't mind," he said, his eyes sparking again. "But yes, we can't do that every night."

I smiled at him, catching his intention but unsure how to respond. I'd enjoyed it, too, even if it was crazy and extreme. I still wasn't sure if I fully processed the idea of them sleeping with me in the bed, and a few of them had already done so.

"You can check the cameras, too," he said. "Do you have your cell phone?"

I paused, trying to remember where I'd put it. Blushing, I tucked my hand inside my shirt, lifting the phone from the cup of my bra.

Victor grinned, taking the phone from me. "Secret pockets," he said. He flipped the phone in his hands and pushed a button. He drew close to show me the illuminated screen. "This here," he said, pointing to an app displaying a pink heart. He touched it. The app activated, showing a map of a cartoon house. It was the side view of two upstairs bedrooms, the bathroom, both staircases, a couple hallways, a master bedroom downstairs, and a kitchen and living room and the garage. "You can press any of these," he said, and he pressed the cartoon bedroom that was colored in pink, "and..."

While he paused, a loading icon circled itself. The screen changed to reveal Victor and I standing together in the room at that moment, from the angle of the camera in the vent. My eyes instinctively went to the vent and back to the phone, as if trying to catch myself.

"It'll make things easier on you, too," he said. "You can check on your mother and Marie without having to risk getting caught snooping."

This made it better. I had access to my own cameras. It was now a tool for me, not just them. "You have this app on your phone?"

He smiled, pulling his phone from his back pocket and pushing a button, showing me the pink heart, dead center on the front. "You're always with me."

I rolled my eyes, unable to smother the smile. "Don't I get your app?"

He shifted, as if debating this. "Maybe later."

Did they not trust me? Or was there another reason?

"But now that's out of the way," he beamed, stuffing

his phone back into his pocket and crossing the room toward the attic door. "There's one more thing."

"Did Luke cut that beam out?" I asked, knowing Gabriel had asked him to. I turned off my phone, drawn to Victor's new surprise.

"Not just that," Victor said. He dropped to his knees, hooking his fingers around the door handle and opening it. "Crawl inside."

I peered in to the shadows of the attic, not able to see far. I twisted the phone around to use it as a light but his hand closed around mine, stopping me.

"Trust me," he said. "Just go a few feet in." The fire flickered in his eyes.

A smile brushed my lips. They might pick on Gabriel for his presentation style, but Victor had a flair for it, too.

I crawled through the open doorway. Not a foot inside, as I expected to feel the rough of the raw wood, I was surprised by softness. My fingers spread out, smoothing over the fibers of a cushioned carpet.

The next part I noticed was the air. It wasn't the warm and thick air, but as cool as the rest of the house. It was still dark and I crept forward, anticipating other surprises.

When I was about halfway to the platform, I stopped, sitting on my heels, and looked back toward Victor.

He hovered in the doorway, a shadow against the light filtering in from the bedroom. He crawled in, closing the door behind himself and casting us into complete blackness.

"Victor," I whispered to him.

"Trust me," he said.

I waited.

A click.

The area lit up around us. A track of lighting had been installed to the side.

The sconces were shaped like roses.

The lighting followed all the way to the back. The plush carpet below me was a deep blue, nearly black. The walls were covered in a dark material. I traced my fingers over the wall, feeling padding.

"It's been soundproofed," Victor said, crawling toward me. He stopped two feet in and pointed to the side wall. "There's this, too."

I knee-walked on the carpet toward him. Against the wall was a miniature wardrobe about the size of a large travel trunk. It was painted a similar dark blue color to the carpet.

Victor opened the front, revealing a tiny collection of the clothing he'd purchased for me yesterday. Skirts, shorts and blouses were hung up on the right side. A few pairs of underwear and a couple of bras were folded neatly into place on shelving on the left.

"I'm sorry about the colors," he said. "We had to keep it dark. The light switch is hidden, but if they ever looked inside on their own, a pink or light color they would probably see and..."

My hand shot out, my fingers falling on his lips. His eyes widened, but he didn't have to keep saying he was sorry. He never had to apologize. They had reasons, and I understood.

As if I needed pink carpet.

"It's amazing," I said.

His mouth shifted into a smile against my fingers. "Still not done," he mumbled. He nudged me toward the platform.

I started crawling. Now that there was light, I could tell the beam had been taken out. There were carpeted steps built up against the opening.

When I got close, I half stood. Another two-person beanbag chair, like the ones at Kota's, filled the space. This one, though, was mostly black, but the top part to sit in was pink.

I turned slightly, looking back at Victor, who had followed me.

"Go ahead," he said, prodding me on the leg.

I climbed the steps that allowed easier access to getting

up and into the beanbag chair. I crawled in on my knees, intending to move out of the way so Victor could join me.

The lighting continued around my head, the rose sconces making a circle above me. The walls had the same dark padding.

I stopped short. A gasp caught in my throat.

Attached to the walls was a collection of photographs.

There they were. All of the boys' beautiful faces. Some were individual portrait shots. Some were taken in places I didn't know, bedrooms and dining rooms of--I assumed—the boys' homes I'd yet to visit.

Some photos had me in the shots. There was the one North had taken with his phone while I was on his back. There was one of me being flung into the pool by Nathan. There was one with Kota brushing my teeth. There were dozens more of us at school. There were even some of Dr. Green and Mr. Blackbourne.

My smile caught again and again as I discovered a new photo. There were so many, I didn't know where to start and I kept going back to look at different ones to make sure I didn't miss any.

Victor was partially standing on the stairs. His head tucked in, and he studied at the display. "Pretty nice, huh?"

I slid over on the chair to give him room.

He smirked, flopping down into place next to me. I drew my legs up, but he hooked a hand over my knees, drawing them into his lap. Our bodies leaned in together. Victor wrapped an arm around my shoulders. I tucked my head next to his, gazing around us at the lights, the photos, at the beautiful work the boys had done.

"I can't believe you guys did this," I whispered.

His free hand dropped onto my knee, his fingers tracing along the kneecap. "We need to keep you safe, Sang. You needed a place to call us." He nuzzled me with his face, cheek and chin pressing to the top of my head. "And we wanted to."

"You didn't have to," I said, taking in a deep breath to swallow back the trembling in my voice. "You've already done so much for me, even before the clothes and everything from this weekend..."

His cheek bunched up as he smiled against my head. "Not quite done yet."

I stiffened against him. What else could there be? I was overwhelmed as it was. I was like a little kid who just got way too many gifts at Christmas and didn't know where to start.

He leaned against me, reaching around to his back pocket, and pulled out a set of keys. The collection varied, from house keys with different colored covers on the top, to a couple that looked like car keys. There was a single keychain, a black and pink plastic heart with a white skull and crossbones in the center.

"They didn't have a prettier pink one," he said, holding up the set in front of me, the keys rearranging as he flipped it over to reveal more of the keychain. "But Gabriel thought you'd like it. Skull and crossbones for Trouble."

I partly knew the answer before I asked, but I asked anyway. "Where do the keys go?"

Victor shifted to pull his arm out from around me and to arrange the keys. "Pink is your house key, green is Kota's house, red for Nathan, dark blue for Silas, white for mine, the baby blue is for Luke and North's house, orange for Gabriel's. And not that you need them yet, but the black key is to North's Jeep, the green car key for Kota's, blue for Silas', gray for mine." He lifted my palm until it was facing up and dropped the keys into my hand. He closed my fingers around the set.

I had keys to their houses and their cars. "I can't drive," I said in a quiet voice.

"Not yet. Soon."

I couldn't wrap my brain around that right now. My fingers massaged one of the keys in my hands. "You'd let me have keys? Kota said I'd probably just get his and Nathan's."

"When Kota gave the order to North to make keys for

you, North did the right thing and made one of everyone's. Kota had to be kidding to think we wouldn't give you one."

A smile teased my lips. "I've never been to your house, but I've got a key to it."

He stretched back again to wrap his arm around my shoulders. "Any time you want, Sang. I mean it."

I tucked my head into his shoulder and dropped the keys into my lap so I could put a palm against his chest. "I don't know what to say," I said. "Victor..."

"One more thing," he whispered. "Last one, I promise."

My body rattled against him. I wasn't sure I could handle any more. "What's that?"

He leaned away slightly, and with his free hand he stretched toward a spot on the wall. There was a click and the lights around us snapped off.

The darkness swallowed us up, but not completely.

Hundreds of stars started to glow. Stars lit up between the photographs, above our heads on the ceiling, in every crevice. There were enough to cast a gentle, eerie green glow on our faces.

"North thought you might like it," Victor whispered.

I sat up and away from him, dazzled by all the stars. Some weren't stars at all, there were heart shapes mixed in. I counted the hearts. Ten. One for all of us, including Mr. Blackbourne and Dr. Green. Our new family.

I extended my fingers to touch one heart painted next to a photograph, giving Gabriel's smile a ghostly illumination. "Victor..."

Victor shifted on the chair, he leaned over to where I was looking, pressing his cheek to the top of my head. "Yes?"

My breath was gone and so was my ability to formulate what I wanted to say. I let go of the star to bring the finger to my lips, pressing to my teeth. "I don't... I can't," I floundered. I mumbled more, but only syllables.

Victor caught my hand at my mouth. He held it, his

fingers warming around mine.

I turned, catching the spark of his eyes in the dark.

"You're not alone, Sang. With us, you'll never have to be. Not anymore."

My fingers trembled inside his hand. Finding the words was only slightly easier in the dark. "I don't know how to thank you. I don't know how to... how could I ever..."

He settled back into the chair, drawing me along with him. This time, he pulled me against him in an embrace. My palms pressed against his chest as my head dropped over his heart, the beating nearly matching my own. His hand brushed through my hair, fingers entwining through the strands. His cheek pressed against the top of my head again. "Promise to stay with us, Sang. It's all we can ask."

Stay? Were they kidding? "What do you mean stay?" I whispered, closing my eyes and breathing in the opulent berries of his cologne. The crease of his polo shirt folded against my cheek. My fingertips traced the angles of his chest, smoothing out his shirt. "Did you think I would leave?"

"You always have the choice," he said. "I've seen it in your eyes. That desire to not burden anyone else with problems, and thinking the best way would be to go home and never talk to anyone again. I did that, too, for a long time."

"You did?"

He sucked in a breath, and let it out slowly before he began. "My father has always been very demanding of me," he said. His fingers traced along the edge of my jaw. "He didn't hit me, but he'd curse and scream. A wrong note during a recital, a misused fork at a dinner party; any small thing would set him off. He'd wait until we got home and spend an hour calling me an 'ungrateful prick who never did anything right'. And that was probably one of the nicest things he ever said."

My fingers clutched at the material of his shirt.

"Victor... that's awful."

"I didn't tell the guys, even after we'd joined the Academy. They had pretty horrible things to deal with, so I felt like my own problems weren't that bad."

I had no idea. If that was how Victor was treated, I couldn't imagine what the others must have gone through. "You said *was*," I said. "Do you mean he doesn't do it anymore?"

Victor's head shifted from side to side against me. "No," he whispered. "No, he doesn't. When Kota and the others found out, they helped me."

"How?"

His mouth twisted to a smile against my head. "That's a story for another day. But it was the hardest thing for me to do to admit something at home was wrong. There were times I considered quitting the Academy entirely and leaving everyone behind so they wouldn't find out and so they'd never know. It might have been the most difficult thing to admit my problems to them, but it was one of the best things, for me and for them."

My hand loosened the grip on his shirt. "I guess that's a hint."

"Running away doesn't help anyone. We'll fix whatever we have to. You just have to tell us." His fingertip traced over my cheek. "Stay with us, Sang. Don't run from us anymore. The only way our group works is if you can be honest with us."

"What if it isn't fixable?"

"There's very little out there that isn't fixable. Death, going to prison... But anything else we can usually figure it out."

"How?"

He laughed, his baritone echoing through me. "You ask me that a lot."

"Sorry."

He smoothed his cheek across the top of my head. "You're not sorry."

I honestly didn't know what I was anymore. I was still

overwhelmed by the gifts. I was still wondering about Victor's story and how he managed to get his father to stop belittling him. I was still curious about what trouble the others were in and how they fixed it together. Wasn't I protecting them by not bothering them over things I could handle?

I had to trust his experience. All I had to do was tell them. Why did it feel like the hardest part? "I want to stay with you," I whispered. That was the easiest to say. I wanted him, all of them, to know.

"Are you sure?" he asked in a quieter tone.

My fingers gripped his shirt again. I wanted to be sure he knew I meant it. "Yes."

The hand at my face shifted to my back, hugging me in close. He breathed in deeply against my hair, his breath shifting the locks against my head. "As you wish."

With my cheek pressed to his chest, my eyes wandered to the pictures around us, the stars above our heads, the outline of the chair we sat in. All the things they did for me seemed like so much, and all they wanted was to make sure I stayed with them. I didn't want to leave them before, but I also didn't feel my place among them. Kota promised, as well as the others promised, that it would happen. I would eventually know where I belonged with them. What I had to trust, what I needed to keep reminding myself, was that I did belong. I belonged somewhere, right? Why not with them?

There in the dark with Victor next to me, and his promise that they wanted me, and the promise from the others displayed before me in the pictures, the stars, the clothes, all the new things, they were doing what they could, before I even knew what I wanted, to ensure I believed it like they did.

We grew quiet together. There were many things I wanted to say. I wanted to thank him again. I wanted to ask him more about his father, his life. I wanted to ask about the others. I wanted to tell him something, a problem, a small one, just to offer something of myself to let him know I understood. My mind was a mess, though. All I managed to do was slip my cheek against his chest and massage my fingertips in a tiny circle along his collarbone.

I didn't want to let go. This was as close as I'd ever been to any of them. A feeling of warmth and belonging was seeping into me through his touch, and I wanted it to last.

His fingers traced along my ribs. "Sang?" Victor whispered.

"Yes, Victor?"

He shifted a hand from my back, sliding down my arm until his fingers found the bracelet at my wrist. He breathed against the top of my head, heating a small circle of my skin. "We should go out." He paused, swallowed, "I mean if you want to, I could take you out sometime."

My eyes widened, focusing on a single heart glowing against the wall. Out as in a date? What about the others? Kota? What would it mean if we started dating? What if something happened and we found out we didn't like each other?

My own heart thundered and my mind whirled trying to grasp the right thing to say. "Where would we go?" It slipped out first and I pursed my lips, unsure.

He released a breath. I felt his mouth smiling against my head. "I'll take you anywhere you want."

It wasn't what I meant. I'd asked the wrong question and it gave him an answer that he wanted and I couldn't take it back. Something inside me didn't want to. I liked Victor. Everything I'd said about him the other night, about being handsome and looking out for me, I admired in him. The only problem was I liked all of them. A yes to him felt like a betrayal to the others. Wasn't dating about choosing one guy to date? "Victor, I... I've never... I mean I don't know..."

He nuzzled my forehead with his nose. "I understand. It's sudden and there's so much going on. Maybe I should have waited. I didn't want to. I'm not very good at waiting."

How long had he been waiting to ask? I didn't want to make him feel bad about asking. Isn't that what he was telling me? To be honest about what I was feeling? I dipped my head down, pressing my fingers to my lips, summoning the courage to say something to clarify things and not disappoint him. "I've never been out with anyone. I mean I'm not sure what I'm supposed to do."

"Well," he said, shifting to sit up a little. I pulled back so I was sitting beside him. His hand found mine, our fingers intertwined. His eyes remained on our hands so I watched our hands, too, assuming that was what I was supposed to do. "First you pick a place. I'll complain that it's girly but I'll take you there anyway because I want to impress you." His tone was matter of fact, as if explaining how to operate a can opener.

I started giggling, shaking my head. "Victor..."

"And then you complain about what to wear. You'll try on a hundred different dresses and go back to the first one you put on. I'll pick you up in my car and we'll go to some place that we'll both hate. It'll probably be some restaurant where the waiter flirts with you and I have to beat him up."

I rolled my head back, laughing. Victor was always so quiet and reserved that listening to this side of him was melting my heart.

His fire eyes sparked against the green glow around us. "And then we'll go see a show, a foreign film in a language neither of us understands. We'll annoy the other people watching by making up the lines as the movie goes on."

"Aw," I said against my laughter. "They'll be mad at us. They might kick us out"

"You're right," he said, tilting his head as if pondering the problem. His thumb started drifting over the back of my hand. "Maybe I should just buy out the movie theater for the night."

I tucked my head back against his shoulder, snickering

against him. "No, you've spent enough on me."

"Are you kidding? I haven't even started yet."

I picked my head up, grinning. "No," I complained. "No more spending money."

He gripped my hand tighter, smirking. "You don't like it?"

Did he want me to be honest now? "I don't want you to spend money on me."

His smile brightened. "Good."

My mouth popped open. "What do you mean, *good*?"

"That's the first thing you've honestly told me you wanted without me prying it from you."

I bit my lower lip, contemplating his meaning. I tried to recall everything I'd ever talked to him about, but with him next to me, it was difficult to think at all.

He picked my hand up, pressing our palms together between us. "Too bad I won't listen," he said.

I scoffed, pulling my hand away. "Victor..."

He laughed but stopped short, stiffening next to me. "No, no, no..." he pleaded as he leaned forward again, hauling out his phone from his back pocket and swiping at the face. "Always perfect timing."

"Academy?" I asked.

He nodded, sighing, tucking his phone away again. "I'm sorry. I can't stay."

"What's going on? It's not fighting, is it?"

He sat up, reaching for the wall. There was a click and the rose sconces lit up over our heads again. "No, not really. Something's broken and I have to fix it."

"Right now?"

He turned back to me; his fire eyes met mine and started to blaze. "Yeah," he said softly, "right now. I wouldn't leave unless I had to."

I rubbed absentmindedly at a spot on my cheek. "Oh I know, I didn't mean... sorry."

His hand found mine, taking it in his and squeezing gently. "If I don't get a chance to come back, I'll see you on Monday."

I smiled, trying to bottle my desire to ask him to stay. I knew better. "Hurry and go before you get in trouble."

He smirked, rolled his eyes, stumbling out of the bean bag chair onto the carpet. I dragged myself up on my hands and knees, intending to follow him out but he stopped short on the stairs. He turned, his head almost smacking into mine.

I pulled back. "What?"

The edge of his mouth curled up. "I lied to you before."

My mouth opened in response. Lied?

His hand drifted above my head. I thought he was reaching to pull me into another hug and without thinking, I leaned forward, expectant.

"There was one more thing," he said, flashing a smile. There was another click as he pressed a button on the wall. Music spilled out around us from unseen speakers.

Mysterious from Yuko Ohigashi.

"I'll see myself out. Stay. Have fun. Call me. No wait, I'll call you. I promise," he said this while rushing to crawl out to my bedroom, opening the door a crack to take a peek out. He turned back to me once, waved and disappeared behind the attic door.

My heart raced. It was the first time I'd been alone in days. The realization settled into me like ice trailing down my spine.

Yet as the piano music tinkered around me like a music box, my eyes fell again on the faces of Kota, Gabriel, Luke, North, Victor, Silas and Nathan, along with a few of Mr. Blackbourne and Dr. Green in the photographs that surrounded me. The spot beside me was still warm, still smelled like berries and moss. The phone in my bra, over my heart, felt more like a connection. All I had to do was call. They'd promised. I'd promised.

I was never alone.

Hoping And Changing

"Sang Baby, yes you can," North urged through the phone as I curled up tighter in the bean bag chair. "You're not going to break it. If you do, I'll fix it. Touch what you want."

I'd hardly moved since Victor left a couple of hours ago. I couldn't stop staring at the photos and when I could finally swallow my heart down from my throat, I called North first to thank him. Only the first thing I'd said was instead of thank you, I admitted I was afraid to touch the things around me.

"I don't know where to start," I said.

"You're in the beanbag chair, aren't you?" he asked, the hint of teasing in his voice. "You've already started."

That was a good point. I knew I was being stupid but I was being honest. "It's amazing."

Pause. "I'm glad you like it."

"I can't believe you got them to put stars up," I said, reaching to flick off the light. The darkness swallowed me up, my senses tingling as the stars started to glow. I recalled the night he came to my window, helping me escape to join him on the roof as we stared up at the stars together. That, too, felt like a long time ago, even though it'd only been a few weeks. "I can't believe you told them about..."

"I didn't tell them why."

My heart stopped. "What do you mean?"

"I thought we should keep our first date to ourselves."

I inhaled, catching my breath and nearly jumped to sit

up straight. Did he mean it? Was that what it was? A date! I'd been on one and I never knew. "North..."

"I know it wasn't ideal."

"It was perfect." After I said it, I realized I'd acknowledged it was a date and that I really liked it. The first I was unsure about, the latter... at least I could say I was being honest there.

Did I lie to Victor? Maybe it didn't count since I didn't know it was a date.

North chuckled on the phone, his deep voice made it seem like the phone was rattling in my hand, or perhaps it was my own trembling. "You're easy to please, but next time maybe we'll go to the beach instead. I did promise."

"Are you going to have time?" I asked, hoping he wasn't going to ask me to do it soon. I needed time to think. "I mean with the diner starting and football and school."

"I think I can spare a few minutes," he said, his tone implying something serious, intense as I imagined his eyes were.

Had I said the wrong thing? Maybe he thought I was questioning his ability to keep up with it all. "Maybe more than a few minutes?" I asked, trying to be funny.

A longer pause. "I'd come for you now," he said, causing my heart to race. He continued, "But neither of us slept well last night, and I don't want you tired at school."

I swallowed. "I'm sorry."

"Stop apologizing," he said. "Your nightmares aren't your fault."

"Well they kind of are," I said, smiling in the dark. "I do dream them."

He groaned. "Will you shut up and go touch your shit, please?"

"North?"

"What?"

I bit my lip, unsure. "Do you still like me?"

He huffed. "Yes."

A warmth rippled through me.

"Do you still like me?" he asked.

"Yes."

"Go play with your stuff. And call me if you have any more nightmares. And when I say call, I don't mean the next morning. I mean when you have them. And call me about any dream. I don't care if it's a nightmare or not."

"How are either of us going to sleep if I'm calling and waking you up?"

"Sang," he said, his tone going dark. "If you don't go touch your things, I'm coming back and I'm going to pilfer through all your pretty stuff and leave dirty fingerprints all over it."

Now who was deflecting? "Fine."

When I hung up, I lingered on the chair for only a moment. I wanted to get up to check on my mother. I'd done it a couple of times with the new app on my phone, but I didn't really trust it yet. According to the video, she was sleeping. The image was surreal, looking in on her from across the room where they'd installed the camera.

I was also getting a cramp in my back from being curled up, inhaling what I could of Victor's scent while he was gone. Why was it so addictive? Why did my heart thud so much thinking of the gold chain on my wrist, or the way he looked so happy after I almost-promised to go out on a date with him? What would I say to him next time, knowing North wanted the same thing? How could I tell Kota or any of the others? North wanted to keep the first date a secret, what about the second?

Because of those questions, I'd hesitated calling anyone else. I couldn't take anyone else asking surprising questions when I hadn't had time to process everything.

I flicked the light back on and I slipped out of the chair, spilling out onto the carpet in a purposeful fall. I stretched out across the deep blueness, feeling the luxury of the padding and fibers tickling my skin. The carpet was new. The carpet was for me. It was our secret and for that reason, it made it feel too special. Surreal.

I crawled over to the wardrobe, opening it up and gazing in at the clothes. I wondered who organized it. Who folded the underwear into such neat piles? I could only guess that it might have been Gabriel. The underwear matched the hanging shorts and skirts and shirts. As I studied it more, I realized he'd paired up everything for me. He was directing me without being here to tell me.

The top of the wardrobe was carved with the same flower and little hearts as the bookshelf. My fingers traced the leaves and a few of the hearts mixed in.

I crawled over to the door, spilling out onto the mauve carpet. At least that was the same.

I stood up, attracted to the bed and drawing back the cover. I groaned and then lit up with pleasure when underneath were brand new, deep pink cotton sheets. It was almost too strong a color, but I really liked it. I slipped between them, burying my head in what I was sure was a new pillow, plump and fresh. The bed was firm, a huge difference from my old one. Would anyone really notice? Would my mother?

With that thought, I sighed, forcing myself to go downstairs to find her. I checked the app one more time to ensure she wasn't walking around before I got up and left my room.

The hallway was empty, as I'd expected thanks to the camera app. Still, I tiptoed down the back stairs, around the living room and through the kitchen to approach my parents' hallway as quietly as possible.

Inside her bedroom, she rested in her bed, where I'd last seen her. She was sweating again. I wondered if she ate. I forgot to ask Nathan, but I assumed he'd say something if she hadn't. I wondered about calling Dr. Green to see if I should do something for her but I wasn't sure what else to do.

On my toes, I drew into the room. I gazed up and to my right, where there was the short hallway. The hallway contained three doors, one on the left and one on the right were matching walk-in closets and the back door was a bathroom. I'd only seen the inside once, the day we moved in. The door was open now. The hunter green carpet was a contrast to the beige of their bedroom carpet. The shower rod had a hunter green curtain hanging from it. The same ivy plant border wallpaper that was in the main bedroom was in the bathroom as well, blending the styles.

This room was different to me, too, somehow. Was it a lingering scent of the boys in the room? Was it that I knew there was a camera and at some point the boys might turn it on at any time? Were they watching now? Victor had promised they wouldn't unless absolutely necessary, but I'd used it a couple of times already in the few hours I'd been home. How easy would it be for them to blink it on? Would I ever know for sure?

Is this what they lived with every day? Was this what it meant to be part of the Academy?

My mother stirred behind me. Years of habit kicked in. I slipped back out into the main hallway, avoiding confrontation.

It felt like eons since I'd last seen her. Something struck me, though. My father was gone. Marie wasn't there right now. She'd been alone. While she was watched over, she didn't know it. I didn't understand why she did it to herself. When there were people out there like Kota and others who could care for someone else, why would someone choose to be alone? Was she happy? Despite her illness, did she like that her world consisted of doctors, two daughters she barely said a word to and a husband who was never home?

I didn't think she could be happy. Yet every time I talked to her, she reprimanded, demanded and punished. I thought of Marie. Did Marie worry? Did she know how bad our mother's illness was? Maybe she didn't, or she would check in more often. Maybe she should know.

Maybe the guys could help. Maybe if I asked, they could figure out why my mother avoided people and could figure out a way to help her. Didn't Kota promise to try the first day we ever met? Yes. He did. Maybe they weren't just protecting me. Maybe they would help. Or maybe they would do more if I asked, like Victor said. And they didn't have to do anything, really. If they could tell me what to do, I'd do it.

Maybe my mother could relax and learn to like other people. If that were true, we wouldn't have to sneak around. Maybe we could be normal, or at least normal enough that she could be happy. Maybe she could get better.

Get family in order. That's what Kota said. I vowed to myself that the next chance I got to talk with them seriously, I'd try to bring that up. Maybe if they had the time, they could help me figure out what to do. Maybe then, when I was in order, I could become part of their family, too, and I would feel it as much as they did with each other. The very idea excited me to no end. I wanted to get started now.

I padded to the kitchen to make my mother some soup.

Sleepless

That evening, I was still awake at eleven, staring at the ceiling in the dark from between the sheets of my new bed. I wore new red shorts and a white tank top from Victoria's Secret. I'd thanked everyone by text and phone calls. I even sent a text to Victor, thanking him again. He never replied, but I assumed he was still doing Academy business.

As I stared off into the dark, I knew Marie was home. She snuck in around nine and went straight to her room. I followed her using the app on my phone. She was in bed now, clothes laid out on the chair nearby for school the next day. Spying was becoming a creepy habit.

I tossed. I turned. I enjoyed the comfort of the new bed. I was far too excited, overwhelmed by what they had done for me. Strangely, I was also lonely. I'd had other people next to me all week and now, my first night alone to give me some peace and without the risk, I was missing them all.

I sat up, suddenly attracted to the window. I got out of bed and sat on my old trunk to gaze out into the evening. Kota's car wasn't back in its place. Was he working late? Was Victor with him?

I turned back to the bed, ready to give it another go and forget trying to call or bother anyone, when I realized this might be exactly what the others meant when they said to talk to them if I needed anything. Didn't Silas command me to call when I was lonely? Hadn't North, Kota and the others constantly nagged me to call for anything? Only I didn't want to call anyone over. It was late. They were probably all sleeping. Except for Kota, who was gone and working.

I sighed, coming up with an idea but unsure if I should do it. Without giving it another thought, afraid if I did, I'd slip back into bed and forget the whole thing, I opened my bedroom door, stepping barefoot into the hallway.

♥♥♥

I skulked my way through Nathan's yard. I had never met his father and I didn't want to get caught in his yard in case he did happen to be home. My heart thundered through me, until I was shaking on my toes.

The air held a crispness as a wind picked up from the ocean nearby, sweeping my hair into my eyes. I breathed in the salt, remembering Silas's cologne. Part of me wanted to stand there and soak in the night. Maybe I should have talked to North. Would he have taken me to the beach? Did I want him to?

I found Nathan's window and tapped at it lightly with a finger. He'd surprised me at my window before. I thought it was fair I got the chance to do so to him. Besides, I was worried if I'd called to ask, he'd tell me not to risk it. The truth was, I didn't want to sleep in my room tonight. I wasn't sure why. Maybe I wasn't used to the cameras. Maybe I was too excited by all the new things. All I knew was, I wasn't going to sleep there. Not tonight.

Silence. I tapped with my fingernail again, peeking in through the slats of the blinds.

The light from his closet was on and a figure stirred in his bed. The maroon covers pulled away. Nathan sat up, a hand pushed to his face, rubbing. I was glad he was home. I'd been worried he'd gotten called into work, too, and I'd made the trip for nothing.

When I tapped again, he glanced over, and wrapped himself at the hips with the blanket as he got up and crossed the floor. He yanked the string to raise the blinds. His bare chest and stomach were exposed. I found myself doing a double take, staring in awe at the definition. He blinked out at me and with one hand he unlocked the window and slid it open.

"What are you doing here?" he said, his voice gruff with sleep.

"I can't sleep," I said, trying to avoid looking at his hips. Was he in his underwear?

He huffed, grinning and shaking his head at me. He thrust the window all the way open. He released it and held out his hand, palm open and waiting. I grabbed it, and he helped me get over the high wall and in through the opening. I landed on the carpet.

He clutched the blanket with his other hand, shifting it higher on his waist. "Turn around," he said. "Face the window."

I did, and closed the window for him and locked it back. Through the reflection in the pane of glass, I watched as he moved toward the closet. With his back to me, he released the blanket, letting it fall to the floor.

My heart stopped dead and I lost the breath I'd been holding.

His bare, fit butt matched the rest of him in exquisite, reflected detail.

I blushed, turning my eyes away to focus instead on the shadows outside. I was embarrassed to have peeked, but I knew the image would be ingrained into my mind forever. Another secret.

Did he always sleep naked when he was home by himself?

He shuffled behind me. I stared hard into the blinds to avoid to the temptation of watching. "Okay," he said eventually.

I turned around as he was fluffing the blanket back over the bed. He'd slipped on a pair of dark boxers. His smile was outlined on his face from the light of the closet behind him. "Oh yeah," he said. "Come see."

I tiptoed around the bed, glancing around his room at the karate posters and his dresser. The stereo on top was playing some rock music from a band I didn't recognize. The volume was soft enough that I hadn't noticed it through my heart beating so loud.

He pointed to his closet. I stepped inside, noting how it had been emptied of the collection of used work out equipment and boxes. Now his clothes were organized, the bars for hanging clothes stretched out on the left and right. I recognized a small collection near the back on the left, with skirts and blouses, in shades of pink and other girl colors. Some underwear and bras were folded neatly on a shelf above them.

I reddened, feeling awkward. It was a strange feeling, like the clothes were for me to wear, but were owned by Victor, with Gabriel overseeing how I wore them, and Nathan guarding them. They didn't really feel like mine at all. In a way it relieved some of the guilt I felt about the cost. "Thank you," I whispered, unsure of what else to say.

"Never thought my first roommate would be a girl," he said. He flicked off the light and through the dark, he shuffled toward the bed, sitting down on the edge. He patted the spot next to him. "Come on."

I crawled onto his bed, moving over to the side closer to the window. I rested on my side on top of his blanket, propping my head up on my arm. "I'm sorry," I said. "I didn't mean to wake you up."

"Don't worry about it," he said. He stretched out next to me, his head propped up, too. I couldn't see the blue in his eyes, but I imagined the serious expression as he spoke. "Why can't you sleep?"

I pushed a forefinger to my lower lip. "I don't know. I like the new bed. I love everything, but I couldn't stop..." I lost the explanation, not that I really had one, but I wanted to give a reason. I did love what they'd done but I didn't understand why I couldn't sleep.

He stretched a hand, taking mine from my mouth and

holding it to his chest. "Too much?"

I nodded.

"It doesn't feel like your own yet, huh?"

"I've never had new things before." Not to mention that they were gifts. The admission surprised me. Was being honest getting easier?

He sighed. "Well, get under the covers."

He scooped up the blanket between us, waiting until I shuffled my feet underneath. I could just make out the outline of his muscled shoulders and wondered if I would ever stop being in awe of his frame. The mere idea of his power made my insides tremble.

He shifted until he was on his side facing the closet, settling in. The scent of cypress and leather filtered to my nose. My eyes widened, focused, looking at the deeper shadows, at the dull blue glow of the light of his stereo, and the red numbers of the digital clock on the side table next to us. I wasn't sure what I was thinking coming over to his house. What made me think I could possibly sleep here any better?

"Shit," he breathed out, flipping over. He propped his body up on his arm as he twisted to reach for something on the side table closest to me, hovering over me. He grinned down at me as he snatched up his phone. "If I don't tell them you're here, they're going to flip if they try to check in."

I hadn't thought of that. It rattled me more that he had to do it. This was a bad idea. They'd think I didn't like all my new stuff. They'd think I'd gotten in trouble. It was a school night. What was I doing here? "Nathan..." I whispered, unsure how to express my fears.

He sat up cross legged on the bed, the phone in his hands. "What?"

"Let them know it wasn't because... I mean I really do love the new things."

He chuckled and his hand found mine in the dark. He guided me to sit up. He tucked an arm around my waist, pulling me into his lap. My butt settled between his legs, my knees hooking over his thigh and he wrapped his strong arms around me, looking down into my face. "You can say it, Sang. It isn't wrong."

My fingers sought my mouth. I wasn't sure what he meant.

He snatched my hand away before I could touch my lip. "Don't do that. I can't stand it. You can say what you're thinking. I'm not going to laugh."

I still wasn't sure what I was supposed to be admitting. In the moment, my mind was muddled with feeling his strong, warm body around me, his serious expression and my own trembling heart.

He pressed my hand to his chest, pushing my palm over his heart, his own fingers warming over mine to keep it there. "You can admit you were lonely. You don't have to hide that. Victor told you the truth. You don't have to wait for an invitation to come over. Call, come over, send smoke signals. If you want me, I'll come for you."

I bit my own lip, swallowing back my heart. "I was lonely," I whispered.

His arms tightened around me again, pressing me close to his body. My cheek fell to the hardness of his collarbone, and I kept my hand over his heart.

He sighed heavily against me. "To be honest, I was, too."

My eyes watered. When I thought about it, it was Nathan that had more reason to feel alone than I did. My mother was downstairs in my house. My sister was there, too. Nathan's father could not be home right now, and might not be for days at a time as he flew helicopters back and forth for work. He saw his father less than I did mine, perhaps. There was no one here. As far as I knew, Nathan was the one who was alone most of all.

He sighed against my head, and pulled back, picking up his cell phone again. "But let me text them before they call in the squad to find you."

I remained against his chest, burying my face into his

shoulder. It was hard to admit what I'd done, and was grateful he was there to tell them for me.

He typed in a message, pushed a button to send it and waited. After a couple of minutes of sitting, cuddled together in the dark, a message returned. "There," he said, "Kota's nagging. So we're good."

"Nagging?"

"Oh you know, make sure you get back tomorrow morning without your mom finding out. Don't be late for school. Don't stay up all night. Don't let you climb up to the roof alone if you need to sneak back in."

My heart warmed. Kota's nagging was caring. It was more than my parents did.

My phone lit up in the crest of my cami bra top and started to vibrate. I'd already forgotten I'd put it there. The phone lit up our faces in the dark.

Nathan laughed. "You've got the best pockets."

I laughed, too, blushing as I removed the phone. Victor was calling. Did Nathan tell everyone I was here? I couldn't not answer him, even though in that moment I wasn't sure I should. Every step I made around them now had me questioning how the others would react. What would Victor think of me sitting in Nathan's lap right now? I was questioning my own loyalties and what was appropriate at every turn.

I pushed the button. "Victor?"

"Are you okay?" Victor asked, genuine concern in his tired voice.

"Yeah," I said, my eyes moving to Nathan's face, wondering if he could hear. "I'm fine."

Victor paused. "Are you?"

That was a challenge. I summoned courage. "I was lonely," I admitted, still blushing, my free hand searching for my lip again. Nathan caught it in his, squeezing it and narrowing his eyes at me. I continued, "After being around everyone all week and suddenly no one..."

"Oh," Victor said, "And you couldn't sleep."

"I tried."

Victor sighed. "Should have left someone with you," he said, though quietly as if noting it to himself instead of saying it to me.

"I didn't know," I said, "I didn't think about it. But we shouldn't be doing that anymore. Tomorrow I'll stay in my room." Was he not mad about me going to Nathan's? He said *someone*. Would he have sent Nathan to me if I'd asked?

"Tomorrow I'll stay the night," he said.

"Victor..." I said, unsure of how to respond.

"Tell him to let us sleep," Nathan complained. "He can talk to you tomorrow."

"Tell Nathan to butt out," Victor said. "But he's right. Go to sleep."

My lips tightened. "Okay."

"'Night," he said, and hung up.

I dropped the phone onto the bed, exasperated and every single nerve ending electrified. "Next time, I'll make you answer. Can we sleep now?"

Nathan laughed. He tucked his arms around me, pulling me back against the bed with him, yanking the covers over our heads. "Whatever you say."

♥♥♥

At first, Nathan slept with space between us. With his bed being bigger than even the new one I had, it was much easier to have some room.

I woke up around two in the morning with his back pressed up against my side. I shivered, my body chilled as his house was cold and the air conditioner was still on full blast. In my sleepy state, I pressed my back into his. It just seemed so natural. His body was warm and I'd slept closer to the others before, so I didn't think it would bother him.

He turned over, mumbled something and his arm fell over me. His hands gripped me by the waist and dragged me until my back was pressing into his stomach. His cheek pressed against my shoulder. I felt the slightest movements of his lips at the curve of my neck as he breathed and settled down, falling back asleep.

I stared at the clock on the bedside table. Nathan was hugging me to himself. My hips and butt felt parts of his body that I was sure friends were probably not supposed to think of. My heart thundered against my chest, rattling me and I couldn't get myself to calm down to sleep.

Only I didn't want to move. Part of me didn't want to wake him. Part of me loved that he had sought me out in the night, hugging me to him. Victor probably wouldn't like this. Neither would North. Would they understand? I pushed the thoughts back. What did I know about friendships, relationships, dating or anything like that? All I had was what they told me was okay.

I willed my heart to slow down. The best I could do was to doze. I did that for hours, occasionally startling awake as his hand adjusted on my waist or slid to lightly clutch at my stomach. His strong fingers spread across my belly, sending different waves of tingles and shivers through my core. It took tensing every muscle to not shake so much.

The night lasted forever.

I was halfway into finally dozing again when his hand relaxed against my stomach, slipping toward my ribs as he pulled himself up to look over my shoulder. "Sang?" he grumbled, thick with sleep.

I yawned, sitting up. I'd been up all night. Utter defeat. Why did I ever think I could sleep next to him?

"It's about five," he said in a whisper.

"I should go," I said, my voice sounding small.

"Do you want me to go with you? I can help you get to your window."

I shook my head, pushing my body to the side of his bed. His bed was high off the ground, enough that my feet were still hovering inches above the floor. I jumped down and wobbled where I stood, still half asleep and wishing I could crawl right back into his bed. I wanted to skip school and sleep all day there. "The back door should still be unlocked." I fished my phone out from the bed, putting it back into the bra top.

"Sang?"

"Yeah?" I turned toward his voice.

He was on his knees on the bed, coming toward me. The muscles in his body shifted as he knee-walked, his arms outstretched toward me.

I opened my own arms to him. His encircled me, holding me around the waist as he hugged me to his muscular body. My arms wrapped around his neck. I liked hugs.

My fingers traced behind his ear. He stiffened against me and drew away. His eyes locked with mine.

Did I do something wrong? "Nathan?"

His mouth twisted, his lips parting to say something, but closed again. I had the sense to understand there was something more he wanted to tell me or ask me, but he had changed his mind.

"I'll be fine," I said. "Don't worry about me."

He smirked, shaking his head. "Says the girl that can't sleep in her own bed."

I scoffed but he crossed the room to the window. He yanked the cord to open the blinds and opened the window. The air had chilled during the night. September was promising cooler days ahead.

I lifted myself through and hit the ground on the other side. I turned around and Nathan leaned out the window, his chest and stomach muscles making weird shadows against the odd glow of the moon.

"Guess you didn't need to go through the window," he said. "Though it's kind of fun, I guess. We sneak in through your window." He grinned. "I'll see you in a little bit."

"In a couple of hours."

He nodded. "Get going before you're caught. Be careful."

Cornered

I ran home, my bare feet sliding against the dew in the grass. A fog had rolled in sometime in the night. The hovering density in the air left my skin electrified as it had the night before. Again it was tempting to stay outside. Monday was here, though, and the guys needed me. I'd see them at school. That thought alone drove me on. I'd get dressed, grab my things and dart right back to Nathan's. No, I should wait and give him time to get dressed. How long would it take him?

I padded across the long driveway up to the door in the garage. My father's car wasn't there. I wondered how much longer he would be away. I wondered if he was in Mexico again. I'd have to find some crackers to leave for my mother.

In my hurry, I twisted the handle, stepping inside.

"Who is it?" My mother called from the kitchen.

My heart froze in my chest as my hand slipped from the door handle. It swung out of reach and crashed against the wall on the other side. The slim chance I'd had of possibly tiptoeing up the back stairs and disappearing as if nothing had happened vanished.

My mother shuffled into the family room from the kitchen. She was awake, and that was good, right? I wouldn't have to call Dr. Green. She was sweating. Her eyes bugged out. "What are you doing out there?" she demanded.

"I... uh... thought I heard something," I said. I let the lies flow from my mouth, too terrified to be concerned with what. "I heard meowing outside my window. I went to check."

"Did you find a cat?"

Was she going to believe me? "I couldn't see one," I said. "I checked the bushes. Is that why you're up? Did you hear me out there? I'm sorry. I didn't mean to scare you."

Her pale face twisted, her dull eyes glancing toward the wall. "Where's your father?"

"He's not here," I said. Did she really not know? "He said there was another business trip."

Her mouth tightened, the creases at her lips deepening. The hair around her face was pulled back. The pony tail was freshly done but the hair was matted together as if she didn't bother to brush it. When was the last time she brushed it? Was it an effort so she ignored it?

"Were you hungry?" I offered in a quiet voice, unsure of her mood. "I've got time before I have to get ready for school. I could scramble some eggs and make some toast."

She swayed on her feet, enough to scare me that she might fall over. "I think I want..." Her head tilted, her eyes widened, staring at my body. It confused me. Was she looking at me now? Did she finally focus on me? Maybe being nicer and trying harder was working.

I thought that until I felt the slight vibration of the phone against my chest. I glanced down, the screen of the phone glowed, giving away its location against my heart. Probably Nathan was calling.

"What is that?" My mother's voice strained with confusion and a rumbling anger bubbling to the surface.

"Nothing," I said, covering my chest to hide the glow. "Just a..." I couldn't think of a lie. I couldn't think at all. Was Nathan watching? What happened? Why would he call? "Something for school," I said.

Her hands balled into fists. Her eyes narrowed at my chest. "Show it to me."

My body quaked. There was no way to hide it. Nathan's call went to voicemail. Either he'd seen what was happening or he was checking in for me to make sure I got in safe. Would he try again in a few minutes?

My fingers trembled as I couldn't think of a reason not to show her, and even if I denied the request, it wouldn't matter. She might punish me and then what? Dr. Green said to do whatever she said as long as it wasn't being tied up in the shower or something equally dangerous. The phone wasn't dangerous.

I untucked the phone from my chest, presenting it to her.

Her eyes narrowed on the iPhone in the pink case. "The school doesn't give cell phones. Where did you get that?"

"I meant," I said, trying something else, "I found it at school. I didn't have time to turn it in to the front office, so I was hanging on to it until Monday when I got the chance."

She snatched the phone from my hands. She tapped at it, illuminating the surface.

A text message caused the phone to buzz in her hands. The message popped up on the screen in front of her face. She scanned the words. "Sang," she read, her voice bursting with anger, and something else... satisfaction? "Hurry back when you can. I've got some of those coffees you like." Her head tilted toward me. "Who is Nathan?"

My hand fluttered up to my lip, pushing to my teeth. My tongue felt glued to the top of my mouth. What do I do? What should I do? Should I run away? If I ran back to Nathan's, could he help?

My mother pointed the end of the phone at me. "Where did you get this? Did you steal it? Or was it from the money you stole?"

I blinked at her, confused. "What money?"

"You know what money."

My eyes flashed at her. "I don't have money."

She scoffed. "Are you telling me this boy bought you this phone? Is that what you're saying? What kind of things did you have to do to get him to buy you one?"

I started to shake my head, but I didn't have an answer for the question it left open. Either someone got it for me or I stole something to get it. What answer was the best?

"I can't believe this," she said. "I tried. I did my best. Here you are. Sneaking into the house. Smelling like a boy. A cell phone. Lying. The tramp of the neighborhood. I knew it when we moved here that it was a mistake. I don't know what to do with you," she spat at me. Her fingers clutched at the phone. She swung her arm, pointing the end of it toward the kitchen. "Start walking."

My eyes opened wide. I smelled like a boy? I couldn't tell but perhaps I carried Nathan's cypress scent with me. This was the worst thing she'd ever caught me at and there was nothing I could say to reverse it. What now? Rice? Should I not kneel like Kota said? Should I wait until she had me kneel and then escape? If I don't answer the phone, they'd come for me when they discovered me on my knees.

I walked through the kitchen as she directed. Instead of looking for a stool or grabbing the rice, she continued to point toward the direction of her bedroom. I shuffled forward awkwardly, my eyes on the phone. I almost wanted to take it from her to call for help, but I also wanted to avoid the worst possible outcome. If I fought her on this, she could call the police on me. I should wait and trust that if the boys did discover I was in trouble, they would know the best way to get me out.

I stood just inside her bedroom door. My mother pushed me aside. Her touch on my arm had me cowering, afraid. How different her touches were from Nathan's or Victor's.

She marched to the closet doors, opening the one to the left. She stopped, her head reeling back. Something caught her off-guard. She stared into the space for several minutes. The door blocked my view. Was that her closet or his? I couldn't remember. I was pretty sure it was his. Was it messy?

Her face littered with pink splotches. Her eyes and

nostrils flared. She spun on me. "You lied about your father. He's not on a business trip."

I stepped back, my mouth parted in surprise. "What... what do you mean? Of course he is. He left a note on my door."

She pushed the door away to open it fully. I remained back, afraid of what it held.

My mother lunged for me, grabbing me by my top and yanking it until it tore at my shoulder. I cried out, mostly out of surprise. My voice choked short. I stumbled next to her, looking in.

The closet was bare. The only things that remained were two plastic hangers, one with an old, worn brown suit coat, the elbows thinned enough that it needed patching. The shelf above the rack was empty, the floor clean, neatly vacuumed.

Her hand continued to grasp at my shirt. "Where did he go?"

I shook my head, tears cutting through my eyes. "I... I don't know," I squeaked out.

She pointed with the phone again toward the empty closet. "Get in there."

The blood drained from my face. Was this going to be dangerous? Should I refuse? I hesitated. They didn't have a camera in the closet, did they? They wouldn't see me if she tried to chain me to something.

Without knowing what to do, and from years of habit, I obeyed. Shaking on my feet, I stepped inside the empty space of the walk-in closet, noting the staleness of the air. My father had moved out his things a long time ago.

The truth of what that meant evaded my mind as my mother glared in at me.

"Take off those clothes," she ordered.

A shiver chased down my spine. "What?"

"Take your clothes off," she commanded. "If you refuse to obey me, I'll tear them off."

I stared at the ground. My mother had never ordered me to strip before. I didn't want her to tear the clothes, so I removed the shorts, holding them out between my fingers and unsure what to do with them. I trembled as I stood in just the bra top and in my underwear.

"All of it," she commanded, grasping the shorts and pulling them from me.

I swallowed against the dryness in my throat. Her eyes shot darts at me while I removed the top and slipped the underwear down my legs. She collected these, too.

"Now," she said, "you're going to sit in there. You won't be going to school today."

Was that it? Was she going to keep me here in the closet until school was over? I stood with my legs close together, and my arms over my chest to mask my body. My shivers rattled through me, like a tornado repeating itself through my spine. "How long do I have to stay in here for?" I asked.

"Until your father gets back," she snarled at me. "If I let him. I might finally send the police after him. Let them deal with him, and you."

Before I could ask her what she meant, she slammed the closet door. There was a click. The light above me blinked out.

I lowered myself to my knees, my breath stumbling from my lips. Nathan would try again in moments. He might even let Kota know I wasn't responding. They would turn on the cameras. I wasn't anywhere to be found. Would they come? If they couldn't locate me, would they even try to attempt it? How could I stop them? She'd call the police on them.

I listened as my mother trailed around in her bedroom. The television was on. Her being awake and on the warpath meant they couldn't sneak in, brown bottle or not.

I fell onto my side on the floor, pulling my knees up to my chest and wrapping my arms around my legs. I breathed in the scent of Nathan on my skin just for some connection to them. Without Kota's command, or Mr. Blackbourne directing, without the others there, I felt lost.

What do I do now?

If I walked out, she'd call the police on me. Wouldn't they put me in some orphanage if that happened? I'd never see Kota or the others again. And she made sure I couldn't just run off because she'd taken my clothes. Why would she do this to me? Was it because she believed I stole her money? I didn't know she had any at all. Did she believe the lies she told my dad?

I wasn't sure what to do. I wasn't hurt. I was alone. That was it. Where was my father? Why were all of his things gone?

Not even a fucking goodbye. That was what Nathan had said when he showed me the note. Did he know about my father taking everything with him? Why didn't he tell me?

Time passed. I wasn't sure how long. From above my head, footsteps squeaked. I recognized Marie's sounds. She was rushing to get into the shower, brushing her teeth at the sink.

My mother's footsteps moved around the room and then changed direction to the hallway. Creaking sounded on the stairwell. Should I try to escape? Should I dart out, check to see if the cell phone was there? No. The others wouldn't want me to do something so risky. If I tried for the cell phone and she found me, she could make good on her promise to call the police. I may not get a call in to the guys before that happened.

For lack of anything to do, I reached for the worn brown coat hovering over me. I covered myself with it. It smelled faintly of staleness and dust. Forgotten. A leftover, unwanted coat was all that was left of my father, and it covered my nakedness demanded upon me by my own mother. My fingers traced over the weave of the fibers, finding the buttons, one missing at the breast. Maybe he was never there for me, like Nathan's father, but I never thought he would disappear. I may have never seen him, but he was always there at night, looking over everything I didn't think about. Now that his things were gone, I felt we were forgotten and discarded like his coat.

I didn't know how to feel about it. Should I be angry? Why wasn't I more upset? Was it because deep inside I didn't really believe it? Did I think there might be another explanation?

Two sets of footsteps returned. I sat up, clutching the coat around my shoulders and holding my breath to listen.

"Sang is staying home," my mother said. "If that... *man* asks you about her, you're to say she's sick and she won't be going to school."

"Where's dad?" Marie asked.

"He's abandoned us," my mother said, monotone, almost matter-of-fact. "I've got to call the bank to see if he left us with any money."

"Why don't you call him?" Marie asked.

"I can't reach him. But text that man back and pretend to be her. Say she's not feeling well. I don't want him coming over and looking for her."

My voice caught in my throat as I gasped. They're going to lie. Marie was working with her. Did she know I was in the closet?

I sank on the floor, stretching to gaze out at the crack between the carpet and the bottom of the door. From the angle, all I could see was the other closet door. I tried it from different angles but the best I could do was see the door to the bathroom.

The bathroom! There was probably a camera in there.

I twisted the handle, opening it a crack. "Mom?" I called, trying to sound humble.

"Close that door," she snapped at me.

"I need to use the bathroom, please," I said.

Pause. "You better be five seconds," she warned.

I let the closet door burst open, stepping out wearing the coat around me. Marie was in the bedroom, my pink cell phone in her hands as she typed in it. Her brown eyes lifted, looking at my face, at my nudity and the brown coat. I was about to flash her a warning look. *Be careful*, I wanted to tell her. *She's not well. She'll lock you in the closet, too.*

Only when I looked at my sister, I didn't see surprise or sorrow. I saw something that made me cower where I stood.

Glee. Pure, unadulterated joy. It was the happiest I had ever seen her. With her shoulders back, wearing Nathan's blue t-shirt on her body and the new red shorts I'd just been wearing. She held the phone like a prize.

All I could think was what could I have ever done to her that she would take such pleasure in seeing me reduced to nothing. Had we not tried to work together over the years? Maybe we didn't get along, but we weren't mean to each other. I got her keys. I tried to help her sneak out when she wanted. I never tattled on her like she often did to me.

"I should hang on to the phone," Marie said. "If they try to text her at school, I could keep telling them she's sick."

My mother nodded, her cracked lips pursed. She held the house phone in her hands. "I don't care. Keep it," she said. "I'll call the school and tell them she won't be in today." She pushed buttons on the phone. "I'm calling your father's office. If he doesn't call me back by tonight, I'm calling the police to report that he abandoned his daughter. If he wants to walk out on me, he'll have to take her with him."

Quick Thinking

I scurried to the bathroom. I didn't know how long it would take for the guys to use this camera or how long it would be for them to figure out what was going on. If Marie was going to text them that I wasn't feeling well, and she would tell them so at the bus stop, they might just believe the lie. What would Nathan think if she was wearing his shirt? What about the shorts? Would he recognize them? They might not check on me at all in person until after school.

What could happen between now and then? What if my mother gave up early and called the police sooner? And why would our father abandon us? Why did she insist he take me wherever he went? What if he was really just on a business trip and had taken all his clothes because it would be a long one? Excuses, conjecture. Not helpful. I didn't have all the answers and I didn't have enough time right now to figure it out.

And why was she shoving me off on him like unwanted leftovers? What about Marie? I understood why she wasn't in the closet with me, but our mother didn't make it sound like Marie was supposed to go with our father, too. Did she hate me that much?

I found the vent on the ceiling. Even after climbing onto the sink to stand, it was too high to reach. I needed a ladder.

What would I do if I could reach it, anyway? I couldn't stay there and make sign language into the camera lens. If Marie was going to do her part, and if they followed procedure, it might be hours before they would even think to check. It might not even be until tomorrow. It would be too late.

I chewed my lip.

"Sang!" My mother called.

I was running out of time.

An idea occurred to me. I didn't have to stand in front of the camera to alert to them that something was wrong. I was the only one who knew the cameras existed. So if I left something that they would know was from me, they'd see it and know I was leaving them a message. What could I leave that they would understand?

The angle of the camera was hard to make out, but it looked angled toward the shower. I yanked the shower curtain back. I opened the cabinet under the sink, looking for something to mark the basin with. I found a bottle of old shampoo, the goo inside was a deep green color. Would they see this against the tub?

I crouched on the edge of the tub basin. She wasn't going to shower. She hadn't done so in a while. I estimated a spot from the angle of the camera. They would see a message but if she came in to use the toilet, she might not notice. It was my only chance.

I opened the bottle, dumping the contents onto the bottom of the tub. With my fingers, I moved the goo around until I had a green heart. Hidden hearts. They had to know it was me. Would they see it? Would they understand? *I'm here. Come find me.*

"Sang!" My mother's voice croaked near the door.

I left the shower curtain open, walking away and flushing the toilet for good measure. I chucked the bottle under the sink and washed my hands. I swallowed, pulling the coat on again and opening the door, doing my best not to give the tub another look or risk drawing attention to it.

My mother stood in the doorway, her wild eyes flared at me. She was shorter than me, but with the demand and anger in her eyes, she seemed a thousand times bigger. She was awake and she was angry, left by her husband. For some reason, I was at the center of her hatred toward him.

"Sorry," I stammered. "I really had to go."

"Get in that closet," she said, each word dripping with venom.

I shuffled forward, heading toward the closet again. Obey as long as it isn't dangerous, they'd said. Lie if I had to. I would trust their advice. Hiding in the closet wasn't dangerous. Maybe it wasn't normal, but I wouldn't die in there.

"Wait," she commanded.

I stopped in my footsteps, my heart in my throat. Did she spot the heart? Did she find the camera?

She pointed at the coat. "Give me that."

I glanced toward the bedroom. Marie was gone. I removed the coat, letting it fall from my shoulders and to the floor.

"Get in there."

I slipped into the closet, naked and alone.

Secret Messeges

Hours later, I was kneeling on the carpet, my butt on my heels. I bent forward, my arms folded on the floor, my head on my forearms. I breathed in the fibers of the floor, listening to the sounds of the house. Every creak, every whisper of air shifting, I hoped it was the boys coming for me and at the same time, I hoped it wasn't. Maybe I'd made a mistake. If they came for me now, the police would be called.

If she called them, I was sure I'd be taken away. Who knows where I'd end up. Maybe inside some foster care place.

I was also running out of time. If my father didn't come home, she'd call the police and have me sent away anyway. Either option was going to end up badly. What would the police do? The fact that I didn't know made me worry so much more. I thought if it happened, I'd probably never see the guys again.

Waiting was the worst. There were so many questions left unanswered and all I had to do with my time was think. My father was gone. She assumed he had abandoned us. His closet was empty, but what did it really mean? Did he leave without saying anything at all? Was it forever?

I could almost understand it and couldn't totally blame him. After at so many years with an ill, possibly dying wife who did nothing but spout misery, rape and evil, he must have gotten tired and disappeared. Wasn't I drawn to the guys because they were nice to me? Wasn't Marie at Danielle's every weekend to avoid the emptiness of the house? I knew it happened to other families. I'd heard it from other students. *Daddy left last night.* Weeks later they might spot him at the grocery store, buying frozen dinners and booze, and sometimes a box of condoms.

What did it matter if he left completely; he was never here anyway? Was that even a concern? Why didn't I feel sadder about my dad not being there? Maybe that was the worst thing. Kota said I was dismissive of things like that. I didn't even care that I was in the closet so much, but was more stressed about putting the guys at risk and that my father might get the police called on him for reasons unknown to me.

And it was all my fault. If I hadn't wanted to go to Nathan's, or if I'd stayed in bed and slept at home like I was supposed to, it wouldn't have happened at all. I would still have my secret phone. I'd have gone off to school. If my dad was gone, I wouldn't have been in the middle of this. Would I?

I felt the guilt of it on my shoulders. I made too many mistakes. Maybe Victor was wrong. Maybe I needed to keep them out of some things. I could have sucked in my loneliness for the night and made it through. It would have been better than this.

♥♥♥

More time passed. My mother made phone calls to the bank like she promised. She rattled off account numbers and she questioned the amounts. She made them repeat information to her. When she hung up, she grumbled. That was all. No revelation as to the condition of the accounts.

A little later, she called my father's office, asking them to leave him another message, and requesting that the secretary try to call through to him. Family emergency.

My mother didn't sleep. It left me without a chance to escape. Cell phone or not, I thought if I could get up to my bedroom, I could at least leave a note. Maybe I could send smoke signals. She never gave me the chance.

A distinct *ding-dong* echoed through the hallway into my parents' bedroom.

It startled me because I'd never heard the sound before. It took a while for me to recognize it as the front doorbell.

My mother shuffled on her feet, pacing back and forth and muttering. Was she contemplating ignoring it?

The doorbell rang again. My heart thundered in my chest. Despite not being able to see, I crawled on my belly toward the light, staring out at the other closet as if doing so would help me hear better.

My mother hobbled down the hallway. I heard the front door open.

A man's voice. Attention demanding. Elegant. Perfect.

Mr. Blackbourne. My heartbeat thundered in my ears leaving me unable to concentrate. I listened, desperate to make out the words he was saying.

My mother replied to him. Something negative. Mr. Blackbourne's voice grew in strength, but despite that, I couldn't make out the conversation. My mother replied, loud, angry and shut the door.

The guys knew something was wrong. They were looking for me. The Academy boys knew.

My mother crossed the bedroom to the closet, opening the door and peering in at me, as if wondering if I was still there.

I kowtowed on the floor, my naked back exposed as I tried to cover everything else. I turned my head toward her, waiting.

Her scowl etched on her face. "Why would your teacher from school come looking for you?"

I had no idea what Mr. Blackbourne told her. "Because I'm not there?" I said flatly, not really caring if that was the answer she wanted. Mr. Blackbourne was outside somewhere! I wanted to hug him, him with his cruel steel eyes and ever-demanding requirement for perfection. I wouldn't care. His voice had drifted to me; it was all I needed to find my courage. I would wait forever knowing someone out there wanted me. The boys did. Even Mr. Blackbourne.

Her eyes narrowed at me. She shoved a paper at my face, flicking the light on. I blinked as the closet light temporarily blinded me. I rubbed my eyes.

"Read that," she said.

Confused, I picked up the paper, drawing myself up to sit on my butt, covering my body with folded legs against my chest. My eyes scanned the square, yellow piece of paper.

The note was mostly in English. It announced a make-up test required in three days or I'd fail.

There was a single line of script at the end. The language was my own secret code, the Korean lettering nearly identical to the way I wrote it.

Bathroom.

That was all. It meant something. That I should go back to the bathroom?

He knew my language. I realized now that writing out his strange little sentence, he was secretly having me teach him how to read it. I hated him for tricking me and loved him for it at the same time. Shrewd, clever Mr. Blackbourne.

"It says I have to take a test," I told my mother.

"I should call the police on you now," she spat at me. "Your father leaves me. I'm ill and he walked out. How am I supposed to run this house with his harpy daughter, running wild in the streets? Getting boys to buy her cell phones. Wearing boy clothes. I saw those clothes in your closet. Boy pants. Boy shirts. I said you would get raped, killed, and tried to warn you. Nothing. No one listens to me. I'll stop this before it starts. You won't bring down this house." She shut the door again, leaving me in the darkness to ponder how she could think such things. I understood it. It looked bad. If she only knew...

But it didn't matter to me. I was no longer alone.

Many Things, But Never Alone

The way the light under the door shifted, I understood that it turned from morning to afternoon. I almost dozed off, but couldn't allow myself to sleep. I was listening and waiting.

Marie returned, stopping in to check with our mother. So I guessed it was after school. It seemed kind of early for it. Did she skip?

She was told to go to her room and remain there. Marie obeyed without question. I listened for her footsteps, giving myself something else to do.

Marie turned her stereo on. I couldn't make out the music type, just the rhythmic beat. It was enough to mask some of her noise.

Mr. Blackbourne hadn't returned. That told me a couple of things. I couldn't tell if he meant from his message that they saw what was in the bathroom or they wanted me to go there. I hadn't risked going to the bathroom yet because I wasn't sure she would let me or if it would be the wrong move.

As the hours drifted by and nothing was happening, I thought I should try it just in case. Maybe there was a message for me or they could tell me what to do from there.

I hesitated a little longer because I was naked.

I cracked the closet door open again. "Mom?"

"What?" she snapped.

"I need to use the bathroom." I peeked around the edge of the door into her room.

She was on her bed. A collection of mail nestled in her hands. Marie must have delivered it. My mother glared over at me, contemplating.

"I don't want to make a mess," I said. I guessed that she didn't want me to pee in the closet.

She released a loud breath. Was this the same person from yesterday? She was so weak last night, sick from the cancer that ate her inside. Now she looked so aware, and full of spite. The anger that radiated from her didn't seem like the illness, or like the usual drug induced paranoia that I was familiar with. Instead, it was like she was fully awake for the first time in years. "You've got five seconds."

I raced to the bathroom, shutting the door. I was here. The heart was still in the tub. Was the camera on?

I dashed to the small bathroom closet, finding a long towel to wrap around myself. I clasped the towel, and stared up at the camera, asking questions with my eyes to people I couldn't see. *I'm here. Now what? What do I do?*

Maybe that's all they needed. They needed to know I was there.

A tap at the window startled me. I spun on my heels.

Gabriel's face, his beautiful crystal eyes, the blond locks lifting against the breeze, mixing with the russet brown, his playful lips... for a moment, I wondered if it was my own hopeful imagination.

Gabriel mouthed words that I didn't catch. He pointed to the lock.

I sucked in some courage, clutched the towel around my body tighter. I turned the lock on the window. Gabriel popped the screen out on the other side, pushing the window up for me. "Come on, Trouble, let's go," he whispered, urgency etched in his eyes and dripping from his voice. His hand stretched to me, wrapping around my arm to pull me toward him.

Was that the plan? To get me to run away? I wanted to. I wanted to run away with him. I knew I should trust them. They didn't know what I knew. They didn't have all the information. "I can't," I said.

He started tugging stronger. "You can fit through the window. It's not that small."

"No, I mean, I can't leave," I said.

"Don't start this again," he said. "You have to. We have to go. Now."

I shook my head, trying to wrestle my arm from his grasp. "No," I whispered, "she's already told me she'd call the police. She's waiting to do it now."

"Sang, we're about ready to call the police on her. She's crazy."

I wrenched myself away. "I can't. They'll find us. They'll put me in some home somewhere. You guys will be arrested."

"You can't stay here."

"I have to," I said, and pouted, not meaning to but I wouldn't let Gabriel go to jail.

"No, Trouble," he pleaded under his breath, "no, no, no. Sweetie, don't... you can't. Please." His eyes darkened, watered. "No, don't you dare."

"Tell them to call my father," I said. "Find him. She's determined to find him. She wants me to go with him."

Gabriel jerked his head back, looking back out toward the yard and then inside at me. "I can't leave you."

"I'm fine," I said.

"Sang!" My mother called. I quivered, worried she'd heard me.

Gabriel's face steeled over. He grasped the edge of the window, hauling himself up and over the side of the wall, sinking down onto the back of the toilet as he stepped into the bathroom. Dark slacks, white shirt, red tie swinging from his neck. Did he come straight from school to here?

"Get out," I whispered to him.

Gabriel put his fingers to his mouth, indicating I shouldn't talk any more.

This was it. He was going to get caught. We'd all go to jail.

He lowered himself onto the carpet, stepping close to me until I could breathe in fresh leaves and sweet fruit. Gabriel, the perfume maker, always smelling different.

"Sang!" my mother called again from the bedroom.

Gabriel signaled with his hands for me to go toward the door. I did, opening it slowly as he closed the window, leaving it unlocked.

I peeked my head out, looking toward the bedroom. My mother's eyes were expectant on me. I sighed, opened the door as Gabriel stood behind it, my shadow.

I shuffled out, clinging to the towel. I opened the closet door, holding it wide. From the angle, it blocked the view of the bathroom. Gabriel slipped against the wall, sliding into the closet. I stepped in behind him, my heart thundering, worried my mother would notice.

"Drop the towel," she said.

Gabriel gazed back at me from the inside the corner of the closet. He turned away, staring off at the opposite wall.

I dropped the towel at my feet, stepped into the closet and closed the door.

When I was inside, I sank onto my butt on the floor, drawing in my knees and surrounding my legs with my arms.

Gabriel's arms found me in the dark, encircling my body. His breath heated my face. Silent, he pulled me into his lap. I wanted to push him away, to tell him to go or hide but his scent, his warmth, the feel of his body made me weak. I was done fighting him.

He held me as he sat cross-legged on the floor. He stripped off his tie, his shirt. He quietly fluffed the shirt out and wrapped it around me. He dressed me, putting my arms through the sleeves and buttoning the front. "Trouble," he whispered against my hair at my cheek. "I swear to fucking god, I'll hate you forever if you ever do that to me again."

"You shouldn't be here," I whispered back, not meaning it at all.

"Like I'm going to leave you alone." He finished the last button and his hand sought out my cheek, bringing my head to his shoulder as he embraced me. "Can't spend the night on her own in her own fucking bedroom and wants me to leave her naked in the dark closet."

"It's my fault."

He stiffened against me. "Don't you say that."

Shuffling noises started in the bedroom. I clutched to Gabriel, my fingers gripping at the ribbed undershirt he wore. Now that I had someone with me, I was desperate to hold on to him.

My mother was dialing on the phone again. Beeps sounded as she pressed the buttons.

Gabriel and I waited, listening. I was so sure she'd heard him and called the police.

She was up, shuffling around the bedroom, sounding like she was marching between the window and her bed. She started talking like she was leaving a message. "I have been trying to reach you all day. I know you're there. Did you think you could run off? Did you think I wouldn't figure out what you've done to me?" Her tone rose. "I don't care if you've left money. What I don't want is her. She's your responsibility, not mine. She stole money to buy a cell phone and now she's sleeping with boys. She'll poison Marie. She's just like her mother."

A rattle swept through me, causing me to miss whatever she said next.

She's just like her mother.

I couldn't breathe. My body slumped against Gabriel. The courage I'd managed to collect to hold myself together through this crazy ordeal, was taken away with one short sentence.

She continued, "If you want to leave me, fine. I'll take the house. Thanks," she spat into the phone, "for being so thoughtful as to leave us what we needed. Now come back and get her or I swear I'll call the police and I'll tell them exactly who she is. I'll give you until nine. I know you have other important things to do."

There was a click as she hung up the phone. The television volume was suddenly turned up, the murmur of news reporter voices filling the air.

I stared at the light under the door.

She's just like her mother. ... I'll tell them exactly who she is.

"Who am I?" I whispered, the words floating away from me.

Gabriel's arms shifted around me, but it was like he wasn't there at all. Not his sweet scent, not his caring whispers to calm down, not his gentle caresses at my back could break through as I felt myself slipping down, drowning in a single question that forced me under.

The connection was made in my head, but it didn't seem real. It was like I was looking at someone else, some other girl's truth was revealed and I was watching, sorry for her, saddened she had to learn it, desperate to know just as much as she wanted to know.

The mother I thought was mine, wasn't. Was my father my real father? Who was Sang?

I was a secret; a secret enough that the police would be interested if they found out. Was that why I was in the closet? All I'd ever known was them, my mother, or the person I thought was my mother, getting ill when I was nine. There was my sister and I who used to play together, and eventually we drifted apart, but were we still sisters? Our father came home on occasion and never talked to us. He disappeared so often.

The years of stress and worry when the punishments started confused me now. The way she never allowed me to have friends, to warn me about going out to get raped or killed… what was that? She warned me about bad guys. I'd always thought maybe it was misguided attempts to keep me safe from harm. I thought it was wrong what she was doing, but some small portion of me understood. She feared for me. I sympathized. I didn't like it, but I was her daughter, and children listened to their parents.

But was it really keeping me safe? Or was it keeping me a secret? If I'd gotten into trouble and had gotten raped or kidnapped, the police would find me or find out the truth. If I had been allowed to have friends like normal kids, maybe this secret would have been exposed. So why send me to school?

Then it hit me. Because home school students are examined closer by the board. If I was registered in public school, I was just a number. Unnoticed.

She controlled me through fear. If someone became my friend and looked too closely, would they see the truth in me? Would they be able to see who I was, even though all this time, I never knew?

Who am I?

"Sang," Gabriel cooed to me under his breath in the dark. "Sang," he whispered, calling me back. "Trouble. Sweetheart. Sang. Don't. Don't slip away." He sniffed.

I felt a droplet meeting my forehead.

Gabriel was crying.

"I need you," he whispered. "Come back to me. I need you."

It was like when North shook me after the nightmare, and I felt myself rising to the surface and waking. My lungs opened up. I gasped, choking on the air, discovering I could breathe again. Gabriel's tears met mine on my cheeks. Trailing together.

I was awake now. My own need for answers had to wait. He was breaking down. I needed to be there for him.

It was the only thing that pulled me from the depths. I needed to protect my family, the only people that I knew wanted me. My father abandoned me. The person I thought of as my mother didn't want me, wanted to shove me off on someone who had already let go. Marie reveled in this for an unknown reason.

Gabriel, Kota, this tender family that had sought me out, they were still in danger. Because of me.

"Meanie. Gabriel," I gasped, as I tried to stop shaking. My fingers found the back of his head, intertwining into the longer parts of his hair. I pressed my cheek to his. How did he know? How did he know I needed to feel needed? "Gabriel."

His lips traced my ear as he whispered. "We have to go. I'll take you with me. I promise. This doesn't matter. None of it matters. You're my Trouble. Let's go. If we run..."

I stiffened against him. "Do you have your phone?"

He sighed. "Yes."

"Text Kota," I said, my mind formulating, calculating. I couldn't worry about myself right now. I had to protect Gabriel. I had to protect them all. "We need to make final plans."

♥

FATHER

Gabriel needed more convincing, but I promised I wouldn't leave until it happened. Gabriel used his phone, and we masked the light of it with our bodies just in case someone looked over and spotted the light. He sent texts to Kota.

Gabriel: I have Sang. She can't leave until her father gets here.

Kota: Get her out of there.

Gabriel: Mother has the phone, ready to call the police.

Kota: We're ready for that.

Gabriel: She's not her real mother. She wants to dump Sang on her father and can't reach him. She's promising to call the police and tell them who she really is if he doesn't show up by nine.

Kota: Gabe, pick Sang up and walk her out of there. That's an order.

Gabriel closed his eyes against the light. I could see the strain in his eyes. Kota was the boss. He had to obey.

I shook my head at him. "Try again," I said softly. This was our only shot to avoid the chaos that would ensue. I knew I needed to trust them, but maybe Kota didn't understand.

Gabriel: Sang won't leave. She wants you to find her father. I'm with her in the closet. Her mother's giving him time to come back and take her. It'll avoid the police if he can show up. Sang wants you to find him.

Moments passed. Gabriel's hand on my waist gripped and regripped me. His shirt fell over my butt, covering my private parts until he'd started grabbing me. He was so focused, I wasn't sure if he noticed but it made me feel strange to be exposed and next to him. I was too scared to move to draw attention to it. In the dark, I wasn't sure if he would see it anyway.

I pleaded in the dark to the phone, hoping Kota would understand. I was safe right now. Leaving meant I wouldn't be. If my father could just come back for a minute, he might be the only one who could straighten this out.

The phone buzzed to life.

Kota: 8.

I stared at Gabriel's phone screen. "What does it mean?"

"It means we have until eight," he whispered. "If your father doesn't show up by eight, I'm to take you out of here."

"Will he help? Will he try to reach him?" I asked.

Gabriel's face broke into a grin. "You're forgetting who we are."

We had time. I relaxed into Gabriel. It might be okay after all. If anyone could find my father, the boys could. I was sure if they could just talk to him, they'd get him to come back. I just didn't want the police called. This was all my mistake. They didn't need to get into that kind of problem with me. Not if it could be prevented.

Gabriel promised Kota if anything changed we would let them know or he'd take me out of here. There was nothing for us to do but to count the time. We had four hours to sit around.

With the drone of the television, it was harder to figure

out the location of my mother. I wasn't even sure if Marie was home for a while. On occasion I heard creaking upstairs and wondered if it was Marie or just the house settling.

Gabriel held me in his lap, occasionally shifting to find some comfort. Eventually, he pulled me with him until his back was against the wall, my body against him as he stretched out his legs. I fell off of his lap, my bare butt landing on the floor next to him. I stuffed his shirt down around my hips.

Gabriel sucked in a breath, pushing my legs off of him. "Turn around."

My heart thundered again. "Where?"

He motioned. "Just look at the wall, will you?"

I turned, sitting on the floor, but faced the wall, staring at it. From behind me came sounds of a belt loosening, a zipper slipping down and cloth shuffling. My back stiffened. He was getting undressed?

Trust him, I willed to myself. Gabriel made a promise. He's here risking his own freedom, at the risk of getting the police called on him, to stay with me. *Trust him.*

More shuffling. A tap on my shoulder. "All right."

I turned. His shoes were off, sitting next to him on the floor. His pants were back on. His belt hung off of his knee as he held up a pair of boxers.

He picked up his phone and hit a button to illuminate the screen. "Hold it up for me."

I took his phone in my hands, holding it over his shoulder. I shifted to block the light from the crack under the door with my own body.

Gabriel held the boxers close to his face, pulling a pocket knife from his back pocket. He measured the width of the belt, and started cutting slots into the material of the boxers, like belt loops. He chewed on the edge of his lip as he worked. "Buy her a fucking new wardrobe, and she wears my clothes," he mumbled.

"I like your clothes," I whispered. His were always so colorful. I couldn't imagine the others wearing the bold oranges and neon greens and having the earrings to match the style he liked.

"Shush or I'll drag you out of here now," he said, his focus on the boxers. When he finished, he threaded the belt through the makeshift belt loops. "Put this on. If we're going to have to make a run for it later, it'll be easier if you aren't completely naked."

I sighed, turning around. I held out my hand, ready to take the boxers from him but instead, he ducked next to me, holding the boxers in place for me to step into. My heart thundered as I stepped into the underwear, and he slid the material up my legs, adjusting them on my hips.

When they were up all the way, he turned me around, yanking the belt together. He tugged it tight at my hips, frowning. "You're too small." He picked up his pocket knife, finding a sharp screwdriver tool and started grinding out another notch.

When he was finished, the end of the belt nearly folded down over itself. He threaded it back again through the belt loops he'd made.

The boxers were a comfort. I felt better prepared to run now, too.

He dropped to his knees again, falling onto the carpet on his back. I slipped next to him on the floor. He held out his hands, wrapping his arms around my shoulder. He pulled me until I was resting on top of him, my stomach on top of his. My knees dropped to the floor on either side of his hips. His hand found my cheek and he held my head against his chest. It was almost cozy.

My eyes drooped. I'd been stressed all night with Nathan, aware and terrified all morning with being stuck in the closet. Now I was with Gabriel. I was warm and exhausted. I knew I shouldn't sleep. I needed to be awake and ready to go in case we needed to fly out or if my father showed up.

"Sang," he whispered.

"Yeah?" I whispered back, staring off at the small

crack of light coming in under the door.

"You're fucking grounded."

I pressed my face to his chest, clutching at his tank top and smothering a giggle. "For how long?"

"Forever."

"Are you mad?"

"Fuck yes."

I shouldn't have been happy about it, but I was. I smiled against his chest.

He tucked his right arm under his head, propping it up. His other hand massaged my scalp, his fingers combing through my hair. "I give you a pretty haircut and paint some stars and do all this shit for you. '*Hey Trouble, come on and let me save you.*' '*No, Meanie, I'm gonna stay here.*' How the hell did you talk me into this?"

"I told you to go back."

"Are you kidding? Kota would shoot me. Mr. Blackbourne would skin me. I'd never live through it."

We fell quiet. I listened for the sound of my mother. It sounded like she was on her bed. Maybe she'd fall asleep.

"Meanie?"

"Yes, Trouble?"

I bit my lower lip. "What's going to happen to us?"

Gabriel sucked in a breath. He carefully picked me up and moved me until I was on my back on the carpet. He shifted until he was on his side, his back facing the closet door as if to put himself between my mother and me. He hovered over me, one arm propping himself up and the other on my stomach. In his shadow, I could only catch the outline of his hair, his cheek, his neck. "I'll tell you what's going to happen. Kota is going to find your dad. I don't know what he'll say, but it doesn't matter. What will happen is you're coming with us."

"I can't live with you," I said.

"You will if you have to." His hand at my stomach gripped me, his thumb smoothing over the shirt.

"Your parents... I mean won't they notice another person in the house?"

"Is that what you're fucking worried about? What my parents' would think? Jesus Christ, Sang. You're being held hostage by your own mo..." He stopped, swallowed. "Sorry."

"How can you be so sure I could stay with you?" I asked, not wanting to talk about her. I didn't know how to think of her right now. "The police..."

His hand slid higher over my stomach, fingers gripping at me and causing a cyclone of warm shivers. "Trouble, will you for once just trust me?" His head sunk down until his forehead was pressing against my shoulder. "Please? Pretty please? I'll take care of you. You can stay with me. You can stay with Kota. You can stay with Nathan. What-the-fuck-ever you want. We'll figure it out. We'll do it together."

His words rattled me. It was what I'd wanted, what I thought of in the back of my mind. I cared about them so I wanted to be with them. Why was I scared when I finally was faced with that? If I left with him now, could they do it?

I lifted my arms, wrapping them around his neck. I wanted to believe. I did. I was just exhausted and couldn't take his begging any more. I knew I'd go wherever he asked, wherever they wanted me. There was so much I was grateful for with them. I was actually kind of sorry they worked so hard on my room. It felt like such a waste now if I did end up living with him or one of the others.

He cuddled me, his nose nuzzled my cheek. "Don't worry so much. I've got you now. I'm not letting go."

I sighed against him, willing myself to believe.

♥♥♥

Time passed. No word from Kota. Gabriel hovered his fingers over his phone several times but never sent a message. He said if they were busy, it could be risky to interrupt. He just really wanted an update.

I dozed next to Gabriel often. I forced myself awake every time, listening. I was worried if I fell asleep and if Gabriel did, too, we would get caught. I didn't know what would happen if she opened the closet now and checked on us.

Gabriel kept his arms around me, as if daring her to find us.

At some point I was drifting when Gabriel nudged me awake. "Trouble, it's time. We've got to go."

I sucked in a breath, getting a lung full of Gabriel's scent. "Hm?" I asked, still half asleep.

"It's eight. Time to take you home with me."

My eyes opened and I sat up sharply. "Did they not find him?"

"I don't know. I haven't heard from anyone."

"Maybe you should text them."

"No," he said. "We've got to go. Kota's orders."

"But he could be here any minute."

Gabriel gave a painful sigh. "Sang, he's not coming. They couldn't reach him or he won't come. Either way, we can't stay here. If we leave, we could get a head start."

"But if we walk out..."

"Oy," he said, his tone growing to the point that I was afraid we would be heard. "We're going."

"Give me a minute," I pleaded, not sure what good it would do. Why was I stalling? If I was honest with myself, I knew why. In my heart, I thought if we left, that it wouldn't be as simple as Gabriel had promised. It was also a crazy feeling of rejection. Maybe I cared what my father thought of me after all. I couldn't believe, even if he had left, that he had truly abandoned us. Part of me wanted to think he really was on a business trip.

I rubbed at my eyes, yawning, stretching, stalling.

"Trouble," he said. "If you don't get that pretty ass of yours up, I swear..."

The house trembled around us as a door was shut hard

somewhere in the house. Footsteps treaded through the house. We both drew quiet, waiting. Was it Kota coming in to swoop us out of there? Did Mr. Blackbourne get tired of waiting and send everyone in?

My mother's voice shot out over the murmur of the television. "Look who decided to show up," she said.

"What's going on?" my father's voice traveled through the air.

My father showed up! My eyes widened, glancing over at Gabriel. I couldn't tell in the dark but he seemed to be frowning.

"You left something," she said.

Footsteps came closer. Gabriel scrambled up, pressing himself against the little bit of wall next to the door, standing out of view. I moved to my knees, kowtowing out of years of habit.

The door opened. My father filled the space. I blinked up at him, shaking. He was wearing brown slacks and a short sleeve polo shirt, two sizes too big. His curly hair had been cut shorter. His cheeks were pink from too much sun.

He frowned at me, turning back toward the bedroom. "You can't keep her in the closet. Her school called me saying she missed some important tests and when they tried to call, you said she moved."

"She is moving," my mother spat at him. "You're taking her."

My father reeled his head back. "No. I'm not."

The silence that fell after sliced through me like a thousand paper cuts in my skin. My mother wanted to get rid of me, and my father didn't want me.

"You're going to take her back, or I will call the police."

"Do it," he said. "Do it and I'll tell them you've got her locked in the closet. I'll tell them why there's scars on her wrists. I'll tell them about how many times I've watched you put her on her knees..."

"I think they'd be more interested in how you raped

her mother."

My head popped up, my eyes locking with Gabriel's.

My father closed the door on me. "Don't you ever say that."

Gabriel slid down to his knees, collecting me until I was standing next to him. He half held me up off the floor, ready to take me. I was ready to tell him to go. I wanted him to run. I'd go with him now. I'd do anything he asked. I didn't want to know any more.

"She was sixteen!" My mother howled at my father. "And she killed herself after she had that girl in the closet. You tell me how it happened. It doesn't sound like she was happy with it."

"Is this why you wanted me back here? To throw it in my face?"

"You bring that girl into my house, swearing she was your sister's and I believed you. I can't believe how stupid I was. I can't believe you had me lie to the doctor about how it was a surprise home birth."

"Stop it," my father shouted, his voice booming. It was the loudest I'd ever heard him. "I came back. What do you want?"

"I want you to take that girl out of my house. You left money for us, good. You're leaving me, go. I don't care. But I'm not going to have her here for another minute."

"She's going to stay here," my father said. "Give me until the end of the school year. By then I'll have enough..."

"She's sleeping around with boys in the neighborhood. She's getting them to pay for cell phones for her. I found boy clothes in her closet. Marie said she's sitting with a group of them at school. I won't have her here. You're not going to leave me with this mess, your mess. She'll end up pregnant and the police will be here after her anyway. I can't look at her face any more, knowing that's what *she* looked like. The whore you slept with. She's a little whore just like her."

Gabriel growled low in my ear, gripping me to him.

"I've left enough money for all of you," my father said. "You don't have to do anything. Just let her go to school. After that, you won't see her again. It's only few months."

"I..." my mom shouted, but faltered. She cried out. There was a thud. She started screaming.

"Don't you give me that," my father shouted at her. "If you're faking it, I swear..."

Her screams filled my senses, drowning out everything else. Gabriel slipped a palm to my ear, bringing my other ear to his chest. I wanted to tear myself away from him to see what was going on but he held me strong against him.

There was more thudding, more screaming. My father started talking quickly, "Hello? Yes, we need an ambulance. My wife is sick." He rattled off the address, repeating himself.

The next few minutes became some of the longest and quickest at the same time. Gabriel held me as the only mother I'd known screamed in pain. My father tried to ask her what was wrong, tried to get her to take medicine but despite this, her screaming continued. Gabriel refused to budge. He didn't want me to see what was happening.

A thunder of knocking sounded at the door.

My father's footsteps echoed through the house. Voices sounded. The crash of a stretcher being brought in followed. Voices spoke. My mother quieted.

Gabriel relaxed next to me when the footfalls disappeared down the hall again.

"Let's go," he said.

He opened the door, peeking out. I followed behind him.

The bedroom was empty now.

Gabriel turned to me, tucking his shoulder into my stomach and hoisted me onto his shoulder.

"Put me down," I said, dangling off of his body. I patted my hands against his waist and butt. "I can walk."

"Fuck you," he said. "I'm dragging you out before you

think of some other stupid reason to stay."

Upside down, I was taken through the house to the side door of the garage. Gabriel stepped out. It was dim. The garage light wasn't on and the sun had just set.

Gabriel marched, carrying me across the garage and out into the open, heading across the drive.

"Wait," I called to him. "Put me down."

"No," he said.

"Sang," my father's voice shot through the air, "hey stop that."

Gabriel ignored him.

"Gabriel," I said. "Put me down." I struggled, poking at his side.

He grunted, stopped, shifting me on his shoulder but moved forward. Orders were given. Orders would be finished.

"Sang," my father called out.

Gabriel stopped in mid-step.

I wriggled. "Let me see what he wants. I'll tell him I'm leaving with you. I'll tell him so he won't call the police or think you've kidnapped me. I'll go with you."

Gabriel grunted but put me down. His hand found mine, his mouth tight, his crystal eyes dark. He squared off his shoulders and turned with me to look at what was happening.

An ambulance was parked in the road in front of the house. The gurney was being hoisted into the back. The paramedics closed the back doors and turned to my father.

My father was in the middle of the yard, staring at Gabriel and I in the drive. "Wait just a second," he said, appearing conflicted over wanting to address the paramedics or to talk to us.

I nodded to him. Gabriel squeezed my hand.

When my father seemed sure we would wait, he turned to address the paramedics, saying he'd follow in his car shortly. The paramedic guys turned to look right at my face as my father turned around to walk back toward us.

Mr. Blackbourne and Dr. Green.

The Academy was taking her. My father had no clue. Did they intercept the call?

Where did they get an ambulance?

My father jogged across the yard toward us. "Sang," he said, stopping a few feet from us, shooting a questioning glance at Gabriel. "Who is that? Is that your boyfriend?"

"Yeah," Gabriel said before I had a chance to respond. "That lady locked her in the closet all god damn day. Where the hell were you?"

My father reeled his head back. "I was at work."

"You weren't," Gabriel barked at him. "We called and you weren't there. What the hell, dude? You don't even want your own fucking daughter."

"Gabriel," I said, squeezing his hand, and pulling. "Don't..."

"Do you know what she's been through? And I know you do because you just admitted it in there! You've seen her scars. And you're walking out and leaving her to that crazy woman? Did you want her to die? Fucking great. No problem. Just let me take her and I'll..."

"Wait," my father said, taking a half step back. "Just wait."

"For what?"

"Let her stay," he begged. "Please." I didn't know him well enough to be able to tell if the sorrow in his eyes was genuine. Footsteps approached. Two figures jumped from the rail barrier of the front porch. Kota and Nathan. They'd been in the house.

Another cluster of footsteps sounded from up the street. A group of guys were dashing down the road in our direction. I recognized North and Silas, with Luke and Victor behind them.

My father took a step back as Kota and Nathan marched around him toward me.

"What is this?" my father asked. "Who are they?"

"My family," I said, the words slipping from my mouth. For a moment I thought maybe that would seem insulting to him. The thought passed quickly. I didn't care what my father thought.

Kota reached me first, wrapping his arms around my waist and picking me up off the ground, hugging me close. I let him take me. I couldn't resist any more. The others surrounded me, I could smell them. I could feel their hands touching my back, my face, my hair.

"Wait," my father pleaded again.

"She's not staying," Gabriel shouted. "Not another second."

"Sang," my father called to me. "Don't leave Marie."

The words stung me. I pulled back from Kota, meeting his concerned face. "Put me down," I said.

"No," he said.

"Please."

He grunted but lowered me until I was standing. The others parted, giving me a clear view of my father.

My father appeared defeated now. His shoulders slouched, like all the times my mother yelled at him and he slinked off to do some laundry or go to work to avoid it. "Sang," he said. "I'm sorry. I know it was hard for you. Will you please stay with Marie? I'm going to the hospital with your... with her." He swallowed. "Don't leave your sister."

"We're not leaving Sang," Kota said flatly to him, the command overwhelming in his voice.

My father blinked, questioning with his eyes at the group around me.

Determined faces stared back at him. Strangers to him. I felt as if I knew them better than I'd ever known him. I'd lived with him all my life and he was the stranger among us.

"I'll stay," I said. Kota and the others started to stir to life, but I spoke over them before they could tell me not to. "I'll stay, but they have to stay with me."

"You can't have boys in the house," my father said.

"They stay or I go," I said, my strength returning. "They stay or I'll tell the police what happened." I had no idea what to tell the police and knew I wouldn't do it, but I wasn't about to be told what was best for me now. He was too late to rattle off parental rules to me.

His eyes narrowed on me. "Fine," he said. "Just stay here until I can get back."

My lips glued back together, but I nodded.

He flicked his eyes once more to the others, eyeballing the seven surrounding me. He jogged over to the car parked in the middle of the drive. He got in, started it and drove away.

"Not a goodbye to either of them," Nathan said.

♥

A New Family

Kota slept in my bed with me. The others were sprawled out on the floor, with blankets and pillows strewn all over. I'd opened my eyes several times during the night, warmed by the sight of them all.

Marie was in her room alone. She'd protested, saying we didn't need to stay, but I'd made a promise and I kept mine the best I could. I wouldn't let Marie sleep alone in the house, despite how she had participated in my punishment. No one deserved to be alone. Not tonight.

Sometime near dawn, the sound of metal striking metal stirred me from sleep. Kota mumbled something next to me but sat up, rubbing his eyes. "What's that?" he asked.

"I don't know," I said. "I'll go check it out." I scooted to the edge of the bed, getting to my feet. When I stood, I swayed, shaking.

Kota stood, finding his glasses. "I'll go."

The others snuggled into the floor. North grunted, rolling onto his back, yawning. "I'll go."

"It's not the boogie man," I said. I stepped over someone's head, tiptoeing over to the door.

The hallway was empty, as I expected, but it felt oddly surreal to me. I went down the front stairs, with Kota behind me and North behind him. Shadows. A wash of shivers swept through me. This would have never happened if my mother was still in the house.

I checked my parents' bedroom. It was in the same state it had been the night before. No mother. No father.

I was still thinking of her as my mother. Habits were hard to break, but every time I did it, the memory that she wasn't renewed itself. I hadn't had time to process it all yet.

The banging noise continued. North pointed toward the back of the house. We gathered in the kitchen, moving together to the windows that overlooked the back yard.

My father sat out in the yard, a large trampoline in front of him in pieces. He was hammering the edges together.

"What the hell is he doing?" North said mid-yawn and scratched at his chest.

"I'll go talk to him," I said. "Stay here."

"Listen to her giving orders. Isn't it cute?" North said.

Kota found my hand, squeezing it. "We'll stay," he said. "We'll be watching."

"Like always," I said.

I left them in the kitchen, padding over to the back door in the back of the family room. I'd hardly used that door, but it led out to the screened-in back porch. I don't think I'd been inside the back porch since we'd moved in. It was too easy to be spotted from the kitchen.

I gazed out into the yard, watching my father piece together the trampoline. What was he thinking? What was he doing here? Shouldn't he be at the hospital? Or at work? He worked all the time. What was wrong?

I opened the screen door to let myself out into the yard. My bare feet slicked over the dew covered grass. The air was thick with dawn scents: of mowed grass and mugginess. The neighborhood was still. A weekday. People were in their homes getting ready for work or school.

I trailed out to the center of the back yard, standing behind my father as he worked. I watched, stepping into view so he knew I was there.

"I was at the super store last night getting groceries for the house when I found this on sale. I always wanted one of these things," my father said, not looking back at me. "When I was your age… I shouldn't say that. You're not that young any more. When I was a kid, I used to beg my parents for one. They said it was dangerous. I'd crack my head on the metal." He was wearing the same dark slacks and polo he'd worn the night before. His eyelids sagged. Was he up all night? "I meant to get one for you two before now but never found the time."

"How is she?" I asked, annoyed. He made me stay the night. He lied to me for years. Now he was deflecting. I was tired of being treated like that.

He sighed, resting the hammer against his leg. "She's still sick."

"Cancer," I said.

He gazed up at my face. "You knew?"

"I learned," I said. "A couple days ago."

His lips pursed. "Did she say so?"

"Nope."

He turned back to the metal bars in his hand, started hammering. "I was going to tell you, you know. I was going to explain it to you one day. I thought when you were older..."

"I turn sixteen in a couple of weeks," I told him. I folded my arms over my chest. I felt horrible, like I was being rude. This wasn't me. But I couldn't stop; I didn't know how to share any sympathy or how else to address him. "How much older were you waiting for?"

He frowned. He started piecing together the frame for the trampoline again.

He wouldn't even look at me.

"Where do you go?" I asked. "You weren't in Mexico." I knew this. I knew it was impossible he'd gone off that far and made it back in time last night.

He picked up another piece and started putting it into place. "If you must know, and you'd probably find out, but I've met someone else. Someone who already has two kids and she wouldn't understand… this." He waved his hand in the air toward the house.

My mouth hung open. “Are you kidding me?”

“Why do you think I’ve been working so much?” He dropped the hammer on the mess of metal bars and stood up. He looked down at me. “And don’t give me any grief. There’s seven boys upstairs in your room right now.”

How dare he? How could he look at me with those accusing eyes, as if I was just like him? He had no idea. He’d never understand. I wasn’t going to waste a moment explaining it to him. His opinion didn’t matter. “What do you want from me?”

“I can’t stay,” he said. “Your mother hates me. She doesn’t want me here. Her illness is bad. She’s getting not just treatment for the cancer but they say she’s being seen by a psychologist today. It might be months before she gets out.”

She’d been in and out of the hospital so much that it didn’t faze me at all to think of her in one. Now here it was. She wouldn’t be back for a while. Was it because of Mr. Blackbourne and Dr. Green taking her? I blinked at him, my mouth clamped shut, waiting for him to get to the point.

“If you run off with that boyfriend, or those boys or whatever, Marie’s going to be alone here. If your mother gets out, it’ll be tough on her. I can’t be in twenty places at once.”

“You want me to stay here with Marie? You want me to stay in this house?”

“I need you to look out for it. Take care of things while your mother is gone. Make sure she has a place to get back to.” His eyes darkened. “Please. I’m not asking for me. I’m asking for them.”

Somehow I doubted that. It felt like he wanted to be assured that he could leave. Isn’t that what he did? He waited until he worked hard enough to collect enough savings so he could run off without telling anyone. He didn’t care. He just didn’t want to feel guilty. I sighed. “Is it true?”

His head tilted at me, an eyebrow lifted.

"Did you rape my real mother? Did she kill herself?"

He reeled back as if I'd struck him. "I didn't rape her."

"Who is she?"

His mouth tightened. "I loved her," he said. "Please. Don't."

"You loved her? Did you love Marie's mother? Is the woman in the hospital her real mother?"

"Yes," he said, his palm brushing against his face. "I mean yes, she's Marie's real mother."

I sucked in a breath. My hands closed into fists. I wanted to pummel him. I knew how. I'd done it before. One chop to the neck and I'd send him to the hospital like I'd did to that kid at school. "And you're leaving her for someone else? You're leaving Marie behind? You're leaving me behind? Just so you can go off and pretend to be normal with another family?"

"Do you want me to stay?" he asked.

The question struck me. Did I? What kind of family did I end up with? Was bombarding him with questions going to bring me any closer to the answers I wanted, or give me what I needed? I didn't know what I wanted at all.

Or maybe I did. What I wanted were the seven people who had said they wanted me. Seven boys. Plus Mr. Blackbourne and Dr. Green. Nine. I had nine people in my family. Not him. Not my father.

"No, you don't have to stay," I said. "Marie might feel differently though. Why don't you go ask her?"

He frowned at me. "I have to go back to the hospital. I have to sign papers. After that, I have to get to work." He turned from me, starting back toward the house.

"What do I do?" I asked, turning to him and following behind. "How do I take care of this?"

"I'll be back," he said. "I'll come back with groceries when you need them and I'll make sure the bills are paid. My phone number is in your mother's side table drawer. If you need anything, call me. I'll bring it over." He stopped, turning to me. "Can you drive?"

"Not yet."

"Find someone to teach you. Those boys drive, don't they? If you want lessons, I'll pay for them. I'll buy you a car. Teach your sister. When you can do that, I'll give you access to the accounts. You'll need it."

"You want us to fend for ourselves?"

"Get through this school year. Just for now. Stay out of trouble and do well in school. You usually get straight As. If you can keep it up, it'll be fine."

"Why?" I asked. "Why this school year? What happens when it's over?"

"I promised I'd take care of you," he said solemnly. "I promised your mother, your *real* mother I'd look out for you. Let me do that. When you're eighteen, I'll pay for college. I'll do it if you let me. I can't bring you two with me, but I can provide for you until you're old enough. I think you're mature enough to handle this. I promised, okay? I promised her."

The blood drained from my face. "Who was she?"

He clamped his lips together again, turning away. He marched over to the car parked in the drive. He was leaving us, with a half-finished trampoline in the yard and unanswered questions. Was it supposed to be a peace offering? Was he trying to make some small connection, leaving a memory that he wasn't such a bad person? He got into the car. He was running away from a life he didn't want, toward a new family he had to lie to in order to keep.

I turned, spotting Kota and North inside the screened-in porch. They'd been watching over me. I didn't want to think the next thought, but I did, and it stuck to my mind like a spider web.

How long did I have before they left me, too?

The unwanted.

~A~

On Friday, Kota parked his sedan at a bar in downtown Charleston. He didn't like that there was an assignment tonight. If he didn't have a family emergency though, the Academy wasn't to be ignored. They'd promised, after all. They'd already been out all week to stay with Sang.

Kota stepped out of his car, tucking a couple of drumsticks into his back pocket to free up his hands. Playing the drums for a faux band at a club was only one of a number of unusual assignments the Academy asked of them. It wasn't his favorite because it meant staying out later than he wanted, especially right now when he preferred to be with Sang.

He flicked his phone on, punching the pink heart and scrolling through buttons as he searched through each camera until he found her. His heart lifted at seeing her face again.

She was curled up on the bean bag chair in the attic. She didn't need to be in there but he knew she liked it. Kota smiled down at the phone, staring at her tiny, perfect features and the way she traced her fingertips over the photographs around her. For good measure, he counted her fingers and her toes, a perfect set of ten for each. It was how he reassured himself that she was really okay, with all digits accounted for.

He closed the app, sliding the phone back into his pocket before he changed his mind about tonight and left to be with her. He shouldn't be looking in on her like this but he couldn't stop himself.

Just like he couldn't stop thinking of that green heart in the tub, and how he knew she was downstairs in the house. He admired her cleverness.

He also couldn't stop thinking of how she'd looked when she appeared in that same bathroom. He'd watched her through the camera before sending Gabriel out to get her. She'd been naked and as much as he wanted to divert his eyes, he couldn't. Her tender, young breasts and the curve of her bare hips aroused him, and had him thinking of things he'd swore he'd never think of with her. Not right now. Not when things were such a mess. She didn't need that now.

Kota tried to refocus. He had other things to worry about. He had Academy business to take care of.

The bar in downtown Charleston wasn't overly crowded for a Friday evening, but they were several hours early. The inside smelled of mildew and alcohol mixes. Rock music played through overhead speakers. Six customers clustered together comfortably at the carved wood bar. Two bartenders leaned on their elbows over the bar top to talk with the patrons. Kota guessed the customers at the bar were regulars. They seemed more at ease than the sixteen other people gathered at seven other tables by the empty stage.

Kota absently touched the bridge of his glasses on his nose. He located the door beyond the far side of the bar marked with a sign: Green Room.

He opened the door, counting off heads as he entered the room. Seven, including Mr. Blackbourne and Dr. Green. They were missing Gabriel and Victor.

He nodded to the others, tugging the drumsticks out of his back pocket and placing them quietly on the table. He sat on one of the available stools surrounding the table in the middle. A family meeting was long overdue.

As soon as he sat down at one end of the table, the door opened behind him and Gabe and Vic walked in. Gabe's hair was spiky in the back today, ready for a night of guitar playing and singing for a crowd. His bright orange shirt had zigzags of contrasting green. They were there to draw attention tonight, and Gabriel was making sure that happened.

Victor was in jeans and a plain black t-shirt he'd borrowed from North. It was one of the few times Victor ever wore something so plain. Victor hooked his finger at the end of the sleeve, tugging as if uncomfortable. Kota knew Victor didn't like playing piano in front of other people in general, although their faux rock band was less of a stressor for Victor than the elaborate concerts his parents demanded he participated in.

Luke's blond hair was swept back into the clip he'd taken from Sang. He and Nathan would trade off bass and second guitar for the night. North would take over drums if Kota wasn't there, but North and Silas needed to set up equipment and work the floor tonight. They were the distraction as the bar owner—an Academy member—had his own important task.

What that was, they didn't know, and they didn't need to. When it came to favors, they did as they were told. They had to trust in the Academy.

Mr. Blackbourne quietly tugged a little black box out of his pocket. Kota recognized the device. With the right frequency, out of human hearing, it could disable recording devices that might have been missed in a security sweep. Whatever they wanted to talk about tonight, they didn't want anyone outside the group knowing about, including the Academy.

They eyed one another. No one wanted to begin.

Her situation was not as straightforward as their family problems had been.

Mr. Blackbourne cleared his throat. "Mrs. Sorenson will be taken to the Mayo Clinic in Florida. She's en route now."

Kota nodded in approval. "For how long?"

"We don't know," Dr. Green said. He propped his elbows on the table, leaning forward. His eyes drooped and his usual warm smile was a little faint. Kota had the feeling he was working overtime at the hospital again, mostly due to Sang's mother. "At least two months, maybe three.

We've ensured that she'll be staying at least that long to give her time away from the girls as well as time to hopefully be ready for surgery and to recover. Apparently when the medicine was corrected, it cleared her mind up. It forced this secret out in the open and she's not in the right place to deal with it."

And poor Sang had to deal with it, instead. "Sang's father," Kota said, "Has asked her to remain in the house to watch over it while her mother is gone. Marie is staying, too. He expects her to get her license, and basically live alone with him paying for it. He's left them for another family." The other seven knew, but wanted to get Dr. Green caught up since he'd been busy with Sang's mother.

"We found him and his new family," North said. His hands made fists against the table. "The woman is at least ten years younger than him, and she has two boys, one our age and one in college. From what we can tell, Mr. Sorenson has been living there for a while. We don't know if the kids are his yet, but I don't think they are. He's claimed the house they live in on his taxes as a vacation home. The woman doesn't know about Mrs. Sorenson or Sang and Marie. Her Facebook status claims she's married to Mr. Sorenson. I don't know if he faked a wedding with her or if she's jumping the gun. He's still officially married to Mrs. Sorenson according to the state. Mr. Sorenson and his… mistress and their family are living on the other side of the state, close to the North Carolina border. This is why it took him so long to get here."

Victor's left hand drifted up, two fingers swaying in the air as if to redirect attention. "He's got four different savings accounts under different names in a separate bank apart from his checking account. He's labeled the four saving accounts. One is marked 'house,' which I'm guessing is for funding the house for Mrs. Sorenson and the girls. There's also one marked 'school'. The others are just initialed; one is marked with an S, the other with an M. You can imagine who those might be for. He funnels money out from each of his paychecks. The amounts in Sang's and Marie's accounts are enough to carry them both through college, unless they become doctors. I'm not sure what the school fund is for. The amount is way too much for them to need for high school books and fees. College, too, maybe."

"We know," Mr. Blackbourne said, and he focused on Kota.

Kota pursed his lips. He hadn't wanted to reveal this to the others, because he didn't want to worry them and he was sure he could figure out an answer to this before now. With everything that had happened though, Mr. Blackbourne silently commanded him with a look to spill it. Kota sighed. "We found letters of acceptance for both Sang and Marie into a…a boarding school of some kind."

"Boarding school?" Gabriel asked, sitting up sharply.

"It's more like a prison," Kota said. "Very restrictive. Very hush, hush. An all-girl school, and she'd be enrolled until she was at least eighteen. If she entered, she'd be forced to stay. I think it's a place for troubled teens. The administrators have a bad reputation. There are a lot of abuse reports that get buried by the local police station."

"And he wants to send her there?" North asked. "Fucking Christ."

"If he's told Miss Sorenson she needs to stay until the end of the school year," Mr. Blackbourne said, "it could be possible he has enrollment established and he just needs to wait it out until then. He may have planned to dump the girls into a boarding school earlier but kept them around because Mrs. Sorenson was so sick. He needed someone to babysit her."

Kota sat back. The others around him shifted uncomfortably. Kota knew the feeling. Sang's life was a twist of complications, most of which she didn't know about yet. Her father had lied to her. He wasn't trying to take care of her. He wanted to stash her away.

"Well that's it," Gabriel said, his fingertips drumming on the table. "We can't let her go to this… thing. No fucking way. She's coming home with us."

"We have to tell her the truth," Victor said. "When she hears her mom's going to come back and her dad wants to drop her into a boarding school, she'll come with us."

Mr. Blackbourne frowned. "From what you've told me, it seems pretty clear Mr. Sorenson wants her to stay at home. I believe the reason is if she goes off to live on her own, and if someone discovers a young girl living on her own, social services might ask questions. If they look into it, they might discover who her real mother is. We need to investigate the details before we can confront Mr. Sorenson. Mr. Sorenson might be opposed to us taking her, as he might be worried we'd draw attention to this. However, the details are pretty buried. The only ones who might know the truth are Mr. and Mrs. Sorenson."

"And Mrs. Sorenson isn't talking right now. She's barely tolerating treatment," Dr. Green said. He raked his fingers through his hair. "And if we take Sang, what do we do with Marie?"

"Marie is trouble," Luke said. "She's sneaking booze from the liquor cabinet from Danielle's house. I found the bottles in her room. Marie isn't doing her homework and failing her classes. I've heard she's selling off some of her mom's pills for money at school, too. She's going to end up in jail before too long."

"But Sang feels responsible for her," Kota said. He didn't like Marie, either, not since she'd lied to them all, and stolen Sang's phone and clothes. He'd pitied her before because of the situation, but Marie was the complete opposite of Sang. "Sang's lost two mothers and a father in one night. How can we ask her to take off on her sister? She's hanging onto the last piece of family she has." Kota admired Sang for trying her best, but it left them with little choice. The silly girl was too loyal for her own good. "And once she learns about this boarding school, she's not going to want Marie to go there, even if she might deserve it."

Mr. Blackbourne sliced his hand through the air.

"We've got two options," he said. "Our first is to tell Sang, and let her know the truth. Marie would be informed and she'll probably go her own way if she hears about the boarding school. Somehow we have to convince Mr. Sorenson to let Sang come with us. If that happens, we need to know what we're dealing with. If Mr. Sorenson did rape a sixteen year old girl, this might become a devil's deal, and we'd have to ensure him that his secret will stay buried if she remains with us."

Kota frowned, and from how the others' faces darkened, he could tell they disliked this option. Not that they didn't want Sang, but if Mr. Sorenson was that kind of person, they wouldn't want him to get away with this. Who knows what else he might have done?

Victor cleared his throat softly. "What's plan B?"

Mr. Blackbourne sighed. "Our only other option is to bring this to the Academy."

"She can't join the Academy," Kota said, frowning. Mr. Blackbourne had to be crazy to think Sang should join. When assignments filtered through to them, they picked which ones they wanted to take on. Academy girls were often asked to play the role of bait. Sang was too sweet, too trusting and too reckless to say no to those dangerous assignments. He wanted to get her out of danger, not throw her back into it. But outside of his desire to keep her safe, there was no way she could join. Not right now. "She doesn't trust us."

"And we don't have time to get her to trust us that much," North said. "Between school and dealing with Mr. Hendricks, we've only got a few months before that mother returns and kicks her out anyway."

"I'm not talking about making her a member," Mr. Blackbourne said. "Besides what you've mentioned, we're also still not ready, unless we were willing to take the risk that she'd join another group."

There was a chorus of grumbles in the negative. Kota knew better. Despite their group being the team lead because they adopted her, she was still new to them.

Another team could easily swoop in and lure her into joining them. Kota was pretty sure Sang liked them, but did he want to risk losing her? If joining the Academy became the answer, the only team he wanted her to join was theirs. As it stood now, the Academy wouldn't allow it. A bird in a dog squad usually never worked out. So that confirmed it for him. He didn't want her to join.

Mr. Blackbourne's mouth curled up in the corner. "I guess that answered the other question I had. So we do want to keep her?"

"Yes," Kota said, though his voice was lost as eight other members, including Dr. Green, all answered the same, some louder than others. There was no question about this. Sang was staying.

"What are we talking about?" Nathan asked. His face was drawn, blue eyes dark. "We'll ask for a favor from the Academy to help us get her out?"

"Correct," Mr. Blackbourne said. "We have them help us find out the truth about Mr. Sorenson. It'll be the fastest possible solution. We could possibly use the Academy's private school façade, and make Mr. Sorenson believe that our Miss Sorenson has been accepted under a scholarship. He might be willing to give her to us if he believes a school is willing to take her in for free."

"If he can put her in sooner," Kota said, almost liking this idea, even though he knew a catch was coming, "if he was told she was accepted before the end of the school term, he'd probably jump on it. Especially if he doesn't have to spend his school fund he's set aside."

Mr. Blackbourne's eyes brightened. He planted his hands on the table in front of him, leaning against it. "We'd have to find an acceptable place for her sister, although that might be a problem because of her failing grades. We'll have to have the Academy pull a few strings for us. With their protection, Miss Sorenson would be out of reach if Mr. Sorenson's past is too horrible to ignore. But on top of Mrs. Sorenson's hospital requirements and dealing with

Mr. Sorenson's past, if we wanted to ensure she stayed with our group, our quickest answer could cost us."

Dr. Green sighed. "Can we afford this? How many favors are we talking about here?"

"From my last count, it'll cost us everything, including the favors we'd earn completing our mission at Ashley Waters. That's if we're successful. We couldn't afford it otherwise."

Kota blew out a loud sigh. This was an impossible choice. The Academy's system worked on a series of favor and financial debt.

Financial debt was obvious. Everyone in the Academy starts out with financial debt. It's the value of the education an Academy student requires to become the best at what he does. If it was a private investigation training class or an eight week boot camp or you were starving and needed groceries to get through a human biology class, the Academy took care of it.

Repaying your debt requires completing various Academy missions. Their particular team specialized in recovery. It was the easiest thanks to Mr. Blackbourne's and Dr. Green's training. A stolen vehicle. Valuable information. A company's prototype. Whatever it was, there was a price tag.

Some member's financial debts were higher than others. Sang's MRI did cost money, but there were several Academy members on the board at that hospital, and the amount was shifted into their team's debt account. Sang's mother was going to cost them several thousand dollars, but money wasn't really a problem for them.

They couldn't pay the debt off directly. Victor couldn't pull out his black card and swipe away what they owed. It wasn't allowed. The Academy trained their teams well. Recovering stolen money and valuable objects was fairly easy. They enjoyed the challenge. And whenever something like an MRI or tuition to a little sister's private school needed to be paid, the hospital bill would be covered by an anonymous donor, or a special sponsorship would open up for just the right student. Always in cash. Always untraceable. Anything they needed was taken care of.

Favors, though, were the real core of the Academy. Favors were anything that didn't have a price. It was usually family problems within the Academy that other members couldn't handle alone. Little brother getting beat up by kids in school? Hire Silas and North to babysit the playgrounds. When the bullies got a taste of their own medicine, Silas and North would walk away with a couple of favors owed.

When you were finally a member, you were in the negative of ten favors right off the bat, just to keep everyone on a level playing field. Favors varied from different situations. Running a background check without anyone noticing you've been snooping around, that was probably worth one or two, depending on how extensive one had to get. Pretending to be a rock band? That was worth three. An operation, like being undercover in a high school for a year, was easily worth at least ten each for the nine team members involved. And since Mr. Blackbourne and Dr. Green didn't have any favor debt, there would have been surplus that they shared with the rest of the team.

Kota was out of favors. Thirty was the maximum anyone could have. This year at the school, plus all the other favors they'd earn on side jobs, would have placed him close to zero. That is, if he didn't end up spending any. He wouldn't have graduated from the Academy, but at least he wouldn't be at the max favor debt.

Sang had already cost them a few favors when they asked for an adoption.

Kota's fingers traced along the grains of the wood on the table. Did Mr. Blackbourne really mean they'd all be back in the negative? Mr. Blackbourne and Dr. Green had already graduated from the Academy, positive on both favors and financials. If they were to revert and go back, what did that mean?

"Why are we playing around?" North asked. His palm flattened against the table. "Let's take Sang. Fuck her dad. Why is she having to suffer because of what he's done? And who cares if the police find out? She's not the one who is going to be arrested. We've got some pull. I bet we could get her emancipated with only a couple of favors. Ten at most. She can move in with me if she wants. If she wants a place of her own, we'll get her one. The police can go chase Mr. Sorenson all day. There's nothing they can do to her."

"I agree," Kota said. "I want to protect her, but if she stays, she's only going to get hurt. It's only a matter of time before Marie gets arrested, her mother returns, or her dad tells her to go to this school. We can't let that happen. The sooner we get her out of there, the quicker she'll adjust if she's with one of us. We don't need the Academy stepping in this far." That wasn't a risk he wanted take. If the Academy was to get involved, it would learn everything about her, and other teams would spread word that there was a new bird of interest.

Kota knew better, and the others did, too. Sang was clever, and surprised him with new talents every day. She was quiet on her feet, honest, and no matter what they were doing, she stepped up and did it with them. And if their team was interested in her, there was no doubt the Academy would be drawn to her, too. Asking for their help would almost be a guarantee the Academy would ask for her to join them.

Mr. Blackbourne's face shifted into a frown. "Stealing her is not a good idea. We can't just rip her out."

"Why not?" North asked. "We don't have time for plan A and I don't particularly want Mr. Sorenson to get away with this. And I don't want the Academy to tell us it'll be in her better interests if we allow her to work with other teams so she has a choice. Fuck that shit. She's ours. We found her. She's with us. Let's just call the cops on Mr. Sorenson and be done with it."

Mr. Blackbourne glanced at Dr. Green.

Dr. Green sighed. "You've got to tell them."

"Tell us what?" Gabriel asked, nearly jumping to his feet.

Mr. Blackbourne touched briefly at his tie. "We'd rather not expose Miss Sorenson to any authorities."

Kota's eyes narrowed on him. "Whatever you're worried about, she can take it. She's strong. She won't…"

"It's not about her emotional state, although that is a concern," Mr. Blackbourne said. "We don't want to expose her because she's a ghost."

Kota blinked after Mr. Blackbourne spoke, because at first he wasn't sure he heard him right.

"It's true," Dr. Green said, as if understanding everyone's confusion. "She's a ghost bird."

The weight of that idea settled into Kota's brain heavily, like a stone in a water bucket. He might as well told him Sang was going to be leaving them forever, because it could be true if anyone else found out. "Shit," he said.

Everyone's eyes widened, especially Gabriel's. "What shit? What do you mean shit?" He pointed at Kota with a lean finger, but turned his attention to Mr. Blackbourne. "If he's cursing, this is bad. What about Sang being a ghost? What does this mean for her?"

"It means she's valuable to the Academy," Kota said, his eyes focusing on the table. Part of him, in the back of his mind somewhere, started counting the lines in the wood grain. Counting was how he calmed himself, but in the moment, his mind couldn't count high enough. "She has no history. No identification. She's untraceable. She doesn't exist to anyone. She could walk into a job, and if anyone tried to ID her, they wouldn't be able to. No one would be able to find her."

"Yeah she does," Silas said, speaking up and surprising everyone, because he was usually quiet during these meetings. "She's got a school ID."

"Not anymore," Dr. Green said. "At least not on the school records."

"What about her birth certificate?" Kota asked, wanting to know all the details.

"Forged," Mr. Blackbourne said. "They seemed to have copied Marie's and just changed the date and the name. Same with the Social Security card. She's never been to the doctor. She's never been mentioned in their taxes. They gave the schools exactly what they needed, and schools just made her a number. They never look too closely at those things. Dr. Green and I have already collected her old school records from her other schools, and gotten rid of any computer information. All that's left is what is necessary at Ashley Waters. We'll get rid of that when she's about to leave. If we did it now, someone would notice."

"But what were they going to do if Sang ever tried to get a job? Or get her license?" Kota asked. "She was bound to find out."

"IDs are stolen all the time," Dr. Green said. "We know that. But you're right, Mr. Sorenson hadn't thought this through. Someone might have discovered eventually that Miss Sorenson's records weren't genuine. If she gets her driver's license, that'd be one solid ID that she could use to get most anything else she needed, up until she tried to apply for a credit card. Either she would have gotten lucky and offices would turn a blind eye and see it as a mistake and issue her new things, or they'd check it out. It might be why he's really interested in this particular school. She'd be eighteen before she was released. That would give him time to figure out the next step."

"But now that we have her," Mr. Blackbourne said, "the ideal situation would be to keep her record completely clean. If possible."

The new realization settled into Kota, and he sat back. This made it incredibly complicated. He wasn't even sure if he wanted to care about this. Not at the risk of her safety. He knew it would never come to that. They wouldn't allow

Sang to risk her life for the hope of keeping her a ghost bird.

But if what they were saying was true, the Academy would do anything to recruit her. And if their group asked for help and paid in favors to save her, they'd find out for sure.

Mr. Blackbourne nodded quietly as the group seemed to come to understand the full significance. "If we turn to the Academy for help, we'll expose her for what she is and there's a strong chance they'll convince her to join and under their terms. Even if she wanted to stay with us, they'd dangle promises to release all of our favor debts and even put us in the positive in exchange for her working with a team they select. Once she realizes she has the ability to command such a price, and with her sweet disposition, she'd agree to it in a heartbeat. We already know she'd put her own life at risk just to save you guys from a fight."

Dr. Green inhaled sharply. "If we let the police handle this, it'll take away one of the most valuable assets…"

"She's not an asset," Victor barked.

"You are an asset," Mr. Blackbourne said. "Every one of you. And like it or not, right now she's worth ten of you."

Victor's head jerked back. "We can't… I mean…" His eyes turned to Kota. "What are we supposed to do?"

"We have to convince Mr. Sorenson to release her to us," Kota said. He didn't like this answer. It was against his morals to see Mr. Sorenson get away with anything. At least Mrs. Sorenson had an excuse, being ill. He had none, and practically caused Mrs. Sorenson's mental state. "If we can do that, we won't need to turn to the Academy. It'll buy us time to win her over and to get her to understand how this works."

"We have to find out the truth, first," Mr. Blackbourne said. "I won't ask any of you to go into this blindly. Whether or not Mr. Sorenson raped anyone, he still had a child with an underage girl. Who knows if there might be more. We already know he's not beyond trying to smother secrets."

Dr. Green nodded. "And we need to keep her where she is for now until we figure it out. We can't let the police in on this. And if we want to keep her with us when the Academy finds out, we'll have to figure out how we can get the Academy to let us keep her with our team."

"I don't want her in the Academy," Kota said. "It's too dangerous."

"We may not have that choice," Dr. Green said. "They'll find out eventually and they'll want her, and she's already interested. You can tell just by looking at her."

"We need to get to work with her," Mr. Blackbourne said. "Stay near her, build her confidence. Trust building has to start now. We might be able to circumvent any long term damage her mother has done to her. You also, though, have to give her a little time alone. Filling her life up only distracts her from processing what has happened to her and puts off the inevitable. There's a strong possibility she'll want to fly solo. We want to avoid that. She's already shown signs of avoidant personality."

"What does that mean?" Nathan asked.

"Emotional distancing," Dr. Green said. "She shows some social isolation. She thinks it's her versus the world. If we want her to feel connected to us, we'll need to break through that. She might continue to keep things to herself for a while."

"What do we do?" North asked. He crossed his arms over his chest. "We have three months to figure out what happened to Sang's mom, try to convince her dad to release her to us, do our Ashley Waters job, and somehow convince the Academy and her that she should stay on our team, with or without her officially becoming a member. They already don't want birds on dog teams."

"We're working on it," Mr. Blackbourne said. "We don't know what will happen. Let's focus on finding out the truth."

Dr. Green cleared his throat. “At any rate, we’ve got a lot to do with her right now. We’ll have to help her adjust to living alone in that house.”

“She won’t be alone,” Silas said.

“No, she won’t,” Kota said. “If we back off now to give her space, she might feel we’re abandoning her, too.”

“It’s too late to back down, and I doubt any of you would, anyway,” Mr. Blackbourne said.

“This is what I thought we should talk about as well,” Dr. Green stated. “I know you boys are trying your best to make her feel included. Goodness knows, she needs it. You have to take it slow with her, though. She’s already admitted that she’s never really been touched or hugged or anything before.”

Mr. Blackbourne nodded. “I think it’s best we establish ground rules now. The first one should probably be no intimate contact of any kind. No dating. Nothing romantic.”

The surge of rejection toward this idea reverberated, surprisingly, from the others in the group around Kota.

“I don’t approve,” Victor called out, using the more formal method of rejection established by the Academy.

“I don’t approve,” echoed Gabriel, in a louder voice, as if trying to establish he felt even stronger about it than Victor. Their eyes locked on each other, and Kota recognized the challenge in their faces.

“I more than disapprove, I reject it entirely,” North grumbled.

Mr. Blackbourne pushed a palm to his forehead. “Good god, don’t tell me it’s already happened.”

Stares zoomed across the table, accusing and daring anyone to speak up and say they’ve done anything to Sang. Kota, most of all, wanted to know exactly what his friends had been up to. He’d dismissed the hand holding, because he did it, too. He dismissed it when she sat in their laps, because he felt a comfort in it. He’d done it with her, so he couldn’t blame the others for doing it. His Academy brothers were friends, yes, and sometimes they shared brotherly hugs. Touching Sang was different. She wasn't a sister or someone out of reach. She was beautiful and sweet and willing to please. When she was near, it was difficult not to reach for her and hang on to her. He didn't do it all the time because he didn't want to scare her.

It was also addicting. The more he touched her, the more he wanted to touch.

He wasn't so sure he wanted her to share more intimate touches with the rest of his family. When he looked around the table, though, the rage in the others' eyes established more than enough proof of something Kota had been worried about since they had brought her in.

Mr. Blackbourne nearly jumped to his feet from the stool, pushing his palms to the table to lean on it. "I can't believe this. This is exactly why we never, ever bring a bird into a dog group. I've warned you. I've warned all of you." He lifted a finger into the air to take stabs in Kota's direction. "You. I've warned you about this."

"I know," Kota said, lowering his eyes at the table. "She needed us, though."

Mr. Blackbourne huffed. "Yes, she needed us." The frown deepened and his critical eyes bore down at the others. "None of you understand what this means, now. You brought her in without thinking. You've moved too fast. Now you all will have to focus. It's bad enough that she's at risk for hero worship with any of us, or all of us. She could equate what she believes to be real feelings of love for helping her. That would be dangerous enough for her at her present emotional state. What we don't need is countertransference on top of it."

"That's not what... I mean that's not how..." Victor said.

"Spit it out, Mr. Morgan," Mr. Blackbourne said.

Victor frowned. "I've already asked her out," he said flatly, his chin lifting to the air. "She said yes."

"Did she say yes or did she divert to figure out what answer you wanted and did whatever would please you?"

"She said she wanted to," Victor countered, but his voice wavered. "She can tell me what she wants or doesn't. She's done it before with me."

Mr. Blackbourne narrowed his eyes at him. "She's hungry for attention. A certain kind, at least. She doesn't know what is too far because she's socially inept. I've seen what she does. She's done it to me, too. She'll fix those eyes on you and lets you touch her, even if she's uncomfortable or unsure, because she doesn't want to disappoint you. And from the looks from your brothers here, I can tell she's done that to everyone."

Jaws became firm, more stares, mostly toward Victor, for daring to cross a line they themselves had probably told themselves they wouldn't. Not yet. Not when she'd gone through so much. Kota felt the heat rising to his face, knowing that while he pushed those same thoughts from his mind, he was always thinking of it.

And he couldn't blame them. She was beautiful, sweet, and they'd all be idiots not to want to get closer.

Mr. Blackbourne didn't have to say it. They could go on dates with girls they met if they wanted to. The problem usually came from the girls they asked out. Academy members often had to disappear because of Academy business, sometimes for as long as a week, and had to lie to cover that up. Most girls couldn't understand and didn't trust them. Often enough, the guys were flat out too busy to date anyone.

They could date other Academy girls, as many Academy members sometimes resorted to doing, but most of the local Academy girls weren't to his taste. He'd dated a couple, but it was short lived. He knew the others sometimes had done so, on and off, but they mostly had the same reaction.

And there were so few Academy girls that they were often taken.

Now they had Sang. Sang was an exception. She knew about the Academy, and she willingly accepted their absences and excuses. She was the only one who had gotten so close. Part of it was because she needed it. And she was so vulnerable. One look at her and you could tell what she wanted without her saying so. Didn't she say she was lonely the night before and stayed with Nathan because of it? She preferred to be with them, even when given the choice to be alone. That meant something, Kota knew. Kota wondered if she would have gone to him if he had been around.

If she had an avoidant personality, like Mr. Blackbourne said, she was breaking through it. She was starting to call them for what she needed. She didn't reach for his hand, he always had to reach for hers, however, she seemed to be warming up to them. He thought showing up at Nathan's house when she felt lonely showed she wanted to break through that isolation.

"This is the problem," Mr. Blackbourne said. He jabbed his finger at the table to make his point. "Supply and demand. There's nine of us and one of her. What happens when more than one person develops feelings, and possibly false feelings, towards her? I'll say what. Anger and resentment and jealousy."

"That's not what's going to happen," Gabriel grumbled.

"It's already happening," Mr. Blackbourne snapped, striking his finger in the air at Gabriel. "You're already fighting over who gets to spend the night with her. You're breaking cover while on missions to text her or respond to her calls. That girl has the power to cause us to crash and burn. Everything we've established, all the things we've done, and it can be over in a moment because of her."

"We don't have to let it happen," Dr. Green interjected.

"No, we don't have to let it," Mr. Blackbourne's voice rose. "Because it's stopping right now."

"We're not getting rid of her," Kota said.

"That's not what I mean," Mr. Blackbourne flashed those silver eyes at Kota's face. "I mean everyone being mature about this and not taking things too far with her."

"If we stop some things, she's going to notice," North said. "We've been holding her hand. I know the rest of you do it. If we back off of that, she might not understand."

"This is what's going to happen," Mr. Blackbourne barked, his order-giving voice dominating over the others. It was the voice Kota often tried to replicate. "You follow the rules, or you bow out of anything to do with her on a group level. It's the only way this can work out. As I see it, there's only one option. Stop where you are, and don't go any further with her."

"How the hell do you come up with this shit?" Gabriel called out. "What do you mean?"

"It's really simple, Mr. Coleman. No one is allowed to become romantically involved at all. Unless you want to risk scaring her, you'll stop at whatever place you are with her. And you'll have to deal with the others still holding her hand and going from whatever level they've already established."

"You mean sharing her?" North said, his head reeling back as he glanced around. "With all of us?"

"That's exactly what I mean," Mr. Blackbourne said. "If you can all agree to share her attention, it might be the only way for her to trust us. You also can't date anyone else right now. She's too susceptible. It's a complicated situation now and bringing another bird into the picture could make her back off permanently."

To Kota, that wasn't a problem. Ever since he'd met Sang in person and gotten to know her, she was all he'd thought about. He'd taken fewer side assignments just to be around her. He wasn't interested in anyone else.

Dr. Green stood next to Mr. Blackbourne. "It's too early to try to date her now, anyway. Feelings are running wild because she's new, she's vulnerable and everyone wants to try to protect her and include her. She may discover she doesn't want to be with us later. That's her choice. If she chooses to stay with us, you'd want to make sure it is her true desire to stay with us and not because she feels it's her only option."

Mr. Blackbourne nodded. "Unless we're willing to approach the Academy and they want to draw her into another group. If they were going to do it, they'd need to do so right now to start establishing trust. I'm not totally opposed to it if it means her safety is assured, but I have a feeling I'd be outvoted in this."

Kota sighed, running his fingers through his hair. This wasn't at all what he pictured this meeting to be about.

Part of him was tempted to go back and talk to her. Maybe he could run off with her. That didn't seem right, either. For one, he wasn't sure she would. The other thing was, he couldn't abandon his family. He cared about her, but he loved his brothers, too. He'd sworn his life to them.

Maybe he should have kept her to himself. It was too late now.

"So it comes down to this," Mr. Blackbourne said. "You can share her or not, that's up to you. You'll have to come to terms with what that means on your own. Until a time when she's less vulnerable and we've got her in a safe position, we have to establish some ground rules. As far as holding her hand and touching, you can take her as far as she's allowed you so far, but every next step she has to initiate herself. Has she kissed anyone yet?"

"No," a few of them said at the same time. Eyes darted around the table, looking for someone who answered affirmatively, but it was pretty obvious. They'd had this argument already. Sang's revelation at the sleepover made it clear no one had tried and in the last couple of days, no one would have attempted it.

"Good," Mr. Blackbourne said. "Here's the rules. No one is to touch her further than already established. Let me make that clear. Holding hands, fine. Letting her sit in your lap, fine. Anything platonic, that you'd do to a sister, fine. Beyond that, she has to make the first move. That means any touch, kiss, everything."

"But she's never done it before," Gabriel said. "She

doesn't know what she's doing."

"Which is why this is important," Mr. Blackbourne said, touching the rim of his glasses. "It's the only way you will be able to establish if she really wants to or if she's just letting you to please you. If she makes the first move, you'll know."

"What about dating?" Victor asked.

"You can take her out, but I prefer you did it with a group or in a public place. If you want something more private, she has to tell you what she wants. Just remember, though, if you're taking her out, you have to allow the rest of us, too. We need time to get to know her anyway."

"So we can kiss her and stuff if she says we can?" Gabriel asked.

Kota's eyes flared. Gabriel wanted to kiss her? He stared at the table, biting his tongue, but his ears strained to hear the answer. He'd wanted to ask the same question.

Mr. Blackbourne shook a finger at Gabriel. "You can't goad her into telling you she wants to. I mean it. No tricks. No trying to talk her into it."

Silas cleared his throat for attention. "What about spending the night? We've already done that. She prefers when we sleep next to her."

Mr. Blackbourne frowned. "Why am I answering questions as if you're all looking for a way to get around the rules and date her? You can't all date her."

Kota leaned against the table, putting his head in his hands. Was he ready for this? He'd been putting the thoughts off for a few weeks... or a month? How long has it been since he first started watching Sang?

He loved his Academy family. They meant everything to him. For years they'd supported each other. They shared a lot. Now they were sharing Sang's attention. How far was this going to go? Would he have to fight off the others?

But didn't he already have that answer? What did Sang do when she was lonely? She found the first available one of them that was close by. And how did he feel about it? Nothing. Well, he missed her. Kota missed her now. However, if he couldn't be there next to her, he wanted Nathan or Victor or any of them with her. He didn't trust anyone but his Academy brothers to take care of her. When he had watched Sang crawling into Gabriel's lap at the party, he was happy she was happy. He did want her in his own lap, but he could wait. She was right there.

He grumbled to himself. This was confusing.

"I think we need to put this off," Dr. Green said. "Focus on the rules and we'll talk about this later when she's in better shape and we're all more familiar with her. It may turn out none of you want to date her. The Academy might learn about her and want to take her into another group. We don't even know if she'll want to stay with us or if she even wants to date any of you."

"That's correct," Mr. Blackbourne said. "So rule one, no one touches her further unless she moves first. Rule two, no intimate date locations unless she suggests it first. Three, until the appointed time where a decision is made, no one should date another girl and no more guys can join the group. Sang's too vulnerable to bring in another member or she could feel hurt if she sees you with another girl."

"So if she kisses one of us? We can kiss her back after that, right?" Gabriel asked, his eyes squinting, as if trying to understand exactly what he could get away with.

"If she really does it first. A kiss on the hand, you can kiss her on the hand. A kiss on the mouth, then you can kiss her there. You can mimic how she touches you," Mr. Blackbourne offered. "And you all have to agree to this. No jealous arguments about who gets to hang out with her. No one fights over who is holding her hand today. If that happens, I'll have to insist you all back off even if she does try to take it a step further."

"I think that's a call for a unified agreement," Dr. Green said, putting his hands behind his back and smiling pleasantly at all of them. "Are we in agreement with three rules in the case of Miss Sang Sorenson? Plus the job of finding out the truth and then deciding if we convince her father to let us take her?"

Everyone turned to Luke, the first in line at the table today. Luke's dark eyes focused on the opposite wall, as if already dreaming up what he was supposed to do. "I am willing," he said in a quiet voice, "and I will obey."

It was an impossible request. The first girl in the group, and they were making crazy promises. It meant Kota couldn't date her until she asked him out. Or maybe he could. Hadn't he kind of already asked her? His mother did, but Sang had said yes. Did that mean he could take her? He couldn't kiss her like he wanted. He thought about all the ways he had touched her before. What could he do with her now?

Victor was next. "I am willing," he said, "and I will obey."

"I'm unwilling," North rushed in. North always had to cast a different vote, Kota knew that. Being unwilling, though, just meant he wasn't happy with the rules. "But I will obey." And there it was. He wasn't happy but he would follow through. It was enough.

"I am willing, and I will obey," Silas said, his voice strong, as if he'd already made his decision for everything and he was waiting for the meeting to be over.

"I am willing, and I will obey," Gabriel said, staring down at the table.

"I am willing, and I will obey," Nathan repeated, flexing his fists. Kota knew this meant he wasn't happy with it.

Kota was last. He could bring this all to a halt right now if he said he would not obey. Three words. I won't obey. The ruling would be overturned. If he did, it would force them all to back off and remain strictly platonic with her. No one could date her if she stayed with their group.

If he did decline though, he would have to establish himself as platonic with Sang for a while, and hope that sometime in the future the others would find other girls they wanted and they could overturn the decision. Maybe Sang would outright say she wanted out of the group and join another Academy family, but she could still date him if she wanted.

It was a big risk. This would assume she was interested in him at all. It would cut off her chance with the other guys if she had feelings for one of them. How would she know they wanted her if they weren't allowed to tell her or pursue her? Could he expect her to wait as a friend in a slim hope she might understand and still want to be with him? If they all established themselves as platonic, what would stop her from trying to date someone else?

All Kota knew was that his need to touch her and to hold on to her was winning out. If he agreed, he could go home to her as soon as their job was over and curl up with her in that damn attic all evening. Someday maybe she'd kiss him and he could then kiss her back.

Could he risk that she might kiss one of the others? What would he do if she did?

Share her or possibly lose her forever.

Kota knew the answer to this. "I am willing," he stated, his voice strong and unwavering. He would not be misheard in this instance. He knew this weeks ago when he first started watching her, before that first night he bumped into her. He wanted Sang, even if he had to share her. "And I will obey."

For new release and exclusive Academy and C. L. Stone information sign up here: http://eepurl.com/zuIDj

Connect with C. L. Stone online
Twitter: https://twitter.com/CLStoneX
Facebook: https://www.facebook.com/clstonex

If you enjoyed reading *The Academy Friends vs. Family*, let me know.

Review it: at your favorite retailer and/or Goodreads

Books by C. L. Stone

The Academy Ghost Bird Series:
Introductions
First Days
Friends vs. Family
Forgiveness and Permission
Drop of Doubt
Push and Shove
House of Korba (October 2014)

The Academy Scarab Beetle Series
Thief
Liar (August 2014)

Other C. L. Stone Books:
Spice God
Smoking Gun

READ AN EXCERPT FROM THE NEXT BOOK IN THE ACADEMY SERIES

The Academy

The Ghost Bird Series

Forgiveness and Permission

Book Four

Written by C. L. Stone
Published by
Arcato Publishing

♥

ONSLAUGHT

If last week you had asked me when my life had changed, I might have said when I met Kota Lee and he dragged me into the world of the Academy with secret agendas and handsome boys who knew how to infiltrate, spy and rescue, and did so on a regular basis.

Today, if you asked me the same question, I would say it was when my mother told me she wasn't my mother.

My name is Sang Sorenson. I was your atypical straight A student who was shy and never had a friend in her life until I met Kota. I had an abusive -- I guess I should call her a stepmother -- who didn't want me and a father who was never there and didn't want me either. The only things my father asked of me before he disappeared back into his double life were to keep my head down and watch out for my older half-sister until the end of the school year, and to take care of my stepmother if she managed to make it out of the hospital. He left us money and the two story gray house on Sunnyvale Court. Outside of that, we were on our own.

And my sister, Marie, didn't want me there, either. After I revealed to her what our father had said, she claimed she didn't need a babysitter and she could handle things herself.

But I made a promise to my father, and following his promise he'd made to my dead mother whose name I didn't even know. He had promised her he would take care of me and I would allow it, for now. I wouldn't abandon my sister like our parents had abandoned us.

But I also had Kota, Luke, Nathan, Silas, North, Gabriel, Victor, Mr. Blackbourne and Dr. Green. Nine friends. Nine members in my own secret family. They looked after me and promised to be there for me, no matter what.

Except, I had a sketchy idea of what family meant, and what they wanted with a girl with such a complicated situation.

I could only wish, with all my heart, they would stay and not leave me alone.

They were all I had left to believe in.

♥♥♥

It was another hot Saturday for late September through the glare of sunlight assaulting me from the window. Having grown up in Illinois, I was unused to the warmth of a southern summer so late in the year. The boys kept telling me I could expect summer days on through November. It seemed impossible, but I'd believe it when I felt it.

I heard the footsteps of a couple of boys in the hallway before they managed to open the door to my bedroom. The footsteps quieted. The handle was twisted, the door had been unlocked. I was under the sheet and thin blanket on my bed, the one Victor had bought for me. I could still smell him in the sheets since he'd spent the night with me. Too bad he wasn't here now. He didn't need to stay with me, none of the boys did, but they did it anyway often enough. Marie and I were alone, but we were never really truly alone. The Academy was always watching.

I'd slept in. Seven a.m. was late to sleep in since the boys were usually up and working at dawn. However, Victor had kept me up late watching a movie, and I was feeling lazy.

My skin electrified. The boys in my room were being sneaky. I had no clue what they were up to. My fingers clutched the blanket, ready to hold tight to it or push it back and jump up and catch them at whatever they were doing.

The edge of my blanket was collected at the foot of my bed in someone else's grasp.

Silence. Both sides were waiting for the other to strike first.

My blanket was yanked from my grasp. I raced to pop up and go after whoever it was.

A spray of ice water smacked me in the face. The edge of a shrill cry caught in my throat but I held it in. Screaming was pointless.

There was a rush for the door. I caught Nathan and Gabriel dashing out, large Super Soaker guns in their hands. Nathan was shirtless. His muscular, tanned body left me breathless. He wore red sport shorts, and was barefoot. His reddish brown hair was wet, sticking up.

Gabriel's leaner frame was also shirtless. He wore camouflage shorts. Two locks of wet blond hair stuck to his cheeks and the rest of his russet brown hair was raked back, hanging behind his ears. White crystal studs hung from each lobe, and three black rings were pierced into his right ear toward the top crest.

Their running, like a roll of thunder, rumbled through the house as they raced down the front stairs. They threw open the front door and ran outside.

My wakeup call had been delivered.

More footsteps rushed up the back stairs. I jumped up on the bed, moving to the wall next to my door, pressing my back to the frame. I'd gotten hit in the face once and I didn't have a weapon. I was outmatched for speed and power by all of the guys, so it didn't matter who it was. I hoped I could garner sympathy from my new assailant.

The footsteps padded closer, slowed, and stopped behind the wall.

I peeked out into the hallway.

Luke peeked back in at me.

His shirt was gone, too. His khaki shorts hung low on

his hips. His tapered shoulders were starting to get a little pink from sun. His longish blond hair was soaked, tied back with a clip he'd probably borrowed from me. He grinned down at me, his brown eyes brightening.

"About time you got up," he said. He stepped back, holding out a second Super Soaker gun. Pink. "Look what the Kota fairy got us."

I grinned. Kota bought us new toys. I took the pink gun, holding it in my hands and feeling the weight.

"I'm going to run out the front door," Luke said. "Head out the back and around the house. I'll try to get their attention. You do that super silent thing you do and sneak up on them."

"Okay." I didn't know what he was talking about. What super quiet thing? Tiptoeing?

I raced back to my bookshelf, snatching up a hair clip to twist back my hair. I checked my clothes: soft gray shorts and a light pink bra cami tank top. I was decent enough for water guns.

I ran down the back steps, listening as Luke did the same in the front and headed out the door. I would have to hurry.

I ran past the side door, flew through the family room and unlocked the back door out onto the screened-in back porch.

The morning greeted me with a wave of thick heat. A basketball was bouncing in the driveway and there was the echo of shuffling tennis shoes meeting the beige concrete. I closed the door behind me, jumping down the brick steps to land on the blue utility carpet.

Silas's tall, strong frame flew into view, nearly hovering as he stood on his toes over North in the driveway. North might have been a few inches shorter, but with the fierceness in his almost-scary face from his intense eyes and strong, two days unshaven jaw, you'd never know it.

North clutched the basketball in his hand, avoiding

Silas. Kota ran in, his black-rimmed glasses sliding down his nose, sweat making the hunter green T-shirt he wore stick to his back. North tossed him the ball. Derrick, a boy from up the road, raced after Kota, trying to block him as Kota aimed for the basket and tried to get off a shot. Derrick was probably the same size as Kota, and wore only a pair of cut off jean shorts that hung low on of his hips, revealing a trace outline of dark boxers underneath. Derrick was deeply tanned from long days spent outdoors all summer. He was a new face, though, as he hadn't been there all week, when the other boys had. Word must have gotten out that the house was no longer a place to stay away from.

I was surprised, too, to find Micah and Tom, a couple of twelve-year-old boys, in the backyard, bouncing on top of a large trampoline. The trampoline had been something like a consolation prize from my father before he last left. He never even finished building it, but North fixed it up. I hadn't been on it yet, mostly because I didn't want to enjoy it. I didn't like the meaning of it. I didn't mind the others using it. In fact, I was glad. At least someone liked it.

My stepmom would have had a fit seeing all these boys running around the yard, through the house, and playing with me.

I ran for the screen door in the porch that led out into the yard. I flung open the door, stepping out into the grass, feeling the heat heavy around me, the water swishing in the gun in my hands.

North stopped in mid-step, glancing over at me, temporarily distracted from his basketball game. He smiled at me, his black hair hanging in his eyes. I gave him a small wave and a wink before dashing off in the opposite direction, heading around the back of the house toward the side yard, taking the longer way around to the front.

I crouched by the bushes surrounding the front porch, glancing over them for Nathan and Gabriel.

Luke was dashing around the front yard. Nathan was on his heels after him. They aimed their water guns at each other, spraying the other one down with a fresh blast every few seconds. The front yard was large and bare, with plenty of space for running around. I didn't have much to block me if I just ran out there. And where was ...

A spritz of cold water caught me in the back. I squealed and without thinking, started to run. I found out where Gabriel was. So much for the surprise attack.

"Oy, Trouble," Gabriel called after me, laughing.

I flew across the yard. My cover was blown. Time for rushing in head first.

I pumped my water gun and aimed for Nathan as he dashed after Luke. I caught him in the back with the spray of my gun. He turned, spotted me and started running.

I cut across the yard; Gabriel was after me, too, taking a different angle. I ran as hard as I could toward the porch but there wasn't much point. Both of them were much faster than I was.

Gabriel managed to cut me off before I made it to the steps. I aimed my gun at him as he started to squirt at my chest and stomach. I caught him in the face as I turned again, intending to run back around the house.

No use. Nathan caught up with me, scooping me up by hooking his arm around my waist and softly tackling me to the ground. I landed on my back. He sat square on my hips. I aimed my pink gun at his face as he aimed his orange one at mine.

"Say 'mercy'," he warned, his eyebrows shifting above his blue eyes, a wide grin splashed on his face. Droplets of water sashayed down the ripples of his abs.

"No," I called out. I pulled the trigger to squirt water at him.

Only I'd forgotten to pump my gun and I got the last of a trickle before the pressure ended.

Nathan made an evil-sounding cackle. "Brave words from a dead girl who forgot to load her gun."

He fired. Icy liquid shot at my face. I dropped the gun to hold both hands up at the muzzle of his, blocking the spray. The water still caught me against the neck and around the top of my shirt.

"No," I squealed, laughing. "Stop."

Gabriel came over, standing over my head, his camo shorts dripping on my face. He aimed his gun at me. "You should know better than to put your gun down." He squirted me in the face point-blank.

I blocked my head with my arms. The water bit into my skin with a sharp chill. "Holy crow, how is the water so cold?"

"We put ice in it," Gabriel said, pumping his gun.

Luke flew over me, jumping over my body and aiming his gun at Gabriel, catching him in the side of his head. Gabriel shot off after him. Luke flew over the rail of the front porch, using it as a bunker as he aimed over it at Gabriel and fired. Gabriel crept around the bushes, slinking up the steps. They both shot streams of water at each other before Luke flew back over the rail, landing in the yard to fly across the grass toward the side of the house. Gabriel went after him.

Nathan laughed, aiming the gun back at my face. "Come on. Say mercy and I'll let you up."

"No," I squealed, giggling and pushing his gun away, reaching for mine.

Nathan let go of his gun, holding it in one hand while with his free hand, he snatched up mine and chucked it a few feet away, out of my reach. "Say it," he grumbled at me, a playful growl emanating from him.

"No," I wailed again, now trying to twist my body around, gripping at the ground to claw my way out from under him. He sank his full weight onto my body, pinning me to the ground. A free hand found my face, and he squeezed my cheeks until I made a fish face.

"Sang," he said, "you've got to learn how to admit when you're outgunned. Now say it."

"No!" My squeaking mumbled through fish lips. I pushed his gun away, poking him in the ribs, trying to tickle my way out.

He laughed, patting my hands away as if he were swatting away flies. "Doesn't work on me, sweetheart."

"Luke!" I cried out.

"Kinda busy," Luke called back, running past my head. Gabriel jumped over me on his heels. Luke was out in the open, crossing the large front yard when he made a U-turn back around, running for a tree in the far corner to hide behind.

"Say mercy and I'll let you up," Nathan said to me. He hooked fingers onto the hem of my shirt, lifting slightly to expose my belly. He aimed the end of the gun there. "Do it."

"Don't you dare," I called out. I had one more plan left, and it was dirty. "Don't or I'll do it."

Nathan's eyebrows shot up in surprise. "What?"

"Let me go or I'll do it."

Nathan smirked at me, curiosity in his eyes. He pulled the trigger. A stream of ice water caught me square in the stomach.

I wriggled under him, trying to block the spray against my bare skin. "You asked for it," I said. "Silas!" I squealed out through my laughing. Part of my shout cut off midway and trailed off and I blamed it on my giddiness, but it was enough to draw the attention of who I wanted.

"You did not," Nathan said, his hand shot out to cover my mouth, his head jerking up to scan the perimeter.

It was too late. Silas was on the warpath, barreling down after us, aiming right for Nathan. Nathan scrambled to get off me, aiming his gun at Silas's broad chest and firing. It didn't deter Silas as he caught Nathan in a full frontal tackle. Suddenly, Nathan was on his back on the ground, Silas sitting on his hips, his wrists pinned to the ground by Silas's knees.

I scrambled to get my gun, stepping up behind Silas, my stomach to his back, as I aimed over his shoulder at Nathan's face.

"Fucking shit," Nathan said breathlessly. "She even

cheats at water guns."

"Yup," Silas called out proudly. "Get him, *aggele mou*."

I pumped my gun and sprayed down Nathan with a long stream, starting from his stomach and ending at his face.

Nathan laughed, stretching to try to pull his arms out from under Silas.

"Thank you, Silas," I said to him, touching lightly at the back of his neck.

"Oy, Trouble!"

It was the only warning I got before Gabriel shot across the yard, aiming his water gun at me. Luke was running behind him, firing, but his gun was out of water.

I laughed, running away from Silas as he was letting Nathan up off the ground.

"Meanie!" I called after Gabriel as I dashed across the yard, heading toward the driveway, thinking I might be able to cut through the basketball game. Maybe I could use Kota as a shield. Gabriel wouldn't dare shoot Kota.

I turned around as a gray BMW pulled into the driveway, parking in the middle of it to give room to those playing basketball. A thrill swept over me. Victor had left early to go to do some work for the Academy. I'd thought he was going to be gone all day but was glad that he was back early.

His car also gave me perfect cover.

I ran right for the car, the plan formulating in my mind. Gabriel hollered after me, but I was flying ahead of him. I had a clean head start.

Prompted by a deep instinct telling me that I could, I ran for the front of the car. I jumped, pushing my body up to vault myself over the front, my butt heating against the hood as I slid across. I landed like a cat on my feet on the other side. I crouched, pressing my back against the wheel as I pumped the pink water gun.

The Terminator couldn't have done it any better.

The car door opened, followed by footsteps coming

around the car. I waited only a moment. Not that I would squirt Victor too much. Just a small spritz to welcome him back.

I caught the shadow coming around the edge of the car, I turned, propping myself up a little as I aimed at a red tie and fired.

And fell back on my butt, when my gaze met with cool, steel-gray eyes.

I dropped my gun to catch myself with my hands before I fell back too far. The gun clattered to the ground.

Mr. Blackbourne finished stepping around the corner of the car, a brown eyebrow shooting up over the rim of his glasses. The dark suit coat he wore was open, revealing the white shirt, probably Armani or Gucci. A wet splotch of water spread across his chest, center mass. "You should know who you're aiming at before you fire, Miss Sorenson," he said, as calmly as if he were explaining a math problem to me.

My heart raced. I'd just iced down the only person I knew who, with just a look, could send me to my knees.

"S–s-sorry," I said, not feeling so confident now.

Mr. Blackbourne stretched out a hand to me, which surprised me enough to make me hesitate; he'd never done that before. I lifted mine, dropping it in his. His smooth, perfect fingers wrapped around mine as he pulled me to standing, inches away from him.

"Remind me to have you trained in gunmanship," he said, the tight corners of his mouth moving up a millimeter.

I released the breath I'd been holding that whole time. I didn't want to make him angry.

From behind him, the other members of the Academy collected: Silas, Luke, North, Nathan, Kota and Gabriel. North held the basketball to his hip. The others stood by, waiting. Derrick had fallen back, standing under the basket, his arms crossed over his chest.

Mr. Blackbourne's eyes remained on me as he spoke. "I came over because I tried to reach certain members of my team by phone. Apparently, they're all ... distracted." The millimeter smile disappeared as he turned toward the guys. "And I can see why."

"Sorry," Kota said. He flicked the sweat from his brow. "I didn't realize."

The others murmured similar apologies.

"We don't have time for that," Mr. Blackbourne said, turning toward his car. "Kota, Luke, Nathan, in the car with me. North, Silas, Gabriel, follow. We've got work to do."

"What about Sang?" Gabriel asked, dropping his water gun to the ground. Playtime was over.

"She doesn't work for me. Let's go," Mr. Blackbourne moved around the car again, heading toward the driver's seat. Was this Mr. Blackbourne's car that looked identical to Victor's? Or was he driving Victor's car? Where was Victor? And why were they all leaving now?

I bit back the questions. I knew better. Academy business was secret. I wasn't a part of it.

Kota, Luke and Nathan found their shoes and shirts quickly and raced toward the car. Mr. Blackbourne pulled the car out of the drive as soon as the doors closed and was down the road again.

I collected the dropped water guns and headed toward the garage. Silas and Gabriel each grabbed the phones they had left on the ground.

North was shuffling a shirt the right way to drop it over his head when he said, "Derrick, do me a favor?"

Derrick had collected the basketball and was taking random shots alone at the goal. "What?"

"Stay with Sang? Until one of us can get back?"

"I'm fine," I said. I thought I was. My mother wasn't there with any more crazy punishments for me. My father wasn't there. There was no one left to do any harm.

"Humor me, Sang Baby." North eyeballed Derrick. "Please?"

"I guess so. Whatever," Derrick said, shrugging and looking at me.

North frowned but nodded. He waved to me as he stalked off, following Gabriel and Silas to North's black Jeep that was parked at Kota's house. They rushed over to it, getting in. The Jeep started up and disappeared down the road, too.

The Academy

The Ghost Bird Series

Forgiveness and Permission

♥

Book Four

♥

Written by C. L. Stone
Published by
Arcato Publishing

ABOUT C. L. STONE

Certification

- Marvelour of Wonder
- Active Participant of Scary Situations
- Official Member of F.A.M.E.

Experience

Spent an extraordinary number of years with absolutely no control over the capping of imagination, fun, and curiosity. Willingly takes part in impossible problems only to come up with the most ludicrous solution. Due to unfortunate circumstances, will no longer experience feeling on a small spot on my left calf.

Skills

Secret Keeper | Occasion Riser | Barefoot Walker | Magic Maker | Restless Reckless | Gravity Defiant | Fairy Tale Reader | Story Maker-Upper | Amusingly Baffled | Comprehensive Curiousness | Usually Unbelievable

CPSIA information can be obtained at www.ICGtesting.com
Printed in the USA
LVOW01s1610090714

393589LV00021B/788/P

9 781492 900016